THE
COAST-TO-COAST
MURDERS

A list of titles by James Patterson
appears at the back of this book

THE
COAST-TO-COAST
MURDERS

JAMES PATTERSON
AND J.D. BARKER

C

CENTURY

1 3 5 7 9 10 8 6 4 2

Century
20 Vauxhall Bridge Road
London SW1V 2SA

Century is part of the Penguin Random House group of companies
whose addresses can be found at global.penguinrandomhouse.com

Penguin
Random House
UK

First published in Great Britain by Century in 2020

www.penguin.co.uk

A CIP catalogue record for this book is available from the British Library

ISBN 9781529125177
ISBN 9781529125184 (trade paperback edition)

Printed and bound in Great Britain by Clays Ltd, Elcograf S.p.A.

Penguin Random House is committed to a sustainable future for
our business, our readers and our planet. This book is made
from Forest Stewardship Council® paper.

PART 1

LOS ANGELES, CALIFORNIA

What is the mind but thin glass?
—Barton Fitzgerald, MD

CHAPTER ONE

MICHAEL

WHERE WILL YOU BE when your life ends?

I was in the grocery store, squeezing a mango.

Sixteen minutes ago, I took a phone call from the woman who lived in the apartment below mine in Wilshire Village, a nondescript mustard-yellow monstrosity just off Broadway on Glendale, a block from Wilshire in Los Angeles.

I left my basket in the aisle and ran the ten blocks from the store, arriving home out of breath and sweating, to find the mailman in our lobby staring at the growing puddle of water under the bank of mailboxes. The steady stream was trickling down the stairs, flooding the first-floor alcove.

I rushed past him and up the steps, careful not to slip.

My phone rang again as I reached my door. Neighbor again.

"I see it, Mrs. Dowell. Must be a burst pipe or something." That happened back east during the winter. I'd had no idea it could happen in California.

The water came out from under my door and into the hall, pooling on the landing.

"Michael? It's dripping down my walls, from the ceiling," Mrs. Dowell said. "My paintings, my furniture…did you call the super?"

I fumbled with my keys, found the right one, and twisted it in the lock for the dead bolt. "I thought you called the super."

"Why would I call the super? It's your apartment."

Because the super could have been here half an hour ago and killed the water. "I'll call him the second we hang up, Mrs. Dowell, I promise."

I pushed open the door and stepped inside. I reached for the light switch but thought better of it—I was standing in at least a quarter of an inch of water.

Mrs. Dowell sighed. "Who's going to pay for all this?"

The hardwood floor glistened in the light of the setting sun. A small river flowed from the bedroom in the back to the living room, down the hall, and out the front door.

I could hear splashing and gurgling. "I think it's coming from the bathroom," I told her.

Mrs. Dowell said, "You didn't answer my question."

"I'll pay for it. Whatever the damage. Don't worry about that."

"My paintings are priceless."

I've seen your paintings. We'll take a trip to the flea market together and replace them.

The bedroom was the only carpeted room in the apartment, and I sloshed through it, my shoes leaving a trail of mushy footprints in my wake.

In the bathroom, water gushed from the sink tap. The bathtub faucet too. Water cascaded over the white porcelain sides of both.

"Mrs. Dowell, I'm hanging up so I can call the super. I'll call you back."

I looked over my shoulder at the bedroom behind me, knowing full well that I didn't leave the water on, so someone else had.

The room was empty, crowded with nothing but elongated shadows.

I turned to the sink, twisted the faucet, shut it off.

A towel was in the basin, blocking the overflow drain. I knew I hadn't done that.

I should have run at that point, left the apartment. I wish I had, because what came next was far worse than a stranger invading my home.

I took the few steps from my sink to the bathtub and looked into the overflowing water, down through the rippling surface at what lay beneath, lit only by the fading light of dusk. I looked down at the most beautiful face staring back at me. Her deep green eyes were open wide, her mouth slightly agape, her blond hair wavering gently with the current.

I found myself staring at her, this nude, lifeless girl in my bathtub. Smooth, flawless skin, the faintest patch of freckles on her nose.

At some point, I shut off the bathtub faucet. I don't remember doing it, though. I only remember sitting on the edge of the tub, my breath deserting me.

CHAPTER TWO

MICHAEL

MY CELL PHONE BUZZED in my hand. Mrs. Dowell again.

I hit Decline and dialed.

I did not call the building super.

She picked up on the third ring. "I'm thinking of a number between one and five."

"Meg, not now, something happened—"

"Ah, ah, ah, you know the rules, Michael. Pick a number."

I shook my head. "Meg, this is really—"

"Do you have any idea how many times I've called you in the past week? You didn't pick up. You didn't call me back. You didn't even bother with a *Hey, I'm still alive but busy* text," Megan rattled on. "Nineteen times. Is that any way to treat your sister? Dr. Bart's funeral is next Tuesday, and you pick this week to drop off the radar? *No bueno,* big brother. Dr. Rose is all over me. 'Where is your brother? Is he coming home? Have you talked to him? He'll be here, right?' It's bad enough you won't speak to her, but you can't shut me out. I know you don't want to be here for this, but you have to, Michael. I can't do Dr. Bart's funeral without you, I

just can't. I know you didn't get along, not all the time—all right, never—but if you skip this, you'll never forgive yourself. This is the kind of thing that haunts you for the rest of your life. You'll regret it, and there's no way to take it back. If you don't want to be here for yourself, think about me and Dr. Rose. I know she can be a bitch, but she raised us. And she's a mess right now. She's barely holding it together. We need to think about appearances too. How will it look for her if you're not here? You know how people at the university talk, her colleagues. She doesn't need this—"

"Megan—"

"Just tell me you'll be here, and I'll drop it. I won't bring it up again. You can even skip my next birthday, my next ten birthdays. Just be here for this. It's too important to—"

"Three."

Megan fell silent.

"The number you're thinking of is three."

"How do you do that?"

"Meg, I need you to listen to me closely. Something's happened."

"Are you okay?"

The girl's blank face stared up at me from the bathtub, the rippling water distorting her features, a shimmer around her pale skin. She looked so calm, peaceful. She had the most beautiful green eyes. A lone bubble floated up from her lips, disappeared at the surface.

I wasn't okay. I wasn't okay at all.

"There's a girl in my bathtub."

Megan replied, "You sound awfully sad about that."

"The water flooded my apartment, Mrs. Dowell... I don't know who..." The words fell from my mouth, incoherent babble. My heart beat hard against my rib cage.

"Whoa, take a deep breath, Michael."

I did. I took two. "She's dead, Meg."

Megan said nothing.

"I . . . I don't know who she is."

My sister remained silent.

"Meg?"

"You're fucking with me, right? Like the time you said you ran over that guy at the truck stop in Kansas City because he was wearing a New Kids on the Block T-shirt? Or the time you said you found a prostitute sleeping in the cab of your truck and decided to keep her? Like the time you said you picked up a hitchhiker in Nevada and left him in Utah, Colorado, *and* Missouri? Now is really not the time for practical jokes, Michael. I need to be able to tell Dr. Rose you're coming home."

"I . . . can't tell how she died. Not by looking at her. I don't see anything wrong. She looks like she's sleeping but she's not, not underwater. She's not breathing. I don't want to touch her. I know I shouldn't, and I haven't."

"Holy hell, you're serious? Did you call the police?"

"I called you."

"You need to call the police. Right now. You need to hang up and call them."

I did.

CHAPTER THREE

MICHAEL

CAN I CHANGE MY pants?"

I was on the couch in my small living room.

From the corner of the room, Detective Garrett Dobbs looked up from his phone. His brow furrowed. "What?"

"When I sat on the edge of the bathtub, my pants and underwear got soaked. Can I change clothes, please?"

"No. Later. I want you to walk me through everything one more time. Start when you left your apartment this afternoon," Dobbs said.

The detective looked like he was in his mid- to late thirties. His brown hair was cropped close on the sides, longer on top, slightly tousled. He wore a black sweatshirt, jeans, and black boots. His badge hung around his neck on a metal chain. He made no effort to conceal the gun attached to his belt. I didn't know enough about guns to identify the make or model. It was black and seemed heavier than it probably was.

He looked familiar, but I couldn't place him. Then it came to me. "You used to play football, right? For Syracuse? Running back, if I remember correctly."

His eyes had been on his phone and they stayed there for another moment. When he looked up, his expression remained blank. "Are you from New York? Not many Orange fans out here in LA."

"I went to Cornell."

He nodded. "Big Red, huh?"

"Not really. I dropped out my junior year."

"Last I checked, you don't need the degree to be a fan."

"You haven't spoken to my parents. Without a degree, you're not much of anything."

"That's harsh."

"You were fast. Always figured you'd head to the pros."

Another detective, I hadn't been told his name, leaned in and grinned. "Dobbs here ran the forty in four point two-seven seconds, the same as Deion Sanders. Fastest guy to come out of Syracuse till he tore his Achilles. Then he was only as fast as the rest of us humans."

Dobbs lowered his phone. "I tore it twice. Junior and senior year. When the NFL scouts came, they saw me as damaged goods. Stepped right on by like I was invisible. Past—"

"Past performance is not indicative of future results," the other detective said. "He always says that. Reminds me of a financial commercial."

Dobbs said, "I saw that phrase next to my name on one of the scout's clipboards. It stuck, I suppose. You hear something like that about yourself, and it gets caught in your head. Coach let me finish out my senior year riding the bench so I wouldn't lose my scholarship, but we all knew I was done with football."

"Wilkins?"

This came from one of the CSI investigators near my bed.

The other detective, Wilkins, crossed the room.

Dobbs turned back to me. "You've got a good memory. I haven't played since 2001. Christ, seventeen years now."

"Some things do stick, I suppose."

My eyes went to the CSI investigator. Through the open bedroom door, I watched him reach down with gloved hands and pick up a woman's purse from the far side of my bed. He set it gently on top of my rumpled navy quilt. I hadn't seen the purse when I came in. He reached back down and brought up a small black dress, panties, matching bra, and a pair of black pumps. He laid each item down on the bed. A second CSI investigator placed small numbered placards next to each—4, 5, 6, 7, 8, and 9. I wondered what had already been tagged 1 through 3. A third CSI photographed each item from multiple angles.

Dobbs watched me watching them, made another note on his phone. "You said you don't know her?"

"I don't."

He tilted his head. "Looks a lot like you know her."

"I don't," I repeated. "I have no idea who she is."

He nodded toward my front door. "We found no sign of forced entry. You said it was locked when you got home, right?"

"It was, yeah."

"The dead bolt, the knob, or both?"

"Just the dead bolt. I don't bother with the other one."

Two other CSIs were busy mopping up the water with large yellow sponges. They squeezed them out into white buckets. On masking tape, across the side of one bucket, printed in black blocky letters, was a case number, my last name, my address, and the number 2; the other bucket had the same information but with the number 3. I imagined yet another CSI studying that water in a lab somewhere, one drop on a slide at a time.

"Hey, Dobbs? We got an ID." Wilkins was busy going through the contents of the purse. He held up a driver's license. "Alyssa Tepper. Twenty-two years old. She lives in Burbank."

Dobbs nodded at me. "Alyssa Tepper. Her name mean anything to you?"

I shook my head.

Wilkins whistled. "Hey, look at this." He held up a baseball card. "This is a '36 Joe DiMaggio from World Wide Gum."

Dobbs went over to him. "Valuable?"

"In pristine condition, they can be worth upwards of ninety thousand. The back is jacked up on this one, though. Half the paper is missing. Left corner is torn. Still worth a pretty penny, but nowhere near that much." He placed it on the bed along with the various other items found in the purse.

Dobbs leaned into his ear and said something I couldn't make out.

Wilkins nodded, took out his cell phone, and made a call.

I knew that baseball card.

CHAPTER FOUR

MICHAEL

THEY FOUND A KEY in her purse. The key fit my dead-bolt lock.

That was two hours ago.

When my building super finally showed up, the uniformed officers standing at my apartment door wouldn't let him in. His eyes met mine from the hallway. I turned away.

The water had been cleaned up, the buckets hauled off.

Dobbs was in my bedroom or the bathroom. He had closed the adjoining door so I could no longer see inside either room. There were at least twelve other people in there.

He'd left me on the couch. The same officers who kept my super out were clearly tasked with keeping me in.

When my bedroom door finally opened, two women from the medical examiner's office wheeled a gurney out, a zippered black bag on top.

Dobbs followed behind them, watched as they went out the front door, then sat beside me on the couch. "Your pants still wet?"

"Damp. It's okay. I'm fine."

He tossed a pair of jeans at me. Underwear, socks, and a worn Big Red sweatshirt followed. All of it had been pulled from my suitcase on the bedroom floor. A CSI investigator stood behind him with a large, clear plastic bag.

Dobbs said, "Change out of your clothes into those. Everything goes in the bag. Do you have anything in your pockets?"

"I told you I didn't the last two times you asked. One of the patrol officers checked before you got here."

His eyes dropped to my jeans. "Turn your pockets inside out. I need to see."

Although frustrated, I did as he asked. Everyone had a job to do.

Dobbs seemed satisfied. He nodded at the CSI.

The man with the clear plastic bag stepped up beside me and held it open.

I frowned. "Right here?"

"If you're shy, we can go into the hallway or the kitchen. Bathroom and bedroom are both off-limits."

I thought about my super out in the hallway. Probably Mrs. Dowell and who knew who else were standing out there too. I turned my back to Dobbs, faced the couch, and stripped off my clothes. Everything went into the plastic bag, and I dressed in the clothes Dobbs had brought me.

The CSI investigator pulled the drawstring on the bag, then took out a Sharpie. He wrote my name, a case number, and 47 on the front. The shoes found beside my bed had been tagged with an 8 and a 9. That meant there was a lot of evidence I had yet to see.

Through the bedroom door, I caught a glimpse of the open drawers, bare mattress, and items pulled from my closet and stacked against the wall—everything from clothing to sports equipment, photo albums, and various boxes I hadn't bothered to unpack since moving in.

Wilkins saw me and closed the door.

Dobbs asked me to take a seat on the couch. "Was anyone here when you left?"

I'd gone over this a dozen times. Not just with him but with the first responders. *He's just doing his job,* I told myself. I drew in a breath and started from the beginning. "I got in late last night and slept until a little after two this afternoon."

"Where were you last night?"

"Working."

Dobbs read from his phone. "You said you're a long-haul truck driver, correct?"

I nodded. "For Nadler Distribution, off Wilshire. I pick up wine here in California and haul it back east. On that end, I load up with craft beer and bring it back."

"How often do you make the trip?"

"Three times per month."

"When did you get in last night?"

"I pulled into the distribution center just after midnight. By the time I finished up the paperwork and offloaded, it was nearly three. I got home around three thirty."

"You didn't stop anywhere between the distribution center and your apartment? No late-night snack, cigarettes at a convenience store, no bar, nothing?" Dobbs had his phone out again, no doubt comparing what I'd said this time to what I'd said the previous times.

I shook my head. "I ate on the road. I don't smoke, and I'm not much for the bar scene. I was tired. Everything ached—sleeping in the cab of a truck for a week will do that to you. I just wanted a shower and my own bed. I came straight here."

"Alone?"

"Alone." I nodded.

"Did anyone see you? Is there someone who can corroborate that?"

"Nadler Distribution will have records of my arrival, offload, et cetera. There's cameras."

Dobbs said, "We'll get that information. That's not what I mean. Can anyone confirm you arrived home alone?"

"At three thirty in the morning?"

He nodded.

I looked down at my hands. "No. The building is quiet that time of night."

Dobbs typed something into his phone: "Let's backtrack a little bit. How did you get home? Where did you park?"

"I walked. It's not very far. I like to stretch my legs after a long haul."

"You walked," he repeated.

"Yeah."

"I'll need the exact route."

I told him. I imagined he would check traffic cameras.

He looked toward my front door. "You don't have a security system. Don't you worry about your possessions, being that you're away from home so much?"

I shrugged. "I don't really have anything worth taking. Nothing that can't be replaced."

"How long have you lived here?"

"About two years."

"Yet you haven't hung up any pictures. Looks like most of what you own is still boxed up. Sparse furniture. A few essentials in the kitchen. Toothbrush, razor . . . not much of anything in the way of personal items," Dobbs pointed out.

"Like you said, I'm not home very much."

"No real security on your building either. No cameras. Your key unlocks the front door. No records, no time stamps."

"It's private. I like that. Sometimes it seems like everything people do is under a microscope. Recorded and cataloged in a dozen different places," I said.

He looked down at his phone. "When we check your social media accounts, are we going to find Alyssa Tepper?"

"I don't have any social media accounts," I said. "I told you, I don't know who she is. You've got my phone. Go through it, I don't care."

Dobbs glanced up at me. "Yeah, we've got your phone." He returned to his notes, then said, "You got home around three thirty, showered, and went to bed? Nothing else? No contact with anyone?"

"I was tired."

"Yeah, you said that. Then what happened?"

"I slept until around two this afternoon. Got up, took another shower to wake up. Ate some lunch, then went out to see a movie."

"What movie?"

"The latest Marvel film."

"I'll need your ticket."

"My ticket?"

"Yeah. Your ticket from the movie. Your ticket stub."

"I tossed it."

Dobbs tapped at his phone again. "Can you log into your credit card account and show me the purchase?"

"I paid cash."

"You paid cash." Dobbs repeated this softly to himself. "Tell me about the movie."

I frowned. "I found a dead girl in my bathtub, and you want me to tell you about a movie?"

He smiled. "I don't need the blow-by-blow, just the major plot points. I love a good Marvel movie."

Frustrated, I closed my eyes for a second and rubbed my temples. *He's just doing his job. He's just doing his job.*

I told him about the film, what I could remember.

When I finished, he said, "Can you tell me something about the movie that I haven't already seen in one of the previews? We've all seen the previews."

The truth was, I had fallen asleep shortly after the film started. I missed most of it. I only went so I could get out of the house, relax, unwind a little. When you're cooped up in the cab of a truck by yourself for a week, sometimes it's nice to get out and be surrounded by people. Parks, libraries, anything to break up the isolation. Sometimes it's a movie. I told him the truth.

Dobbs studied his notes. "So even though you slept nearly ten hours and got up only two hours earlier, you couldn't keep your eyes open—that it?"

I nodded.

"Anyone see you there? Anyone you know?"

"No."

He sighed. "What time did the movie end?"

"Five fifty. I checked the time on the way out."

"And then you went where?"

"Big Six Market on Sixth and Rampart."

Dobbs said, "You walked?"

"Yes."

"And that's when your neighbor called?"

"Mrs. Dowell said there was some kind of water leak, so I dropped everything and came straight back. That's when I found her."

"And you called 911."

"Correct."

"After you spoke to your sister."

"Yeah, I called her first."

He had grilled me on that earlier, unsure why I would call her before calling the police. Now he said, "I want you to think long and hard before you answer me this one *last* time. Do you understand?"

I nodded.

He looked me directly in the eye. "Are you sure you don't know Ms. Tepper?"

I returned his gaze; I didn't hesitate. "I'm certain."

Dobbs shook his head, turned back to his phone, and scrolled through his notes again. After nearly a minute of silence, he stood. "Get up. We're going to take a ride."

CHAPTER FIVE

MICHAEL

DETECTIVE GARRETT DOBBS PLACED me in the back seat of a white Ford sedan parked between two Los Angeles PD vans in the yellow zone in front of my building.

Although it was nearly one in the morning, a surprising number of my neighbors had been up and about, their apartment doors open, as we walked past. Harvey Wilfong from two doors down had set up a lawn chair in the hallway and sat there with a six-pack of beer. I smiled awkwardly at all of them. Most turned away. Mrs. Dowell met my gaze, but her face was so full of disappointment, I found myself looking down at my hands.

The Ford was unmarked, but the floodlight on the driver's side gave it away as a police car. There was no barrier between the front and back. An ancient Panasonic laptop was bolted to the dashboard. Fast-food bags littered the floor. The back seat was upholstered in some kind of black vinyl. Two metal eyebolts protruded from between the cushions, no doubt for fastening handcuffs. Detective Dobbs had not handcuffed me. He had not read me my rights. When we left my apartment, I'd expected him to do both.

"Who is Megan?" Wilkins said, climbing into the front passenger seat. He held my phone, sealed inside a plastic bag.

"My sister."

"She's called about a dozen times."

"Can I call her back? Let her know what's going on?"

Wilkins tossed the bag aside and fastened his seat belt. "Nope."

"Am I under arrest?"

Before Wilkins could respond, Dobbs got in and started the car. He got us out from between the vans and onto Rampart. We turned on Sixth and drove past the park.

"Where are we going?"

Dobbs glanced at me in the rearview mirror. "You tell me. You don't recognize the route?"

I shrugged. "I know MacArthur Park."

We got on the 110 for about twenty minutes. There was a surprising amount of traffic for the late hour. He took an exit just after the 101 flyover. "Chinatown?"

"Lookie there, it's all coming back to him now," Wilkins said.

"What's in Chinatown?"

Neither man answered.

Dobbs took several more turns—a right here, a left, two more rights. He knew where he was going—he didn't use a map or GPS. On Cleveland, I spotted two LAPD patrol cars and another van, similar to the ones parked in front of my building.

Dobbs pulled up behind them, shifted the Ford into park, and looked up at me again in the mirror. "Where are we, Mr. Kepler?"

I frowned. I had no idea. I hadn't been to Chinatown in at least a year.

Someone dressed in white CSI overalls exited the van nearest us and went through the open door of the building to our right. Beyond the door was a narrow staircase. On one side of the door there was a laundromat; on the other, a pizzeria. A sign on the open door said STUDIOS AND ONE-BEDROOM APARTMENTS FOR RENT! and gave a phone number.

"Michael?"

Dobbs again.

I said, "I . . . I've never been here."

Wilkins pulled his wallet from his back pocket, took out a dollar bill, and handed it to Dobbs. "Double or nothing inside?"

Dobbs pocketed the money. "You're on."

I leaned forward. "What's going on here?"

Both men got out of the car.

Dobbs opened my door. "Want to lead the way?"

I just stared at him, puzzled.

He rolled his eyes. "Christ. Okay, come on, we're going inside."

CHAPTER SIX

MICHAEL

DOBBS WENT FIRST.

I followed him through the door and up the narrow stair-case, Wilkins right behind me. An ancient floral-print wallpaper covered the wall, peeling in some places, torn away in others. The wood steps and railing were covered in so many layers of paint, I could barely make out the intricate carving on the banister. The heavy-gloss white paint on the steps was marred with scuffs and grime. The stagnant air stank of old cheese and chemicals from the businesses below.

The top of the stairs opened into a hallway with six doors. The one at the end on the left stood open with an overweight uniformed officer perched on a wooden chair next to the door, a half-eaten burrito in his hand. He gave Dobbs and Wilkins a nod and gestured toward the open door. "In there," he mumbled, bits of beef tumbling from his full mouth.

"You're a pig, Horton," Dobbs said, walking past him and into the apartment.

I had stopped in the hall.

Wilkins gave my back a push, forced me inside.

A man in a white dress shirt, khakis, and a loosened dark blue tie came over when he spotted Dobbs. His gray hair was cropped short on the sides; he was bald on top. He was probably in his fifties. He held a clipboard in his hands, used it to point at the room behind him. "We left everything as is, just like you asked. I can't keep my team standing around, though—we need to process this place. I've got another one downtown after we finish up here."

"We won't be long," Dobbs said. "Ian, this is the man I told you about, Michael Kepler."

Reflexively, I offered my hand. "Pleased to meet you."

The man only stared.

Dobbs looked at me. "Ian Dantzler here heads three of LA's crime scene investigative teams. Been with LAPD for twenty-two years now."

"Twenty-three," Dantzler corrected him.

Wilkins dropped a heavy hand onto my shoulder, looked at Dantzler. "Mr. Kepler says he found the vic in his bathtub after going out for a movie. Says he has no idea who she is. Says he's never seen her before in his entire life. Figured we'd bring him down here, see how that goes."

I absorbed about half of what he said.

My eyes were fixed on a framed photograph sitting on a small table near the door beside a bowl holding several loose keys and some change. A wood frame, stained a deep cherry. It was the image within that frame that had caught my eye, though, the image that held me. A photo of me with a very much alive Alyssa Tepper standing outside gate 4 of Yankee Stadium in the Bronx. My hair was a little longer; I hadn't worn it that way in some time. We both smiled at the camera, our hands entwined.

"This is her apartment," I said softly.

"Wait for it," Wilkins said, his grip tightening on my shoulder.

"I don't...understand. I've never met her."

"Fuck me." Wilkins released my shoulder, pulled out his wallet, and handed two more dollars to Dobbs.

Dobbs pocketed the money but his gaze never left me. His lips were frozen in a sort of half grin. "Are you seriously going to deny that's you?"

I felt my face flush. My cheeks grew warm, hot. "It's fake...got to be. Photoshop or something. Some kind of trick or a joke."

On the floor, between the small table and the front door, were several pairs of tennis shoes. Two of those pairs were obviously female; the third I recognized. Size 11 Nike Air VaporMax LTRs. The right one had a dark smudge near the toe where I had spilled coffee. By the time I'd tried to scrub it out, the stain had set. I hadn't seen them in a while; they'd been misplaced somewhere in my closet.

Dobbs caught my millisecond glance at the shoes. "When we pull DNA, it's going to match yours, right?"

I didn't say anything.

"Your brain is no doubt chewing through a million thoughts," Dobbs said. "While you're being quiet, and it's probably best that you do, I'd like you to consider one more thought. Possibly *the most* important thought you will ever consider in your life. If you tell us the truth now, if you cooperate, everything will be far easier for you. When we file charges, and we *will* file charges, they will be lesser charges than if you continue to deny your involvement in the death of Alyssa Tepper. LA County has some of the nastiest prosecutors in the country. They're bitter, angry, fed up with all the bad press they receive, so when they get a case they see as a slam dunk, they take it to the rim. They milk it. They'll make an example out of you and they'll do it publicly. California is a death-penalty state when it comes to capital offenses, so you might find yourself standing in the gas chamber when the dust settles. Even if they don't actually kill you—the last execution was more than a decade ago—they'd have no problem keeping you on death row for the rest of your life. You're, what, twenty-six? That's a long, long time. You cop to all this, you tell us the truth, and you're probably looking at only twenty to thirty years, maybe less if you keep your head down, stay out of trouble. That's not bad. You'd be out in your forties or fifties. Plenty of time to pull a new life together. Because you could still have a future, if you chose to."

Dobbs turned back to Dantzler. "Do you mind giving us a tour of Ms. Tepper's apartment? I think Michael has a right to know what else we've found."

CHAPTER SEVEN

MICHAEL

THERE WERE SEVERAL OTHER photos.

On the coffee table, there was one with Alyssa Tepper and me kissing outside a Hard Rock Café. In a silver frame beside the couch, one of the two of us with the famed Hollywood sign in the distance. Four of me alone, grinning, smiling, laughing. I remembered none of them being taken. In the small kitchen, held to the refrigerator with a Pizza Hut magnet, was one of me standing in the open door of my truck. Alyssa Tepper sat sideways in the driver's seat up behind me wearing a white tank top and shorts, her legs wrapped around my chest. She had a Nadler Distribution ball cap perched at an angle on her head. My tongue was sticking out, and I had a goofy expression on my face. The photo was crinkled, faded, worn, as if it had been carried in a pocket for some time before finding a home next to a to-do list and a calendar from a local real estate agent.

I stared at that last one.

I stared at my own eyes looking back at me. Familiar, yet not.

I'd had only two girlfriends since moving to Los Angeles and I hadn't shown either of them my truck, where I worked. I wasn't ashamed; I loved my job. Security at Nadler was tight—nonemployees were not permitted on the lot for insurance reasons, and when I had the truck out, I was on the road. I didn't linger in LA long enough to visit with anyone or take pictures.

"She looks happy there," Dobbs said. "You make a cute couple."

"*Made,*" Wilkins said from behind us.

Dantzler cleared his throat. "Yes, well, there's more for you to see in the bedroom."

He led us down a narrow hallway—bedroom on the left, small bathroom on the right. I stopped and looked in the bathroom. A CSI investigator was busy bagging up two toothbrushes—one pink, one blue—a men's razor, a half-used bar of soap, and several other items I couldn't see from where I stood. When she noticed me watching her, she pursed her lips and closed the bathroom door.

"In here," Dantzler said from the bedroom.

The bedroom was small, no more than eleven by thirteen. A full-size bed was pushed into the corner opposite the door, a scratched and worn nightstand beside it. There was a dresser against the wall to our right. There were more photos in here—I stopped looking at them; my gut was churning. The bed was unmade, white sheets tangled in a brown quilt at the foot. Rumpled pillows tossed about.

An empty tripod stood near the back of the room. The video camera that no doubt had been perched atop that tripod was now on the dresser; wires trailed from the front of the camera to the back of a small flat-panel television. The screen was on but blank.

Dantzler looked to Dobbs.

Dobbs nodded.

The lead investigator pressed several buttons on the camera and an image appeared. Grainy. The only light in the room came from candles on the nightstand. It was a side shot of the bed. On it, Alyssa Tepper, naked, her back arched, eyes closed, writhing as she slowly rose and fell. She rolled her head to the side, her hair moving from one shoulder to the other. Hands came up from beneath her, slid up her bare belly to her breasts, brushed her nipples. Hands I knew, arms I knew. When one of those arms came back down and pushed the quilt aside, then pushed it to the floor, I wanted to turn away. I didn't want to watch, but I couldn't look away. Like everyone else's in the room, my eyes were fixed on the screen, my eyes locked on my body beneath hers, my own face glancing at the camera briefly before turning back to her and smiling, my voice whispering her name before sitting up and pulling her against me in the dim light.

"Turn it off," I muttered.

Again, Dantzler looked to Dobbs.

Again, Dobbs nodded.

The screen went blank.

Dantzler pulled open one of the dresser drawers and stepped aside.

Dobbs nudged me toward the open drawer. "Take a look."

Inside were several pairs of jeans, socks, underwear, a couple T-shirts. Some folded, others not. The drawer was nearly full.

"I think we've all had a drawer like this at one point or another," Dobbs said. "A little home away from home. You're not quite ready to bite the bullet and move in, but you're spending enough nights with her to warrant some space. I don't know about you, but I always found that moment nice, when a girl gives you a corner of her place. It shows she trusts you, finds comfort in your presence. I suppose it also means she drops her guard a bit, sometimes a little too much. Do you recognize the clothing, Michael?"

I didn't reply.

"I bet you do," Dobbs said. "I bet you remember the day she gave you that drawer."

All three men watched me close, studied me. I didn't look in the drawer—I wouldn't give them the satisfaction. The top of the dresser was cluttered with headbands, jewelry; earrings and necklaces sat in an open wooden box. My eyes fell on one particular necklace near the bottom—a bird feather attached to a thin leather strap. A sparrow feather.

I quickly looked away.

CHAPTER EIGHT

MICHAEL

THEY TOOK ME TO LAPD headquarters on First Street.

This time, Dobbs did handcuff me, although I wasn't read my rights.

None of us spoke in the car.

Inside the building, Dobbs and Wilkins guided me past the front desk to a bank of elevators on the east wall. We got in one, exited on the third floor, and crossed through a large bullpen humming with activity despite the ungodly early hour. The dozens of desks, tables, and chairs were filled with people from all walks of life—gangbangers and prostitutes and men dressed in drag; old people and screaming children; a man in a four-thousand-dollar suit with a twenty-something woman wearing an equally expensive dress, both shouting at two uniformed officers. Their hair was disheveled, and he had a tear in his right jacket sleeve. At first I thought they were the victims of a mugging but then I realized they were both in handcuffs with a ziplock bag of colorful pills on the desk between them and the cops. At the far end of the room, I was photographed and fingerprinted. The female officer, clearly proficient, rolled my fingers one at a time over the digital reader.

When she was finished with me, Dobbs tugged at my arm and Wilkins gave me a shove. They led me down a hallway, deeper into the building, leaving the noise behind us.

Dobbs opened a door marked INTERVIEW ROOM 7—DO NOT ENTER WHEN RED LIGHT IS ON and ushered me inside. "Get comfortable."

He left. The door locked with a loud *clack!* and I was alone.

I sat there for two hours.

I had never been in an interrogation room before, but nonetheless, the space felt familiar. I'd seen enough of them in films and on television and it was clear that those in Hollywood didn't travel farther than LA for their inspiration. The room wasn't very large, maybe ten feet square, with a drop ceiling and fluorescent lights beaming down. The cinder-block walls were painted a muted gray. A metal table was bolted to the wall and the floor with two black cloth chairs on one side and a single chair on the other. A large one-way mirror filled the wall to my left, and a camera faced me from the corner above. I tried to sit in the single chair but with my hands cuffed behind me, I had to sit on the edge of the table instead.

Two hours.

Dobbs returned alone carrying two cups of coffee. He set them down on the table and closed the door with his foot. "Turn around."

He removed the handcuffs and told me to take a seat.

I rubbed at my wrists. "I'm supposed to get a phone call."

"In a minute."

"You haven't even read me my rights."

"I haven't arrested you." Dobbs slid one of the coffees toward me. "Take a seat."

I lowered myself tentatively into a chair. "I need to call my sister. She's got to be worried."

Dobbs pursed his lips, turned his own coffee cup counterclockwise, and took a drink. "Have you thought about what I said?"

I looked him dead in the eye. "I have no idea who that woman is. I've never met her. I've never been to her apartment. I've certainly never slept with her. Somebody is trying to set me up."

Dobbs looked down at his coffee cup, turned it slowly again. "Give me a DNA sample."

"Why would I do that?"

"Why not? If you're innocent, there's no reason not to, right?"

I shook my head. "Not until I talk to my sister. I want my phone back."

"Your phone has been logged into evidence. You can file a petition to have it returned to you but I can tell you, it won't be released until this case is closed." He pushed the second cup toward me. "Drink some coffee. Relax. Let's just talk, okay? Just the two of us. Try to clear this up."

"Right. Just the two of us. Who's behind the window there? Who's watching the camera feed?"

Dobbs glanced up at the one-way window. "Nobody's in there and the camera isn't on. No blinking red light. It's just us now."

"Right." I smirked, took a sip of the coffee. "I know how this works."

"Have you been arrested before?"

"You said I'm not under arrest."

He waved a hand. "You know what I mean."

"I've never been inside a police station before."

"Really?"

"Never."

"Never been in any trouble at all, huh? Perfect citizen?"

"I do my best."

"Tell me about Alyssa Tepper."

I took another sip of the coffee. "I'm not gonna kill a girl in my own apartment, then call the police to report it."

"You're on the road for, what, two-thirds of the month? Everyone's got needs. Did she cheat on you? Did she catch you cheating on her? Tempers flare, emotions take over, bad things happen. I've seen it before, Michael, more times than I can count. You can be straight with me."

"I've told you the truth from the beginning."

Dobbs head tilted to the side. "Have you?"

"Yes."

"You told me your name is Michael Kepler. Since we're being honest with each other, why don't you start by telling me your real name."

CHAPTER NINE

MICHAEL

THAT IS MY REAL name."

"Your prints came back as belonging to Michael Fitzgerald," Dobbs said. "You're in the system because of your commercial license."

"I'm adopted. Fitzgerald is their name, not mine. I was born Michael Kepler."

"Legally, your name is Michael Fitzgerald."

"Well, that's not me. Never has been."

"You're not fond of your parents, are you?"

"What does that have to do with anything?"

Dobbs shrugged. "I looked them up when your prints came back. The Fitzgeralds are well known back east, a family of considerable resources. Both shrinks, right? I found their names on dozens of websites. Academic stuff, mostly. Over my head, for sure. Well respected in their fields, tenured professors at Cornell, your alma mater." He lowered his eyes. "Sorry to hear about your father. Aneurysm, right?"

"Adoptive father."

Dobbs twisted his coffee cup again. "They're a family of considerable resources."

"You said that already."

Dobbs curled his fingers around the edge of the table. "I suppose that's why you called your sister first? Give her a chance to run some interference?"

I looked at him, puzzled. "I'm not sure what—"

Two knocks at the door. Swift. Hard.

The door swung open.

Detective Wilkins came in, followed by a heavyset man wearing a charcoal-gray suit so perfectly fitted that the tailor might well have come marching in behind him holding a needle and thread. The man's salt-and-pepper hair was slicked back, appropriate for an evening out, not walking into a police interview room at four in the morning. His sharp eyes held the wisdom of a man in his sixties, but his face and his even sharper, beak-like nose belonged to a much younger man, late forties at the most. He carried a slim leather briefcase, which he set in the middle of the table between me and Dobbs. He turned his gaze first on the detective, then on me.

"Is it safe to assume you haven't said anything to this upstanding public servant or his colleagues?" A deep voice, all bass. His manicured fingers triggered the latches on his briefcase; he reached inside, removed a notepad and pen, then closed the case. "Never mind, don't answer that." He turned to Dobbs and Wilkins. "Gentlemen, can you give me a moment with my client?"

Dobbs nodded reluctantly and stood. When he reached the door, he knocked twice, then turned back to me. "I know you're guilty, Michael. Know how I know?"

I only looked at him.

"You never once asked me how she died."

The man in the gray suit raised his hand. "No need for

jabs, Detective. You've traumatized my client enough. Out. Both of you."

An officer opened the door and stepped aside. Young guy, short dark hair.

Wilkins smirked and seemed about to say something, then apparently thought better of it. He pushed past Dobbs and went out the door. Dobbs lingered a moment longer, his eyes still locked on me, then he left too. The door closed behind him.

The man in the gray suit dropped into Dobbs's seat; the frame groaned under his weight. "An overdose of propofol."

"What?"

"That's what killed the girl in your bathtub. An overdose of propofol. She was injected here." He touched the left side of his neck. "It's a drug typically used by anesthesiologists, a sedative."

"I know what propofol is."

He frowned. "I wouldn't tell anyone else that. Ignorance is bliss, and you, my friend, need some bliss."

"Who are you?"

"Philip Wardwell. Our firm has done a significant amount of work for your father over the years. After you spoke to your sister, she talked to your mother, who in turn called our New York office," he said. "I'm based in Los Angeles, so I was dispatched."

I lowered my head and ran my hand through my hair. "I didn't want my mother to find out about this. Megan shouldn't have said anything."

Wardwell shrugged. "Well, she did, and I'm here. I plan to help you avoid a jail cell for the foreseeable future—try not to get too dizzy with gratitude." He flipped through several pages of notes on his pad. "I just spent the better part of an hour reviewing the evidence with those two detectives. It is substantial but primarily circumstantial."

"Primarily?"

"They have one witness. One of Tepper's neighbors, a Velma Keefe. She told them she saw you with Alyssa Tepper twice—two days ago and last week. Says she passed you both on the stairs. She ID'd you from a photo lineup."

"That's ridiculous. I've never met Alyssa Tepper. Somebody is trying to set me up," I insisted.

He gave me a sideways glance, then returned to his notepad. "They told me about your field trip to Tepper's apartment. If we need to discredit this Keefe woman, we can say she saw you when the police brought you through. I'm not worried about her." He flipped the page. "I saw the photographs, video, clothing. They're rushing DNA on a number of the items they pulled out of there. Did they tell you what they found in your building? Beyond the items that were near your bed? Did they tell you about the garbage chute?"

I shook my head.

"They pulled out a trash bag, same brand as under your sink. The bag was stuffed full of women's clothing, Tepper's size. One of the blouses, purple with white trim, matches her outfit in one of the photographs with you they found at her place."

I had no idea what to say to that so I said nothing.

When it was clear I wasn't going to respond, Wardwell went on. "They found a phone too. A disposable cell. The log showed calls and texts dating back nearly three months."

"Not with me."

Wardwell said dismissively, "Circumstantial, anyway." He placed his pad and pen back inside his briefcase and snapped the lid shut. "The phone was wiped clean, no prints. Nothing on the bag itself or any of the items found inside. They're pulling a warrant to check your truck at Nadler. I imagine they'll have that by the time the sun comes up."

"This is crazy," I muttered. "What do we do next?"

Wardwell stood and knocked twice on the door. "We get you out of here."

The door opened and the dark-haired officer looked in. "Yes?"

Wardwell grabbed the man by the collar, pulled him inside, and slammed his head against the cinder-block wall three times. The officer crumpled to the ground, blood trickling from his ear.

CHAPTER TEN

MICHAEL

WHAT THE FUCK!" I jumped up from my seat and backed into the corner.

"Get his gun," Wardwell said, sliding the toe of his shoe into the doorway before it could close and lock us in.

I shook my head. "No way."

Wardwell rolled his eyes. "You're some kind of Boy Scout now? We don't have time for a crisis of conscience."

He jammed his briefcase into the opening, freeing his shoe, then knelt down beside the unconscious officer.

"Is he dead?"

Wardwell stood with a grunt, fumbled with the leather strap on the officer's gun, and pulled it from the holster. He tucked the gun under his belt at the small of his back and smoothed his suit jacket down over it. "Walk directly next to me, don't make eye contact with anyone but me. Look like you belong, and nobody thinks twice."

"I'm not going anywhere with you!"

"Do exactly as I say, or I'll start shooting people. It's a Glock twenty-two—fifteen rounds in the magazine, another in the chamber. I'm a good shot. I'll take out at least five to ten people before someone gets a bead on me. You want that on your head?" Wardwell picked up his briefcase and held the door open. He quickly glanced into the hallway, then back at me. "Come on, move."

I went.

I knew I shouldn't but I went anyway.

I stepped out into the hallway, fully expecting a dozen cops to jump me. A female detective walked by, her head buried in a folder, gun slapping at her hip.

Wardwell pressed his free hand against my back and steered me to the left. At the end of the hall, he turned us to the right. "Good," he said in a low voice. "Keep moving. Make a left up ahead."

Wardwell was leading us deeper into the building, in the opposite direction from Dobbs, Wilkins, the officer who took my prints.

"End of this hall, make another right."

We passed a janitor emptying trash cans, lost to some song in his earbuds.

Two more lefts.

A right.

A service elevator.

Wardwell pressed the button. "Almost there."

I started to turn, see what was behind us.

He squeezed my shoulder. "Don't."

The doors opened.

We stepped inside.

He pressed the button marked P2.

When the elevator doors opened again, we were in the parking garage. "The blue Ford, over there to your right."

The level was only about a quarter full. I spotted a Ford Escort parked beside a concrete support pole. A wreck of a car, at least fifteen or twenty years old. The hubcap was missing from the right front wheel. Faded navy-blue paint, pocked with dings and dents and patches of rust.

I glanced over at Wardwell. His suit was probably worth more than the car. "Are you even an attorney?"

He fished the keys out of his pocket and tossed them to me. "You're driving."

The car wasn't locked.

I climbed into the driver's seat. The tattered beige material was patched with duct tape.

Wardwell took out the gun, got in the passenger side, put his briefcase on his lap. The door squealed and closed with a thunk. Sweat trickled down his brow, the fast walk taking a toll on his large frame. "Go, damn it. Start the car!"

"Why are you doing this?"

He appeared puzzled. "This is what you paid me to do."

A wetness slapped against my face before I registered the sound of the gunshot, heard the shattering of the passenger window. Wardwell jerked toward me, then fell forward, his eyes blank.

CHAPTER ELEVEN

MICHAEL

I DON'T KNOW HOW long I sat there, my limbs paralyzed, my heart thudding wildly. The shot echoed off the concrete and faded away, replaced with the sound of rapidly retreating footsteps. Then the garage was quiet except for my breathing. My gasping, quick breaths.

Wardwell's empty gaze seemed to focus on the gun in his own hand, still resting atop his briefcase, his finger less than an inch from the trigger.

I touched the side of my face. My fingers came away slick. Not with my blood, though. Wardwell's.

The bullet had entered the front right side of his head and exited the back left. Owing to either a carefully placed shot or an extremely lucky accident, I was alive and unhurt.

I wiped my hand on the side of the filthy seat.

Instincts took over in that moment and I let them. If I thought about what I was doing, I wouldn't do it. I wouldn't do what needed to be done.

I twisted the key.

The engine sputtered, caught, and came to life with an aggravated groan.

I put the Ford into drive and followed the exit signs from the second level up to the first, toward daylight. Not one of the officers in the several police cars that passed me gave me a second glance.

Wardwell had left his parking ticket on the dash. I fished Wardwell's wallet out of his jacket pocket and paid the twelve-dollar fee with his Visa card.

The name on the card was not Philip Wardwell.

An alarm went off as the arm went up, a wailing through the structure. I didn't know if someone had heard the shot or found the officer down in the interview room, but I didn't care. I made a left on North Main Street and didn't look back.

CHAPTER TWELVE

MICHAEL

ROLAND EADS," I SAID into the pay phone.

I had circled the block around the police station, then made a left onto Fourth toward Sanford. From there, I drove to the fish market. Nobody followed me.

I knew I couldn't go back home. I couldn't go to my truck—that was the first place they'd look.

The Los Angeles fish market officially opened at six in the morning, but the restaurant buyers, tourists, and locals lined up long before that.

What I needed was a crowd.

Someplace I could disappear.

Someplace I could dump the Ford.

I drove behind the old Edward Hotel and nestled the wreck between a Dumpster and a large pile of trash partially covered by a blue plastic tarp.

The engine sputtered a few times, then dropped off.

The dead man beside me was large. Too large for such a small car. He had shifted during the drive, but his slumped body remained wedged between the dashboard and the passenger seat. His ruined head lolled toward me.

I pulled the briefcase from his lap, careful not to touch the gun. Inside, along with the notepad and pen, I found a cassette tape. I must have stared at the handwritten label for at least a minute, my heart pounding at the sight of it, before finally shoving it into my pocket.

I kept his wallet.

I searched his pockets for a cell phone but found nothing.

With napkins from a discarded McDonald's bag on the floor, I wiped my face, the steering wheel, the dashboard, my door, his briefcase, anything I remembered touching.

And I left him there.

I didn't want to, but I had no idea what else to do. What else *could* I do?

The gas station on Fifth had a bathroom around back. I bolted across the parking lot, locked myself inside, fell to the ground beside the grimy toilet, and threw up into the bowl.

My hands were shaking.

My heart was pounding.

I couldn't get enough air.

I threw up a second time, nothing but yellow bile. My stomach churned, wanting to get rid of more, but there was nothing left.

I rolled to the side and closed my eyes.

I had to calm down.

I forced my breathing to slow.

Deep breaths—in through my nose, out through my mouth, as Megan had taught me. The burn of adrenaline began to ebb. My heart slowed. When I finally managed to stand, my legs almost folded under the sudden weight. I stumbled over to the sink and got a good look at myself in the mirror. The eyes staring back at me were not my own but those of a much older, very tired man.

I pulled my stained sweatshirt off and scrubbed my face and hair to get rid of the red. The white and gray too—I tried not to think about that. The water swirling around the drain ran red, pink, and finally clear. I did my best to clean the sweatshirt. I tore off the tag and turned it inside out, then pulled it back over my head.

By the time I'd finished, twenty minutes had passed. I found a pay phone on Stanford and dialed Megan collect.

"I can barely hear you. Where are you?" Megan said. "Who did you say?"

"Roland Eads," I repeated into the pay phone. I covered my other ear and tried to twist away from the people pushing past me on the sidewalk. "I'm at the fish market."

"I didn't call anyone," Megan said. "I've been worried sick, calling you all night, but I didn't talk to anyone else. Not about this."

"So you didn't tell Dr. Rose?"

"I'd never do that. At least, not unless you told me to. Christ, Michael. You've never met this girl? Are you sure?"

"I don't know who's doing this or how, but someone is setting me up."

"But it was you? In the video?"

Two patrolmen walked by me. I turned away. "If you didn't send this guy, somebody else did."

"Why would someone frame you for murder?"

"I have no idea."

I pulled out Roland Eads's wallet and picked through the contents.

Ninety-three dollars in cash, the Visa card, and a driver's license. Nothing else. The address on the license told me this man lived in Needles, California—a small town on the Nevada border nearly four hours away. I knew it from my route. I kept the driver's license out and shoved the rest in my pocket. "Megan, I need you to do me a huge favor."

"Of course, anything."

"I need you to get into Dr. Bart's office and see if his Joe DiMaggio baseball card is still there."

Megan grew quiet.

"Meg."

"I'm here."

"Can you do that for me?"

After a moment, she said, "His office is locked, Michael. Dr. Rose has the key. Nobody has been in there since he died. She won't even let Ms. Neace in there to clean."

Ms. Neace had been our parents' housekeeper for the better part of thirty years, but nonetheless, Dr. Bart had rarely allowed her into his office—she could go in only on Friday mornings, when he was at the university. Even then, Dr. Rose watched over her as she worked.

"Please, Meg. This is important. The police found a card just like it in Alyssa Tepper's purse," I told her.

"It can't be the same one."

"A 1936. Half the paper on the back was missing, and the left corner was torn."

"For real?"

"There's something else," I told her. "She had a sparrow feather. I saw it in her apartment. It was on a leather strap, like a necklace."

Megan said nothing.

"Meg, please," I pleaded.

"Are you sure it was a sparrow feather? There's, like, thirty-seven million kinds of birds, Michael, and they've all got feathers."

"I'd recognize one of those feathers from a hundred feet."

"You need to come home, Michael. Right now. Just come home."

I looked down at Eads's driver's license in my hand. "I can't. If I run, they'll find me. I need to figure out what's going on."

"Maybe we should tell Dr. Rose."

"No way."

"She can protect you."

"Promise me you won't."

Megan didn't reply.

"Meg? Promise me."

Finally, she said, "Promise *me* you'll come home, then I'll think about it."

"I will," I told her. "As soon as I can." I hung up before she could object, because Megan *would* object.

At a small drugstore, with money from Roland Eads's wallet, I bought a baseball cap, sunglasses, and a T-shirt. Not much of a disguise, but all I could put together. I also bought a disposable phone. I changed in the alley behind the store, stuffed my sweatshirt deep into a Dumpster, then dialed Megan from the disposable phone. The call went to voice mail.

I fished the cassette tape out of my pocket and glared at the handwritten label.

Dark room—M. Kepler—August 12, 1996.

Dr. Bart's handwriting.

I was four in 1996. The year I went to live with the Fitzgeralds.

I needed a cassette player, and I knew where to find one.

CHAPTER THIRTEEN

WRITTEN STATEMENT, MEGAN FITZGERALD

To Special Agent Jessica Gimble, the lovely Detective Dobbs, and their friends in law enforcement—

Okay, fine, I'll write it all down. Every last word of it. Not because you asked me to, but because I think it may be the only way all of Michael's story gets out there. The truth of it. The nuts and bolts. I'm certainly not going to leave it up to any of you to piece together. I've spent the past two days watching all of you try to gather evidence and figure out what really happened, and while that was pretty entertaining, I can't let you twist in the wind forever. You're clowns in a circus car. Our tax dollars at work—what a joke. I owe this to Michael. I've got no intention of throwing him under the bus—he managed to crawl under there all by his lonesome. But when the dust settles on these last forty-eight hours, I do want to be sure the facts are straight. And you clearly need a little help in that department.

So here it goes, all that you've missed, spelled out nice and neat on a legal pad. I'll try and keep it between the lines and in tight cursive just as Dr. Bart would have wanted. The language of a lady, as Dr. Rose would insist. Pay attention, kids—it's time to go to school.

My shit of a brother hung up on me!

He called me from a pay phone somewhere in LA not only to repeat that he'd found a dead girl in his bathtub but also to tell me how his attorney had decided to bypass the court system and bust him out of jail. He finished with the attorney catching a bullet in the head soon after exiting said police station.

He rattled all this off, then he hung up on me! I hit Redial from my call log but the line just rang and rang, a dozen times at least. I couldn't call him back on his phone; he said the police had that. I did the only sane thing I could—I rolled over in my bed and screamed into my pillow.

I felt better after that. Nothing like a good scream to clear the head. You all should try it, maybe you could actually do what you're paid for.

That's when I caught the smell of breakfast wafting up from downstairs—bacon, eggs, English muffins...Ms. Neace, no doubt. It seemed odd for such a normal thing to fill my senses after Michael's phone call.

I pushed back my sheets and down comforter, sat on the edge of my bed, and caught the naked girl staring at me from the full-length mirror in the corner of my room. Even from that distance, I spotted the bags under my eyes, the tangled mess of my brown hair. At least my boobs looked good. I gave the nips a tweak. I could always count on the girls.

I had spent the entire night dialing Michael over and over after he'd found that body. I'd texted too. Dr. Rose always insisted I get at least eight hours. I probably slept half that. *No bueno...*

No way I could let Dr. Rose see me like that. She'd know something was up if I planned to help Michael, and that wasn't an option. I snatched my robe from the back of my dressing-table chair, threw it on, and fumbled with my hairbrush.

One hundred strokes, fifty per side.

Better.

Little concealer under the eyes—much better.

I glanced down at my desk at that point, and I'm not gonna lie, I stared at it a few minutes.

Dr. Bart bought me that desk when I was a kid. An antique Cutler rolltop, more than one hundred years old, in perfect condition.

"This desk belonged to a schoolteacher in Buffalo during the First World War," he told me on the day he presented it. He'd guided me down the hallway and ushered me into my bedroom blindfolded. "Her husband left to fight in the war, and she sat here every night writing him letters, praying for his safe return. He never did come home, though. When she passed at the age of eighty-one, she left the desk to her grandson, an attorney in the city. It remained in his office until I purchased it at an auction last week. This desk has seen the birth of equal rights, the Great Depression, multiple wars, the rise and fall of nations, the deaths of Kennedy and King, and the destruction of the Twin Towers. Imagine the secrets held within that polished mahogany. This desk is a witness to history, and now it's part of your history to own, to cherish—you will write its next chapter before passing it on to your own children one day."

I was five.

WTF, right? Who says that to a five-year-old?

Twenty minutes later, I wrote my name across the front with yellow crayon. Dr. Rose cleaned it before Dr. Bart saw what I'd done. I never did like antiques much, anyway.

There's a hidden compartment under the center desk

drawer—that's where I kept the sparrow feathers Dr. Bart gave me over the years. Soft and pressed tight between the pages of *Wuthering Heights*.

Have you ever read that book, Detective Dobbs? I doubt it. You look like a jock who probably avoided books without pictures. I bet Jessica read it, though, when she was a girl, all curled up on a bench at her window in her perfect room on a perfect street in a perfect little town.

Not all homes are perfect, Jessica. I think you have to live in toxicity to understand it. And that's why you suck at your job.

CHAPTER FOURTEEN

DOBBS

DOBBS STOOD IN THE interview room, staring at the two red spots on the cinder-block wall, then at the larger puddle on the tile floor. "Is Sillman gonna be okay?"

"Concussion," Wilkins said. "They took him to Good Sam. Waynick rode with him and the paramedics. Said he came around by the time they got to the hospital, swore it was the attorney who hit him, not Kepler. Said he sucker-punched him. Sillman's expected to make a full recovery, but he's taking it pretty hard. Said to tell you he's sorry he dropped the ball."

Dobbs glanced up at the camera. It had been his call to leave it off while talking to Kepler. He preferred to leave the camera off until the start of an actual interrogation; the little red light blinking to life tended to rattle a perp.

This camera hadn't recorded anything, but others had. In the security office, he watched Kepler and his attorney hustle through the building, go down the service elevator, and walk out into the parking garage. The camera lost them there but picked Kepler back up when he exited the structure in an old Ford, the attorney riding shotgun. The tags were bogus, but they had an APB out on the car. Rush hour in LA started at five, gridlock lasted until ten. Traffic cams might pick up the bogus plate, but if Kepler had half a brain, he'd ditch the car, maybe swap it for another or maybe go on foot.

"Get his picture out to all the bus stations, train, TSA over at LAX. We can't let him out of the city," Dobbs said.

"Already done," Wilkins replied. "I also put it out to the taxi services, Uber, and Lyft. They got a pic of the attorney too."

"He's armed. Do we go to the press? Get his picture out in the public?"

Wilkins bit his lower lip. "He escaped from LAPD headquarters. You don't want to put that out there unless someone up the totem pole signs off."

Dobbs's phone rang. He took it from his pocket and glanced at the display—Dantzler. He walked to the far corner of the room and answered. "Yeah?"

"Hey, I'm at Kepler's truck over at Nadler Distribution. Do you have a second to talk?"

"What'd you find?"

"Well, for starters, Kepler's an audiobook fan. He's got about a dozen of them in here, CDs checked out from his local library. Not exactly the kind of thing I'd expect. It's all highbrow stuff— nonfiction philosophy texts, sociology, ideology, and two books by a guy named Lawrence Levine. The book currently on deck is called *The Interpretation of Dreams* by Freud. Good book, but personally I prefer Jung over Freud."

"I'm more of a Jack Reacher fan myself," Dobbs said.

"No popcorn fiction for this guy. He's burning the miles educating himself."

"Why doesn't a guy like this finish college? He's got Mommy and Daddy footing the bill. Why drop out to drive a truck?"

"Did you pull his transcripts? Maybe there's something there," Dantzler suggested.

"I'll get to that. Does the truck have a transponder?"

Dantzler said, "A Trux Data. They recently switched from CarrierWeb. I've got my guys downloading the data. Kepler's boss said the box records thirty days. He's dropping the rest on a thumb drive from some central server. Said he can go back to the day Kepler started, about two years ago. For what it's worth, his boss said Kepler never gave him any trouble. Showed up on time. Delivered on time. Everything by the book. The ideal employee. We're getting the security-camera footage too. I don't expect to find much there. Sounds like he pulled in at midnight, unloaded, and left around three in the morning, just like he told you."

"What else did you find in the truck?"

"Couple changes of clothes. Toothbrush, shaving kit. Our guy's neat. You could eat off the floor. No garbage. Ashtrays look like they've never been used. He's got one of those extended cabs with a small bed in the back—he actually makes the bed. Sheets are tight and white, reminds me of my army days. I was beginning to think we wouldn't find anything worthwhile, but then we pulled the mattress out and got a good look at it. Found a small slit in the back corner, just big enough to get stuff in and out."

Dobbs pressed the phone closer to his ear. "Tell me you found something."

"We found a ziplock bag full of bird feathers."

Dobbs frowned. "Feathers?"

"Sparrow feathers. About two dozen of them."

"Why would he have sparrow feathers?"

Dantzler said, "I suppose it's not weird to collect bird feathers. It *is* weird to hide them inside your mattress, so we plugged the bird-feathers thing into NCIC and got a hit. An FBI flag. When we hang up, you need to give them a call. I'll text you the information along with a few pictures. You'll have the rest of my file inside an hour."

"What about a personal vehicle? Between his apartment and work, have you seen any evidence of some kind of car or truck? Nobody lives in LA without a vehicle."

"I asked, and nobody here has seen him with a car. He walks in and walks out. His apartment is less than a mile away. It's possible he doesn't have one. Did you check the DMV?"

Dobbs said, "Nothing registered in his name. *Either* name."

They hung up, and a moment later, his phone buzzed with a series of text messages from Dantzler. He used his thumb and forefinger to expand one of the images of the feathers in a bag. Fucking weird. Then he dialed the FBI special agent who'd put out the alert on NCIC—a Jessica Gimble—got voice mail, and left a message.

He needed coffee.

CHAPTER FIFTEEN

WRITTEN STATEMENT, MEGAN FITZGERALD

What was your mother like, Jessica? I bet she was a nice lady who spent half the day in a kitchen that always smelled of freshly baked cookies and the other half with her arms around you, telling you how much she loved you. Even Dobbs probably had a father who liked to toss a football around with him occasionally. Maybe helped him rebuild a '65 Mustang so he could roll into high school at sixteen all king-of-the-hill-like.

My home life wasn't quite like that.

Our home life wasn't like that.

Although I was too young to remember when the Fitzgeralds adopted me, they were never shy about reminding me. Me or Michael. There was no mom or dad in our house. Not really even a mother or father. Such things, such terms, were deceptive, and when you're raised by not one but two doctors, those falsities don't fly. They insisted we call them Dr. Bart and Dr. Rose. The term *mother* never left my lips unless it was part of a compound word not quite as charming but perfectly appropriate for both my adoptive parents.

"Megan, dear, you're not eating."

Dr. Rose knew how to get under my skin. I looked up to

find her watching me from across the table, her head tilted slightly to the side.

Even on Sunday mornings, she dressed to the nines in clothing no doubt purchased at Mint Julep, her favorite boutique in town. Usually she wore a cream-colored two-piece suit with a white blouse beneath, buttoned to her neck. A silver brooch to match the silver hair she pulled into a tight bun, the kind of bun that gave me a headache just looking at it. She spent hours applying her makeup, finishing moments before coming downstairs.

The day her adopted son was accused of murder was no different.

I looked back down at my plate.

Ms. Neace had loaded me up with bacon, eggs, and a grapefruit sprinkled with sugar. I managed to take a few bites, but mostly I just shuffled the food around with my fork. "Not hungry, I guess."

"You guess?"

"Sorry, Dr. Rose. I'm not particularly hungry this good morning, kind madam."

Her gray eyes narrowed and she gave me that look, the one that made her hawklike nose appear a little longer. The look that dramatically positioned shadows from the room around her solemn face just so. "Perhaps it's time we put an end to the late-night phone calls," she said. "Such distractions lead to lack of rest, and lack of rest will rob one of one's appetite."

Dr. Rose had insisted Ms. Neace set a place for Dr. Bart— plate, utensils, glassware—as if he were going to join us. I might still be an undergrad, but even I understand this is unhealthy, creepy behavior. Dr. Bart was in a drawer somewhere, a cold metal drawer, probably with a hole in his head and his brain in a bin, removed to get a better look at the aneurysm that had killed him without warning. In a few days, he would be buried, gone forever, yet Dr. Rose persisted in these games. Last night, I saw her carry two glasses of water up to their bedroom.

I plucked the grapefruit from my plate and set it on Dr. Bart's. He always did love his grapefruit.

Dr. Rose watched me quietly.

My cell phone vibrated on the chair beside me. Cell phones were not permitted at the dining table. I glanced down at the display—I didn't recognize the number.

"Is that your brother?"

"Telemarketer, I guess." I expected her to scold me, but she didn't.

"But that was your brother last night?"

It was my turn to fall silent.

When Michael dropped out of school and ran off (had it been six years already?), he didn't tell our parents where he was going—didn't so much as leave a note. He had this nasty fight with Dr. Bart, and the following morning he was gone. Nearly a month passed before he even contacted me— from Wyoming that time, the first of many places. Over the years, I'd boxed up some of the stuff he'd left and mailed it to him whenever he did anything even mildly permanent, like paying two months of rent in advance. First just clothing, then more obscure items; I was hoping they might remind him of home, maybe guilt him into some kind of return. I sent track trophies, drawings we did as kids, old Halloween costumes, whatever I could find. Whatever I could ship. No way he'd talk to Dr. Rose. He certainly wasn't going to talk to Dr. Bart. But he talked to me.

Dr. Rose said, "Will your brother be attending Dr. Bart's funeral?"

Ms. Neace came in to refill our coffee mugs, eyed the grapefruit on Dr. Bart's plate as she circled the table, then returned to the kitchen.

"He knows the funeral is Tuesday," I told her. "I asked him to come."

"He should be there," she said. "It would be wrong for him not to attend. Dr. Bart raised him. Put a roof over his head. Offered him an education, even if he didn't take it."

My phone buzzed again. Same number.

"If that's him, you should answer it."

"It's not him," I told her.

Dr. Rose dabbed at the corner of her mouth with a cloth napkin. "Tell him to put his differences with Dr. Bart aside long enough to attend. That would be the proper thing to do. If not for me, he should do it for you."

The only reason Dr. Rose had her girdle in a twist was appearances. Oh, the gossip if Michael didn't attend! What would her university colleagues say behind her back? A boy raised by two of the most prominent doctors in the country who would not speak to his mother or attend the funeral of his father?

Did you know he ran off six years ago?

He dropped out of school? I thought he'd just transferred!

I heard he's a truck driver, of all things! Can you imagine?

On and on.

If word got out about Michael, his actions would clearly be seen as a failure on the part of Dr. Rose and Dr. Bart, and neither of them failed—not in anything. Not ever. Dr. Bart in particular had never hesitated to point that out.

"You need to tell him how disappointed you will be if he doesn't attend," Dr. Rose insisted.

"Are you seeing patients today?"

She smiled that Cheshire cat grin of hers. "Trying to get rid of me?"

I nodded. "I need to break into Dr. Bart's office, and I'd prefer it if you weren't here to stop me."

"You think you're funny. I see. As if this were a time for jokes."

"I'm sorry, Dr. Rose."

Dr. Rose added creamer to her coffee, stirred, and took a delicate sip. "I prefer not to work on Sundays, but yes, I have two appointments today at my university office, at twelve and one. Later this afternoon, I'm meeting Gracie downtown. You're welcome to join us if you'd like."

Tea time and girl talk with one of Dr. Rose's friends—I'd rather go to the gyno. "Can you drop me at the university library? I really need to study. I have an exam tomorrow in Professor Spradley's class."

"Dr. Spradley can be tough."

My phone rang again. I pressed Decline.

"Are you sure that's not your brother?"

"Positive."

But I was beginning to think it might be.

CHAPTER SIXTEEN

MICHAEL

THE STOW 'N' GO warehouse complex off Alameda reminded me of a prison repurposed as a place to store the crap people never use. Signs advertised 120,000 square feet of secure storage at rates as low as $19.99 a month. The top floor of the three-story outer building was painted bright blue; the lower half was a creamy beige. Within the center courtyard stood three rows of smaller buildings. Each of the first-floor units boasted large garage doors painted the same blue as the topmost brick that opened onto strips of blacktop just wide enough for loading and unloading.

A key card was required to enter the building whether you were in a vehicle or on foot. My key card was in my wallet, which was back at my apartment or in an evidence bag with the LAPD.

From one of the four Dumpsters on the west side of the building, I fished out a flattened cardboard box that had once held a wine refrigerator. I found three smaller boxes, put them on top of each other, then picked up the whole pile. When a woman followed by a little boy of around eight years old approached the glass double doors toting a box of her own, I fell in step behind them. The woman held her key card awkwardly between two fingers. She said something to the boy, who snatched the card, ran to the reader, unlocked the door, and tugged it open.

I closed the distance, bending my knees slightly as if struggling under the weight of the boxes. "Can you hold that for me?"

I wedged my shoulder against the door, shouted a thanks, and made my way down the hallway on the right to one of the doors leading to the outer courtyard. Cameras were mounted everywhere.

In the courtyard, I left the largest box just outside the door and quickly carried the three others to the third row, the second-to-last storage unit on the left, thankful I'd decided on a combination lock when I'd rented the space a little over two years ago.

I raised the door just enough to get inside, pulled it down behind me, and turned on the light.

CHAPTER SEVENTEEN

DOBBS

AT HIS DESK AT LAPD headquarters, Detective Garrett Dobbs scrolled through the hundreds of photographs taken at Alyssa Tepper's apartment earlier in the day. CSI had uploaded them to a secure cloud storage folder. Pictures of Tepper and Michael Kepler, or Michael Fitzgerald, or whatever; seemingly random photographs of her kitchen, living room, bedroom. Still shots of the video featuring her with Kepler. Near the end, he found what he was looking for. "There it is."

Dobbs raised his phone and held it out to Wilkins.

Wilkins, sitting at the desk across from his with his own phone pressed to his ear, waved him off.

Dobbs looked back down at the screen and enlarged the image of the feather attached to a thin leather strap, some kind of necklace. On the flat-panel computer monitor on his desk, he had a picture of the bag of feathers found in Kepler's truck. A tech had removed one of the feathers and photographed it alongside the bag and a ruler. The example feather was a little over four inches long, similar to the one on Tepper's necklace. Dobbs was by no means

65

an expert, so he called one. Mirella Sunde at the Griffith Park Bird Sanctuary dropped into lecture mode, and Dobbs scrambled to take notes on at least thirty-five sparrow species in North America. Fifteen of those were common throughout the country, half a dozen were common to the eastern United States, ten more were common to the central part of the country, and two particular species were common to western North America—the Baird's sparrow and the golden-crowned sparrow. Dobbs finally got her to consent to identify the species if he had a feather brought to her by a uniformed officer.

Across from him, Wilkins scribbled on a notepad, then ended his call. "I've got something from Kepler's credit card records. He rents a warehouse space off Alameda. Maybe ten minutes from here."

Dobbs snatched his keys from the corner of his desk and stood. "I'm driving."

CHAPTER EIGHTEEN

WRITTEN STATEMENT, MEGAN FITZGERALD

By the time Dr. Rose brought her silver Mercedes CLS to a stop in front of the campus library on West Avenue, my call log recorded six missed calls from the California number along with one voice mail I didn't dare listen to in front of her. I clutched the phone in my sweaty palm—thank God they made these things waterproof.

"Will you need a ride home?"

I shook my head and unbuckled my seat belt. "I'm sure someone in the library can drive me back. If not, I'll Uber."

I was halfway out the door when Dr. Rose said, "Don't forget about our session. Five p.m., my home office."

"Sure."

I grabbed my backpack from the rear seat, closed both car doors, and started up the sidewalk to the library. Approaching the entrance, I watched the reflection of Dr. Rose's Mercedes. She pulled away as I stepped into the vestibule.

I dropped my backpack and tapped the voice-mail icon on my phone. The message had been left twenty minutes ago.

Michael's voice, thin and tinny through the small speaker. "Damn it, Meg, where are you? I bought a burner phone. The police still have mine. I'm getting my car. Call me back!"

I pressed Redial, but my call went straight to voice mail. I wasn't able to leave a message. A recording said the mailbox had not been set up.

I went back out the glass double doors and rounded the side of the library at a sprint, heading for the science building on the opposite side of the campus—where Dr. Rose saw her student patients.

CHAPTER NINETEEN

DOBBS

SHORTLY BEFORE NINE A.M., Dobbs pulled up in front of the Stow 'n' Go.

"How you doing on a warrant?" Dobbs asked.

Wilkins frowned and scrolled through the e-mail on his phone. "Nothing yet."

"Did you call Judge Fleming?"

"No—Fleming's in Tahoe until Tuesday."

Dobbs tossed his LAPD placard up on the dash. "Guess we're winging it."

Inside the office, they found a teenager manning the blue Formica counter. His spiky black hair jutted out in all directions. He had at least half a dozen piercings in his right ear, twice as many on the other side. A silver hoop hung from his nose. He had another in his lip. He wore a T-shirt that read THIS IS WHAT AWESOME LOOKS LIKE.

The kid glanced up as they entered, said, "Morning, Officers," before Dobbs had a chance to pull out his ID.

"That obvious?" Wilkins said.

The kid shrugged. "Nobody rocks a Ford Taurus like the po-po." He nodded at Dobbs's belt. "And the bad guys have the decency to hide their guns."

Wilkins stepped up to the counter, took out his phone, and scrolled through the pictures. "We're looking for someone."

"Damn, I thought you were here to take advantage of our nineteen-ninety-nine move-in special. Could have used that commission."

Wilkins's face soured, and he leaned slightly over the counter.

The kid shrank back and raised both hands. "Whoa, just playing with you. It can get lonely up in here. What've you got?"

Dobbs nodded at the ancient Dell on the corner of the desk. "Need you to look up a unit number. Should be under the name Michael Kepler. If you don't see a Kepler, try Fitzgerald."

Wilkins found the photograph of Michael Kepler and held his phone out to the kid. "You're billing this guy's credit card four hundred ninety-nine dollars a month."

The kid took the phone and studied the image, chewing the ring on his lip. "Four hundred and ninety-nine dollars would be one of the garage units on the first floor, a ten by thirty." He handed back the phone, walked past the computer, and pointed at the security monitor. "Think that could be your guy?"

Dobbs stepped closer. The security-camera footage was frozen on a man carrying a large box, his face only partially visible. He wore a Los Angeles Angels baseball cap and dark sunglasses, and he looked a lot like Michael Kepler.

"He ducked in behind another customer, didn't swipe a key card." The kid clicked on a food-encrusted keyboard under the screen. "I got another shot of him outside a minute or so later."

In the second image, the man was kneeling down at a garage door, working a lock.

"Box is gone," Wilkins pointed out. "Where'd it go?"

"He left it out in the courtyard, just outside the door. A lot of weirdness going on. I was checking him out when you guys came in." He clicked a button on the keyboard, and the video advanced in slow motion. They watched the guy on the screen remove the lock, raise the door, and slip inside. The door rolled back down behind him.

"When was this recorded?" Dobbs asked.

The kid brought up the time stamp. "About twenty minutes ago."

"He still in there?"

The kid shrugged. "I didn't see him come out..." His voice trailed off. He was gazing at a small television on the counter, stuffed back behind the security monitor. The sound was off, but images flickered across the screen. "Isn't that him too?"

Dobbs leaned over to get a better look. Michael Kepler's image stared back at him from the local NBC affiliate. Looked like a DMV photo. Below Kepler was the headline "Escape from LAPD?"

"Shit," Dobbs muttered. "That didn't take long."

"What unit is that? Where is it?" Wilkins asked, still staring at the security monitor.

The kid didn't answer.

"Kid! Over here. What unit?"

He reached for the phone. "I need to call my boss."

Wilkins smacked the top of the monitor. "Where is that unit?"

Dialing, the kid nodded toward an open doorway to the right. "Follow that hall to the end, go out to the courtyard. Third row, second-to-last garage door on the left, D-forty-seven."

CHAPTER TWENTY

WRITTEN STATEMENT, MEGAN FITZGERALD

This is probably totally illegal. I'm not up on the latest breaking-and-entering laws, particularly when the room you're breaking-and-entering into is in your own house. If what I share below is illegal, I plead the Fifth, or defer to my lawyer, or assert my right not to self-incriminate, or whatever. Also, this is off the record. Like the rest, I'm telling you this only to help you understand Michael's full story. How he got from A to B to D. I can't skip it—there'd be a gaping hole in my statement and you, being the bulldog that you are, you'd ask me about it anyway. Consider this my way of saving us that time and trouble. Not an admission of guilt. Now that I think about it, I don't think what I did would be illegal, anyway. At worst, it might subject me to a solid grounding. Dr. Rose and Dr. Bart were never shy about doling out punishments. You'll see that soon enough. Back to it, then—

The two of them shared a two-room office near the back of the northeast corner on the first floor of the science building. Rather than separate offices, they opted to set up facing desks in one and a couch and a chair in the other in order to create a private space for their sessions with patients.

I arrived at the science building about a minute before noon and slowly navigated the hallways. Dr. Rose had said her appointments were at noon and one p.m.

As I rounded the corner and her office came into view, I moved even slower, on the tips of my toes, holding my backpack at my side. The glass door was closed. The door to the secondary office was closed too, the blinds drawn. She would be inside with her first patient.

Dr. Rose's purse was on her desk. Dr. Bart rarely kept more on top of his desk than an old landline phone and a white coffee mug filled with pens. The phone was still there, but the pens were gone. His collection of framed degrees was gone from the wall too. There were no boxes. I wondered what she'd done with everything.

I opened Dr. Rose's door slowly. It squeaks if you open it too fast. I'd learned the sweet spot between fast and slow the first time I'd snuck in. Behind me, in the secondary office, I heard Dr. Rose's muffled voice followed by some girl's.

I tugged open the purse's zipper just far enough so I could reach inside for her keys.

I nearly dropped them when my phone vibrated in the back pocket of my jeans. I snatched it with my free hand and hit Decline before it could vibrate again.

Michael.

I quickly texted, Can't talk.

His response came a moment later. Did you get into his office?
Working on it. Where r u?
Warehouse.

I thumbed out, Call later, and put the phone back in my pocket.

I set Dr. Rose's keys on the desk and reached down into my backpack. I took out a lighter, a roll of clear packing tape, scissors, my old bank debit card, and a pair of tweezers.

Dr. Rose kept about a dozen keys on her ring—keys for the house, the university, and her various vehicles. She would never keep an outdated key. Each served a purpose. The dead bolt on Dr. Bart's office was a Medeco. I remember sounding out the word as a kid, reading it in the polished silver from the hallway outside his office as his deep bass voice resonated inside, the occasional reply from one of his many patients filling the space between.

Dr. Rose had one Medeco key, the only key on her ring with a square head. I held my breath, pried open the ring with my thumbnail, and slid the key off, doing my best not to jingle the others. I set it on the desk.

With the scissors, I cut a piece of the packing tape equal to the length of the key and placed that on the desk too, sticky-side up. Using the tweezers, I gripped the edge of the key.

When I flicked the lighter, nothing happened.

I flicked the small wheel again. The flint sparked, but no flame. I cursed myself for not buying a new one. The lighter finally came to life on my third attempt, and I quickly ran it along the side of the key until the metal was black with soot.

I killed the flame, waited a moment, then pressed the key into the sticky packing tape. When I pulled the key away, much of the soot remained on the tape—a perfect duplicate. I carefully applied the tape to my debit card, preserving the image.

In the room behind me, I heard a girl laugh, then Dr. Rose's voice. I couldn't make out the words.

I wiped the remaining soot from the key on my jeans and put the key back on Dr. Rose's ring. Returned the ring to her purse. Slipped the items I'd brought with me back in my pack and left the office.

Four minutes total, my best time yet.

* * *

What's *your* best time, Jessica? Do they teach this sort of thing in the FBI? I bet you cheat and use one of those automated lockpicks. They're called snap guns, right? You'll need to get me one of those. The holidays are coming up—it's never too early to start buying those stocking stuffers.

CHAPTER TWENTY-ONE

DOBBS

DOBBS CALLED FOR BACKUP as he ran, barking orders into his phone. He pushed out through the glass door at the end of the hall into the courtyard, drew his weapon, and got his bearings.

The courtyard was larger than it appeared from the outside. Three long rows of garages stood in the center, the building on one side and a tall cinder-block wall on the three others. Arrows painted on the blacktop indicated the flow of vehicular traffic. Signs identified rows A through D, D being the last.

Wilkins shielded his eyes with one hand, held his gun in the other. "You go in from this side, I'll circle around to his row from the far end, and we'll box him in."

Dobbs nodded, ran past the first two rows, and rounded the corner at D in a low crouch. Wilkins came around the opposite end, his gun pointed at the blacktop.

The row was deserted. Kepler was gone.

Dobbs knew the moment he saw the combination lock secured on the bottom right of the garage door.

Wilkins turned in a slow circle. "He can't be far."

"Get back to the main entrance, wait for backup, then comb everything—every inch. I'll—" Dobbs's phone rang. He didn't recognize the number. "This is Dobbs."

A female voice, slight Southern accent. "Detective, this is Special Agent Jessica Gimble with the FBI. I need you to listen to me carefully. I believe the suspect you have in custody might be responsible for multiple homicides in at least ten states. He is to be considered extremely dangerous. I've got marshals en route. They're about twenty minutes out from LAPD headquarters."

Dobbs blew out a breath. Apparently he wasn't the only person who didn't have time to watch the morning news. He lowered himself to a squat and fumbled with the combination lock on the garage door. "Are you in Los Angeles, Agent Gimble?"

"Santa Monica. I'm right behind them, about forty minutes away. The marshals have instructions to hold the suspect until—"

Dobbs ran his hand through his hair. "You'll want to reroute. I'll text you the address. A warehouse complex off Alameda. We've had a . . . complication."

CHAPTER TWENTY-TWO

WRITTEN STATEMENT, MEGAN FITZGERALD

The Uber dropped me at the start of our long, winding driveway. I chose to walk from there. Not because I had a problem with Uber drivers pulling up to the house, but because Ms. Neace was somewhere inside or on the grounds, and I didn't want her to know I was home just yet.

I entered through the side door off the laundry room, took off my shoes, tiptoed up the back stairs to my room, and gently closed the door behind me.

I placed my backpack on the corner of my bed, fished out the scissors and debit card with the image of the key, and settled in at my desk. I took my time cutting it out. I knew from past experience that one slip, and my DIY project would be toast. Dead-bolt locks in particular were tricky, far more unforgiving than a simple door lock. Cuts needed to be exact. Ten minutes later, the key cut from the plastic, I took a nail file from my makeup table and smoothed the edges. Then I blew away the dust and admired my handiwork.

Security is such an illusion. Every night, we seal ourselves up in our homes, these boxes filled with windows of fragile glass; we set alarms that ring to call centers in far-off places like India or the Philippines. We tell ourselves we're safe because the police patrol the streets and our neighbors watch and our Wi-Fi cameras and motion-activated lights diligently stare with unblinking eyes. The world might look glossy and safe, but that's just paint, a shimmering clear coat. Windows break, call centers are slow to respond, an interruption in electricity disables nearly all gadgets, and locks can be picked.

Makeshift key in hand, I stood, went to my door, and pressed my ear against the wood.

From down the hall, a vacuum droned. Ms. Neace in the master bedroom.

I opened my door, crept down the hall, and descended the stairs.

Dr. Bart's home office sat across from Dr. Rose's on the opposite end of the house, past the kitchen and informal living room, through a thick oak door, and down a hall that led to a small waiting area complete with a separate entrance. Both Dr. Bart and Dr. Rose routinely saw patients here, and those patients were not permitted into the main house. Although the oak door wasn't typically locked, a heavy-duty arm at the top of the door kept it closed. As I pushed through, I felt as if I were stepping into a forbidden space. Ms. Neace and the sounds of her cleaning efforts disappeared. The air grew still. The hallway grew longer, and I was suddenly a kid again, tiny shoes clicking on hardwood.

As with the hallway, the walls of the waiting area held a shrine to the doctors' greatness: framed degrees, newspaper and magazine articles, large posters of their book covers. Several photographs of them together, just the two of them, and with various local celebrities—the mayor and such. None of me. None of Michael. I asked Dr. Rose about this once, and she told me some bullshit about how it wasn't appropriate to display photographs of children in the workplace. Come on. I'm a psychology major—this was about intimidation. These pictures were meant to belittle people, make them feel inferior in the presence of their eminences the Doctors Fitzgerald.

Like the lock on a bedroom door.

They didn't control me. Their world was a movie and I controlled the house lights.

Dr. Bart's door was on the right.

I slipped my homemade key into the dead bolt carefully, finessing the plastic into the slot, passing the tumblers a little at a time. When it jammed, I resisted the urge to force the key deeper. Patience—a vital habit of highly effective lockpickers. I pulled it back just enough to work it free, then gave it a gentle nudge. I repeated this maneuver several times until the plastic was buried to the handcrafted hilt.

I closed my eyes.

And twisted.

The plastic began to bend. The colorful bank logo on the front of the card turned white at the stress point, I kept the pressure steady and easy. If this sucker broke off in the dead bolt, my career as a thief, not to mention my freedom, was on the chopping block.

Nobody entered Dr. Bart's office. That was his private space, and you had to respect that.

I would never violate Dr. Bart's private space, Dr. Rose.

I kept twisting the plastic key.

Forced it to turn.

Easy, easy. Like Sunday morning.

It didn't break.

The tumbler turned, and I heard the bolt slide from the jamb and retract with a quiet click.

I turned the doorknob and stepped inside.

The room smelled like Dr. Bart's sessions.

CHAPTER TWENTY-THREE

DOBBS

THE MOMENT DOBBS SAW the two black Chevy Suburbans pull up to the LAPD roadblock on Alameda just outside the Stow 'n' Go warehouse complex, he knew they belonged to the feds. The driver flashed some kind of identification at one of the patrol officers, and the officer guided them around the barricade, into the complex, and toward the back of the courtyard where Dobbs now stood. The officer motioned to his right and watched them park.

Four men got out of the first SUV dressed in full tactical gear, U.S. MARSHAL stamped across the front and back of their vests. From the second SUV three men and a woman emerged. Two of the men wore white button-down dress shirts, sleeves rolled up, with dark slacks. The third, at least ten years younger, wore a black T-shirt and jeans. The woman, early thirties with chestnut hair pulled back, wore a white tank top, jeans, and mirrored sunglasses. Petite. Attractive. At about five two, she was dwarfed by the men, but from the moment she stepped out of the vehicle, it was clear she was in charge.

She crossed the blacktop at a swift pace and took off her sunglasses. "Detective Dobbs?"

"Yes, ma'am." He held out his hand, but she didn't take it.

"Special Agent Gimble, Agent Gimble, or just Gimble, but never 'ma'am,'" she said with the hint of a Southern drawl. "Where do we stand?"

He told her. A SWAT team had arrived at the Stow 'n' Go twelve minutes after Dobbs placed his initial call. Wilkins had ushered them inside, and within fifteen minutes, they completed a search of the entire structure. The few patrons in the building were escorted out to the sidewalk as each hallway and open storage unit was thoroughly searched.

They'd found no sign of Michael Kepler.

"Who's running SWAT?" Gimble asked.

"Darrick Atkinson. He should be in the main office." Dobbs pointed to the door leading back inside.

Gimble turned to the U.S. marshals at the first Suburban. "Garrison, you and your team check in with Officer Atkinson, figure out where they need you, follow his lead. Understand?"

A tall, stocky African-American man with a shaved head nodded at her and gestured to the three men behind him; all four took off in the direction of the door at a jog.

Gimble glanced at Dobbs, then at the building behind him, at the open garage door. "This his storage space?"

"Yes, m—y-yes," Dobbs stammered.

The warrant had come in about thirty minutes ago, but Dobbs hadn't waited. With the bolt cutters from the trunk of his car, he had snapped off the lock and gotten inside.

Gimble pulled a pair of latex gloves from her back pocket, slipped them on, took several steps toward the opening, then stopped. "Pretty obvious we've got something missing here, Detective, don't you think?"

Dobbs came over to her and looked inside.

Kepler's storage space was ten feet wide, thirty feet deep,

and more orderly than most units Dobbs had seen. Uniform-size cardboard boxes labeled with neat handwritten script and clear plastic storage bins lined the walls on the right and left. At the back, there were more boxes at least two rows deep, floor to ceiling. A workbench and a metal clothing rack with several plastic garment bags hanging from the rods fronted those, creating a U shape, with the center of the storage unit empty. Two tire tracks were clearly visible in the dust, leading out the front.

"Do we know the make and model?" Gimble asked. "We've gotta have cameras, right?"

Dobbs led her to the end of the row, back near the front of the complex, and pointed up. A small cardboard box covered the security camera mounted on the wall. "We've already checked the footage," Dobbs said. "Before pulling the car out, he covered up this one, another across the courtyard there, and a third at the exit gate. We've got nothing."

Gimble didn't seem surprised by this. "What about traffic cams? Anything out there on Alameda?"

"One camera two blocks down at Seventh Street and another at the freeway overpass; that's about a half a mile."

"Sammy!" Gimble shouted toward the second Suburban. The lanky man in the T-shirt glanced at her, his phone pressed to his ear. She snapped her fingers and started rattling off orders. "I need you to pull all camera footage in a two-mile radius starting with Alameda, pull all footage from inside this place, isolate some images of Birdman, then run facial and try to make a match. We need to identify his vehicle. He would have left"—she turned back to Dobbs—"what's our window?"

"Eight thirty to nine thirty," he told her.

"Pull everything from eight a.m. to ten a.m. Probably made a beeline for the freeway, so focus on that, got it?" she shouted.

"Already on it!" the man in the black T-shirt shouted. He pressed his free hand over his other ear and returned to his call.

She took several steps toward the Suburban. "You two, why are you standing around? Get some gloves on and get in that warehouse. I want a complete inventory of everything in there within an hour, understand?"

Both men nodded and started toward the open garage door.

"What did you call him?" Dobbs asked her.

Her brow furrowed. "Who, Sammy? That's Sammy Goggans. He specializes in IT forensics. The other two are Special Agents Waylon Begley and Omer Vela—they're all on the task force."

"No, not him. Kepler, Fitzgerald—your unsub."

"Birdman. Vela came up with the name, and it stuck. On account of the feathers—he's left one with each body." Gimble must have seen the confusion in his eyes. She took a step closer, placed a hand on her hip, tilted her head. Her shampoo smelled like cherries. "You have no idea who he is, do you?"

CHAPTER TWENTY-FOUR

WRITTEN STATEMENT, MEGAN FITZGERALD

As I pressed my back into the door, my eyes fell on Dr. Bart's desk across the room. He had been sitting there when it happened. You know, the long nap. Reading through patient notes, preparing for his three p.m. appointment, then a sharp pain in his temple, a bright flash, a switch turning off, and then head to the desktop. Like one of those cartoons—facedown in the soup.

I made up that last part. Nobody had been in the room when it happened, but in my mind, I imagined that was how his final seconds played out. I like to think he shit himself, but if he did, nobody told me.

His three p.m. appointment, Latasha Gillock, a sophomore at Binghamton, sat out in the waiting area until nearly four o'clock waiting for him to summon her into his office. She finally knocked because soccer practice was at five, and when he didn't answer, she opened the door. Latasha found him slumped over his desk, his eyes wide open, the left eye facing forward and the right staring at the short bookcase. I don't know her, but she wasn't shy about sharing what happened with anyone who would listen and pretty soon it got back to me. Whether or not she embellished, I suppose I'll never know. She said she froze there for at least a minute before running off to get help. She said she didn't touch anything. Latasha Gillock said a lot of things. Her unchecked diarrhea of the mouth was probably the reason she was seeing Dr. Bart in the first place. Had I been asked to diagnose her, pathological liar would have been my first guess.

Dr. Bart's home office was fifteen feet by twenty. I knew that because Dr. Rose once complained that her home office was thirteen feet by twenty—forty square feet smaller. His desk sat in the back left corner facing the room and two plush leather chairs. I still remember when Dr. Bart bought his desk chair—an Eames Executive fashioned after the ones designed for the Time-Life Building back in the sixties. He paid a little over five thousand dollars for that single piece of furniture. I had been around nine or ten at the time and couldn't imagine spending so much on a chair. In my mind, that was enough to buy a car or a house or maybe a horse.

I don't remember being adopted—I was just a baby—but Dr. Rose and Dr. Bart had never hidden the fact that I was. When Michael and I were growing up, they brought it up regularly. Dr. Bart caught me sitting in his new chair on the day it was delivered, and he immediately reminded me of where I had come from. He told me my real parents couldn't have afforded a five-thousand-dollar chair. He said my real parents left me at the orphanage door in a box with nothing but a filthy diaper and a rash—they couldn't even afford to clothe me. He said I was never to sit in his chair unless I asked first. Every time I did ask, I was told no. He said I had to earn the right to sit in a chair like that.

I crossed the room, rounded his desk, and plopped my butt firmly in his prized fucking seat.

How about today, Dr. Bart? Today a good day?

His office did not smell like piss or shit, as I'd hoped, but the stale coffee still sitting on his desk in his favorite mug gave off a ripe odor and was mixed with his lingering scent. A film of some kind of nastiness floated in the liquid, congealed creamer or something, an island of lumpy white, green, and yellow in a sea of black. Beside the mug sat a plate with the remains of a ham sandwich, the bread covered in mold, the edges of the meat crusty with dried rot. This smelled too but, oddly, not as bad as the coffee. I found it strange to think Dr. Bart had taken a bite of that sandwich just last week, that he'd been the last to touch it. It made me wonder about the condition of his body in that drawer today, waiting for his hole in the ground.

Dr. Rose hadn't allowed anyone to enter this room since his death, not even Ms. Neace, judging by the science experiment on that plate and in his cup. Yet something felt off.

His baseball collection filled three glass cases along the east wall. Beside the cases was a door. Although painted white to match the other doors, I knew it was made of steel, the frame too. Dr. Bart once told me that the room behind that door was originally meant to be a safe room. Someplace we could hide if people decided they wanted to break in and steal a nice office chair and some diplomas from elite schools.

A safe room.

I couldn't help but wonder if he'd somehow taken joy in that description. Just looking at it made my skin crawl and my stomach churn. My fingers twitched as I thought about just how cold the surface of that door and the room on the other side was. Nothing safe about that room.

I shook off the feeling. No time for that.

I stood, went to those glass cases, tried not to look at that door.

Dr. Bart told patients and colleagues alike that he was an

avid baseball fan and had been since childhood. He would share stories about how he'd stood outside Yankee Stadium as a kid and listened to the crowd, how he'd scrounged pennies in hopes of eventually having enough for a ticket. He would go on to say that his parents barely got by and his humble beginnings had forced him to strive, to achieve, to become the man he'd become. As Dr. Rose stood beside him, he'd point out the various items in the glass cases he'd collected over the years: Bats once held by famous Yankees such as Babe Ruth and Alex Rodriguez. A glove worn by Yogi Berra. A Mickey Mantle jersey and a cap signed by Whitey Ford. There were about a dozen baseball cards too, both old and new, some signed and some not. Balls from various games sitting on wooden stands with brass plaques identifying their origins. Dr. Bart's eyes would often become glossy with tears as he recounted how and when he'd acquired each item, how each represented a moment in his life where he clawed his way up from poverty to his current elite stature.

What a load of horseshit.

He held season tickets to Yankee Stadium but never attended the games. The stories he told so fondly of the players— meetings, autographs obtained, balls caught—none of it was true. He'd purchased everything over the years from stores in the city or online, and while the collection was extremely valuable, it was so only in the financial sense. The items carried none of the emotional weight he so diligently described. The collection was nothing more than window dressing for him, part of the well-crafted persona Dr. Bart wished others to see. At times, I think even he believed these little tales; he'd told them so often, they eventually seemed true.

The cases themselves had been designed, built, and installed by a Missouri company that specialized in displays for jewelry stores. Dr. Bart had once told me the glass wasn't actually glass; it was something called Lexan and couldn't be shattered, not even with a sledgehammer. The locks were biometric, requiring his thumb to open, and each case was wired with sensors connected to the house's extensive alarm system.

None of this changed the fact that Dr. Bart's 1936 Joe DiMaggio baseball card was missing, nor did it explain the sparrow feather resting in the place the card belonged.

CHAPTER TWENTY-FIVE

DOBBS

BEGLEY, WHERE'S YOUR TABLET?" Gimble called into the storage unit.

The older of the two agents looked up from one of the plastic bins. He cocked a thumb out toward the courtyard. "Suburban, back seat, passenger-side door pocket."

Gimble crossed the blacktop, opened the back door, and retrieved an iPad. She set it on the hood of the vehicle and began tapping at the screen.

Dobbs caught a glimpse of two marshals and someone from SWAT examining the first row of garages on the opposite end of the courtyard. When they turned down the second row and disappeared from sight, he joined Gimble at the SUV.

She didn't look up. Instead, she swiped back through several photographs to an image of a map of the United States with more than a dozen points marked with virtual red tacks. "Like I said on the phone, we've got homicides in at least ten states—California to New York. The earliest dates back a little over two years, about the same time Kepler started working for that Nadler outfit."

Gimble turned the tablet toward him, traced a slender finger from Los Angeles to the East Coast. "When we pull the GPS data from Kepler's truck, I'd be willing to bet we get a map that looks a lot like this one."

When Dobbs didn't reply, she turned the tablet back, opened up a different folder, and swiped through a series of crime scene photographs. "No discernible preference in race or gender on any of the vics. We've got both men and women, Caucasian, black, Hispanic. Only commonality appears to be age — late twenties to mid-thirties, every one. Initially, he presents an organized dichotomy." She weighed this for a moment, then continued. "He appears to identify his victims long before any attack. Observes them. Plots out a strategy. No signs of struggle at the initial abduction, which suggests he determines the ideal moment for a grab before he moves. In the few instances where security systems are in place, he takes the time to disable cameras and sensors in advance. He's highly adaptable, patient. At least when it comes to stalking his victims. Then the profile flips, and he leans toward disorganized when he goes in for the kill."

Dobbs frowned. "Aren't serials usually one or the other, not both?"

"Nothing usual about this guy," Gimble said. "Aside from the occasional use of propofol to subdue or kill his victims, he tends to improvise and use items found on scene for each murder. He's used electrical cords for binding and strangulation. I've seen him puncture the femoral artery with a screwdriver. Suffocate with pillows." Gimble quickly swiped to the left and brought up a photograph of a woman with short red hair in a T-shirt and panties, splayed out at the base of a staircase. "With Darcey Haas here, bruising indicates he picked her up with one hand under her left arm and another under her right leg and threw her down these stairs into her basement — three times. Kept picking her up and carrying her back to the top for another go. On the third, he finally got the angle right, and her neck snapped."

Gimble scrolled forward three images to an African-American man sitting at a dining-room table, his head tilted back, a fúnnel in his mouth. "With Issac Dorrough, he bound him to this chair with Saran Wrap from the vic's kitchen, broke two teeth forcing that funnel into his mouth, then poured nearly a quart of Drano down his throat."

"Christ," Dobbs said.

"He doesn't leave prints. Not ever."

"Just the feathers."

"Just the feathers," Gimble repeated slowly in that Southern drawl. She looked up at Dobbs with deep blue eyes. "Here's the thing about those feathers. Not only are they all from the same species of sparrow, Henslow's, he *licks* each feather before leaving it with the body."

"What?"

Gimble nodded slowly. "This crazy, careful, no-fingerprint-leaving son of a bitch gives us a DNA sample at every murder."

Dobbs wasn't sure how to respond to that. Finally, he said, "How many?"

"Murders?"

He nodded.

"Eighteen."

"Eighteen? Why haven't I heard of this guy?"

Gimble said, "No two murders are alike. Spread out over thousands of miles. Multiple states, jurisdictions. We've kept the feathers under wraps. Going public with this guy would only create panic, possibly get him to change his MO, stop leaving the feathers, go underground. A guy like this can disappear. I'm not about to give him a reason to." She glared up at Dobbs, and her face tightened. "No talking to the press, understand? As far as your local media is concerned, he's responsible for one death here in LA and has escaped police custody."

Dobbs nodded reluctantly. "Christ, eighteen dead."

"Nineteen, counting the girlfriend."

"Alyssa Tepper."

"Right, Tepper." Gimble shut off the iPad and turned back to him. "I'm gonna need access to his apartment, the Tepper scene, his work truck, a full report detailing every second he was in your custody," she said, ticking off the items on her fingers. "Everything you got so far."

"Whatever you need."

"Our working theory is that Tepper somehow figured out what her boyfriend was doing, who he really was, so he shut her down."

Dobbs considered this. It didn't add up. "If he's so careful, then why call the cops? Why not kill her someplace other than his own apartment and cover it up?"

Gimble turned back toward the storage unit. "Hey, Vela? You're a clinical psychologist, right? Why does Birdman do the things he does?"

Vela had three boxes open and surrounding him on the floor. "Because he's a fucking nut!" he shot back.

"He's a fucking nut," Gimble agreed, turning back to Dobbs. "Same reason your boy bothers to wear gloves while purposely leaving DNA at every crime scene. Same reason he calls the cops with his dead girlfriend still warm in the tub. He thinks this is some kind of game, and he's decided it would be fun to toy with the local yokels. Up the stakes. See your faces while you try to figure it all out." She shrugged. "I don't know his motivation, and I don't care. Now that we got a bead on him, my only focus is bringing him in."

"How do you know it's his DNA?"

Gimble smirked. "You think he's got someone else licking his feathers, Detective? Some kind of surrogate licker in the mix?"

Dobbs said nothing.

She shrugged. "We found a hair at one of the crime scenes—number four—root still attached. At scene number twelve, his victim, Selena Hennis, managed to get in a good scratch before he strangled her. We pulled his skin from under her nail. In both cases, the DNA found matched the DNA on the feathers."

Dobbs said, "We bagged numerous items from his place. Got a toothbrush and razor from Tepper's apartment that most likely belong to him. Pulled another razor and toothbrush from a travel kit in his truck. He drank from a coffee cup at the station. We bagged that, too."

"Has it gone out for processing?" she asked, then she shook her head. "Doesn't matter. Pull everything, get it to my team. I'm sure I can get it processed in the Bureau lab much faster than you running it through FSC."

Dobbs nodded. The Hertzberg-Davis Forensic Science Center was fast, but not Bureau-fast.

Gimble tossed the tablet onto the rear seat of the Suburban and started back toward the storage unit at a quick pace, calling out over her shoulder, "Let's see what kind of secrets our boy keeps in his rented closet, Detective!"

CHAPTER TWENTY-SIX

WRITTEN STATEMENT, MEGAN FITZGERALD

I imagine by now you've found my phone and pulled all the text messages between Michael and me. You seem thorough like that. My memory is pretty solid, but it's probably best you refer to the actual texts from my phone rather than what I have below for this sort of thing. I'll try to get it right but a girl can sometimes make mistakes. Right, Jessica?

Standing in Dr. Bart's office, staring at his display case, I pulled my phone from my back pocket, then quickly wrote out a text.

Michael, r u there?

"Come on, come on," I muttered.

My phone vibrated. Yes.

Where r u? R u safe?

Nearly a minute passed before his reply. Did you get into his office?

Yes—you were right, the baseball card is gone. Someone left a feather in its place.

How'd they get in?

Can't tell. Nothing broken.

Anything else missing?

I looked back at the display case. I didn't see any other

feathers. And for each engraved display plaque, there was a corresponding piece of memorabilia.

I don't think anything else is missing, I typed back.

When Michael didn't reply for several minutes, I typed, Still there?

I looked at the clock on my phone and realized I had already been in here for nearly thirty minutes.

Thirty minutes was too long.

My phone vibrated, and I glanced at the display.

Can u get in the dark room?

My chest tightened.

No way!

The feathers, Meg—this is about the dark room.

No, no, no.

Please!

I quickly fired back, You said there's a tape—did you listen to it?

Michael's reply came much faster this time. Not yet. Soon. No opportunity yet.

I needed to change the subject. R u coming home?

Michael went silent again.

One minute.

Two minutes.

Then—

If you won't go in the room, get Dr. Bart's files. There'll be a file on Alyssa Tepper—must be a connection somewhere. And maybe Roland Eads.

I turned and looked at Dr. Bart's desk and the matching credenza behind it. I'd seen him reach into those drawers a hundred times, a thousand. Plucking out one file, returning another.

Patient files.

I typed, Do you have any idea how much trouble we could get into if someone found out we looked at those files?

Again, his response came fast. Not look—take! Get the files. Important!!! Hide them. Buy burner phone. Next contact from that only. Not your regular phone. Not anymore.

I stared at the message. A burner phone? WTF?

A second later: Meg, please!

My finger hovered over the keyboard. I don't know when it started trembling. I should never have agreed to come in here.

When I finally typed a response, my hand had gone from trembling to downright shaking. My heart felt like it might burst through my rib cage. I sent back a single letter, all I could manage—

K.

You'd do it too, wouldn't you, Jessica? If your brother asked?

CHAPTER TWENTY-SEVEN

DOBBS

WHEN DOBBS AND GIMBLE reached the open storage unit, they found Special Agent Begley crouched over one of the dusty tire tracks on the concrete. He glanced up and nodded. "I sent photographs back to the lab. They're running it. I want to try and lift one too."

Dobbs frowned. "You're not bringing in CSI for collection?"

"Begley here was a lab geek before I pulled him for this task force," Gimble told him. "Twelve years with the Evidence Response Team Unit at Quantico. He's my mobile lab. I call in for an ERT, and we have to wait on them, then watch that same half a dozen people traipse around my crime scene, moving a quarter as quickly and a third as effectively as Begley. No time, no need."

Begley had apparently heard all this before. He was studying the track again. "We've got a very narrow wheelbase. That suggests something small. Wide treads might mean we're looking for some kind of sports car. He kept it alive on a trickle charger and fuel preservative."

Gimble had already moved on. She was studying a label on

one of the cardboard boxes. "What's this address in New York? Looks like all of these were shipped to Kepler by a Megan Fitzgerald."

Dobbs told her what he had learned about Kepler's family.

"Think that's where he's heading?" Gimble asked.

The detective shook his head. "I doubt it. He's adopted and had some kind of falling-out with the parents. His only family contact appears to be with the sister. The entire time we had him in custody, all he wanted was to talk to her. Meanwhile, she lit up his phone."

"Somebody text Sammy and tell him we need a warrant for a data dump on the sister's phone—all calls, texts, GPS." Gimble snapped her fingers in time with each item.

"On it," Vela said.

She turned to Vela. "Where's my inventory? What have we got in here?"

"You said an hour."

"I lied. He's moving with a two-hour jump on us. We don't have an hour. When I say an hour, I mean ten minutes ago."

"Figured as much," Vela said. "About half the boxes I've been through are full of books. Mostly nonfiction, heavy stuff—psychology texts, self-help. A lot of Freud."

"Sounds like your dream collection," Begley muttered.

"He was majoring in psychology at Cornell before dropping out his junior year. His father was a psychiatrist, mother's a psychologist, and his sister is majoring in that field too," Dobbs said. "We found similar audiobooks in his truck."

"What else?" Gimble said, snapping her fingers again.

"I've got bins with socks, underwear, shirts, jeans. All look like they've been rifled through." He pointed at the garment bags hanging from the metal clothing rack. "Those are all suits. Expensive—Armani, Kiton, Brioni. We've got dress shirts, ties, shoes, and matching socks in those bins under the rack. He definitely went through those."

"So our boy fugitive dressed to the nines for his road trip," Gimble said. "Anything to indicate he had cash stashed here?"

Vela bit his lower lip. "Nothing conclusive."

"What about inconclusive?"

"You don't like inconclusive."

"I do today."

Vela indicated the far right corner. "I found a safe back there. The door was closed but not locked. It's empty."

Gimble looked at Dobbs. "Did you get his passport?"

He shook his head. "We still have his wallet back at LAPD. Credit cards, driver's license. My team didn't find a passport in his apartment or his truck."

Gimble looked up at the ceiling. "We've got to assume he's got cash, possibly a passport, maybe even fake identification," she said, thinking aloud. "He's got wheels. Two hours on us. He's not going to risk an airport. No need to take the bus or a train if you've got a car. He's going to try and get away from here fast, so the real question is where would Mr. Kepler go? Port or highway?"

"If he makes the port," Dobbs said, "he might be able to bribe his way onto a tanker. Any commercial travel and he's got the same problem as an airport—cash transactions are monitored, and he's got to assume we're watching for his name or passport."

Gimble's eyes narrowed. "Please tell me somebody had the sense to flag his name? *Both* names?"

Dobbs nodded. "TSA and the other agencies were all notified when the BOLO went out a few minutes after he escaped LAPD custody."

"Good boy," Gimble said.

Special Agent Sammy Goggans appeared with Detective Wilkins

behind him. Goggans balanced a small laptop in the crook of his elbow and typed with his free hand.

Gimble crossed over to him. "Tell me you got something off the cameras, Sammy."

Agent Goggans frowned. "I got nothing on his exit from this place and nothing on facial recognition off the cameras on Seventh Street or the highway overpass down the block."

"They scan every car, correct?"

Goggans nodded. "It's not foolproof. They only get a view of the front seat, and with glare from the morning sun distorting images, I'd say only about sixty percent of what they capture is usable. It's possible for someone to slip through."

Gimble started snapping her fingers again, her mind clearly churning. She turned around, knelt, and studied the tire tracks carefully, then looked back up at Agent Vela. "Could these be fake? Some kind of ruse? Could our boy be on foot?"

"I don't see how. I'm confident there was a car here and it was moved this morning. This guy seems smart. I think if he wanted to try and pull some kind of bait and switch, he would have given us a shot of the car, something to chase. He went through too much trouble to get a vehicle out of here unseen. He's on the road."

Gimble considered this, took out her phone, and dialed a number on speaker.

Dobbs leaned over to Goggans. "She always second-guess everybody?"

"Yep," he replied.

"Heard that, Sammy." Gimble winked at Goggans.

Her call was picked up on the second ring.

"U.S. Marshal Garrison."

"Where are you on your search of this place? Turn up anything?"

"Nothing yet. Checked everything but your row. I don't think he's here," Garrison replied. "The video footage I reviewed with

Goggans indicates he made a beeline for his own storage unit, covered the camera, then left."

Gimble glanced at Goggans, who nodded. Into the phone, she said, "Check the rest anyway. No unturned stones."

"Copy."

She hung up, shoved the phone back in her pocket. "Somebody get me a map."

Goggans turned his laptop toward her, a map of California on the screen. "Already working on it. With a two-hour head start, accounting for traffic, I'd put him somewhere within this yellow band."

Gimble's face fell. "Christ, that's a big grid. He could be halfway to Tijuana by now in an unknown car with an altered appearance."

PART 2

NEEDLES, CALIFORNIA

Try a little experiment. Dress a millionaire in
rags. Observe him. Watch the shift in his personality. This unintentional shift. The clothes
do make the man. Thoughts alone don't define
us—we're a complete package defined by the
wrapping.

—Barton Fitzgerald, MD

CHAPTER TWENTY-EIGHT

MICHAEL

YOUR CAR WILL BE ready in about five minutes, sir. They're just finishing up the interior."

Having memorized the address in Needles, California, I placed Roland Eads's driver's license in the breast pocket of my Armani jacket, glanced up at the cheerful young woman, and smiled. "Thanks, I sure do appreciate you squeezing me in without an appointment."

She returned the smile. Suzy, according to her name tag. "It's a beautiful car. The guys are fighting over it out there. What year is it?"

"It's a 1969."

She glanced over her shoulder at the man in white overalls getting a drink of water from the fountain in the corner. "A '69, Brad. You win."

I pulled back my right sleeve and glanced down at the Breitling Navitimer. Nearly eleven in the morning.

I'd been here for a little over two and a half hours.

Devil in the Detail had had no trouble fitting me in right away when I told them I wanted their VIP detail package along with several à la carte items I'd rattled off from their menu of services on the wall above Suzy's head—around five hundred dollars in total. She told me it would take several hours. I told her I wasn't in a hurry and didn't mind waiting.

They quickly ushered my black 1969 Porsche 911 into the center bay, closed the large door, and got to work. This was fortunate for me because Devil in the Detail was located directly across the street from the Stow 'n' Go facility on Alameda. From their waiting area, with a six-month-old copy of *Road and Track* in hand, I had a clear view of the storage facility's front entrance, and whenever the large gate opened, I could see my unit. While enjoying a complimentary coffee and several chocolate doughnuts, I watched Detectives Dobbs and Wilkins arrive about ten minutes after I'd left; they were followed soon after by a SWAT team and then two black Chevy Suburbans that were so obviously federal vehicles, they might as well have had FBI painted in big white letters on each of the doors and an American flag fluttering off the antenna.

I knew they'd quickly locate my storage unit.

I was certain they would hone in on the tire tracks and missing vehicle.

I'd found all the cameras in the storage facility years ago, and I was confident that by covering the few I did, I'd prevented them from getting an image of what I drove, so they'd have no means to identify the car.

I was well aware of the cameras located on Seventh and at the freeway overpass a few blocks down Alameda in the opposite direction, the only two traffic cameras nearby. I'd seen enough movies and television shows to know they'd assume I'd run. Based on estimated departure time, they would create a rolling window, a target search area. They'd most likely try to find an image of me behind the wheel of their mystery vehicle.

Rather than run, I waited.

In my head, I imagined their search area, a giant doughnut slowly expanding out from the center at ground zero.

I watched as the SWAT teams and U.S. marshals raced around the storage facility like ants on a hill. I watched as they picked through the various boxes and bins I kept there, no doubt wondering what was missing. There was nothing of real importance there—not anymore, anyway. I'd grabbed all the cash I had, nearly six thousand dollars, and whatever clothes I could fit in the trunk of the Porsche. When I'd left home, that car might have been the only thing I took that I actually cared about.

"You're all set, sir," Suzy said, back behind the cash register. "That will be five hundred twenty-three dollars and eighty-seven cents."

I stood, pulled out my money clip, and peeled off seven crisp hundred-dollar bills. "Please divide what's left over among the people who worked on the car."

Suzy's grin widened. "Thank you! Come back soon."

A heavy yawn rolled over me and I realized I hadn't slept in nearly a full day. I'd need some rest for what was to come.

I pulled out of Devil in the Detail and made a right on Alameda heading toward the freeway, resisting the urge to wave at the growing number of law enforcement officers across the street.

CHAPTER TWENTY-NINE

DOBBS

HEY, GIMBLE? WHAT DO you make of this?"

The shout came from Special Agent Vela inside the storage unit.

Dobbs and Gimble found Vela in the back corner. "How old was Kepler when he was adopted?" he asked.

"Don't know," Dobbs said. "We put in a warrant for the records this morning, but the judge kicked it back. Cited relevance. Why?"

"This box, it's packed full of old uniforms for an orphanage called Windham Hall. Got everything from toddler sizes all the way up to adult size pants. I've got three problems with all this. The first is why would Kepler have any of them? Orphanages recycle clothing—something doesn't fit, it goes to someone else. You don't keep old uniforms. And two, I got the impression he was adopted at a young age. Why would he have these large sizes?"

Gimble looked up at Dobbs. "Did he mention a place called Windham Hall to you?"

Dobbs shook his head.

She turned back to Vela. "You said three problems. What's number three?"

Vela reached into the box with his gloved hands and pulled out a pair of pants. The material was in tatters, nearly shredded. "I think someone cut these up. A few are in this condition, shirts too."

Gimble knelt down beside him to get a closer look. "Do you think they belong to victims?"

"I'll have them tested, but I see no outward signs of human trauma, no blood, no staining of any kind. Just the cutting."

Wilkins tapped Dobbs on the shoulder. "I just got a call on a car fire down at the fish market—a blue Ford Escort. Sounds like Kepler's attorney's car. There's a body."

CHAPTER THIRTY

WRITTEN STATEMENT, MEGAN FITZGERALD

I'm not proud of this, Jessica, but I think you'll understand—you freaked me out. Who wouldn't be freaked out? This happened before I got to know you, realized what a kind and generous person you are. Your sense of fashion may need a little work, but that's neither here nor there. I was more concerned with protecting my brother and my own butt at this point. Can't fault a girl for that, right?

My phone rang twice while I was still in Dr. Bart's office, one more time while I was making my way back through the house, carefully avoiding Ms. Neace and her roving vacuum, a stack of patient files in my hands.

California number.

Not the number belonging to Michael's new phone.

The third time my phone rang, the caller finally left a message rather than hanging up.

Inside my room, I set the files on my bed, quickly closed the door, and listened to the voice mail.

"Megan Fitzgerald, my name is Special Agent Jessica Gimble. I'm with the Federal Bureau of Investigation and I need you to call me back immediately at this number regarding your brother."

I deleted the message.

(Sorry, Jessica!)

Michael was right. They knew my phone number. If they knew my phone number, they could use my phone records to get Michael's number. Burner phone or not, they could probably trace his phone once they had the number.

I started keying in a text, then thought better of it. They'd see that, right? Cops in the movies always find stuff like that.

I deleted the text and called Michael instead.

Got his voice mail and left a quick message.

Wait. Would they be able to get the voice mail? I was getting nervous and sloppy. Live calls only!

I dropped the phone on my bed and went back to the files. I'd used a letter opener from Dr. Bart's desk to open the lock on his file cabinet. The older metal bent a little bit, but nobody would be able to tell I'd jimmied it. The damage could easily have come from years of wear and tear.

Dr. Bart had hundreds of files. No way I could take them all.

Nothing for Roland Eads or the fake name the man had used, Philip Wardwell.

He did have a file on Alyssa Tepper. Not very thick. Not much more information than he had in my file. I pulled out both and set them on the desk. Dr. Bart had two files on Michael; one was labeled *Michael Kepler/Fitzgerald* and the second said *M. Kepler*. I took both of those too.

I set Michael's files down on the desk beside my own and Alyssa's. The names lined up and that's when I noticed that each was marked with a small blue dot, barely a smudge. I quickly thumbed my way through the rest of the drawer, pulling every file with a blue dot. Eleven in total, counting mine, Alyssa's, and Michael's.

I started with Alyssa's.

Alyssa Rena Tepper, court-ordered to seek therapy after a

series of shoplifting incidents back in 2008. She was fifteen. She'd taken clothing, mostly, from a few high-end boutiques in New York City.

Rookie. If you're gonna steal clothes, everyone knows you hit a big department store.

Dr. Bart's notes were vague. Alyssa had seen him half a dozen times, completing the court order. He attributed her thefts to her recently broken home—her parents had divorced a year earlier. She was acting out. Wanted attention. Blah-blah. So predictable.

Three pages of notes, and that included his standard patient record sheet filled with useless data.

I dropped Alyssa's file and grabbed another.

Cassandra Shatley.

Boring.

Nineteen, suffering from depression and anxiety issues. You and every other sophomore. Cry me a river, Cassie. Four pages of notes, nothing but broad-stroke clinical analysis. No real opinion. Just a recap of each session. Boyfriend problems, self-esteem issues. A photo was clipped to the inside of the folder—pretty girl, with dark, curly hair, hazel eyes, nice smile. According to the notes, Dr. Bart saw her five times in total over a two-month period back in 2009.

Nicole Milligan, nineteen, date-raped at a frat party. Disgusting, but common. I've been to my share of frat parties. She'd filed charges. Good for her. Dr. Bart had encouraged her to move on with her life, put the incident in her past, not let it rule what she could become. Eight sessions in 2010, then nothing.

Darcey Haas.

Issac Dorrough.

Selena Hennis.

Jeffery Longtin.

Katrina Nickols.

All more of the same. Typical problems, sparse notes, dating back nearly a decade.

My file was even worse. No notes at all, only a copy of my adoption records. No secrets there—Dr. Bart had given me a copy when I was nine.

Like mine, the Kepler/Fitzgerald folder had nothing but a copy of Michael's adoption records (which Dr. Bart had given to Michael and which Michael had shared with me), no notes. The M. Kepler file was a duplicate.

Fuck. Either Dr. Bart took shitty notes or he purposely left stuff out and just wrote enough to get by. Double fuck. I'd just risked God knows what to get these, and there wasn't a single bit of useful information in any of them!

My phone rang. I snatched it up.

It was you again, but my only thought was *FBI! FBI! Oh, shit, FBI!*

I clicked on Decline, then bounced through the call menu and selected Block This Caller.

Double fuck.

My MacBook was on my nightstand. I grabbed it, opened the lid, and waited a moment for the computer to come to life. From the launchpad at the bottom of the screen, I clicked on the calculator icon, which loaded my Tor browser. Most people use Safari or Chrome. Smart people use Tor. The Tor browser hides your identity with something called onion routing, encrypting traffic and randomly bouncing communication through relays around the globe. According to the information box in the right corner of my screen, I was currently in Munich, Germany.

Dr. Rose scrolled through my browser history the way

some people scroll through Facebook, so I used Chrome and Safari for school and communication with friends and used Tor, hidden safely behind the calculator icon, for anything I didn't want her to see. I wasn't building bombs or anything, but a girl's got her secrets and a right to privacy.

I keyed *Alyssa Tepper* into the search box.

The screen filled with about a dozen stories, all rehashed pieces of what Michael had told me. Photos of her apartment building. A photo of Michael under the headline "Escape from LAPD?" Nothing new there.

I typed in *Nicole Milligan,* the girl Dr. Bart had treated after her rape. Over a million results came up. The first few were typical—Facebook, LinkedIn, Twitter—because it was such a common name. On the image tab, there were hundreds of pictures, so many different girls. Hopeless.

I flipped through Dr. Bart's files and pulled out Cassandra Shatley's. Her file had a photograph. Her name also brought up a zillion results. This time, I went straight to the image tab and scrolled through the pictures—I found her on page 3. Not the same photograph, but the same girl, older by at least ten years. A woman now. There was no mistaking her sharp nose and hazel eyes and curly hair, although she wore it a little shorter than she had in college.

I clicked on the picture.

CASSANDRA SHATLEY, TWENTY-SEVEN, FOUND SUFFOCATED IN HER WILLIAMS, ARIZONA, HOME

The story was a little over a year old.

Shatley was discovered by her boyfriend of three years in the kitchen of their two-bedroom apartment in the Canton District, her hands and feet bound with strips of a towel, a plastic garbage bag over her head and twisted tight at her neck. The boyfriend, Russel

Logan, 36, was quickly ruled out as a suspect; several employees and patrons of Hooligan's Bar and Grill, where Logan works as a bartender, confirmed his whereabouts for six hours leading up to the estimated time of death.

The story went on to say the police had no leads. There were several follow-up stories over the next month, then nothing.

I had less trouble finding Darcey Haas, more of a unique name. My throat tightened as I read through the first of many links. Repeatedly thrown down the stairs until her neck broke.

My God.

Selena Hennis.

Issac Dorrough.

Both dead too. Both murdered.

When Ms. Neace knocked on my door, I nearly fell off my bed. "What?" The single word came out harsher than I'd meant it to. "Sorry, just changing clothes. What do you need?"

"I've got to get in there to clean," Ms. Neace said, her voice muffled by the door.

"Give me a second." I made a list of all the names on the files with blue dots, then gathered up the folders and hid them in a box at the back of my closet under my high-school yearbooks.

I grabbed my MacBook and called for an Uber as I passed our housekeeper and went down the stairs.

"You can clean now! Sorry, gotta go!" I called out behind me.

I'd finish this downtown.

I needed to buy a new cell.

Then I needed to get my pain-in-the-ass brother on the phone.

CHAPTER THIRTY-ONE

MICHAEL

IT MIGHT HAVE BEEN the lines on the road racing past me at seventy-two miles an hour. I didn't remember leaving the I-10 for I-15 North. I barely remembered leaving Los Angeles two hours earlier. Hell, even getting dressed back at my storage unit, I hadn't been thinking; at first I'd put my watch on my right wrist rather than my left.

The car swerved for the third time, rolling over the rumble strips along the shoulder and slapping me awake.

Shortly after that, I pulled into a rest stop just past the I-40 East interchange, parked in the far back corner, killed the motor, and closed my eyes.

My eyes didn't open again for another two hours, not until the deep bellow of a tractor trailer's horn yanked me from my dreamless sleep. I got out of the car and went into the building, used the toilet, splashed water on my face, and returned to the car.

Alyssa Tepper, the police, all the events of the past twenty-four hours seemed like some distant memory or a nightmare.

On the seat beside me sat Roland Eads's driver's license and my cell phone; I'd missed three calls from Megan and had no service.

Next to the phone was the cassette tape I'd found in Eads's briefcase.

Dark room—M. Kepler—August 12, 1996.

Dr. Bart's handwriting.

His voice was on that tape, waiting to talk to me from beyond the grave. This man I so wanted out of my life—his fingers were in the doorjamb, prying it open.

I started the Porsche and got back on I-40.

With my speed hovering in the low seventies and Needles, California, less than two hours away, I finally reached for that tape and slipped it into the Porsche's cassette player, knowing if I didn't do it right then, I never would.

The tape hissed.

Static.

The crackle of someone moving the recorder?

His voice then, deep. The Porsche speakers rumbled. "This is Dr. Barton Fitzgerald. The date is August 12, 1996. Initial patient therapy session with Michael Ryan Kepler, age four. Although placed due to recent traumatic events in the custody of Windham Hall, he has been remanded by the courts to my personal care and transported by me and my wife, a practicing clinical psychologist, from Windham to our home yesterday afternoon. Although he answered questions—none regarding the incident—he made no effort to communicate unless prompted. He does smile when joked with, but he appears to do so out of politeness rather than a genuine response to humor. The boy is clearly intelligent. Not only was he able to name the current president, but he performed simple math—addition, subtraction, and even multiplication—with relative ease. He understood the concept of division but struggled to answer the several problems we put forth. Still, rather astounding for his age and challenged upbringing.

"Upon arriving at our home, he was shown to his room and permitted to rest until dinner at six, at which time he joined my wife and myself for probably the first balanced meal of his life— yogurt-marinated chicken with mushrooms and sweet potatoes and chocolate mousse for dessert. He devoured all as if he'd gone unfed for months. Following dinner, he was bathed and returned to his room, where I observed him periodically via a closed-circuit video system installed for this purpose. He remained awake until approximately four in the morning, at which time he finally drifted off into a fitful sleep.

"On the surface, Kepler appears relatively unscathed, willing and able to go through the motions of life. Today's session will mark my first with Kepler regarding his mother, Janel Kepler, and her boy-friend, one Maxwell Pullen. I've decided to conduct this discussion in the dark room in an effort to minimize outside stimuli and mitigate any apprehension he may harbor when speaking with an adult or authority figure."

Dr. Bart cleared his throat, then continued. "As per my agree-ment with the New York State Police, Cortland County law enforcement, and the Department of Child Services, copies of all records related to the treatment of Kepler will be sealed. At my dis-cretion, and taking into consideration all aspects of doctor/patient confidentiality upon drafting, summary reports will be provided to Judge Henry Larson of the Twelfth Circuit. Unless ordered by an appropriate court, copies of these reports may be provided to the aforementioned parties only if deemed necessary to the open investigation by Judge Larson and cleared by my office. As both his doctor and legal guardian, I restate here for the record: Kepler is a minor placed in my care by the courts. Sharing of information related to his care without my express written consent is a criminal offense, and I will not hesitate to prosecute anyone who violates that sanctity."

There was an audible click followed by a pop as Dr. Bart either paused the tape or stopped and restarted the recorder.

The next voice I heard was my own—thin, quiet, and distant. An unsure child.

I swallowed the lump in my throat and remembered to breathe as I turned up the volume.

CHAPTER THIRTY-TWO

MICHAEL

WHY DO WE HAVE to sit in the dark?"

"Do you like the dark?"

"Sometimes."

"I like the dark," Dr. Bart said. Although still the voice I knew so well, the hard edge had dropped away, as so often happens when an adult speaks to a child. "I find it easier to talk in the dark. Only your voice and my voice. Nothing else. Two grown-ups having a conversation."

"The dark is scary."

"It can be," Dr. Bart agreed. "But it can also be comforting, like a thick, warm blanket. What we can't see can't hurt us."

"That's not true."

"This room is the safest place in the world. I promise you that. You have nothing to fear here. Whatever you say here, in this place, will remain between us. And I want you to understand that you can ask me anything and tell me anything. Think of me as your best friend. Someone you can trust."

"You're a shrink. Mama said never to talk to shrinks."

"She did, did she?"

"She said shrinks want to take me away from her, and if they ask me questions, I'm not supposed to answer."

Dr. Bart sighed. "Well, if you don't answer, it will be hard for you and I to get to know each other."

"I don't want to get to know you."

"I'd like to know you."

"I want my mama. Where is Mama?"

"She's gone, son."

"Gone where?"

"Heaven, I'm afraid. That's why you came here yesterday to live with us."

"I don't want to live here. I want to live with Mama."

Dr. Bart fell silent, then said, "You want to live with her back at the motel with her boyfriend Maxwell Pullen?"

"Just with Mama. I don't like Max. Max is mean."

"Mean to you, or mean to your mama?"

"Mean to everyone."

"Is that why the police found you in the closet? Because Max was being mean to you?"

Silence.

"Michael?"

"It was dark in the closet, like in here."

"And you went in there because it was safe, like here. Nothing can hurt you in the closet, and nothing can hurt you here."

"Max sometimes found me in the closet, but not all the time."

"Not *that* time."

Silence again.

"Where was your mama when you were in the closet hiding from Max?" Dr. Bart's voice had grown slightly louder, like he'd leaned in closer to the recorder.

Again, I was quiet.

"Michael? Where was Mama?"

"Mama was sleeping in the bathtub."

"Your mama was sleeping in the bathtub when you hid in the closet? She wasn't in the bed?"

"In the bathtub. Mama likes baths."

"Where was Max?"

"Max wasn't home."

"But he came home, didn't he? Did he come home while your mama was in the bath?"

My little voice, barely audible: "Yeah."

"What happened when Max came home? This is important, Michael, so I want you to think about it carefully before you answer. Can you do that for me?"

"Okay."

"You said your mama was *sleeping* in the bathtub. A lot of important people are trying to figure out if she was already sleeping when Max came in or if he *made* her go to sleep. Do you understand?"

I didn't answer.

"If you heard her speak to Max, then we know *he* made her go to sleep."

"I don't know."

"Did Max speak to you when he got home?"

"I don't know."

"You're a smart boy, Michael. I know you understand the question. Did Max speak to you when he got home?"

My reply came softly. "Yeah."

"What did he say?"

My little voice dropped nearly an octave in an effort to imitate Max. "He said, 'Not a fucking word outta you, you little shit.'"

"Were you in the closet when he said this?"

"No."

"Where were you?"

"I was sitting on the bed watching the TV. Max came in, was mean to me, and went to mama to be mean to her. He was loud."

"Did he close the bathroom door?"

"Yes."

"What did your mama say when he came in the room?"

Silence.

"What did Max say to your mama?"

"He said she was supposed to be working. He said, 'We wouldn't be so fucked right now if you went to work when you're supposed to!'"

"Your mother worked for a restaurant, right? As a waitress?"

"Waffle Castle. I like waffles."

Dr. Bart said, "You're being a good boy. If you keep answering my questions, maybe we can have waffles when we're done."

I said nothing.

"Max worked in construction, right?"

"Mama said Max was a lazy shit who couldn't hold down a construction job 'cause he drank so much."

"She said that from the bath?"

"No. She was sleeping. She always said that, though."

Dr. Bart went on. "Max blamed your mama for losing the house, having to move into the motel?"

"That's what he was yelling about. Max was always yelling."

"In the bathroom?"

"Yeah."

"Did your mama yell back?"

Nothing.

"Michael? Did your mama yell back at Max?"

"I heard splashing. Lots of splashing."

"But not your mama?"

"Max screamed. Max screamed so loud. So loud! Max screamed. I couldn't hear nothin' else." My little voice screamed then, my voice on the tape, in order to show Dr. Bart, make him understand. Loud enough to reach out from the past and rattle the speakers in my Porsche. Loud enough to reach through my chest, yank at my heart, and threaten to pull the organ out mid-beat.

I nearly drove off the shoulder of the highway; the wheels spun, grabbed gravel, then found the pavement again.

I scrambled for the volume knob and turned down the stereo.

Neither Dr. Bart nor the younger me spoke for a moment. The seconds ticked by. When my four-year-old voice came back, it was a whisper.

"That's when I went into the closet."

CHAPTER THIRTY-THREE

DOBBS

IT SMELLS LIKE BARBECUE, Detective. It's okay, you can say it. We're all thinking it. This isn't my first car fire, and they all smell this way," Special Agent Gimble said. She chugged a Red Bull, crushed the can, and set it on the bumper of her Chevy Suburban. "The nasty smell, the one that really turns your gut, that comes from the tires. I always thought that seemed a little backward."

"I'm a homicide detective in Los Angeles," Dobbs replied. "When I started out on patrol, I probably caught one of these a week."

"With a body?"

Dobbs shook his head. "Most around here are kids torching stolen wheels after a joyride. A couple with bodies. Usually gang-related. The smell doesn't bother me, not anymore."

The Ford Escort had been doused in gasoline and set ablaze. By the time the fire department had responded, there was nothing left but a burned-out hull. The body of Philip Wardwell was still in the passenger seat, the remains of his suit fused to what was left of his body, two holes clearly visible in his skull—the entrance and exit wounds of a bullet fired at close range. The stolen Glock from the police station lay in his lap.

"If it's not the smell, why's your nose all scrunched up like that?"

"I'm thinking."

"That's your thinking face?"

"Kepler's actions don't add up." Dobbs picked up Gimble's empty Red Bull can and turned it in his hands. "Sillman—that's the cop who got attacked in the interview room back at headquarters—he swore up and down it was the attorney who hit him. He was shaken up, though, slight concussion. I figured it had to be Kepler, and Sillman just remembered it wrong. Then we've got the two of them walking out of the building—Kepler's not forcing him, he's not forcing Kepler. They get in this car, Kepler drives, not the attorney. Drives to here—"

"And shoots his attorney in the head," Gimble interrupted. "What kind of attorney throws away his life and career for a client?"

Sammy Goggans poked his head out of the SUV's back door. "The kind of attorney who isn't an attorney."

Gimble rounded the side of the Chevy with Dobbs behind her. "What'd you find, Sammy?"

"I've got one Philip Wardwell licensed to practice law in the state of California, but unless he somehow managed to morph from a ninety-three-year-old black man to an overweight white guy half his age, the cooked man in the Ford over there ain't him."

Gimble faced the various law enforcement officers and investigators in the Edward Hotel parking lot, her eyes darting around. "Begley! Where are you?" She started toward the burned-out Ford. "Begley!"

A hand went up from a group of FBI agents huddled at the ground near the side of the Dumpster. Dobbs followed her over to them.

Begley was poking at a bundle of crumpled napkins in the

grass with a pencil. "We've got blood on these. They haven't been here long."

Gimble's eyes narrowed. "Blood? As in Kepler's injured?"

Begley shook his head. "Not unless he's dead. There's brain matter too. My guess is he used these to clean up after shooting Wardwell."

"Wardwell's not Wardwell," Dobbs said.

Gimble explained what Sammy Goggans had found.

Dobbs neared the burned-out husk of a car, carefully avoiding the water pooled on the ground, and studied what remained of the man in the passenger seat. "Are you able to print him?"

"No way," Begley said. "Too much damage from the fire. I can run dental, but we'll need someone to match to." With a gloved hand, he placed the napkins in an evidence bag.

Gimble turned to Dobbs. "What kind of ID check would they have done before letting him in to see Kepler?"

Dobbs shrugged. "Driver's license, business card. Tough to say."

"Business card," Gimble repeated.

Dobbs realized what she was getting at. "Wilkins would have it. I sent him back to Tepper's apartment for something." He took out his phone and dialed his partner on speaker.

Wilkins picked up on the second ring. "It's gone."

"How's it gone?" Dobbs replied.

"What's gone?" Gimble asked.

Dobbs pulled up the photograph of the sparrow feather on a leather strap taken at the Tepper crime scene earlier and showed it to her and Begley.

Gimble frowned. "The girl from the bathtub had that?"

"When we found the feathers in the truck, I remembered seeing this. It was just sitting at the bottom of a jewelry box. I told Wilkins to go back and get it, put it in evidence," Dobbs told her.

On the phone, Wilkins said, "He either grabbed it when we

walked him through the place or he somehow came back for it, but it's definitely gone."

"Fuck," Gimble muttered.

"Kepler's attorney. Please tell me he gave you a business card," Dobbs said.

"Kepler's attorney gave me a business card."

"And you still have it?"

"Yeah, why?"

Gimble started pacing, snapping her fingers.

Dobbs said, "I need you to run it for prints. Philip Wardwell is not Philip Wardwell."

"Of course not," Wilkins grumbled. "What else can go wrong today?"

Dobbs disconnected the call.

"We need to get in front of this," Gimble said, her fingers snapping so quick it pained Dobbs to look at them. "I think I'm gonna have the sister picked up."

Dobbs bit his lower lip. "A family like that, they'll lawyer up before you get a chance to talk to her. She's not going to sell out her brother."

"Adoptive brother."

"Whatever. She's got no reason to talk to you. We'll continue to watch her phone, wait for him to make contact, then work backward. That's the move. I'm still not sure you should have called her."

Gimble stopped pacing, took out her cell phone, and made a show of dialing Megan Fitzgerald again. When the call went to voice mail, she left another message, then slipped the phone back into the pocket of her jeans. "We want her spooked. People who are spooked make mistakes. Spook, rattle, then roll—that's the plan until we pick her up."

She turned and her eyes locked on Special Agent Vela, leaning on the wall of the Edward Hotel near the service entrance, scrolling through something on his phone. She started toward him, Dobbs following, and shouted across the parking lot, "Vela? Where are you on a profile? You've had half a day since we ID'd this guy. You should be able to tell me what color underwear he's wearing at this point. I need to know where he went from here!"

Vela held out the phone to her. "You'll want to read this."

"What is it?" She took the phone, began scrolling through the text.

Vela looked at Dobbs. "You said his adoptive family was Fitzgerald. I didn't make the connection at first, not until we saw all those books back at the storage unit, the audiobooks you found in his truck. Several were written by the Fitzgeralds. He was adopted by *Rosela and Barton Fitzgerald*."

"They're shrinks, teachers at Cornell. Why does that matter?"

Vela nodded toward his phone in Gimble's hand. "He wasn't just adopted, he was *placed*. That's a copy of the police report from the last night he spent with his real mother."

Gimble glanced up at Dobbs and Vela only long enough to whisper, "My God, this is horrible." She went back to the small screen, lost in the text.

CHAPTER THIRTY-FOUR

MICHAEL

THE TAPE CONTINUED, NEITHER me nor Dr. Bart speaking, only a delicate hiss from my car speakers. When Dr. Bart's voice came back, it was less steady but intent on pressing on.

Dr. Bart said, "Did your mama scream, too? When Max screamed?"

"Mama couldn't scream."

"Why not, Michael?"

"Because Mama was sleeping."

Silence again. Nearly ten seconds. Then: "What happened next?"

"Someone knocked on the door."

"Your closet door or the motel-room door?"

"A man knocked on the front door of our room, and Max came out of the bathroom to answer."

"Who was there?"

"I couldn't see."

"Because you were in the closet?"

"Uh-huh."

"But you heard him? What did he say?"

"He wanted to know if everything was okay. He heard Max being loud. Max told him it was all okay. He told him it was the TV. The man must have believed him, because he went away."

"What did Max do after the man went away?"

"He sat on the bed for a long time."

"You could see him?"

"I laid down on the floor of the closet. I could see his shoes from under the door."

"What did Max do next? When he got up from the bed."

"I don't want to talk about that."

"We need to, Michael, it's very important."

"No."

"Is that when Max went out to his truck? The police report said he kept his tools in his work truck."

"No! No! No! I don't wanna!"

Silence again.

"Michael." Dr. Bart lowered his deep voice; it sounded calming, soothing. "I want you to take a deep breath."

I turned up the volume again. I couldn't help myself. Barely audible, deep in the background, I heard myself breathing in fast, gasping breaths, nearly hyperventilating.

"You're safe here, Michael. This is a safe place. Max can't hurt you. Max can't hurt anyone, not anymore."

"Max is dead."

"Yes, Michael. Max is dead," Dr. Bart said. "Take another breath, calm yourself. Nobody can hurt you here. Not Max, not anyone."

A minute passed.

Two minutes.

Three minutes.

Nearly five before Dr. Bart spoke again. "Do you feel better, Michael?"

No reply.

"Michael?"

"I'm not—"

The tape clicked. Then came a loud clunk as it reached the end of the side and reversed. The second side was blank. I let it play anyway. Thirty minutes of the loudest silence.

At some point, my foot sank on the accelerator. I realized I was doing nearly ninety. I slowed as the first sign for Needles, California, flew past on the right. Not much longer now.

CHAPTER THIRTY-FIVE

DOBBS

WHEN GIMBLE FINISHED READING the police report, she lowered Vela's phone to her side. Her face had gone pale. "What does something like that do to a kid?"

"Something like what?" Dobbs asked, eyeing the phone.

Vela's gaze met Gimble's, and then he turned to Dobbs. "Back in 1996, when Kepler was only four years old, they found him in the closet of a run-down motel room outside Dryden, New York. He'd been in there all night. Not locked in, mind you; he was hiding. On the other side of that door, a tweaker named Maxwell Pullen started to dismember the boy's mother with a hacksaw. He wrapped the pieces in plastic painter's tarps and lined them up on the floor. The investigating officer thinks he planned on disposing of her remains once he'd finished but then got cold feet. They found a high concentration of methamphetamines and alcohol in his blood, and there's no way to know what was going on in his head, but when he'd cut up about half of her, he sat on the edge of the bed, put a thirty-eight in his mouth, and pulled the trigger. If anyone heard the gunshot, they didn't report it. A cleaning woman stumbled into the mess and found Kepler the next morning."

"Shit."

Vela went on. "According to the medical examiner, the actual cause of death for the mother was drowning."

"Drowning?" Dobbs repeated.

Gimble handed him Vela's phone. "Page three, second paragraph."

Dobbs studied the text. "Drowned in the bathtub. Unlikely accidental. No drugs or alcohol found in her system."

Vela nodded. "But here's where things get weird—rigor had started to set in before Pullen made his first cut. Normally, rigor starts to set in about two hours after death and lasts for about eight to twelve hours. The ME set the time of death somewhere between four and seven p.m. Security footage for the motel has Maxwell Pullen leaving at just a little past one in the afternoon and returning at six thirty."

"So he wasn't there when the mother drowned?" Dobbs asked.

Vela shook his head. "Guess who was, though."

"Kepler."

Gimble's fingers were snapping again. Softly this time. A nervous tic. "If she drowned in the tub, how would the water temperature affect time of death?"

Dobbs said, "I caught a bathtub drowning two years ago— a mother in East LA swallowed a handful of pills, passed out, eventually went under the water. The ME measured the water temperature versus air temp and figured in both when calculating TOD. She was confident within thirty minutes. They probably did something similar here."

"No way a four-year-old kid drowned a grown woman," Gimble replied. "How about someone else? Another unsub in the room before this? Before Maxwell Pullen got back?"

Dobbs was studying the report again. "The security footage only covered the office and the parking lot, no line of sight on the room. Anyone could have come and gone."

Vela retrieved his phone from Dobbs and dropped it back in his pocket. "That doesn't explain Pullen's actions. If he didn't kill her, why try to cover up the crime?"

"Distraught about losing her, maybe?" Gimble said.

Vela shook his head. "Maybe that's why he killed himself, but dismemberment is an act of desperation, concealment. His actions suggest remorse too. Possibly an attempt to cover up for someone else."

"Like the kid?" Dobbs suggested.

Gimble was pacing again. "If the kid killed her, and that's a mighty big *if*, and this guy wanted to cover it up, that suggests he had much more of a vested interest in their little family than the report implies. This goes way beyond tweaker boyfriend crashing with mom and little boy. That brings me back to my original question—what does something like this do to a kid?"

Vela chewed on the inside of his cheek, his eyes roving the ground. "Most adults can't remember anything prior to five years old. Children form memories, retain information, but not efficiently. I read a study of early-childhood development where kids were asked to recall documented events that had taken place when they were three or younger. Between five and seven, they recalled approximately sixty percent of the events. That number dropped to forty percent by eight, and lower as they got older. With an event this traumatic, the mind's natural defenses move to block it out entirely, regardless of age. It's also very possible that every second of that night got permanently etched into his subconscious or even conscious memories, meaning those events might have played a role in shaping every decision he's made since whether he's aware of it or not."

"Which might explain why we found Tepper in his bathtub," Gimble said.

Dobbs turned to Gimble. "You said you have at least eighteen other victims connected with the feathers—any others found in bathtubs?"

Gimble shook her head. "None. Alyssa Tepper would be the first."

Vela's eyes grew wide when he realized what Dobbs was suggesting. "Something triggered him. Brought this back."

"You said he was placed with the Fitzgeralds after his mother's death in the motel and treated by his adoptive father," Dobbs said. "Barton Fitzgerald just passed away. Aneurysm."

Gimble tilted her head. "According to the report, Fitzgerald's sessions with Kepler were recorded and sealed by a Judge Harry Larson."

"I looked him up. Larson retired nearly a decade ago. We'd need someone else to overturn his original order. That will take a while. We've got a better shot at getting his adoption records," Vela said.

Gimble stopped pacing. "We need all of it. Every scrap of paper. Whatever we can find on this guy's real parents too. All of them. It's all relevant. Find me a judge who will understand that and be willing to sign a warrant."

Vela bit his lip. "Rines, maybe?"

Dobbs said, "If the adoptive father's death was a trigger, Tepper was only the first. The eighteen bodies you've already got were nothing but a warm-up for what he'll do next. This is the endgame."

Gimble turned back toward the burned-out Ford and shouted, "Begley! Finish up. We're regrouping at Kepler's truck!" To Dobbs, she said, "We need to look at where this guy's been if we want to figure out where he's going. You're with us until this is over."

CHAPTER THIRTY-SIX

MICHAEL

I ARRIVED IN NEEDLES, California, in a daze. The desolate landscape of the Mojave Desert rolling past outside, the Colorado River—I saw none of it. I listened to all thirty minutes of the blank side of the cassette, then listened to the first side again. The tape repeated for a third time before I made the turn onto Dunes Road, found number 78, and finally registered that I had arrived.

I drove past the small, neglected mobile home, turned at the end of Dunes, came back around, and parked across the narrow street. I picked up Roland Eads's driver's license from the passenger seat and confirmed I had the right address.

A rusty Mazda sat under the sagging carport. Several planters lined the cracked sidewalk, filled with nothing but weeds. There was no lawn, only a small rock garden to the left of the driveway— the source of the dusty white film coating the concrete and the dull metal walls. An American flag, torn and faded, fluttered on a pole near the door.

I slipped a finger under the collar of my shirt and tugged the material away from my neck.

A few hours ago, I remembered thinking it felt good to wear nice things again. Now, the shirt had grown stiff and uncomfortable. The Armani jacket was in a ball on the floor. And I kept thinking about the tennis shoes in the trunk—I wanted to swap them for the Berluti loafers on my feet. I reminded myself who the police were looking for, what they expected that guy to be wearing. It was why I'd donned these clothes in the first place.

My burner phone vibrated on the passenger seat. For much of the drive, I didn't have service and I'd given up on it.

"Meg? Why are you calling me from your phone? I told you to get a burner before you called me again!"

"Didn't you listen to my messages? The FBI keeps calling me! The FBI! If they have my number, they can get my records. And once they have your number, they can trace you."

"Whoa, calm down, Meg." I regretted the words the moment they left my lips. I pictured Megan's reddening face in my mind.

"Life is totally Zen now. I feel so much better," she said mockingly. "What if they're listening right this second?"

"They'd need to get a warrant first, and they haven't had enough time," I told her.

"Where are you getting your intel? Jason Bourne movies? I don't think we should take any chances. As soon as we hang up, you need to destroy that thing."

"How will I reach you? You'll need a new phone too," I told her.

"I already bought one." She gave me the number. "You got it?"

I committed it to memory.

Megan went on. "Don't call my new phone until you have a new burner too."

I tried to change the subject. "What did you find in Dr. Bart's office?"

"Man, you really suck at this. Are you listening? We need to be sure they don't have either number."

"Yes. I got it. Loud and clear. What did you find?"

She told me about the blue dots on some files but not others. "Do you know any of these names? Nicole Milligan, Darcey Haas, Issac Dorrough, Selena Hennis, Cassandra Shatley, Jeffery Longtin, or Katrina Nickols?"

"No."

"None of them?"

I thought I recognized one name but I wasn't sure from where. The memory was like water—when I tried to grab it, my fingers just passed through.

"Michael?"

"No. None of them. Why?"

Megan's voice dropped to a hush. "They're all dead, Michael. All but two."

I heard voices behind Megan, then a girl laughing and some guy shouting something. "Where are you?"

"The Starbucks near campus."

Good. Away from the house. "Which two?" I asked her.

"Don't you want to know how they died?"

"Not right now. We don't have time for that."

"Murdered, it looks like. Each one."

The two of us were quiet for a few seconds, then I said, "Which two are still alive?"

Megan didn't reply.

"Meg, come on."

"Nicole Milligan and Jeffery Longtin."

"We need to find them. Can you track them down?"

Again, Megan was quiet.

"Meg."

"Okay, okay."

My eyes drifted back to the mobile home. "Was there a file on Roland Eads?"

She sighed. "No. Nothing with that name. Nothing under Philip Wardwell either."

I'd thought for sure Dr. Bart would have a file on Eads.

"Michael? How did you know Alyssa Tepper was one of Dr. Bart's patients?"

I thought I saw movement inside the mobile home across the street.

"Michael? Are you still there?"

"I saw the feather, Meg. I told you. The baseball card too."

"You didn't know her? You'd never met her before?"

"You don't believe me?"

"You just seemed so...sure. You said there'd be a file, and there was."

"Meg. Someone is trying to frame me," I said. "Someone connected to Dr. Bart, his patients, his research. This is about the dark room. It has to be. I need you to believe me, Meg. You're all I've got."

"I believe you, Michael." The weakness in her voice betrayed her real feelings, though. She *wanted* to believe me.

The two of us were quiet for a long while.

Megan broke the silence. "What was on the tape?"

I told her.

"Whoa."

"Yeah."

Megan said, "Come home, and we'll figure this out together."

"I'll text you as soon as I have a new phone. Then send me whatever you can find on Nicole Milligan and Jeffery Longtin."

Before she could reply, before she could try to talk me into doing something else, I hung up.

I killed the Porsche's engine and got out of the car. I stretched my arms and legs right there in the deserted street.

In the mobile home, a curtain was pulled an inch or two to the side, then dropped back. The front door opened a moment later, and a heavyset woman in a floral-print muumuu frowned at me. "What the hell are you doing here? Where's Roland?"

CHAPTER THIRTY-SEVEN

MICHAEL

WHERE'S ROLAND?

I didn't recognize her—I was certain I'd never seen her before.

Short gray hair. Mid- to late fifties. Dark, leathery skin lined from years of sun damage. A cigarette sagging between her lips. She glanced up and down the street before turning her frown on me and gesturing inside. "Get your ass in here before somebody sees you."

My body didn't want to move, my arms and legs stiff.

I'm not sure what I expected to find in my search of Roland Eads's house, but another person complicated the matter.

Significantly.

Her frown deepened. She pinched the cigarette between her fingers, threw it on the faded doormat, stamped it out. "Damn it, get in here!" She surveyed the street, her neighbors, her teeth clenched.

I closed the car door, crossed the street, and stepped through the lingering smoke into the mobile home.

Behind me, she closed the thin door and twisted the dead bolt.

"Christ, you're all over the news. What a shitstorm. Where the hell is Roland?"

"He's still in LA," I told her. Having no idea what she was talking about, I needed to improvise.

"He's okay, though, right? Nothing happened? I worry about that boy."

"He thought it would be better if we didn't stay together. He said the police would be looking for the both of us." It seemed like the logical answer. *Why else would Roland stay behind after breaking me out of LAPD?* "He told me to meet him back here. I must have beat him."

She pulled back the curtain again, looked across the street. "Car like that, it's no wonder. You couldn't find something a little less conspicuous? What is that, a Porsche?"

"Yeah. A Porsche."

She shook her head. "Not registered to you, I hope. You're not that dumb."

"It's registered under one of my parents' LLCs, not my name."

"You should dump it, first chance you get. You're pushing your luck driving something flashy like that." She dropped the curtain and turned back to me. "How far behind you is he?"

"I don't know."

The frown finally faded and she sighed. "Are you hungry? I imagine you're famished. When was the last time you ate?"

I thought about that and realized I hadn't eaten anything in nearly twenty-four hours. "Not since yesterday," I told her.

As if in acknowledgment, my stomach growled, a low, deep rumble.

The interior of the mobile home was larger than I'd expected, but I could still smell stagnant dishwater in the sink in the tiny kitchen. A sixty-inch television filled much of the living-room wall, too large for the small space. Although muted, the television was tuned to one of the twenty-four-hour news networks.

The woman followed my gaze. "The local news in LA has been running stories on you practically nonstop. Nothing on national yet but I keep flipping back."

From a small built-in table near the kitchen, she picked up the television remote and switched to KNBC out of Los Angeles. My driver's license photo popped up next to some reporter I didn't recognize. On the opposite side of his perfectly combed hair was an image of Roland Eads and me in the hallway at LAPD. I thought it came from a camera near the elevators but I couldn't be sure.

She set the remote down on the table about a foot away from a chrome-plated nine-millimeter pistol; a box of ammunition was beside the gun. Then she went to the refrigerator and started rooting around inside. "I've got ham, roast beef, and American cheese. Will that work?"

"Sure."

"Ham or roast beef?"

"Can you do both? I'm starving."

My eyes hadn't left the gun.

She lit another cigarette, then scooped up several items from the refrigerator, including a jar of mayonnaise, and set everything on the counter. She pulled a plate from the cabinet above her on the left, parked the smoke in the corner of her mouth, and began to assemble a sandwich. "You can turn the sound back on if you want. I just got tired of listening to them drone on. They don't know much." Her voice dropped into a bit of a singsong as she said, "Michael Kepler killed Alyssa Tepper. Michael Kepler escaped LAPD custody with the help of his attorney. Michael Kepler, Michael Kepler, Michael Kepler." She paused for a second, slicing the sandwich. "They found the warehouse. Looks like the television crews got there about the same time the local yokels were wrapping up." She whistled. "The feds were there, U.S. marshals. Roland said this would be big, but I don't think anyone expected all that."

I took up the remote and pressed the mute button, bringing back the audio. The camera zoomed in, the image shaky, shot from outside the Stow 'n' Go complex. I spotted Detective Garrett Dobbs. He was talking to a pretty woman with chestnut hair pulled back in a ponytail. Although she wore jeans and a white tank top, she was clearly FBI.

"That's Special Agent Jessica Gimble," the woman told me from the kitchen counter. "The reporter put her name out there about an hour ago, but nothing else. I ran her through Google but got nothing." She waved a hand at the screen.

I returned the remote to the table, setting it much closer to the nine-millimeter than it had been. My little finger brushed the cold metal.

She turned from the counter and set a plate down on the table in front of me, then went back to the refrigerator, retrieved a can of Coke, and set that beside the plate. "Sit, eat!"

I pulled out the chair and sat. I didn't eat the sandwich as much as inhale it. The can of Coke I downed in large gulps.

She stubbed out the remains of her cigarette in a filthy MGM Grand ashtray and stared at me in awe. "My God, it's like you've *never* eaten."

My eyes drifted over to a stack of unopened letters piled on the far end of the table. Bills, Publishers Clearing House ads. I lifted the empty Coke can and shook it. "Mind if I have another?"

"Yeah, sure."

When she stood and went to the refrigerator, I glanced at the topmost envelope. It was addressed to Erma Eads.

"Erma, did Roland tell you why Alyssa Tepper had to die?"

When my eyes danced over to the nine-millimeter on the table, I forced them back on her.

She popped the top on the can of Coke with a satisfying hiss and placed the can in front of me. She glanced at the gun too. "Roland didn't give me a lot of detail on that," she said. "Only told me it had to happen. No other way to see this through."

I took a sip of the Coke. "Aren't you going to eat?"

Her eyes darted over the gun again, then she smiled. "I'll wait for Roland."

On the television, the reporter was in the middle of describing my escape route from the LAPD building when he stopped mid-sentence. From the corner of my eye, I caught him placing a finger on his left ear, no doubt listening to a voice in his earbud. When he looked back up at the camera, his face had gone solemn. "We have a report of a car fire earlier in the day near the fish market, and we're going to cut over there live—sounds like there may be a connection."

The screen flickered and a shot of the parking lot behind the old Edward Hotel came up. The camera focused on a redheaded reporter straightening the collar of her blouse speaking to someone off-screen. When she realized she was live, she dropped her hand and stared into the camera.

I didn't hear what she said. I was too busy studying the smoldering remains of the car parked behind her.

Roland Eads's car.

When the reporter said the victim found in the passenger seat of the Ford Escort had been executed with a single shot to the head, both Erma Eads and I dived for the nine-millimeter in the center of the table, sending the television remote skittering.

CHAPTER THIRTY-EIGHT

MICHAEL

THE REMOTE FLEW OFF the edge of the table, slid over the linoleum floor, and cracked against the wood-laminate cabinet about three feet behind Erma Eads. Her plump form crossed with it in the air, moving at a speed that seemed impossible for someone of her size and age. Her fingers found the nine-millimeter, but she came at the gun from an odd angle, and rather than gripping the cold steel, she sent the weapon spinning.

I stood up fast, sending the wooden chair crashing to the floor behind me as I dived for the gun. If not for the spin, I would have missed it, but the butt of the gun rammed into my palm and I scooped up the pistol in a series of moves more lucky than skillful.

This didn't slow down Erma Eads. With the howl of a banshee coming from her lips, she grabbed the edge of the table and yanked up. My sandwich plate, her ashtray, and the can of Coke flew through the air. The table careened toward me, and she followed behind in an uncontrolled tumble; two hundred and fifty pounds of blubber and bone crashed into Ikea's finest, and both table and woman slammed into me. I tumbled backward, tripped over an end table, and went down next to the couch.

Erma got to her feet first and came at me again, half stumbling, half thrusting. She fell on top of me, and as her shoulder crunched down into the center of my chest, I heard a horrible cracking sound.

The air left my lungs and I thought for sure she had broken several of my ribs before I realized the sound had come from the end table, now in pieces under her meaty thigh.

Somehow, I managed to maintain my grip on the gun. I swung my arm around and smacked the butt of the nine-millimeter against the side of her head with a satisfying *thunk*. This slowed her for only a moment. Her long fingernails grabbed at my arm and sliced through the skin just above my wrist, and spittle flew from her lips as she growled like a rabid dog.

I brought my knee up while simultaneously punching her kidney. Once. Twice.

I kept hitting her, drawing strength from her garbled grunts, and finally her flailing diminished into lumbering, weak thrusts, her energy gone.

I twisted away and managed to roll out from under her before she could strike again. I half stepped, half stumbled to my feet. I raised the gun and pointed the barrel directly at her snarling, gasping face. "Enough!"

"What did you do to my Roland?" she screamed, a crumpled heap of flowered muumuu on the floor.

I twisted the gun sideways to get a better look at my wrist. She had drawn blood, but the scratches weren't deep.

"You shot my brother!" she spat. "You killed Roland!"

"It wasn't me!"

On the screen, the redheaded reporter was still talking. "The vehicle behind me, a 1992 Ford Escort, matches reports of the car used by Michael Kepler in his escape from LAPD earlier today with the aid of a man posing as his attorney. At this point, we don't know if the body found in the car is that of Kepler, his attorney, or someone else. We have learned the person was shot in the head before the vehicle was doused in gasoline and set aflame. A gun was recovered at the scene, but the police are not willing to confirm whether or not that gun is the murder weapon." The reporter gazed into the camera, her face solemn. "One thing is certain, Brett—a killer is on the loose. Residents of Los Angeles County are strongly cautioned to remain careful and vigilant until he is back in police custody."

"Erma, you've got to believe me," I said. "I didn't hurt him. I wouldn't shoot him, and I didn't set the car on fire. Why would I do that?"

Her eyes narrowed as they darted from the television to me. "You're him, aren't you?"

"Who?"

"Nobody calls me Erma."

"I don't understand. Who are you talking about?"

She glared at me from her position on the floor. "Anyone who knows me calls me Bunny. Nobody calls me Erma. You're him. I know it. Roland told me, but I didn't believe him. Fucking crazy."

"What are you talking about?"

"Just shoot me. I ain't telling you shit."

"I don't want to hurt you."

She smirked and nodded toward the television. "Is that what you told him?"

"Get up."

"No."

The two of us stared at each other for a long time, neither one looking away.

I crossed the small living room to the lamp on the floor,

unplugged it, and yanked the cord out the other side. Then I did the same with the matching lamp. I used one cord to tie her hands behind her back and the other to bind her legs. From the coffee table, I grabbed the lighter sitting with a pack of Marlboro Reds and used it to heat the plastic cord at the knots.

"You're burning me!"

"No, I'm not. Stop squirming."

When the plastic cooled, the knots on the cord had fused. There would be no untying it. It would need to be cut away. I helped her to a sitting position on the couch.

I pressed the barrel of the gun against her cheek. "Tell me what the fuck is going on."

"Shoot. Me." After the two words, she pinched her lips shut tight and turned her head away from me, reminding me of a child refusing to eat.

"Which room is Roland's?"

She only glared at me.

"Did he kill Alyssa Tepper?"

This seemed to confuse her, but she still didn't speak.

I straightened and went to the bedroom on my left.

I had a fifty-fifty shot.

Erma's room.

Bunny.

Whatever.

I tore the room apart. I yanked open every drawer and dumped the contents. Pulled every article of clothing from the closet and flipped the mattress and box spring. Several pictures hung on the wall—Erma in her younger years—I yanked those down too. I moved in more of a blind fury than anything resembling an organized search, but I continued, each destructive motion eating away at my anger and confusion.

After twenty minutes, I had found nothing meaningful in her

room. I stomped the length of the mobile home to the bedroom on the opposite side, stepping over Erma Eads, who had managed to roll back onto the floor but had made little headway with her bindings.

"There would be no need for this if you just told me what was going on, Erma," I said as I stood at the open door to the second bedroom. "You have a lovely home. I take no pleasure in this."

The second bedroom was a mirror image of the first, about twelve feet wide and ten feet deep. A double bed, unmade, was crammed in the far corner. The once-white sheets were now a muted yellow. A small air-conditioner unit chugged at the window, but it did little to diminish the musty odor of sweat and mildew in the air.

I rubbed at my temples. I wasn't exactly sure when the headache had started, but the dull throb behind my eyeballs had grown to the point where it could no longer be ignored.

"Erma, do you have any Tylenol?"

When she didn't answer, I went back down the hall to the small bathroom. "Never mind, I'll find them."

Above the pedestal sink, I opened the mirrored medicine cabinet and rummaged around inside. I didn't find any Tylenol, but she did have a bottle of Excedrin Migraine.

I took two, swallowed them dry. Started to put the bottle back, thought better of it, and slipped it in my pocket instead. As if in retaliation, the pain behind my eyes intensified. My ears filled with a low hum.

I tried to ignore it and give the medicine time to work.

I returned to the second bedroom, Roland's, and stepped inside.

CHAPTER THIRTY-NINE

WRITTEN STATEMENT, MEGAN FITZGERALD

As I had earlier, I asked the Uber driver to drop me at the start of our long driveway rather than at the house. The sun had set nearly an hour before, and the last thing I needed was Dr. Rose or Ms. Neace spotting headlights coming up the drive.

I bolted through the yard, my backpack bouncing under my right arm, dodging all but the last motion-activated light, this one above the laundry-room door.

The interior of the house was dark, and I kept it that way. I removed my shoes and felt my way up the back staircase and along the hall. I slipped into my room and gently closed the door, cringing as the hinges squeaked the last few inches.

When I turned on the light, I found Dr. Rose sitting on the edge of my bed.

"Shit!" I dropped my backpack and covered my mouth.

Dr. Rose stared at me with those steel-gray eyes, her lips pursed. Both her hands were at her sides, her fingertips digging into my duvet.

"You scared me half to death!"

Dr. Rose licked her lips. "Our appointment was three hours ago. Where have you been?"

"Studying. At the library."

"I called campus security and had them check the library.

Four times. You weren't there." She rose from the bed. "Where have you been?"

"I...I wasn't at the library the whole time. I went to Starbucks to get a snack and some coffee. That's all. They probably missed me."

Dr. Rose glared at me.

"Really, that's the only place I went. Where else would I go?"

"Why didn't you answer your phone?"

I had turned off my phone after speaking to Michael. That FBI agent kept calling, and I didn't want her to be able to track me. "The battery died."

"Let me see it."

"Seriously?"

"I'm not going to ask twice."

I reached into the front pocket of my backpack, pulled out the phone, and handed it to her.

Dr. Rose studied the blank screen for a second, then pressed the power button. "You've got fifty percent left on the battery. Why was it off?"

"Are you sure? It died hours ago."

"I'm not an idiot, Megan. Don't patronize me. It's unbecoming."

"I didn't mean—"

"What's your pass code?"

"You have no right—"

She glared at me. "What is your pass code?"

I told her.

Dr. Rose keyed in the number and began opening various apps.

"What are you doing?"

Without looking up, she said, "I'm checking your call log, your texts, your pictures, and whatever else I decide I'd like to look at." She tossed her keys to me. "Go wait for me in my office."

I felt my face flush. I squeezed Dr. Rose's keys hard enough to draw blood and stomped down the stairs.

I had no idea what Michael was about to do, Jessica. If I had, I would have tried to stop him. I swear.

CHAPTER FORTY

MICHAEL

LIKE ERMA'S BEDROOM, ROLAND'S had two windows. He had covered both in newspaper, haphazardly taped over the glass—not enough to block the sunlight entirely but enough to make the space feel smaller, claustrophobic. A milk crate beside the bed served as a nightstand. No other furniture.

I stepped over the dirty clothes, went to the milk crate, and flicked on his lamp. The bare bulb came to life, sent the shadows scurrying.

An empty garment bag from Roselli's in downtown LA hung from the back of the bedroom door; no doubt it had once held the suit Roland was wearing today. An old pair of tennis shoes were lying on the floor atop a couple of stained T-shirts and a pair of dusty jeans.

Beside the lamp on the makeshift nightstand was an old alarm clock, a stained water glass with a thin layer of dust, and several prescription bottles, including Ambien and mirtazapine, an anti-depressant. All the medications had been prescribed for Roland Eads.

With my left hand, I held the lamp. With my right leg, I kicked the side of the milk crate, punting it toward the wall. It rolled several times before coming to a stop on the opposite side of the small room. The pills, clock, and water glass scattered in various directions.

He hadn't hidden anything under or behind the crate.

I set the lamp down on the floor, slipped both hands under his mattress, and tossed that aside too. The box spring followed. Nothing.

Systematically, I made my way around the room, kicking at the threadbare, filthy clothing, thumbing the pages of each book, every magazine.

I found nothing.

My headache intensified, the dull hum growing to a steady grumble. It felt like someone was squeezing my left eyeball, the pressure slowly building.

I swallowed another migraine pill.

I went to the closet and slid the door open.

On the floor sat a bowling ball, several pairs of shoes, and some old hiking boots. A couple of stray hangers had fallen down there too. I checked the finger holes of the bowling ball before throwing it through the bedroom wall. I even reached into each fragrant shoe on the off chance he'd hid something inside.

I found nothing.

I threw the shoes behind me, getting little satisfaction in the thumps as they slammed into the far wall.

The shelf at the top of the closet held only a couple pairs of jeans and dust.

My headache grew worse.

I think I groaned as I began rifling through the hanging clothes. If I did, I couldn't hear it over the roar in my ears. I tugged at each garment, throwing it to the floor behind me as I went—several wrinkled button-downs, faded slacks, a—

I stopped.

I stared.

There were three of them.

I pulled them from the hangers and stomped back into the living room.

Erma "Bunny" Eads was lying on her side, twisting like a beached cod, still attempting to break the cords around her hands and feet. She managed to do nothing but work up a sweat. She looked up at me as I came in, her hair matted against her forehead.

I threw all three shirts at her, watched them flutter to the ground.

I returned the kitchen table to its original position, grabbed one of the chairs, and fell into it. I took the bottle of Excedrin Migraine from my pocket, popped the top, and swallowed two more.

My head screamed.

Elbows on the table, I held my head between my hands and rubbed my temples.

Fuck, it hurt.

The three shirts on the floor around Erma Eads were all embroidered with the same text:

WINDHAM HALL—STAFF

ROLAND EADS

Windham Hall—the orphanage where I stayed briefly before being placed with the Fitzgeralds. Megan had been adopted from there too. Both Dr. Rose and Dr. Bart served on the board.

"What does Roland have to do with Windham Hall?" I spoke the words softly, yet each syllable felt like the tip of a rusty fish knife digging into the side of my skull.

Bunny Eads smirked; her eyes narrowed, and she slowly shook her head.

I closed my eyes and sucked in tepid air. "Goddamn it, Erma, you don't want to shut me out. That won't end well for you."

She licked at the blood trickling from her cracked lip. "Fuck. You."

I wasn't proud of what I did next.

CHAPTER FORTY-ONE

DOBBS

DOBBS WAS BEGINNING TO understand that whenever Special Agent Jessica Gimble faced a problem, she retreated into her own world, pacing, finger-snapping, and occasionally barking an order, as she attempted to puzzle it out.

He stood under a tent in the Nadler Distribution parking lot listening to Sammy Goggans talk. Dobbs tried not to watch Gimble, but as Sammy Goggans droned on, he kept finding himself stealing glances as she circled Kepler's truck, following the wide perimeter taped off by LAPD around the eighteen-wheeler. He knew she was a runner by her posture, her stride, her overall muscle tone and level of fitness. Her white tank top and jeans clung to her, and she seemed comfortable in the thin layer of sweat brought on by the activity; her cheeks, forehead, and arms glistened in the setting California sun.

Sammy paused a moment and plugged the small black box he had removed from the truck into his MacBook via the USB port. "This one is made by a company called Trux Data," he said. "Unlike the hardwired models made by Xata, Cadec, and CarrierWeb, it's meant to be mobile. This unit just needs a power supply, the transmitter plugs into the vehicle's ODBC port, and it's ready to record everything—"

"My guys pulled all this," Dobbs said.

Sammy nodded toward Gimble. "If she found out I'd relied on a third party when I had access to the data myself, she'd tear me a new one."

Dobbs glanced back at Gimble. Her pace had quickened toward a sprint-walk with each lap. He'd lost track of how many times she'd gone around.

Sammy sighed. "Yes, she's single. Yes, she's attractive. She is deeply involved in a passionate relationship with her career. We assume she has a family somewhere, although I wouldn't be surprised to hear she was grown in a lab. All I know for sure is she grew up somewhere outside Charleston, did her undergrad at Vanderbilt on some kind of full-boat athletic scholarship, then went right into the academy at Quantico."

Sammy lowered his voice. "She doesn't talk about her home life, and we learned long ago not to ask. Speculation is, it was rough, and she clawed her way out. Ran and didn't look back."

Dobbs stole another glance at her.

Sammy shook his head. "She goes out of her way to avoid any kind of attachment. I think she lives out of a go bag. Put her in your spank-bank and move on." Sammy's MacBook dinged and he looked back down at the screen. "Now we're talking."

"What is it?"

"I'm combining data," he said as a map of the United States filled the screen with a red line running from Los Angeles to New York. "This is Kepler's most recent run, which ended day before yesterday, just like he said. If I do this"—he hit a series of buttons, and dozens of other overlapping red lines appeared—"we've got all the runs he's made since he started with Nadler."

Dobbs leaned in closer. Although it appeared Kepler stuck to the same three or four cross-country routes, he diverged on small runs north or south. "These detours—"

"I'm on it," Sammy replied. His fingers moving quickly over the keyboard.

Nearly two dozen red dots appeared on the screen, each lining up with the route data, most at the point of each detour.

"We got him," Sammy said.

"Those are the murders?"

"Each dot represents a homicide where a feather was found." Sammy turned and shouted over his shoulder, "Gimble! You'll want to see this!"

Dobbs frowned. "He knew his GPS data was being recorded. I don't get it."

Special Agent Vela came up from behind them and set a stack of audiobook boxes on the table along with several dog-eared paperbacks. He'd heard what Sammy said. "Most serials know they'll eventually get caught. It's like the feathers—Kepler wants us to catch him, just on his terms. Kepler knows he's looking at the death penalty once he's in custody. This is him securing his legacy. Making sure he gets credit for his kills."

Gimble came over. She leaned toward the laptop, lifted her right foot behind her back, and stretched. As she realized what she was looking at, she began to nod. "That's our boy. Better than bread crumbs. He diverted from his route long enough for each kill, then got back to business as usual."

"Is that a smile?" Dobbs said.

"I don't smile." She glanced at Vela. "I need an updated profile. I need it yesterday. Where are you on that?"

"Rines denied our warrant for Kepler's adoption and treatment records. He says he'll reconsider if we can demonstrate it's necessary to track him down. He thinks we can catch him with traditional methods and doesn't feel we need to break confidentiality."

Without missing a beat, Gimble said, "Work with Sammy. Get Judge Rines copies of this data. Share the DNA. Press him. Press him hard. Kepler's our guy. We need to get in this guy's head."

Vela gave her a frustrated glance, then nodded. "I'm on it."

Gimble snapped her fingers. "What about that Windham Hall place? The orphanage. Shredded uniforms. Would they have records?"

"I've got two calls in to the director"—he glanced down at his notes—"a Lawrence Patchen. I haven't heard back yet."

"Only two? Make it ten. If you have to, send someone from the local field office in…"

"Lansing, New York," Vela said.

Gimble's eyes went to the ceiling and she thought about this for a second. "The Ithaca field office would be closest. Ask for Paul Grimsley. He runs that branch."

Vela nodded. "You got it."

Dobbs's phone rang. He glanced down at the display, then answered on speaker. "Wilkins, you get an ID on the attorney?"

Wilkins said, "Just came in. His real name is…was Roland Eads. I've got an address—Seventy-eight Dunes Road, Needles, California. He's got several priors for B and E. Did six months for identity theft about a decade ago. Nothing recent. We also confirmed the gun found in the car is Sillman's Glock, the one he took from the interrogation room. We can't find the damn slug that killed him, though."

"Where is Needles?" Begley said.

"Oh, hell."

This came from Sammy Goggans, who was frowning down at his MacBook. He had keyed in the address on Google. The top search result was from the local NBC affiliate, an article with the headline

"Possible Homicide" followed by the address and a picture of a run-down mobile home. The time stamp was one hour ago.

"Needles is about four hours from here," Sammy said. "Just this side of the Nevada border."

Gimble took out her own phone and started dialing. "I'm getting the chopper. Dobbs, Begley, you're with me. Vela and Sammy, alert Garrison with the U.S. marshals, let him know we have a possible location on Kepler. Contact the locals, bring them up to speed, then meet us there. Tell them we're taking over. Don't let them trample my crime scene. Text me the name of whoever is in charge as soon as you have it."

She was halfway to the SUV before she finished the last sentence.

CHAPTER FORTY-TWO

DR. ROSE

DR. ROSE FITZGERALD FOUND the door to her office open.

What she didn't find was Megan.

The girl's phone was still in her hand, and she damn near crushed it as she glanced into the empty room.

All three drawers of her file cabinet, normally locked, were open.

She hurried inside and found her desk drawers open too. The appointment book on top of her desk was turned to the wrong date; the various envelopes and papers that had been in her in-box were scattered about. Her trash can had been dumped; the contents of her shredder littered the floor.

"The little bitch," she muttered. "The goddamned little bitch."

She went to the file cabinet, already knowing what she'd find. Her face burned anyway as she peered down inside at the various empty spaces.

"Megan! Where are you?" she shouted.

Of course there was no answer. The house felt empty. She knew the girl was gone. One glance out the window confirmed it— Megan had taken her Mercedes.

I gave her the damn keys. To my office, to my car.

The little bitch.

Back at her desk, she picked up her phone and pressed number 3 on speed dial.

He picked up on the fourth ring. "Yes?"

Dr. Rose sighed. "We have a problem."

"What?"

"Megan is gone."

Lawrence Patchen said nothing.

"She's got the Kepler files. The others too. She raided my office and took off in my car."

"Report it stolen."

"That will just draw more attention; we don't need that."

"Better than her getting away."

Dr. Rose said, "And what if they find the files in the car? Then what?"

"What does she know?"

"Nothing."

"She knew enough to take the files. She clearly knows something," Patchen said. "Is she going to him?"

"Probably."

He remained quiet for a long while. Then: "This experiment is over."

"I'm not ready to give up yet."

"I'm not asking for your opinion; I'm stating a fact."

"Barton wanted—"

"Barton is dead," Patchen interrupted. "You find the girl, I'll take care of the rest."

"What are you going to do?"

"Don't contact me again. I'll see you at the funeral."

"I'm coming over there," Rose said. "We need to talk. Not on the phone. In person."

"I don't want you anywhere near here. Not right now."

"You can't—"

The line went dead.

She was about to call him back when the phone in her other hand, Megan's phone, began to ring. A Los Angeles area code.

Michael?

She answered. "Hello?"

"Is this Megan Fitzgerald?"

Something loud whirred in the background. *Helicopter?* "Who is this?"

"I'm Special Agent Jessica Gimble with the FBI. Am I speaking to Megan?"

Dr. Rose hung up.

When the phone rang again, she clicked Decline. It took all her willpower to keep from dropping the phone to the ground and stomping it to dust under her shoe.

CHAPTER FORTY-THREE

PATCHEN

NINE MILES AWAY, IN his office at Windham Hall, Lawrence Patchen hung up the phone and looked at the man sitting across his desk. "It's worse than I thought. With Barton gone, this will unravel fast."

The man considered this without a word. His dark eyes gave away nothing.

Patchen had always admired a man with a good poker face. Emotions, involuntary actions, everything from the way a person breathed, blinked, or positioned his arms or legs—any one of these things could give away more than an entire conversation. During his years dealing with the children, Patchen had learned never to listen to them. Not a single word. Their verbal responses to his questions were irrelevant. It was the unspoken that told him what he needed to know. Most learned to lie long before they arrived here—children could be incredibly skilled at spinning lies—but they rarely learned how to hide the signs of deceit. For most, a simple glance gave them away. Full of tells. All of them. Patchen believed he had a good poker face. This man put him to shame. "The offer you made, to clean up, I take it that still stands?"

"If it didn't, I wouldn't be here," the man said.

Patchen handed him a folder containing several photographs of Kepler.

The man glanced at the pictures and slid the folder back. "I don't need these. He's all over the news. I know who he is." This man was tall and lanky with dirty-blond hair, slightly tousled, probably a month or so from its last cut. He wore a pea-green jacket even though it was warm enough to go without. There was a slight bulge under his left shoulder—no doubt a gun of some sort. He had an old, ragged scar on his left hand, nearly an inch and a half long. Patchen tried not to look at it.

"Does that complicate matters? Kepler's current profile?"

"Nope."

Lawrence Patchen nodded and took out his wallet. He fumbled through the various pictures in the back, removed one, and slid it across the desk. "This one too. She'll be with him. She's my goddaughter."

He stared at the photo for several seconds, then slipped it into the pocket of his jacket. "Anyone else?"

"There may be one more. A woman. Barton's wife. I'm not sure yet."

"If you're not sure, don't tell me about her."

Patchen nodded, considered asking for the picture of Megan back but didn't. Instead, he retrieved a leather bag from under his desk and placed it in front of the man. "This is all I have."

Without opening the bag, the man replied, "There's two now, which means this is only half of what I plan to collect, what you'll owe me if I walk out that door. When this is done, I'll be back for the rest. I don't give a shit where you get it, but I suggest you do. Understood?"

Again, Patchen nodded. He'd figure it out. He had no choice. He scribbled two addresses on a piece of paper. "Kepler's heading to one of these."

"Which is most likely?"

Patchen pointed to the first address. "This one. He'll save the girl for last."

CHAPTER FORTY-FOUR

MICHAEL

I WOKE IN A bed.

A dark room.

My head throbbing.

The thin veil of light creeping in from around the heavy curtains on the single window felt damn near blinding.

I squeezed my eyes shut again.

During the headaches, and even after, light was the worst. Like thousands of rusty nails digging around my eyeballs, scraping behind, going deep into the sockets, relentlessly scratching at my brain, my thoughts. This was joined by an immense pressure, a band around my head slowly tightening until there was nothing but the pain.

Lying there, I knew the worst was behind me. The headache of earlier was ebbing, fading, but it was not willing to release me altogether, not yet.

So I lay there for at least another thirty minutes, maybe more, before forcing my eyes to open again and finally sitting up.

My eyes adjusted.

A motel room.

Not a very nice one.

The pain receded to a dull, cold ache.

The blinding light faded to what it truly was, only the minute glow of a distant street lamp somewhere, brought to life by the occasional headlights racing past, barely enough to set shadows stirring.

I pulled back the musty quilt and sheet.

I wore nothing but my underwear.

From the corner of my eye, I spotted my clothes in a pile near the bathroom at the back of the room.

I didn't remember removing them.

I didn't remember coming here.

I remembered nothing after tearing apart Roland Eads's bedroom.

My watch, which I knew I had moved to my left wrist, was back on my right again, the band cinched tight enough to dig into my skin and turn the flesh pink.

I moved the watch back to my left, checked the time: 8:40 p.m.

Three hours missing.

Lost.

This was not the first time I had blacked out from one of my headaches. It wasn't the first time I'd woken in a strange place.

But knowing it had happened before, telling myself that it would most likely happen again, did nothing to soothe the anxiety inching along my bones.

I forced myself to my feet and stood there feeling light-headed, slightly off balance. A wave of nausea washed over me, but I choked it back, made myself move.

On a small table near the front door, I found my leather duffel. Beside that were my car keys and a new disposable phone, still in the plastic packaging. I tore it open, powered on the phone, and ran through the automated activation prompts.

A minute later, my thoughts still muddled, I strained to recall the number Megan had given me.

I dialed, ready to hang up if I'd gotten it wrong.

"Hello?" Megan's voice was barely a whisper.

I glanced at the time on the phone and realized it was nearly midnight where she was.

"Did I wake you? I got a new phone." My throat was dry, full of gravel.

Somehow, she managed to drop her voice even lower. She rushed the words out at me: "Did you kill that woman?"

"What? No, I told you I didn't. I just found her in my—"

"Not Alyssa Tepper," Megan interrupted. "Erma Eads. It's all over the news. They're saying you killed her."

I closed my eyes for a moment and rubbed at my temples. "She's dead?" Everything was still soft, out of focus. I tried to remember. "She recognized me somehow . . ."

"So you killed her?"

"No . . . no, I didn't. I wouldn't . . ."

"Recognized you from where? From television?"

"Before."

"Before?" Megan repeated. "Before what?"

I felt the headache seizing the moment and attempting to creep back in. "I . . . I don't know. When I got there, to Roland's address, she acted like she'd expected me to show up, but *with* Roland, not alone."

"That doesn't make any sense."

"She was alive when I left, Meg. I tied her up. Scared her. That's all. Why would I kill her?" I squeezed my eyes shut. "You know me. I wouldn't hurt anyone. Someone is—" From somewhere behind Megan, a recorded message played over a loudspeaker, first in English, then in Spanish. I opened my eyes. "Was that TSA?"

Megan said, "I'm at the airport."

"The airport?"

She told me what she'd done. What she'd taken.

I ran my hand through my hair. "Christ, Meg, what if she calls the cops?"

"She won't. She'll try and find me herself before she calls the police. Hold on a second." She must have placed her hand over the phone; I heard her talking to someone, both voices muffled. She came back a moment later. "Where are *you* right now? You sound funny."

"A motel. I got one of my headaches so I stopped to sleep it off," I said. "I'm all right now. Just a little groggy."

"Are you..." Megan's voice trailed off.

"Am I what?"

She hesitated for a moment, then asked, "Are you...taking your meds?"

She had never asked me about the medication before. She never asked me about my sessions with Dr. Bart, his prescribed "treatments." But I wouldn't be some medicated zombie. The pills made me feel like I was an observer of life rather than someone living; they numbed me to everything, good and bad. They made me half a person. "I don't need the meds."

"Maybe you do, Michael. Maybe not all of them, maybe not the doses Dr. Bart prescribed, but just enough to...to stop the headaches. Did you black out?"

Megan knew about the blackouts. Aside from Dr. Bart, she was the only person I had ever told about these periods of lost time. She was the only person I trusted. Had ever trusted. But at moments like these, I wished I had never mentioned any of it. I could imagine her looking at me, her expression meant to be caring but her eyes holding something else—fear, worry, even pity. That last one hurt the most.

"I slept it off," I finally said. "I'm fine."

"Michael..."

"Really, Megan. I'm fine. Please, let's not go there right now."

I pulled back the curtain and took a look outside. The motel was one story, L-shaped, with the manager's office on the opposite end. There were only a few cars in the parking lot. My Porsche was in a space near my door. The building was set back about a hundred feet from a two-lane highway, the offending street lamp on the opposite side of the road. A filthy neon sign glowed with green letters near the entrance. "I'm at a place called the Lutz Motel."

"Still in Needles?"

I fumbled with a pad of motel stationery on the table, read the address. "Yeah, Needles."

"Can you stay there? I'll come to you."

"It's too dangerous. I don't want you mixed up in this."

"Little late for that, don't you think?" Megan shot back. "What did you find at Roland Eads's house?"

I had no idea what I'd found at Roland Eads's house. I rubbed my temples. "He lived with his sister, Erma. She..."

It was all so cloudy.

Then I remembered his closet. The image of the uniforms popped into my head along with a stab of pain. "I think he worked for Windham Hall."

"The orphanage?"

"Yeah. I found uniforms in his closet."

I saw something in my leather bag under one of my shirts. A sheaf of paper. I took it out. A stack of log sheets from Windham Hall.

Did I take these from the Eadses' house?

Megan said, "But that's here in New York. That doesn't make sense. Maybe it's a different Windham Hall?"

I flipped through the pages. Dozens of entries were highlighted, dating back years. Dr. Bart's name. My name.

The headache clawed.

I shoved the logs back into my bag.

Windham Hall. Roland. Alyssa Tepper. Dr. Bart's patients. All connected. Somehow.

I rubbed my temples again, dug my knuckles in. "Did you find addresses for those two . . . what were their names?"

"Are you sure you're okay? You really don't sound okay."

"I'm fine."

"It's going away, right?"

"Yeah," I said. But it wasn't.

Megan said, "I've got addresses for both Nicole Milligan and Jeffery Longtin. Dr. Rose had them."

"Text them to me."

"No way."

"Come on, Meg. We don't have time for this."

"You stay put. I'll come to you, and we'll go together."

I couldn't drag her deeper into this.

Another stab of pain, behind my left eye. "People are dying, Meg. Whoever is doing this . . . I don't want you anywhere near it."

Megan went quiet for a little bit, then said, "Remember when we were kids, when I used to have that nightmare all the time? Seemed like every night for nearly a year. Guess I was around five."

I nodded. "The man with the yellow eyes. You thought he lived in the tree outside your window. You used to say you could hear him scratching at the glass. If your window got foggy, you swore it was him. His arms were so long he could reach inside the house and scoop you right out of your bed."

"I'd hide from him. I'd come to your room and spend the night with you. You'd hold my hand and tell me you'd never let anything hurt me. You said you wouldn't let go even if he tried to pull me away. He'd have to take both of us."

"I remember."

Megan said, "You've always been there for me. Let me be there for you. Don't shut me out. Not now."

"Meg, it's too dangerous."

"Stop saying that. Either you meet me or you figure out all this bullshit on your own. Let me help you."

I closed my eyes again, shut out the light. The pain came back with a vengeance, like a two-by-four to the side of my head. I nearly dropped the phone. My knees almost buckled. "I can't risk losing you, Meg. You're all I have. I need to know you're someplace safe. That's how you help me. That's how you hold *my* hand." I opened my eyes.

Megan went quiet again.

"Meg?"

"I'm so worried about you."

"I know."

Neither of us said anything for a long while.

My phone dinged with a text message. An address in Arizona. "Which one is that?" I asked.

"Can you get there?"

I was sweating. My palms and face were slick with it. I remembered the bottle of Excedrin Migraine in my pants pocket. "Yeah, I think so. Which one is it?"

"Neither," Megan said. "It's where you meet me. Call me when you're close."

Megan hung up before I could reply.

My head buzzed with pain. I set the phone down and nearly missed the table. I pushed it back from the edge.

With each step I took across the room, the pain behind my eyes intensified. Each footfall was a hammer hitting the inside of my skull, cracking against the bone, building pressure.

I stumbled to my discarded clothes, fumbled with the pants. They were wet, sticky. My shirt too. My fingers found the pocket, the bottle of migraine medicine. I took it out, nearly bit off the childproof cap when I couldn't get hold of it. Finally, I got it off and pushed three pills into my mouth.

The bottle fell from my hand, dropped to the ground, pills spilling everywhere. My clothes, my hands, were covered in blood.

CHAPTER FORTY-FIVE

WRITTEN STATEMENT, MEGAN FITZGERALD

Michael couldn't do this alone, you get that, right, Jessica? He was already making a huge mess of everything. We look out for each other. So, yeah, I stuck it to Dr. Rose. Borrowed some things. I mean, she gave me her keys. I always knew those two were hiding something from us. And he didn't sound good. Not at all. You wouldn't abandon your brother, right? When he was hurting? I couldn't either.

I hung up with Michael, forced a smile on my face, and turned back to Roy, the twenty-something guy manning the airport's Sharper Image counter who had taken the opportunity to stare at my legs. I had to admit, they were looking nice in my new Tahari sundress and Christian Louboutin heels.

"Sounded intense," he said, remembering where my face was. "Boyfriend?"

Subtle. "Brother."

He nodded slowly. "I've got a little sister; she can be a pain too. If you'd like to talk about it, I'm off at midnight."

We were standing in the far back corner of the store, beyond the massaging chairs and travel cases that looked strong enough to take a bullet. I watched as he unlocked the glass cabinet and removed a small box. He handed it to me. "This is the only cassette player we still carry. It's meant to plug into a computer so you can convert tapes to digital. There's a cheap pair of headphones in the box—they're okay for voice stuff. I've got better ones if you're planning on listening to music."

"Just listening to some lectures."

"Thought maybe your boyfriend went old school and made you a mixtape." He grinned.

My legs must have looked even better than I'd thought. I returned the grin. No reason to be rude—he was kinda cute.

I followed him back to the counter, watched him ring me up. "That's thirty-one dollars and twenty-two cents."

I pulled a credit card from my new purse, accidentally dropping a checkbook in the process.

Roy picked it up and glanced at it before giving it back to me. "*Dr.* Rose Fitzgerald?" His eyes narrowed mischievously as he took the credit card—also in the name of Rose Fitzgerald—and ran it through the machine. "You look a little young to be a doctor. Mind if I see your ID?"

"I'm a bit of an overachiever, I suppose." I handed him my driver's license.

"'Megan Rose Fitzgerald,'" he read aloud. "That's a beautiful name." He gave the license and the credit card back to me. "Beautiful name for a beautiful girl. I don't suppose you'd like to get coffee sometime?"

I smiled, tilted my head. "If you upgrade my headphones, I'll give it some serious thought, Roy."

Five minutes later, I was in a seat at gate 11, reading the instructions for my new cassette player and the pair of Bose noise-canceling headphones Roy had slipped into my bag. Considering it was nearly midnight, the terminal was pretty crowded. I had my backpack on the seat to my right and Michael's file spread out on the seat to my left.

I'd gotten to the airport at about half past ten and left Dr. Rose's Mercedes in a handicapped-only spot on the top floor of the parking garage with the keys in the ignition. Fuck her.

Once inside the airport, I began hitting the ATMs. I withdrew the maximum amount of cash I could from each of Dr. Rose's credit and debit cards, thirty-three hundred dollars in total. Who uses her own birthday for a PIN code? Double fuck her.

From there, I purchased a one-way ticket to Flagstaff with cash. This set me back two hundred eighty-three dollars and fifteen cents. The cops could probably still trace me if they wanted to, but I figured using cash would slow them down a bit. I knew Michael would meet me; I didn't plan to give him a choice.

Ticket in hand, with nearly an hour before my flight, I hit the shops. I got a nice Tumi bag from Luggage Etc.; jeans, blouses, and undergarments from Airport Express; several dresses (including the one Roy admired), shoes, and a watch from Montauges. Each time someone rang up the card, I expected a problem—some kind of security flag—but that didn't happen. Dr. Rose routinely shopped at airports; I suppose that was enough to prevent a security alert. Triple fuck her.

By the time I heard my flight called over the loudspeaker, I had read most of Michael's file.

Fragile. Dr. Bart had used that word more than once.

Some parts were more horrifying than I'd expected. I thought Michael had told me everything.

When boarding started, I shoved the papers into my

backpack. I kept the three cassette tapes that had been in there along with my new tape player and headphones—I'd listen to those on the trip.

As I followed the line of passengers to the plane, I blew a kiss in Roy's general direction. Maybe I'd thank him when I got back, maybe not. I was sure he'd be there waiting for me either way.

CHAPTER FORTY-SIX

MICHAEL

MY HEART RACED.

I stared down at the clothes in my hand. A part of me believed that if I wished for it, the blood would vanish, and this would prove to be some kind of hallucination, something related to the headaches. The blood didn't disappear, though. A coppery scent drifted up, filling my nostrils, and the hammer in my head beat away.

The pants and shirt were soaked, primarily in the front. I glanced down at my bare chest, and even in the dim light, I didn't see any blood. Most likely, I'd cleaned up before getting in bed, but I had no memory of it.

Several minutes ticked by, me on the floor, cradling my soiled clothing, before I finally found the will to stand and make my way to the bathroom sink.

I didn't turn on the light. I twisted the faucet and scrubbed my hands in the icy water. The blood was stubborn but eventually came off. I cupped water in my palms and brought it to my face, then ran my hands through my hair.

When I finally looked at myself in the mirror, I saw someone else, someone I didn't want to know. I squeezed my eyes shut again, forced myself to calm down.

Eyes still closed, I fumbled for the switch on the wall, flicked on the lights.

I opened my eyes again, slowly, afraid of the pain sometimes brought on by the light.

Better, though. A little better. The Excedrin was finally helping.

That's when I saw the bathtub to my right, next to the toilet.

Water filled it nearly to the rim.

A lone feather floated on the surface.

And beneath the surface—

Oh God...

CHAPTER FORTY-SEVEN

MICHAEL

I THOUGHT IT WAS a woman.

My mind somehow took in what was there and filled in the gaps—long legs, the curve of slender hips and waist, a flat stomach. Brown hair floating around a beautiful, angelic face and neck.

I even saw her watching me, bright blue eyes staring up from beneath the surface. A full mouth parted slightly, prepared to whisper, yet silent forever.

I saw her fingers splayed at her sides, her arms gently floating in the still water.

I saw all of this in what must have been a split second although it felt like an hour, a lifetime.

I squeezed my eyes shut.

The hammer in my head thumped with a newfound frenzy.

My heart beat against my rib cage, threatened to explode.

When I opened my eyes again, when I forced myself to look into that bathtub, I realized it wasn't a woman there floating in the water beneath that feather; it was *women's clothing*—jeans, a white V-neck sweater, black panties, and a matching lacy black bra. All laid out in the perfectly still water. Pinned to the sweater, shimmering beneath the surface, was a plastic name tag that read MOLLY.

The name tag contained only a first name. No surname, no company name, nothing to identify where she worked.

Molly.

The feather floated lazily past the place her head belonged, across her invisible cheek.

The exhaust fan, which had come on with the bathroom light, whirred above me. Not the steady, even drone of a new fan but the click-filled choking of an old one.

Had I done this?

Had I hurt this person? This Molly?

I knew nobody by that name. I didn't remember meeting anyone recently with that name, but that didn't mean much, not with the blackouts and headaches.

Where was Molly?

At some point I had gone to my knees, but like so much else, I didn't remember the movement. I remembered turning on the light, grabbing the door frame for support, but not falling to my knees. But there I was, on the floor next to the bathtub.

An odd thought popped into my head at that moment, a question I had no answer to, one nearly as perplexing as Molly's missing body: *Where are her shoes?*

White canvas sneakers. Molly was wearing white canvas sneakers.

Somehow, I was as sure of this as I was about her brown hair, the slight pucker of her lips on the left side as they curled up in a smile, the flirtatious tilt of her head.

She had stood on her left leg for a second while scratching at her right calf with the tip of her white canvas shoe. Then she settled back, cocking her hip to the side.

No! I knew nobody named Molly, had never met anyone named Molly. This was my brain playing tricks on me. Filling in gaps, making things whole. My mind wasn't willing to accept the missing time and was crafting a narrative all its own—a fiction was better than nothing at all.

Molly had the cutest laugh. This light chuckle.

No!

I forced myself to stand. I pushed these thoughts out of my head and searched the room. There wasn't much to search. From the sink, I could see nearly every square inch, but I wandered around anyway. I lifted the mattress and found nothing. I pulled back the sheets, expecting to find blood, but there was none. I lowered myself onto the orange shag carpet and looked under the bed— nothing but ancient dust bunnies and cobwebs.

No body.

No Molly.

No missing shoes.

Not in the room, no.

I went to the window, pulled the curtain aside.

I had backed my Porsche into the parking space. From the window, I faced the tail end. Still, I could see enough of the front seat through the rear window to know it was empty. The car had two trunks, one in the front, one in the back, but neither was big enough to hold more than a suitcase or two. Even if I'd wanted to hide a body in there, God forbid, I couldn't have. There was no room.

Not a whole body, anyway.

I shook this thought out of my head.

Somebody was trying to frame me. This was no different than Alyssa Tepper in the bathroom back in my apartment. Somebody had drugged me, staged the room, bloodied my clothing. Nothing else made sense.

Somebody was fucking with me.

As if in response, the hammer in my head took another whack

at my skull. It was fading, though, the hand holding that hammer growing weak.

Whatever *this* was, I needed to clean it up. I knew that, and before I could change my mind, I pulled the plastic trash bag from the can next to the table, crossed the room, and stuffed my soiled clothes inside.

In the bathroom, I drained the tub and placed those clothes in the bag too, along with the feather. I soaked a washcloth and then wiped every inch of the bathroom—the tub, the tile walls, the toilet, even the floor. After that, I wiped down the counter, the nightstand, the doorknob, and the various locks.

Back at the table, I threw the packaging from the disposable phone into the bag, then got dressed with clothes I pulled from my duffel bag—jeans, a Boston Celtics sweatshirt, and a matching ball cap. I moved the bag to the floor near the door, placed my keys and the disposable phone on top of it, then wiped down the table too.

By the time I finished, the rag was filthy black with grime. The room hadn't really been cleaned for months, or possibly years. I thought about all the DNA on that rag from who knew how many visitors that was now spread all over the room, and I was perfectly okay with that.

With one more look out the window to confirm the parking lot was still deserted, I used the tail of my sweatshirt to open the door, careful not to leave prints. I placed my duffel and the trash bag in the trunk and slammed it shut.

I climbed into the driver's seat and tossed the phone beside me.

On the floor of the passenger side were two white canvas shoes, one missing the laces.

CHAPTER FORTY-EIGHT

DOBBS

THEY ARRIVED IN NEEDLES a little under two hours later; the Bell 407 helicopter landed in the far corner of a Days Inn parking lot two blocks south of the police station. Two uniformed deputies stood by two police cruisers waiting for them.

They had a possible ID on Kepler's car. Neighbor had seen it—black sports car, old. Possibly an MG, Fiat, Porsche, Karmann Ghia...not much to go on, but something. They'd put out a tristate BOLO from the air.

Gimble was out the door the moment they touched the ground. The rotor blast kicked up dirt, dust, and sand and slapped her ponytail against her back, shoulders, and face. She ignored it and ran at a crouch toward the cruisers.

As Dobbs got out, he shielded his eyes and took in the surroundings. It looked to him like the Mojave had started to reclaim this small town years ago, gotten distracted, and left but planned to return soon enough to finish the job. The few buildings he could see were in desperate need of a coat of paint. The cars in the parking lot were ten years past their prime, as were the handful of people who stepped outside at the late hour to find out what all the hubbub was about.

Dobbs grabbed one CSI case, Begley took the other, and they both chased after Gimble.

When the three of them reached the deputies, the older of the two officers shook their hands. "I'm Deputy Ben Labrum. That there is Cole Bulloch. Sorry you had to land so far from the crime scene here. The golf course is much closer, but we couldn't get clearance on account of the time of night and it being residential."

"How far away are we?"

"Five, maybe ten minutes at most," he replied. "Let's get loaded up. Cole and I will get you out there as quick as we can."

Deputy Bulloch nodded at the three of them and opened the trunk of his cruiser.

The drive took seven minutes with lights flashing, sirens off.

They raced down the narrow streets at nearly twice the posted speed limit, bouncing over speed bumps fast enough for Dobbs to bang his head on the ceiling of the cruiser—he hadn't fastened his seat belt. Deputy Labrum took a hard left onto Dunes Road and finally slowed down. He came to a stop about half a block from the crime scene, unable to get any closer. Dobbs stepped out of the car and counted two more sheriff vehicles, three from the state police, an ambulance, a fire truck, and a van from the coroner's office. There were also two television vans, satellite antennas up, and at least two dozen residents standing around in the nearby yards. A few had even set up chairs and tables to take in the spectacle. The entire area had been roped off with yellow crime scene tape, and large floodlights were positioned all around the small, run-down mobile home at 78 Dunes Road.

"Holy hell," Gimble muttered.

Begley blew out a soft whistle. "You'd think the Manson family were having a block party by the looks of this."

Deputy Bulloch unloaded Begley's cases from his trunk and set them in the street while Labrum rounded his own car and gestured toward the mobile home. "That's the sheriff over there under the carport. He's talking to the coroner."

"What's the sheriff's name?"

"Burt Moody."

"I'll stay with these until you get situated," Deputy Bulloch said, gesturing toward the two black cases and speaking for the first time since they'd landed.

Gimble took one more look at the large crowd, shook her head, and ducked under the tape with Dobbs and Begley close behind.

Sheriff Moody saw them approach, said something to the coroner, and walked toward them. "You must be Special Agent Gimble?" He gave Dobbs and Begley a wary glance. "This your team?" Moody looked to be in his mid-fifties. His neatly cropped brown hair was peppered with gray, and he was in surprisingly good shape for his age. His beefy arms strained at his uniform, and his stomach was flat.

Gimble said, "Part of my team. The rest are coming by car. I've got marshals en route too. They're probably still an hour or two away." She glanced nervously toward the mobile home. "Please tell me you didn't let anyone in."

His brow furrowed. "As instructed. I've kept everyone standing around out here with their thumbs up their asses waiting on you to come and save the day. Think we gave that Kepler fellow enough time to get away? I can hold my boys back another hour or two if you think that makes sense."

"Who told you this was about Kepler?"

He held up his phone. "Google, Reddit, MSNBC, and Lou Jacobs from our local CBS affiliate. If this is supposed to be a secret, somebody dropped the ball and gave it a swift kick over to the press hours ago. All the major networks are probably right behind your people, coming in from Vegas."

Dobbs glanced down at Gimble's fingers, expecting them to twitch. He figured she'd lash out, but she said only "What have we got inside?"

"A complete clusterfuck, and I couldn't be happier you called dibs," he replied. "Follow me."

CHAPTER FORTY-NINE

DR. ROSE

WHEN THE PHONE RANG, Rose Fitzgerald nearly knocked the lamp off her desk scrambling for it. She hadn't planned on sleeping, had just wanted to lay her head down for a few seconds. According to the grandfather clock in the corner of her office, it was a little after one in the morning.

Her fingers closed around the phone as the shrill ring cut the night again. She fumbled with the lock screen, hit Answer. "Megan, where the hell—"

"Not Megan."

"You?"

"Me."

"What do you want?"

"I missed you, Dr. Rose," he said. "Wanted to hear you. I've got exciting news."

He always spoke in short sentences but dragged each word out—two syllables became four, four became eight. There was no emotion there, no feeling.

Dr. Rose stretched her legs under the desk, her tired bones

creaking. "I'm hanging up. I can't talk to you when you're like this."

"Like what, Dr. Rose?"

"Like this, with this cat-and-mouse bullshit of yours."

"I'm on the mark, Dr. Rose. Finally. You should be happy for me. It feels...wonderful. So free. I felt the need to celebrate," he said. "I met someone tonight, Dr. Rose. Someone...special. She helped me celebrate. She had long brown hair and the most beautiful eyes."

"Had?"

"A wonderful listener, like you. How are you sleeping these days?"

"I sleep just fine."

"So alone, though. Half the bed cold. Half the bed still made when you crawl out in the morning and wander the halls of that tomb you call home."

"I'm not alone. I have Megan."

"Do you?"

She looked around her office at the mess Megan had left behind.

He said, "Do you miss him, Dr. Rose? I do. I miss our little chats. Dr. Bart would be so proud, don't you think? Of my progress? His star pupil, shining bright. Why do you think he ate the gun, Dr. Rose? Was it you? I think he got tired of listening to your nagging. Your constant berating. A bullet, the only way to silence your whiny banter, and now Dr. Rose is all alone."

"He didn't shoot himself. He died from an aneurysm."

"His body pulled the trigger, that's the only real difference."

"Why did you call me?"

"To tell you I'd be home soon. For the funeral. Back where I belong. To see you. To say hello to Mr. Patchen. So many reasons. I have a feather in my pocket. Can't wait to give it to you. Feathers for everyone. You sick, twisted bitch of a—"

Dr. Rose ended the call and slammed the phone down on her desk.

CHAPTER FIFTY

DOBBS

FOR DOBBS, CRIME SCENES always carried a certain silence, a stillness. Like walking into an abandoned house. The Eads house had been ransacked—the couch overturned, the cushions slashed, stuffing removed. Every book, framed photograph, and knickknack had been pulled from shelves and left on the floor. The carpet crunched underfoot with broken glass. In the small kitchenette, the table was overturned, every drawer pulled out, the contents spilled. The cabinet doors were all open. Broken plates, shattered glasses, pots, and pans littered the linoleum floor. The refrigerator and freezer were both open; half the food was on the ground.

"Vela can weigh in when he gets here, but to me this goes well beyond a search. There's anger here," Gimble said.

"I've got some blood," Begley said, crouching down and studying the edge of the table with the help of a penlight. "Not much. Probably someone grabbed it with some kind of cut on their hand."

"The victim has a cut on her right hand, right here," Moody said, gesturing toward the meat near his own thumb. "Every room in the place looks like this. Your man tore up every inch."

"You said a neighbor called this in?" Begley asked.

Moody nodded. "Florence Ostler, across the street. She wandered over when Erma didn't show up for their Sunday-night card game. She gave us the description of the car and ID'd Kepler as 'that handsome boy from TV.' I figured you'd want to do a photo lineup, so I've got someone sitting with her back at her place. She's seventy-five, a bit shook up, but she seems sharp."

Although light streamed in from the floods outside, the only light in this room came from the freakishly large television. It was tuned to one of the cable news channels and paused on a close-up shot of Gimble and Dobbs at the car fire earlier.

"Well, that's a little creepy," Gimble said.

"Gets creepier." Moody took several giant steps across the room, picked up the television remote, and pressed a button; the screen went dark. Scratched across the surface from the bottom left corner to the top right were seven words:

I SEE YOU—DO YOU SEE ME?

When the sheriff pressed the button again, bringing back the frozen image, the words vanished, became nothing more than smudges barely visible in the bright, colorful scene. He flicked it off for a second time, and the words were readable again. He did that several more times.

"Okay, we got it," Gimble said. "You can stop that now."

He set the remote back down on the floor.

"Is this the murder weapon?" Begley asked. The beam of his flashlight was focused on a chrome-plated nine-millimeter on the kitchen floor.

The sheriff shook his head. "Nope. He didn't shoot her. Come on."

He led them down a short hallway to a small bedroom.

Erma Eads's large body was sprawled on the bed, a stained

comforter bunched around her. Her hands and feet were bound with what looked like electrical cords. She stared forward, her eyes bulging from their sockets and lined with blood.

Begley leaned over her. "We've got hypoxic damage, petechiae." Using the penlight, he studied her face. "Oh, hell."

"What is it?" Gimble asked.

"He glued her mouth shut. Her nose too. She couldn't breathe—must've died from asphyxiation."

"There's a bottle of superglue on the floor over here," Dobbs said.

Gimble knelt down beside the bed. "I see something under her."

CHAPTER FIFTY-ONE

WRITTEN STATEMENT, MEGAN FITZGERALD

Roy was kind enough to include batteries for my new cassette player, but unfortunately he didn't give me a baseball bat, which was what I desperately needed to keep the leech sitting beside me in 2B from bothering me when I unboxed my newly acquired hardware.

"Would you like me to help you with those?" He fondled his own pair of headphones with the unabashed fervor of a fourteen-year-old boy getting his fingers on his first pair of moist panties. His sweaty hands left glossy streaks on the plastic. He kept wiping them on the seat.

Big strong man save helpless girl from technology.

What a tool.

The gate agent had upgraded my seat to first class when I told him this was my first time flying—the same thing I say every time I hand over my boarding pass—but I was seriously considering moving back to row 17 to get away from this guy. "I'm fine, thank you." I gave him a smile, and that was a mistake—you don't smile at guys like this.

He wasn't bad-looking. Twenty years ago, he might even have been hot, but I'd be willing to bet he hadn't set foot inside a gym in about a decade, and his gut was happy for it, straining against the seat belt as he turned toward me. "My name is Warren. Heading to Flagstaff, huh?"

No, Warren. I'm actually heading to Poland, but I like the food court at Pulliam Airport, so I figured I'd make a quick stop. "I'm visiting family."

When I leaned forward to put the empty boxes under the seat in front of me, I caught Warren looking down my dress at my lacy black bra. He didn't avert his eyes; he just smiled. "You know, I met my second wife on a flight just like this. We were both flying back from Barbados. Didn't talk for the first hour, but once the ice broke, you couldn't shut the two of us up." He leaned closer and lowered his voice. "By the end of the second hour, we were up there in the first-class bathroom banging away like rabbits in the spring."

"Really?"

He nodded. "She orgasmed so loud, we thought half the plane might applaud when we came out. If you slip the flight attendants a couple hundred, they'll watch the door for you."

"I've heard that."

He leaned even closer. He smelled like beer and onions. "Have you ever…"

My fingers went to one of the buttons on my dress, but I didn't look at him. I lowered my voice. "I think it's best when you do it with a stranger. Someone you know you'll never see again. Everyone thinks about it when they get on a plane. You can tell by the way they check out the other passengers, size them up, pick one out." I licked my lips. "I've done it twice; it was incredible."

Warren didn't seem quite prepared for this; sweat started to trickle down from his temples. He nodded toward the bathroom. "It's empty. I've been watching."

I fiddled with the button on my dress—unbuttoning it, then sliding it back in, then out again. I still didn't look at him. "First class isn't a challenge. Meet me in the bathroom at the back of the plane. The one on the left. I'll knock twice so you know it's me. Give me a few minutes, though; we don't want anyone to figure out what we're doing."

The breath Warren drew in was audible, this nasally inhale. He nodded quickly, fumbled with his seat belt.

"Oh, and Warren?"

He turned back to me.

"Take off your wedding ring. I won't be able to look at that."

He nodded again and tugged at the ring as he made his way down the aisle toward the back of the plane.

I figured this bought me at least twenty minutes.

I took one of the cassettes from my purse. The label read *Dark room—M. Kepler—August 13, 1996.*

I slipped it into my tape player and pressed Play.

There was a moment of static, a soft hiss, then Dr. Bart's voice: "I'd like to give you something, Michael, something special for talking to me yesterday. For sharing what happened at the motel."

"What?"

I almost paused the tape at the sound of Michael's voice; he sounded so young, just a child. A little kid. I did the math— only four years old.

Dr. Bart went on. "Whenever one of my friends shares something with me, a secret, something personal, I give them a sparrow feather. What you shared with me yesterday, what you told me about your mama and Max, that earned you a feather."

"And I'm your friend?"

"I'd like to think so. I think you and I could become great friends."

A rustling sound.

"It's soft," Michael said.

"That's from a Henslow's sparrow, my personal favorite. They make the most beautiful sounds. We have several nests on the grounds. Perhaps later I'll show you one."

"And I can keep it?"

"Yes, Michael. That one is for you. I'm hoping you'll share another secret with me today. And if you do, you'll get another feather."

"How many can I get?"

"As many as you want."

"I'd like that. I'd like a bunch of them."

"I'm going to turn out the light now so we can talk."

"With no distractions," Michael said. "Like last time."

Although Michael was able to say the word, he stretched it out, emphasizing each syllable. *Diz...track...shuns.*

"When we talked yesterday, Michael, you were extremely helpful. I'd like to continue our conversation, if that's okay with you."

Michael didn't reply.

"You told me your mama was sleeping in the bathtub. Can you tell me what she did before she went to sleep?"

"Yeah."

"What did she do, Michael?"

"She took off her clothes and washed them in the sink."

"That's good, Michael. Let's start there and slowly move forward through what you remember. What were you doing when your mama was washing her clothes?"

"I was sitting on the bed."

"Watching TV?"

"No, watching Mama. I wanted to see where she would hang her clothes. She already washed some of my clothes and some of Max's clothes and hung them up everywhere. I wanted to see where she would hang her clothes 'cause there was no places left."

"And where did she put them?"

"On top of the air conditioner. She said they'd dry fast there."

"That's very smart."

"Mama is smart."

"What did she do next?"

"She turned on the TV for me and said she was going to take her medicine. She asked if I remembered what I was supposed to do after she took her medicine, and I told her I did."

Dr. Bart said, "And what was that?"

"I was supposed to wait for a commercial, then take the rubber band off her arm. Mama said if I don't, it's bad for her cir...cir...lation."

"Circulation?"

"Yeah. I was supposed to take the needle out, too, if it got stuck. Sometimes it gets stuck and Mama falls asleep, so I have to take it out. That's gross, but I do it."

"Your mama, she took her medicine in the bathtub?"

"She likes the water. Her medicine works better in the water."

"And did you do these things, Michael? When the commercial came on, did you go into the bathroom and take the rubber band off her arm...and take out the needle?"

"Uh-huh."

"You took out the needle?"

"I put it on the counter so it wouldn't get stepped on. One time, Max stepped on it and Mama got mad."

Dr. Bart cleared his throat. "Michael, do you know what an autopsy is?"

Michael didn't answer.

"You need to speak aloud, Michael, for the recording. Do you know what an autopsy is?"

"No."

"It's when a doctor checks someone after they die to figure out how they died."

Michael still said nothing.

"The doctor checked your mother, and he found no evidence of medicine in her system. In fact, he didn't even find traces of medicine from past use," Dr. Bart said. "I do know from the police report that Max regularly used heroin—do you know what heroin is? I think you do. The needle, the rubber band, these are all things you've probably seen Max use. I think that's why you're able to describe them to me. But you never saw your mama use heroin, did you?"

Silence.

"Why are you lying to me, Michael?"

Silence.

"I thought we were friends?"

"Mama's medicine made her fall asleep."

"Your mama drowned," Dr. Bart replied. "Did Max tell you to say these things if someone asked you? To protect him?"

"No."

"If we're going to be friends, you need to tell me the truth. I'd never lie to you, Michael. It's important you're honest with me."

Silence.

"Did you ever help Max do heroin? Take medicine?"

Nothing from Michael.

Dr. Bart sighed. "If you're not going to talk to me, I'm afraid I'll have to take my feather back and give it to one of my real friends."

When Michael finally spoke, his voice was so low it was

barely audible. "Mama was sad. She was crying. He said if we gave her some of Max's medicine, she'd feel better. I wanted Mama to feel better."

"Max said that?"

"Not Max."

"Who then?"

"We couldn't find Max's medicine, but he said there was still a little left in the needle and that would be enough."

"Who, Michael?"

"When we tried to give it to her, Mama started to yell, and he got scared and he pushed her down until she stopped."

"Michael, who are you talking about? Who pushed her down?"

"Mitchell."

CHAPTER FIFTY-TWO

MICHAEL

I DROVE.

From the motel in Needles, I drove like a goddamn madman—twenty, thirty, sometimes forty miles an hour above the speed limit. I didn't give a shit. If the cops pulled me over, if they locked me up, if they put a bullet in the center of my forehead...anything was better than looking down at the floor of my passenger seat and seeing that pair of shoes sitting there.

Molly.

I saw her in my mind, clear as day. Wearing the clothes that were in my bathtub. Wearing *those* shoes.

Smiling at me. A laugh.

Shit.

Shit.

Shit.

On the dark road, the deserted highway, as long as the car remained dark, I *could* make those shoes go away, make them disappear, but each time I approached a rest stop, every time an exit came up, there were lights, and the interior of the car became just bright enough for me to glimpse them, those white shoes.

Molly's shoes.

Twenty minutes outside Nowhere, Arizona, I pulled over.

I slammed my foot down on the brake, locked up the rear wheels, and skidded to a halt on the gravel shoulder, the dirt and dust creating a cloud; I smelled rubber smoldering. The engine stalled, ticked with heat in the otherwise silent night.

The shoes, refusing to disappear no matter how many times I blinked or looked away, tumbled across the floorboard.

A voice in my head whispered, *She wasn't part of the plan, Michael. She was just for fun. Wasn't she fun?*

I pressed my palms to my ears, tried to shut it out.

Focus, Michael!

Not real.

Not real.

I remembered her then. Where I'd seen her.

She was real.

Just you tonight? You look like you're ready for a soft bed.

I didn't hurt her.

I wouldn't.

I threw open the car door and vomited into the dirt.

CHAPTER FIFTY-THREE

WRITTEN STATEMENT, MEGAN FITZGERALD

The flight attendant smiled at me from the aisle. Gestured toward her beverage cart. Said something.

I clicked the Pause button on my tape player and removed my headphones.

"Would you like a complimentary beverage or perhaps a menu?" she said.

No. I'd like you to leave me the fuck alone. Can't you see I'm in the middle of something? I gave her a smile. "I'd kill for a Grey Goose and cranberry."

She smiled back. "What about your friend here? Any idea what he's drinking?"

"My—" I glanced at the empty seat next to me. Warren still hadn't returned with his Viagra-laced tail between his legs.

I leaned a little closer to her and whispered, "He said something about going to smoke pot in one of the bathrooms. I told him he shouldn't, but he's a nervous flier and said it's the only thing that calms his nerves. He's been gone a while. I hope everything is okay. Last time, he gave himself a horrible shock fiddling with the smoke detector."

The smile never left her face. "Perhaps I should check on him."

I nodded in agreement. "You need to knock twice or he probably won't open up. He's silly like that."

After mixing my drink from the ingredients on her cart, she returned to the small alcove at the front of the cabin and spoke to two male flight attendants, then the three of them rushed down the aisle to the back of the plane.

My vodka was divine.

I slipped my headphones back on and pressed Play.

Dr. Bart's voice, sounding confused. "Who's Mitchell?"

"Mitchell pushed Mama under the water until she stopped crying. Until she went to sleep."

"Michael, I've read the police reports. I know you were alone with your mother at this point."

"Not alone. Mitchell too."

"What did I tell you about lying, Michael? You don't have to make up stories for me. You can tell me the truth. I won't tell anyone. Whatever you say will stay just between us. Even if you did something wrong. Even if you did something *really* wrong, I won't tell anyone. You won't get in trouble. Not with me."

"Not lying. It was Mitchell. Mitchell is mean sometimes. Like Max."

Dr. Bart cleared his throat. "You told me you were alone on the bed when Max came back to the room. Where was Mitchell then?"

Silence from Michael.

"Was he on the bed with you? Watching television?"

"Mitchell was in the closet when Max got home. Mitchell quiet."

"You lied to me about your mother and the medicine. Now you're lying to me about this. You can tell me the truth,

Michael. You'll feel better if you do. Lying is hard. It's bad. Nobody likes a liar. Telling the truth makes you feel good." Although firm, Dr. Bart's voice remained steady, patient. "Friends don't lie to each other."

Michael's voice didn't falter. "Mitchell always helps Max with his medicine. Mitchell helped Mama sleep."

Both voices fell silent; there was only breathing, Michael's quick, high rasps and Dr. Bart's lower, deeper intakes and exhales.

Dr. Bart spoke first. "Michael, did Max ever hurt you?"

"No." The response came fast, barely enough time for him to consider the question. Too fast.

"Did he ever give you some of his medicine?"

"No."

"Did he ever touch you in a way that made you feel uncomfortable?"

"No."

"Did he—"

"No!" Michael shouted. "No! No! No!"

"Take a deep breath, Michael. Calm down."

"I don't wanna talk about this. Not no more!"

"Calm down, Michael."

Silence again.

"Michael, did Max ever do anything to hurt Mitchell?"

Michael screamed then, a horrific shriek. I almost tore off the headphones, and I would have if Dr. Bart hadn't stopped the recording on his end.

The scream gave way to silence, then several clicks, before continuing.

"This is Dr. Barton Fitzgerald. Summary report, session two, with Michael Kepler. Although clearly traumatized, Michael Kepler doesn't present with the markers typically found in a patient suffering from schizophrenia or dissociative disorder. As an expert in both, I'm comfortable ruling those diagnoses out, and I mention them here only because someone listening to this tape, someone less qualified to make such a diagnosis, may consider one or both viable. For the record, I am adamantly stating they are not. I imagine, if circumstances hadn't changed, if he had continued to live in that hostile environment, it's very possible a disorder might have developed. At this point, though, I have no reason to believe this Mitchell is anything more than an imaginary friend created by Michael to help him deal with the horrible conditions in which he was forced to live. A common toddler developmental solution. At his current weight of forty-three pounds, I find it hard to believe he forced his mother beneath the surface of her bath and held her there long enough for her to drown. Although that scenario does fit with the medical examiner's findings for cause of death, I believe it to be only a partial explanation of events."

Dr. Bart paused for a moment, then added, "For those of you who have not reviewed all the relevant data, I do feel it's important to mention that the clinical examination of Michael Kepler revealed signs of both sexual and physical assault. Scarring and bruising indicate these abuses date back at least a year, with the most recent incident no more than a week ago. It's common at this point for the patient to deny such abuse, particularly at his age, but I feel, given time, he would be open to discussing the details. I'm hesitant to push too hard on this. At his current age of four, the memories of these traumatic events will most likely recede and be completely forgotten by the age of six. I have yet to decide if it would prove more beneficial for him to remember and confront these memories or to bury them."

The recording came to an end. I removed my headphones and finished the last of my drink.

The two male flight attendants helped Warren back into his seat. His face was flushed red and dripping with sweat. Without looking at me, he muttered, "You're a bitch."

"I love you too, Warren."

CHAPTER FIFTY-FOUR

DOBBS

SPECIAL AGENTS OMER VELA and Sammy Goggans arrived by car shortly before midnight; the U.S. marshals were five minutes behind them. Gimble had a map spread out on the hood of one of the SUVs. U.S. Marshal Garrison stood beside her, his fingers tracing the various arteries out of the small town. "We've got clear shots to Arizona and Nevada. He could double back to California, no way to know."

Sheriff Moody said, "We've got a small regional airport, a bus stop, and a train station. I've got men watching all of them on the off chance he ditches the car and opts for public transportation."

"He knows LA," Dobbs said. "He could get lost there. All these highways run through nothing but wide-open spaces. That's too dangerous; I think he's heading back to the city."

Gimble's fingers were snapping again. "If he wanted to hide in LA, I don't think he would have gone through the trouble of securing a vehicle. I smell road trip. I think he's heading east. You said he was from New York. Maybe he's running home."

Garrison said, "No way he makes it across the country."

"He's got at least a two- to three-hour jump on us. I want to widen the BOLO—Texas, Kansas, Oklahoma...all these surrounding states." She drew a large circle with her finger.

"Without a plate?"

"Can't rely on plate readers to catch every bad guy," Gimble told him. "Go old school. Stay on highway patrol. Small, black sports car, old. MG, Fiat, Porsche...that's gotta stand out."

Vela came out the mobile home's front door, Begley behind him, carrying a cell phone and several evidence bags. He set the bags down on the hood of the SUV next to the map and handed the phone to Sammy. "We think this is Erma's, but it's got a pass code. Can you break it?"

Sammy studied the phone, then plugged it into his MacBook. He brought up a program, keyed in the serial number, and studied the screen. "It's an Alcatel Pixi Avion running an older version of Android called Lollipop. I can get in, but it will take a little while."

Gimble was leaning over the bag with the chrome-plated nine-millimeter, now grimy with black powder. "What'd you find here?"

"Kepler's prints are on it, but it hasn't been fired recently. I found his prints all over the interior of the house too. Where I didn't find them is on this." He held up the bag containing the bottle of superglue. "I've got Erma's, Roland's, and an unknown's thumbprint. No Kepler."

"So he put on gloves for the kill?" Dobbs said.

Begley shrugged. "Seems odd, considering he wasn't concerned about touching anything else in that place."

Gimble looked down at the third evidence bag. "What about the book?"

The book.

They had found the book wedged under Erma Eads's body on the bed, a sparrow feather marking one of the pages.

Begley picked it up, flipped through the pages, then went back to the cover. "*Fractured*, by one Barton Fitzgerald, MD."

Vela said, "It's a case study of one of his patients with dissociative identity disorder."

Gimble smirked. "Multiple personalities. Is that a real thing?"

Vela nodded. "Rare, but real."

"Tell me this book isn't about Kepler."

"It's not. Fitzgerald refers to his patient only as John, but the book was published in 1982—that's ten years before Kepler was born."

"So why did Kepler leave it under the body?"

Vela opened the book to the page previously marked with the feather. One sentence was underlined: *Who is on the mark?*

"Fitzgerald uses this phrase throughout the book to identify which of John's thirteen personalities he's speaking to," Vela explained. "David is on the mark, Joey is on the mark, John is on the mark...the personality in control is the one on the mark."

Dobbs said, "Kepler didn't come out here just to leave us a book with some bullshit taunt."

"Kepler came out here for information," Begley replied. "Erma Eads has signs of severe bruising. She was beaten shortly before death. He glued her nose shut at least thirty minutes before he started on her mouth. He took his time—glued her lips on the left, then slowly worked his way around, one drop at a time. I can tell by the tearing. He glued, she ripped it open with her jaw muscles. He glued again. He tortured her. He came here for information. Possibly to silence her. Maybe both."

Gimble took this in. "Get me background on Erma and Roland Eads. We need to figure out the connection."

The sheriff's phone rang. He pressed it to his ear. "Moody."

He spoke for several minutes. When he hung up, his eyes fell on

Gimble. "Your clusterfuck just expanded. We have another body. About three miles up the road at the Lutz Motel."

"Gimble!"

The shout came from Marshal Garrison. He rounded the SUV at a run. "Your BOLO—I phoned it in, and the computer matched it to three seventy-seven calls in the past hour."

Gimble's eyes narrowed. "What's seventy-seven?"

"Civilian traffic calls," Dobbs said. "Reports of aggressive or erratic driving."

Garrison nodded. "About three hours east of here on the inter-state in Arizona. Black Porsche, late-sixties model. We've got a state trooper on him about a mile back. I ordered him to hold visual but not to pursue."

Gimble considered all of this. "Begley, finish here, then get to the Lutz Motel, process the scene. Work with the locals. Garrison, I need you to mobilize marshals in Arizona. Come down I-40 west, close the distance from the opposite side, then take your team from here. Pin him down from both ends. Got it?"

"Understood."

She turned back to the sheriff. "How fast can you get the rest of us back to the chopper?"

CHAPTER FIFTY-FIVE

WRITTEN STATEMENT, MEGAN FITZGERALD

Warren snored.

Not only was this beast of a man both physically and morally repugnant, he came with matching sound effects.

One of the flight attendants had offered me earplugs, but I declined; I waved him off and held up my headphones. When he left to tend to Warren's other offendees, I took another cassette from my bag.

Dark room—M. Kepler—September 12, 2007

Michael had been fifteen years old in 2007. Eleven years after the last tape.

I had taken everything I found in Dr. Rose's files, but surely there was more. I knew from personal experience that Dr. Bart taped all sessions, and he'd seen Michael several times per week. Possibly hundreds of tapes were missing. Either Dr. Rose had hidden them somewhere, or they were still in Dr. Bart's office, or someone else had them.

Where were *my* tapes?

I hadn't found any of mine.

I put on my headphones. Slipped the cassette into my player and pressed Play.

* * *

Dr. Bart cleared his throat. "I have something special for you today."

"Oh yeah? What?"

It was weird, hearing Michael's voice, older now. Not quite his current voice, but somewhere in between the child of the other tape and the present. A voice from my past.

"You'll need to go into the dark room."

"Why can't we just stay out here and talk at your desk?"

"You know why."

"Your research?"

"Yes."

"Have you ever wondered how your research would play out in the light? Would you get the same results or something different?"

"If the research was conducted in the light, it wouldn't be the same, now would it? You change such an integral variable, and the experiment is compromised."

"Or possibly improved."

"Or degraded."

"Different, though," Michael pointed out. "Sometimes different is good."

"Are you afraid to go into the dark room?"

"No. Of course not."

"But you always come up with excuses to put it off."

"Did I say I *wouldn't* go in?"

"It was implied in your comments."

"But I didn't say I wouldn't."

Sound of a drawer opening and closing. "You'll need these."

Michael didn't respond.

"Go on, take them."

"Why do I need scissors? Aren't those Megan's?"

"I'll return them when we're done."

I paused the tape. I remembered my missing scissors, the ones with the purple handle. When I told Dr. Rose I couldn't find them, she blamed me. Said I was always losing everything because I didn't put things back where they belonged.

Thanks, Dr. Bart. Steal from kids much?

I pressed Play again.

The sound of scissors slipping across the desk. I could almost see them.

"Pleasure or pain?" Michael asked.

"You know I can't tell you. Not in advance."

"Your research."

"My research. You need to go in of your own free will, regardless of what is to come."

"And what if I say no?"

"That is your right. I won't force you. You know that."

Michael went quiet for a second. Then: "How long this time?"

"Thirty minutes."

Michael exhaled.

The sound of scissors opening and closing.

When Michael spoke again, his voice carried the blind confidence held by every fifteen-year-old boy. "Okay, I'll do it."

A drawer opening and closing again.

"You can remove the blindfold once you're inside."

Michael sighed but didn't push back.

A crackle filled the tape. Somebody picking up the recorder, carrying it. I heard the sound of Dr. Bart inserting his various keys into the locks of the dark room's door. The twist and click of a dead bolt. I always expected the door to squeak when he opened it, make some foreboding high-pitched whine, but it never came. When I closed my eyes, though, I could see it.

The door slowly swinging open. Dr. Bart guiding Michael inside as he had with me on so many occasions.

"Sit here," Dr. Bart said. "I've placed a stool for you. That's my boy."

The door closed then. The click of the latch. The twist of the dead bolt.

Dr. Bart knocked twice on it, as was his practice. "Can you hear me okay?"

"Yes," Michael replied, his voice muffled from the other side.

"You may remove your blindfold now."

I knew it wouldn't matter. The room itself was pitch-black, always was. Not the slightest bit of light allowed in. The blindfold's only purpose was to ensure you didn't see anything while the door was open, while you were stepping into the room.

"What's that smell?"

Dr. Bart said, "You're not alone in there, Michael. Four hours ago, one of my other patients entered the room, and she's still inside. Unlike you, she is not only blind but deaf. I won't go into how I was able to block both senses, that's a discussion for another time, but it's important you understand she doesn't know you're in there with her. She has water, should you become thirsty. Although I don't know how she'll react if you try and take it. I suggest you keep those scissors handy in case she doesn't react favorably to your presence."

His voice dropped off momentarily, then he continued. "I gave her something else, Michael. Something I went through a great deal of trouble to secure. Obtaining evidence from a homicide can be a costly endeavor. I had to call in numerous favors, but I felt it was necessary to ensure the success of this experiment. It's the hacksaw Maxwell Pullen used to dismember your mother. When I gave it to this girl, the one in there with you, I told her it was her only means of defense and she shouldn't be afraid to use it. You see, she was violated recently in ways not unlike Maxwell Pullen explored with you. She was unable to fight back. She is in the dark room in order to revisit that experience and hopefully achieve a more favorable outcome. She wishes to regain the strength and self-respect she feels she lost. You can help her, Michael. And I believe she will help you. I've determined three hours should be ample time for this test."

"You said thirty minutes."

"I've adjusted."

"I'm not gonna hurt her, Doctor," Michael said, his voice muffled by the door.

Dr. Bart replied, "Mitchell would."

CHAPTER FIFTY-SIX

WRITTEN STATEMENT, MEGAN FITZGERALD

The tape ended abruptly. Just a click, then nothing but the hiss of blank tape.

"Shit," I muttered.

Warren stirred, slurped, and drifted back off to sleep.

I removed the tape from my player and found the last one in my purse.

Dark room—M. Kepler—April 8, 2009

Michael's seventeenth birthday.

This tape didn't contain a preamble. Nothing from Dr. Bart. At first, I thought it might be blank, then I heard several clicks—the locks on the dark room's door.

Breathing then. Thin gasps.

The recorder had been placed on the floor. I closed my eyes and pictured it. The spot to the left, just inside the door. I had seen Dr. Bart put the recorder there more times than I could count.

"Would you like some water?"

"Yes."

"Yes what?"

"Sir. Yes. Water, please, sir," Michael said. He sounded weak, barely audible.

"Who is on the mark?"

Shuffling.

"Who is on the mark?"

"Me."

"Who is on the mark?" Dr. Bart repeated, the frustration in his voice mounting.

"Michael."

The door closed.

Locks clanked back into place.

The tape clicked and clicked again a moment later—the recording had stopped and restarted. I couldn't tell how much time had passed.

"Who is on the mark?" Dr. Bart said again.

"I need water," Michael said, voice muffled by the door. "Please…"

"Not until you stop lying to me."

"How long?" Michael said softly.

"You've been in there thirty-three hours. About to become thirty-four."

"I'm not lying."

"I can easily wait another hour, or two, or ten. I'm a patient man. You know better than to try me."

"Michael is on the mark."

"You little shit."

"Not very professional, Doctor," Michael said.

Dr. Bart cleared his throat. "Why didn't you kill Maxwell Pullen? You could have ended all the abuse."

"I was a child."

"That didn't stop you from putting your own mother out of her misery."

"So you say."

"We all know the truth. You somehow overpowered her—

maybe it was the angle or your weight or maybe you caught her by surprise, but however it played out, you somehow managed to kill your own mother. You forced her under that water, held her there until she was dead."

"I didn't."

"At any point, you could have taken Pullen's heroin, got a nice needle full of it, and plunged it into that man's arm. God knows you were alone enough with him passed out in some corner. Instead of ending the life of the tormentor, you kill your own mother. Was she awake? Did she look up at you through the water? Did she somehow find a way to plead with you to spare her life in those final moments? Maybe just with her eyes? *My little boy—how could you?*"

"Stop," Michael said.

"Who is on the mark?"

"Screw you."

"You know why I think you spared Max and killed your mother? I think you liked it. The things he did to you. I think you felt your mother was in the way. Maybe she was getting between the two of you. Couldn't have that. Maybe you were jealous. Mom had to go so you could have Max all to yourself."

"You're worse than Max ever was."

"Who is on the mark?"

"Why don't you open the door, and I'll show you?"

A loud click again, but this time, there was nothing else but white noise.

My eyes still closed, I pressed my head back into the seat and listened to the soft static of that final tape as the plane touched down.

PART 3

FLAGSTAFF, AZ

People who accept defeat become stepping-stones for those of us who don't.

— Barton Fitzgerald, MD

CHAPTER FIFTY-SEVEN

DOBBS

THE RAIN CAME AT them from the east. At first, only a few drops against the thick curved glass of the Bell 407's windshield, then multiple heavy thuds, followed by an onslaught—water smacked into the glass and rolled over the sides with such ferocity, visibility dropped to only about 20 percent.

Dobbs glanced over at Sammy, buckled into the seat beside him. His face was green and his knuckles white; he was clutching his MacBook, attached by a USB cable to Erma Eads's cell phone, as if it were a parachute. The man's eyes were closed, and his lips moved soundlessly. He did not inspire confidence.

Vela, oblivious to the weather, sat in the seat opposite, his face buried in the book they'd found under Erma Eads.

In the copilot seat at the front, Gimble leaned forward and peered through the haze at the faint outline of I-40. "I'd prefer to hold this altitude, but if you need to pull up and get back over the storm, do it; we have GPS coordinates on our target."

Her voice sounded thin, tinny over Dobbs's headphones.

The pilot, a Gulf War vet named Cory Harland, shrugged. "Night flight like this, I'm running mainly by instruments, so it doesn't matter to me. Rain looks scary, but it doesn't have much of an impact. Wind can be a bitch, but a little rain does nothing but give the bird a bath."

Lightning skittered across the sky up ahead, illuminating the churning dark clouds, as if to remind the chopper's passengers of just how insignificant they were.

Gimble nodded and flicked a switch on the board at her left. "Trooper Winkler, you still on him?"

Winkler's voice came back a moment later. "I-40 eastbound, just past mile marker seventy-two. Closed the distance slightly on account of the weather, didn't want to lose visual. Hanging back about a quarter mile. Our boy is still all over the road—he's bouncing off the lines like a pinball. Speed is anywhere from seventy to ninety."

Thirty minutes earlier, Winkler had considered pulling Kepler over. The Porsche had drifted far enough to the right to drop off the pavement and slide in the gravel. When the driver corrected with a hard pull left, the car fishtailed and nearly spun into the oncoming lane. While there wasn't much traffic at this late hour, there was *some* traffic, and the Arizona Highway Patrol, not the FBI, ultimately had jurisdiction when it came to public safety on the highway. If Winkler determined a move on Kepler was justified, there was little Gimble could do other than cite the current situation—U.S. marshals had dispatched a team from Flagstaff and set up roadblocks on I-40 about thirty miles east, and Garrison's team was about twenty minutes behind and closing. As long as Kepler continued east, they'd snare him. If Winkler gave chase, Kepler might panic, and someone could get hurt. Following him into the roadblock was the safest bet.

"Oh, Christ," Winkler muttered.

Gimble pressed the button again. "What is it?"

"He just blew past a tractor trailer. Must have broken a hundred. Missed a station wagon in the oncoming lane by a car length. Drove it off the road."

"But everyone's okay, right?"

"We've got nothing but desert out here. Nothing to run into. Vehicle hit the dirt, spun at least twice. It's still now."

"Stay on him, Trooper."

"I should see if the passengers are okay."

"Trooper . . ."

Dobbs knew she couldn't order him; that would be overstepping. She sure as hell wanted to, though.

Winkler said, "I radioed another car behind me. They'll stop. Staying on him. I'm increasing my speed to one-ten to pass the truck. Closing the distance to an eighth of a mile."

Gimble's fingers began twitching. "Not too close. If you can see him, he can see you."

"I'm well aware, I . . . oh, shit!"

"What is it?"

No response.

"Winkler?"

His voice crackled a moment later. "There was another tractor trailer in front of this one. Didn't see that one. Had to pass them both. I'm okay now. I see Kepler again. Rain's picking up, and he slowed down a little. Looks like he dropped to around seventy. I'm matching speed."

Harland tapped Gimble on the shoulder, then pointed out the windshield. "I think that's them at your one o'clock."

Dobbs followed his gaze and spotted two tractor trailers nearly on top of each other, another car just in front, and several more up the road ahead of that one. Although Winkler didn't have his strobes on, Dobbs could make out the faint outline of numbers on the top of the highway patrol car as the helicopter reduced altitude.

Gimble said, "Winkler, we have visual. We're coming up behind you."

"Copy."

"There's your roadblock," Harland said, pointing about ten miles up the road at a line of stopped vehicles.

"He's slowing down a little bit. Coming up on another car," Winkler said. "Should I close distance or hang back?"

Gimble was practically standing in her seat. "What are all those lights? Up over there?"

Harland said, "Flagstaff coming up on the right, the Flying T Truck Stop on the left."

"What am I doing here, Agent?" Trooper Winkler again.

Gimble flicked the switch at her side. "Garrison, what are your coordinates? How far are you from Flagstaff?"

His voice came back a moment later. "I'm tracking your trooper. We're about ten minutes behind him."

"Tell me you've got roadblocks set up at all the exits approaching the roadblock."

"I do," Garrison said. "On your word, we'll lock those down. Kepler will have no choice but to continue east into the net."

"Do it now."

"Copy."

She flicked the switch again. "Stay back, Winkler. We've got U.S. marshals on your six and the roadblock coming up ahead of you. All exits are going into lockdown."

"Understood."

"Who's that?" Dobbs said, pointing at another car flying up fast behind the state trooper.

"Get closer," Gimble told Harland.

The helicopter dipped, and Dobbs's stomach churned. They

closed their altitude to only a few thousand feet. Dobbs leaned over to get a better look. He caught sight of the taillights as the speeding vehicle careened past the highway patrol car.

Winkler's voice came back over their headphones. "Agents, I just got lapped by another black Porsche."

CHAPTER FIFTY-EIGHT

DOBBS

STAY ON THE FIRST one," Gimble said.

"This guy is driving nearly as bad as the other one," Winkler replied.

"*Stay* on the first one," Gimble repeated.

Dobbs peered down through the rain. From this distance, it was impossible to tell the two cars apart; they were nothing but two hazy black blurs.

"This guy is gaining fast. He's nearly on top of Kepler," Winkler said. "Scratch that—he just passed him."

"What the hell?" Gimble muttered. "What's he doing?"

Dobbs watched as the second Porsche got out in front of Kepler and slammed on the brakes. Kepler avoided rear-ending him by swerving into the oncoming lane, then drove up parallel to the other car. He stayed there briefly, then gunned the engine, roared past, and swung back in front of it.

The helicopter jerked up, its nose momentarily pointing toward the clouds. Dobbs fell back into his seat, his hands gripping the leather. Beside him, Sammy let out a single chirp.

They rocked slightly, then leveled off.

"Sorry about that," Harland said. "That would be the wind I mentioned earlier. It's kicking up. We're okay."

Vela looked up from the book, glanced out the window, and went back to reading, unfazed.

When Dobbs looked back down at the road, one of the cars was passing the other again.

Winkler came back over the radio, frustration mounting in his voice. "They keep trading places. I don't know which is which anymore. I need to get closer, maybe read the plate."

Gimble said, "Doesn't matter, they've got nowhere to go. We'll take down both, then sort it out."

Sammy's MacBook beeped, a series of happy chimes.

"What is that?" Dobbs said.

Sammy opened the computer and studied the screen. His face was a pale shade of green in the light. "Erma's phone—I've got her pass code." He picked up her mobile and keyed in the six-digit code and began cycling through the screens. His eyes went wide.

"What is it?" Dobbs said.

Sammy looked to the front of the chopper. "Hey, Gimble, she's got a number for Kepler programmed in her contacts."

Gimble, without taking her eyes off the cars below, shot her hand back. Sammy placed the phone in her open palm.

With one hand, Harland fished his own phone out from a compartment in the dash, unplugged a cable, and handed the free end to Gimble. "If you plug into this, audio will feed through your headphones."

Gimble attached the cable, clicked several buttons on the phone, and Dobbs heard the line ring twice over his own headphones. A voice answered, one he recognized. Had it really been less than two days since he'd met Michael Kepler?

"I didn't leave Erma in a position to phone a friend, so I'm going to have to guess this is either Special Agent Jessica Gimble or possibly Detective Dobbs throwing a Hail Mary my way. The real question is, are you in the car behind me, up ahead in that roadblock, or bouncing around in the storm above my head?"

"Michael Kepler, this is Special Agent Jessica Gimble with the FBI. Pull over immediately, place the car in park, get out of the vehicle, and get down on your knees with your hands on your head!"

"It's raining, Agent, and I don't have an umbrella. I think I'll stay put for now."

"You've got no place to go."

"Is Detective Dobbs with you?"

Gimble turned in her seat and met Dobbs's eyes. She nodded.

"I'm here," Dobbs said.

"Did you get off watching my video with Alyssa? I bet it's hard to come by a piece of ass like that on a cop's salary. I bet you watched it with all your buddies and had a jerk-fest in the locker room."

"Giving up on the whole 'That wasn't me' defense, Kepler?"

"She was so damn sweet. You know she climbed into that bathtub *willingly*? Such a team player, that one, always was. Of all of them, she was the hardest for me. I almost couldn't bring myself to do it. I powered through, though. I got the job done. Had to, for the greater good. She wanted her feather. She deserved it, *earned* her feather. Didn't even fight back. Not at first, anyway, and that really threw me. They *always* fight back. Makes sense, right? I know I would. I've learned to expect it, maybe even crave it a little bit, like some kind of Freudian power trip; that last bit of fight feeds me. But Alyssa only looked up at me from beneath the water and waited. At one point, she even smiled." Kepler paused for a second. "Have you ever put a sick pet to sleep, Detective? For me, that's what it was like with Alyssa. Like I was putting a sick pet out of its misery. It was like she welcomed the relief that was to come and knew I was doing it out of love."

Dobbs glanced back out the window. Both Porsches were still jockeying for the lead. Trooper Winkler had given up all pretenses of stealth; his lights were flashing, and he was right behind both cars. The roadblock was less than a mile ahead. They flew past the last exit, no place else to go.

"Slow down, Michael. No reason to risk getting hurt," Gimble said.

"I appreciate your concern, Agent Gimble. It's heartwarming," Kepler said. "I'm afraid I need to hang up now. I'm gonna need both hands in a minute."

Vela, who had put the book down at some point during this exchange, cleared his throat and looked out the window at the cars below. "This is Special Agent Omer Vela. I'm a clinical psychologist with the Bureau. I've studied your father's work."

"Adoptive father."

"Adoptive father," Vela agreed. "Mind if I ask you a question?"

Kepler didn't reply.

Vela glanced at Dobbs, then said, "Who is on the mark?"

The line clicked and went dead, and two things happened.

One of the Porsches sped up, barreling toward the roadblock.

The other Porsche veered hard to the left, dropped off the pavement, and tore through the flat desert toward the lights of the Flying T Truck Stop.

CHAPTER FIFTY-NINE

DOBBS

GIMBLE DIDN'T MISS A beat. The moment one of the black Porsches veered into the desert scrub toward the truck stop, her finger clicked the toggle on her microphone. "Winkler, stay with that one! Stay on him!" She flipped the switch to a third position. "Marshals, target coming in hot from the west. He may attempt to bypass the roadblock; be prepared to evade impact and pursue."

She turned to Harland. "Stick with the one running for the truck stop."

Harland nodded and twisted the stick. The helicopter banked hard left, circled around, and steadied with the nose pointing toward the north. He flicked several switches on a panel to his left, and the large floodlight under the chopper burst to life, illuminating the desert beneath them. He nodded at Gimble's left hand. "That joystick there controls the flood. I'll get us closer."

Gimble took the control and maneuvered the light until it landed first on the flashing lights of the state trooper, then on the black car ahead of him. Both were moving fast, far too fast for the slick dirt. Rooster tails shot up behind them, the Porsche spraying the patrol car with mud and water. Winkler's wipers slapped the mud aside only to be met with more.

"Get us closer!" Gimble ordered. "Can you get out in front of them?"

The chopper dived forward and down. Dobbs's stomach lurched up into his throat, then settled back at his gut. They spun around 180 degrees in one swift, fluid motion. Gimble trained the large floodlight directly on the Porsche's windshield.

The tail end of the black car locked up as the driver hammered the brakes. Rather than slowing, the Porsche only slid, regained control, then accelerated again.

A gruff voice came over the helicopter's radio. "This is U.S. Marshal Tanner. Target approaching our roadblock at ninety miles per hour, still accelerating. Quarter mile out. I've got six cars on him—two on either side, two more in back. They're blocking, forcing him down the center of the road."

There was an audible click; the voice fell off, then came back a moment later. "Deploying spike strips in five, four, three, two..."

Dobbs looked out the window. He couldn't see the highway anymore. They couldn't be more than fifty feet off the ground, flying backward with the nose of the chopper pointing at the black Porsche. The floodlight filled the windshield, obscuring the driver inside.

"We have impact," Marshal Tanner said. "All four tires shredded. He's slowing. Sliding, but maintaining control."

Harland, whose eyes were locked on an eleven-inch monitor, said, "I need to pull up. We're too low. We're approaching power lines and other hazards." He didn't wait for Gimble to weigh in before tugging back on the stick and adjusting position on his pedals. The chopper shot nearly straight up.

Dobbs glanced at Sammy, fairly certain the color in his face matched the other man's.

Gimble struggled with the light control. The beam crisscrossed the desert but finally found the car again. "We can't let him reach that truck stop. Can you set down in front of him?"

"Too dangerous. I'm not risking that."

The radio squawked: "Vehicle stopped. Driver door opening. Someone getting out, hands first."

"Is it Kepler?" Gimble said into her microphone.

No response.

"Marshal? Is it Michael Kepler?"

"Negative. Looks like some kid. Late teens at the most."

The helicopter swooped up and around, came up behind the state trooper. The bright lights of the truck stop filled the horizon. It looked more like a small city than some gas station. Close now. Too close.

"Attempting a PIT maneuver," Trooper Winkler said from below.

Dobbs watched as the patrol car sped up and tried to get beside the Porsche in hopes of a controlled hit into the other car's left rear fender. If executed properly, it would cause the Porsche to slide sideways, possibly spin. He wasn't fast enough, though. The Porsche pulled ahead, and a moment later, they watched helplessly as the black sports car shot from the dirt and scrub onto the pavement at the outer edge of the Flying T Truck Stop, nearly clipping the tail end of an eighteen-wheeler—one of hundreds in this maze of trucks.

CHAPTER SIXTY

DOBBS

GIMBLE SAID, "THIS PLACE is huge. Why is it so busy? It's the middle of the night."

Harland stayed with the car, following from an altitude of about five hundred feet. "This is one of the largest truck stops in the country. Every truck heading east or west makes it a point to stop, and the tourists do too. Twelve restaurants, showers, motels, a dozen or so stores."

"What are those tents?"

"Flea market and a small circus."

"Christ."

"He's going to kill somebody," Dobbs said.

The Porsche flew through the trucks, slid as it turned hard left through the parking lot, then accelerated again.

"Winkler, look out!" Gimble shouted into her microphone.

An eighteen-wheeler coasted past a stop sign directly into Winkler's path. The back wheels of the patrol car locked up, filling the air with black smoke and steam. He came to a stop several feet in front of the trailer. Without hesitation, he threw the car into reverse, only to find another truck blocking his path from the other direction.

"I've lost visual," Winkler said.

The black Porsche crossed another intersection and disappeared beneath a large roof covering the fuel pumps. As Harland circled in a broad arc, Dobbs counted six pumps per row, twelve rows in total. Seventy-two pumps. A steady stream of cars entered and exited, but the Porsche didn't come out. "Every car and truck from the interstate must be down there," he muttered.

Marshal Tanner came over their headphones. "The kid driving the second Porsche is named Raymond Hine. He said some guy gave him a thousand dollars to get that car to Albuquerque in seven hours. He ID'd Kepler from a photo lineup. The car is stolen. Belongs to a plastic surgeon from Vegas."

"Understood," Gimble replied. "I need you to reposition your men immediately. I don't want a single vehicle leaving this truck stop."

His vehicle's light bar flashing, Winkler pulled under the canopy three lanes to the left of where Kepler entered. Red and blue light pooled out from the sides.

"Agent, that's not just a truck stop. There's a small airport in the back. Bus terminals too. Your warrant covers the I-40 corridor eastbound only. At any given time, you've got a thousand trucks down there. We lock down the Flying T, we affect interstate commerce; that means lawsuits by suppliers. You need an updated warrant for that."

From the window, Dobbs counted two lanes of incoming traffic and two more exiting, and that was just for I-40. A smaller highway butted up against the west end of this place with vehicles coming and going that way too, and there was some kind of service road on the far end that looked like it went to the airstrip in the northwest corner of the plaza.

"Nothing else gets in, nothing leaves, understood?"

"I can't do that, Agent. Not on your authority."

"Shit." Gimble fumed. She flicked the switch on her microphone again. "Garrison, I need—"

Garrison came back before she finished the sentence. "I heard. We're on it, but we're still two minutes out."

Gimble looked out of her window at the gas pumps below them. People were racing out from under the canopy. "Winkler, do you see him? What's going on?"

"Kepler's on foot—pulled the fire alarm. I'm going after him."

"Look," Sammy said, pointing out the window.

People were streaming out of the motels, the restaurants, and the shops, flooding the walkways and parking lots.

"They're all heading to their cars or trucks," Dobbs said, watching the swelling crowds through the rain.

Sammy opened his MacBook, logged into emergency services. "Someone phoned in a bomb threat. Fire alarms are going off everywhere, not just at the gas pumps—twelve of them, thirteen, fourteen. Every building is lighting up."

"Set down somewhere now," Gimble ordered Harland.

CHAPTER SIXTY-ONE

DOBBS

THEY LANDED IN A grassy area about a hundred yards from the pumps. Rain was still coming down in sheets.

No sign of Kepler.

His Porsche was parked at pump 19, the driver's-side door left open, keys in the ignition. No sign of Trooper Winkler either. His patrol car was parked behind the empty Porsche, lights flashing.

Dobbs pointed toward the interstate. "We need to lock this place down before he gets out. If we stop the first vehicle in each lane, everyone else will be stuck behind them."

"You get eastbound, I'll get west," Gimble said, taking off at a run.

Dobbs sprinted across the muddy field. He pushed until his leg muscles burned. Icy rain stung his face. Cars, trucks, RVs, and tractor trailers were all lined up in the exit lane, slowly feeding back onto the highway. He pulled his badge out as he ran and held it out toward the vehicles. A pudgy little kid with freckles sitting in a station wagon stared at Dobbs as he bolted past, the kid's face pressed to steamed glass.

At least six eighteen-wheelers got back on the highway before

Dobbs neared the front of the line. One driver looked down, saw the badge, and quickly turned away, pretending he hadn't seen him. He shot out onto the highway. When the next one tried to rush past him, Dobbs stepped out in front of the large truck. The wheels locked, screamed in protest, as the semi lurched to a stop.

The driver leaned out his window. "You crazy shit!"

A white panel van peeled away from the row of cars, pulled onto the shoulder, and accelerated. Dobbs stepped out in front of that one too, but it didn't slow down. "Stop!"

The van swerved.

Dobbs dived to the side.

A blur of white rushed past him and got back on I-40.

He fumbled with his phone, dialed Marshal Tanner. When the man picked up, he shouted, "White van, eastbound, just got back on the interstate!"

"On it," Tanner replied.

The driver of the semi hit his horn, three loud blasts.

In the muddy bank on the side of the road, Dobbs shook his head and held his badge up in the air.

CHAPTER SIXTY-TWO

DR. ROSE

DOORBELL.

Dr. Rose Fitzgerald rolled onto her side and glanced at the clock on the nightstand—four thirty in the morning.

She had fallen asleep atop the covers, still in her clothes. She hadn't brushed her teeth. Megan's cell phone and her own were the only items on Barton's side of the bed.

Closing her eyes, she reached over and ran her hand over the sheets, imagined the warmth of him there, the sound of his soft snore. She tugged his voice from her mind, the memory already trying to fade away. She remembered the smile on his face as he held up his degree all those years ago, his eyes somehow finding hers in the crowd as he crossed the stage. "I'll change the world, Rose," he had told her that night at dinner—Café Moulin, their favorite French restaurant. Then he'd dropped to one knee and held up the small box that had so obviously been burning a hole in his pocket. "Change it with me?"

The doorbell again, then three quick knocks.

Rose's eyes snapped open.

Megan had a key, and if the little slut came home tonight, she wouldn't announce herself. She would scuttle in through the back door, as she always did, and sneak off to her room.

She wasn't coming back.

Not tonight.

Maybe not ever.

Rose knew that, and the thought sent a shiver through her tired body.

Another knock, louder than the last.

Rose left her bed, made her way downstairs to the front door, peered through the peephole.

A man in a suit. A woman beside him.

"Are you aware of the hour?" Rose said through the door.

"Ma'am, we're with the FBI. We need to speak with Megan Fitzgerald."

Rose reached for the dead bolt, then thought better of it; her fingers rested on the cold metal. "My husband recently passed—"

"So sorry to hear that."

Rose cleared her throat and repeated, "My husband recently passed, and I'm not comfortable opening this door in the middle of the night."

"Would you like to see our identification?"

"Identification can be faked."

"I assure you, it's not."

"I'm sure you're quite confident in that, but I have no reason to take your word for it," Rose said. "Why do you need to see Megan?"

"Ma'am, you are aware of the incident that took place in Los Angeles regarding your son, Michael?"

"Adopted son. Estranged now."

"But you've seen the news?"

Rose *had* seen the news. She'd watched the coverage for nearly forty minutes before she could stomach no more. Barton's mess, left for her to clean up. Barton and Patchen.

The man continued. "We have reason to believe your daughter has been in contact with Michael. If she is aware of his current whereabouts and conceals that information, she could be charged with a crime. We're here to give her the opportunity to tell us what she knows."

"She's not here."

"Where is she?"

"Out with friends, I imagine. She's a grown woman. It's not my place to keep tabs on her."

Through the peephole, Rose watched the woman lean over and whisper something to the man.

"May we come in?" he said.

"Do you have a warrant?"

"We can get one."

"I suggest you do that."

The woman whispered again.

The man nodded. "Dr. Fitzgerald, are you aware of the whereabouts of Michael Kepler Fitzgerald?"

Rose didn't respond; she only watched them through the peephole. She didn't move; she made not a sound.

Seven minutes passed before they left.

CHAPTER SIXTY-THREE

WRITTEN STATEMENT, MEGAN FITZGERALD

People were running.

There were at least four car accidents as everyone attempted to leave the Flying T at the same time, law enforcement be damned. The movement was feral, instinctive.

Perfect.

I pulled another fire alarm, this one just inside the door of the McDonald's. I ran to the Arby's next door, pulled that one too. Then the one in the Dunkin' Donuts. Other alarms went off, probably because of the bomb threat I'd phoned in a few minutes ago. People poured out of the motels carrying suitcases, their children in tow.

I found Michael sitting on the curb outside a small shop selling souvenirs and custom truck accessories. People ran past him, stepped over him, went around him. His head was buried in his hands.

"Michael!"

He didn't look up. He didn't acknowledge me at all.

I ran into the shop, pulled the fire alarm, and came back out.

I knelt beside him. "Michael, we need to go," I shouted in his ear, my hand in his hair.

When he finally raised his head and looked at me, there was nothing but confusion in his eyes. He looked so lost. "Megan?"

He was drugged. Out of it.

I pulled him to his feet, grabbed his bag. "We don't have much time," I said.

I had parked my rented Toyota SUV near the far edge of the parking lot to avoid the swelling traffic, but that meant it was farther away than I would have liked. More distance to cover increased our odds of getting caught.

"I'm here," Michael said in a slow drawl. "Right where you told me."

I nodded, planted a kiss on his cheek. "Come on."

I dragged him in the direction of my car, pushing through the crowd.

His pupils were dilated. Drool dripped from the corner of his mouth. He'd taken something. Something bad.

CHAPTER SIXTY-FOUR

DOBBS

RAIN COMING DOWN IN sheets.

Dobbs was halfway back to the fuel pumps when his phone rang. He fished it from his pocket and swiped at the wet screen. "Yeah?"

"It's Tanner. Your white van was full of illegals, sixteen of them. That's why they ran. No sign of Kepler."

Dobbs hung up without replying, ducked out of the rain, and made his way back to the others at Kepler's Porsche. "Garrison's team is here. They locked down the exits and they're searching vehicles one by one now, but a few got through. Four-wheel-drive SUVs are just crossing the desert back to the highway. A few cars too." He wiped his face on his shirt, leaving streaks of mud, and glanced down at his watch.

Thirteen minutes.

Thirteen minutes had passed since Kepler left his car.

He could be anywhere.

"You're limping," Vela pointed out.

"Tweaked my ankle," Dobbs said. His eyes darted over the manic crowds, people running everywhere. The cars bumper to bumper, everyone trying to get out. His gaze landed on the state patrol car. Someone had shut down the motor and lights. "Where's Winkler? He was on him—where the hell did he go?"

"He's not responding," Vela said.

Agent Gimble stood in the far corner of the fueling pumps, her back to them, yelling into her phone.

Both the front and rear trunks of the Porsche were open. Several items had been placed on plastic tarps around the car.

"Begley called," Vela said. "The body back at the Lutz Motel is Molly Fellman, twenty. She ran the night desk. I started processing the car. We've got her clothing here. Kepler must have taken it as some kind of souvenir."

"Anything to indicate where he might be going?"

Vela shook his head.

"How did he . . ."

"Cut her femoral artery," Vela told him. "They found her in a small closet off the lobby. No feather. He bagged his clothing too—stuffed everything in with Molly Fellman's clothes. An Armani suit soaked in her blood. Well, most likely hers. If not, we've got another vic out there somewhere."

"Armani? How many truck drivers wear Armani?"

Vela shrugged. "Matches what we found back at his warehouse."

Dobbs leaned down in front of a pile of tattered material. "These are like the ones we found in his warehouse too."

Vela nodded. "Windham Hall uniforms. All shredded."

Sammy had set up a makeshift desk on a tower of bottled water near one of the pumps. Without looking up from his Mac, he pointed at the corner of the roof. "I'm working on the camera footage. Maybe we'll get lucky."

Gimble returned, shaking her head. "Bureaucratic bullshit. All of it. The judge who signed our warrant won't approve a full lockdown on this place. He's giving us thirty minutes, then I have to pull the marshals from the exits. Says he's already gotten three phone calls—this little pimple on the ass of the American highway system accounts for nearly eighty percent of the local income, and a lockdown will put the Bureau on the hook for the lost revenue. We can't guarantee Kepler is still here, so he won't risk giving us more than a half hour."

"He's probably right," Dobbs said.

"Oh, boy," Sammy muttered while typing feverishly.

Gimble turned on Dobbs, her face red. "Think so? That what your extensive experience in fugitive apprehension is telling you? Aren't you a homicide cop? Not hard to chase down a dead body."

Dobbs raised his hands. "All I mean is Kepler is smart. He'd know we'd want to lock this place down the moment we could, so he would have tried to beat us. He could have hitched a ride, stolen a car. Hell, he knows how to drive these rigs—he could have taken a semi."

Gimble's fingers began to twitch as she processed this, then she patted her pockets and pulled out Erma Eads's phone. "Let's just call and ask him where he is."

She dialed on speaker.

The phone began to ring.

Another phone began to ring. Distant, muffled.

It was coming from the trunk of the state patrol car.

Gimble drew her weapon as Dobbs popped the trunk.

Winkler lay folded inside, his neck at a grotesque angle, a feather protruding from his mouth. The ringing phone glowed in his shirt pocket.

Dobbs stared down at the man's body and blew out a defeated breath. "I need a minute."

Before anyone could reply, he walked off and pushed through the swinging door of the men's restroom at the corner of the fuel complex. He went to the sink, ran his hand over the faucet's electronic eye, splashed cold water on his face.

Dobbs didn't see the man lower himself down from the dark alcove behind the exposed heating and air-conditioning ducts. He didn't hear him either. It wasn't until Kepler grabbed him by the hair and slammed his head into the mirror that Dobbs realized he wasn't alone.

CHAPTER SIXTY-FIVE

MICHAEL

PEOPLE WERE SHOUTING.

Alarms were shrieking.

I squeezed my eyes shut, blocked it out, and my world changed.

I was in a motel lobby.

Needles, California.

"I need a room," I said.

She grinned at me from behind the counter. Not the fake grin people in hospitality wore so nonchalantly, but the genuine grin of someone happy, someone enjoying life.

MOLLY her name tag read.

"I'll need to see your ID and a major credit card," Molly said.

I took out my wallet, thumbed through the bills. "I'd prefer to pay cash."

Molly shifted her weight, right leg to left, and produced a logbook from beneath the counter. "In that case, it's seventy-nine dollars for the night, and I'll need an additional hundred as a deposit. It will be returned to you in the morning when you drop off your key, providing you don't burn the building down. What is your name?"

"Mitchell. Mitchell Kepler."

"Mitchell," she said, scribbling it down in the book.

She turned and took a key from the pegboard on the wall behind her. An actual key, not one of those electronic credit card–looking keys, but a real one with teeth. I took it from her, my fingers brushing her soft skin.

"What are you taking, Mitchell?"

"What?"

"Those pills in your other hand—what are they?"

I looked at the bottle, felt the smooth plastic, the loose cap. I should take another. "Migraine medicine," I said, the words falling loosely from my lips. "I have the worst headache..."

"Give me those!" She reached out, snatched the bottle from my grip. "Where did you get them?"

Not Molly's voice anymore. Megan's voice.

Not in a motel lobby.

"Michael!" she shouted. "Where did you get them? How many did you take?"

Not Molly.

Not the motel lobby.

In a car. Megan driving.

How did I get—

Megan was shouting at me but the words no longer made sense.

"I pulled the fire alarms, Meg. Just like you said."

My thoughts turned to soup then, and everything went black.

CHAPTER SIXTY-SIX

DOBBS

DOBBS WOKE ON THE bathroom floor with a female paramedic leaning over him, Gimble kneeling at his side.

"It was Kepler," he muttered. "Ceiling...hiding in the ceiling."

"Kepler?" She shook her head. "It was just some guy dealing meth. We grabbed him when he ran out. He saw your badge and attacked. Can you sit up?"

Dobbs forced himself into a sitting position. His brain felt like it was sloshing around in his skull; there was a sharp stinging on his forehead. When he reached for it, the paramedic smacked his hand away.

"You have a small laceration. Nothing serious, but I want to clean it up." She held her hand out before him. "Follow my finger."

Dobbs did, his eyes roving back and forth, up and down. "I saw his face. It was Kepler."

The paramedic said, "You might have a concussion. You should probably go to the hospital and get a CT scan, make sure you don't have a head bleed."

Dobbs shook his head, which he immediately regretted, and

stood. He expected the mirror to be cracked, but it wasn't. Most likely made of something more durable than glass. His forehead was beet red, and there was a bump over his left eye. A small cut was closed with a butterfly bandage. "Where is he?"

Gimble led him from the bathroom to a man sitting on the concrete, his back against the wheel of Winkler's patrol car. His hands were bound with a thick zip tie. He held them up defensively, blocking his face. "It wasn't me, man! I told them. You were on the floor!"

Dobbs took out his phone, loaded a picture of Kepler, and thrust it in front of the man. "Did you see this guy?"

His eyes narrowed. His head quickly bobbed up and down. "He hit me with the door, he ran out of there so fast. Heading toward the courtyard. You were already on the ground, I swear!"

"The bathroom has two entrances, one on this side facing the pumps, one opening onto the courtyard facing the restaurants," Gimble said.

The man nodded again. "I came in that way; he pushed past me. Your people grabbed me when I came out this side. I told you. Either let me go or get me the hell out of here—somebody planted a bomb. This whole place is gonna blow!"

"There's no bomb," Dobbs said, putting his phone away.

"Hey!" Sammy called from his makeshift desk. "You need to see this."

They left the man on the ground. He dropped his bound hands back into his lap with a frustrated sigh.

Sammy pointed at his MacBook. The image, shot from above, showed several gas pumps and was frozen on a man. "That's Kepler pulling the fire alarm, right over there." He pointed to the far corner of the structure. The alarm box was centered on the wall near the bathroom entrance. "Got it?"

Gimble frowned. "We know this already. Where does he go next?"

"I'm getting to that," Sammy said. He clicked several buttons and brought up another photo, Kepler again, an orange and brown wall behind him. "Here he is pulling the alarm at Burger King. He disables the camera right after."

Sammy paused a moment to give them a chance to view it, then brought up another image. "Here he is at the truck service center." After a few seconds, he loaded up yet another. "Here's Kepler at the CAT scales."

Vela walked up and watched over Dobbs's shoulder.

"This one is at the truck wash."

"We get it," Gimble said with frustration. "He pulled a lot of fire alarms. What's the point of this?"

"Nineteen alarms went off in total, plus the phoned-in bomb threat. I've got two points," Sammy said. "The first is this—"

Another image filled the screen, this time a woman with her hand on an alarm trigger, her gaze focused on something off camera. "That's Megan Fitzgerald in the lobby of the Carriage Motel." The image switched to another shot of her. "Here she is again at one of the supply stores."

"So she's here, not in New York. They coordinated this," Gimble said. "Michael and Megan. We need to get her photo out to everyone—"

"Already done," Sammy interrupted.

"That explains how he was able to trigger so many alarms," Vela said.

Sammy was shaking his head. "No, actually, it doesn't. That brings me to point two."

He brought up another image. A map of the Flying T Truck Stop littered with virtual red and green thumbtacks filled the screen. "Red is Kepler, green is Megan. Seven for him, twelve for her." He ran his finger over the screen. "See how Megan's are all grouped? She primarily hit the motels and the restaurants in this tight little spot in the northeast corner, all right next to each other. Kepler is all over the place."

Dobbs studied the map. Sammy was right. Kepler had pulled the alarm here at the fuel pumps, at buildings on the opposite side of the large truck stop, and at several more buildings in the far corner of the plaza. "What kind of distance is that? How did he get around so fast?"

"That's what I said," Sammy replied, "so I added time stamps to help plot out some kind of path."

He clicked several buttons, and time stamps appeared next to each pin.

They all saw it, but Gimble was the first to say something. "So the time stamps on the cameras are off. Must be. They can't be right— these three alarms went off before the one here at the fuel pumps. *Before* Kepler even got here. Are you sure those weren't Megan?"

Sammy shrugged. "We've got video of Kepler at each, not of her. And the cameras have Megan at the food court within seconds of this alarm at the weigh station. She can't be in two places at once."

"Well, neither can Kepler," Gimble said.

"Maybe somebody tampered with the feed," Vela suggested.

"Maybe."

Dobbs said, "Can you load up the feed from here at the bathroom? When I got attacked?"

Sammy nodded. "Already did."

The MacBook screen split into two images. The one on the left showed the door leading back to the fuel pumps; the right one showed the courtyard side. They all watched as Dobbs walked in. About twenty seconds later, the meth dealer pushed through the door and scrambled past one of the gas pumps, disappearing from the screen. A moment after that, another person exited, this time from the courtyard door. Sammy slowed the video, but the man's back was to the camera. He too ran offscreen.

"Build and hair color look like a match for Kepler, but there's no clear shot of his face," Sammy said.

"It was Kepler," Dobbs insisted.

Sammy froze the screen and pointed at the time superimposed in a white font at the bottom corner. "That would put him here less than thirty seconds after pulling the alarm at Burger King."

Gimble sighed, frustrated. "We need to stay on task, can't get distracted by all this smoke-and-mirror bullshit. Use the camera footage to trace both of them to a vehicle. If they're in the wind, we need to know what they're driving. I want to know where they're going, not where they've been."

"I think I know," Vela said, staring at his phone.

All eyes turned to him.

CHAPTER SIXTY-SEVEN

DOBBS

GIMBLE TURNED TO VELA. "You had a theory in the helicopter—that's why you threw out that line."

"'Who is on the mark,'" Vela said, nodding. "From the page marked with the feather in this." He held up the book they'd found under the body of Erma Eads: *Fractured.*

"The book *not* about Kepler," Gimble said flatly.

Somewhere in the distance, two of the fire alarms shut off. The crowd had thinned substantially. The Flying T had gone from complete chaos to a ghost town in a matter of minutes.

Gimble's fingers began to twitch. She was growing impatient. "Spit it out, Vela. What's the connection?"

Vela glanced over at Kepler's Porsche. "When Judge Rines denied our warrant for Kepler's adoption and treatment records back in LA, I submitted a request for whatever public information I could pull on Dr. Barton Fitzgerald—state medical boards and licensing, that sort of thing. I expected most of what I got back, the accolades, awards from his peers. I've read many of his published papers in the trades. He was highly respected. Here's the thing—over his career, nearly forty years, only one complaint had been filed against him. That's remarkable. In today's world of online reviews and anonymity, people file complaints at the drop of a hat; they feel emboldened to do so. I expected to find a dozen or so complaints, maybe more. That would be normal. The fact that he had only one stood out."

Vela loaded a document on his phone and handed it to Gimble.

She expanded the text. "J. Longtin, in 1985. Sued him for malpractice. Not much here. No case details. No outcome."

"That's over thirty years ago," Vela said. "Just a blip in a database somewhere. Frankly, I'm surprised it's there at all."

She returned the phone to him. "So how does it help us?"

Vela opened the book to a page near the back containing Dr. Fitzgerald's bio and photo. "Look at the photo credit."

She took the book, squinted at the small print. "'Author photograph copyright Jeffery Longtin.'"

"Early on in this book, Fitzgerald says that John, the subject's pseudonym, was a photographer, made a living at it before his illness presented. I think Jeffery Longtin is John."

Gimble handed the book to Dobbs.

Vela hesitated a moment, then said, "I also think Jeffery Longtin is next."

Dobbs returned the book to Vela. "That's a big leap."

Gimble held up a hand. "Vela's not one to leap. How did you get there?"

Vela fidgeted with the book, his thumb flipping the pages. "You're not going to like this."

Gimble's eyes narrowed. "What did you do?"

"I dug," he told her. "As a licensed psychologist, I have avenues open to me that are not necessarily available to an FBI agent."

"What kinds of *avenues*?"

"I used something called the Gordon Act to pull Fitzgerald's insurance records," he told her. "When a doctor passes away, the

Gordon Act allows other medical professionals to access certain information pertaining to the deceased's practice. We can't get full treatment files, but we can get patient lists. The point of the act is to ensure that the treatment of patients won't lapse if they lose their doctors. With psychiatry and psychology in particular, some patients, especially the ones most in need, won't seek a replacement on their own. We use the act to work with the insurance companies to identify at-risk patients and ensure their treatment does not get interrupted."

"You use it to poach clients from dead doctors," Gimble said.

Vela shrugged off her comment. "With the mentally unstable, a break in treatment can lead to horrible consequences for the patient; it can also leave the insurance companies exposed legally. The act allows everyone involved to be proactive in the best interest of the patient."

"Let me see the list."

Vela pulled up a second document on his phone but held the device out of her reach. "We're on dangerous ground here. If I show you this, and a judge deems the means I used to obtain the information unlawful, he or she could consider everything it leads to inadmissible. Everything from here on out. Kepler could walk."

Gimble considered this, then turned to Sammy. "Do you have anything from the security cameras? Something else we can go on right now?"

Sammy looked up from his MacBook, frustration all over his face. "Time stamps are all off. I've got Kepler in multiple places; nothing matches up. It doesn't look like any of the cameras in the parking lot are active. I lose him before he gets to a car. At first, I thought Kepler or the sister disabled them, but the head of security shot me a text saying they intentionally shut them down a few years ago—apparently, recording the happenings of a truck-stop parking lot leads to liabilities they didn't wish to be party to."

"So you can't tell where they went?"

"They're gone," Sammy said.

Gimble's fingers twitched again as she processed this. "By telling me you made the connection, we're already compromised. I can't *unknow* that. None of us can. We've got Kepler on the murders. He can't beat the evidence. If his attorney manages to get this thrown out, it won't matter. Let me see your phone."

Vela handed it to her.

As Gimble scrolled through the list, she began nodding. "They're all on here—Darcey Haas, Issac Dorrough, Cassandra Shatley, Selena Hennis, Molly Fellman . . ."

"What about Alyssa Tepper?" Dobbs asked.

Gimble nodded. "Others too. Names we don't know." She turned to Vela. "If you're right—"

"Kepler has been systematically killing off Fitzgerald's patients, and anyone still alive on that list is a potential target." Vela raised the book. "With Longtin most likely next. I think he got Longtin's address from Erma Eads."

"Why leave the book?"

"A taunt," Vela said. "Same reason he talked to you on the phone."

"Where is Longtin?" Dobbs asked.

"Just outside St. Louis. I matched current DMV to the insurance records with his DOB and Social."

Gimble snapped her fingers several times. "Take all of this back to Judge Rines. Don't skirt the issue—explain exactly how you got the client list so he doesn't have wiggle room later. Press him for all of Fitzgerald's patient records—you can tell him they're all in danger. Every person on this list. We need their files and current addresses in order to protect them. We need a search warrant for Fitzgerald's offices and residence too. If he denies any of it and someone else dies, it will be on him. Tell him I said that. Tell him I said I'll make sure everyone knows he dropped the ball if there is another death. I'll go on CNN and shout about it. He won't hang himself. When he's fuming over that, push him for Kepler's adoption and treatment records."

"He won't give us those," Vela countered. "Adult records, maybe, but nothing sealed as a minor."

"I know he won't. But if you push for those too, he'll give us everything else as a compromise. He'll see that as his out." She glanced over at Kepler's car, at the evidence piled around it. "Call Begley too—when he's done in Needles, I want him on a plane to New York ready to pounce on the Fitzgeralds the moment that warrant comes in."

Vela nodded.

Gimble looked up at Dobbs. "How's your head?"

Dobbs rubbed at the growing bump on his forehead. "I took much harder hits in college. I'll live."

"Are you okay to travel?"

"Yeah, sure."

"I want you to meet Begley out there," she said. "He's a solid investigator, but I want someone with interview experience to talk to the mother."

"Aren't local agents already on-site?"

"They don't know what to look for and we don't have time to explain. I need someone who knows this case, someone I can trust. Someone who's sat across the table from Kepler and will know if the woman is lying."

Dobbs said, "You'll need to clear it with my lieutenant."

"Done." She turned back to Vela. "Jeffery Longtin. Are you sure?"

"I'm certain."

Her fingers twitched. "Okay."

A moment later she was on the phone with U.S. Marshal Garrison—they'd need a plane.

They'd get to Longtin first.

PART 4

ST. LOUIS, MISSOURI

How many times must you repeat a phrase before it's fully committed to memory? How many times before fiction becomes fact?

—Barton Fitzgerald, MD

CHAPTER SIXTY-EIGHT

THE MAN WITH THE scar on his left hand gathered his bags and stood in the aisle as the train lumbered into Gateway Station in downtown St. Louis. There were only a handful of people in his car—an older woman knitting in the back corner, a mother and infant daughter one row up and across from him, a man reading the paper, his eyes drifting shut as sleep slowly claimed him. None appeared to be getting off at this stop. The mother was breastfeeding; a thin shawl was draped over her shoulder and the child. The baby's little legs kicked beneath it, kept pulling it down, and the mother would replace it, covering herself, then patiently repeat the motion a few moments later.

The baby cooed, thrilled with milk. All she probably knew at such a tender age.

So innocent.

Uncorrupted.

Unaware.

He traveled with only two items.

He needed nothing else.

There was the Roosevelt travel duffel that had been with him for nearly twenty years. The worn brown buffalo hide was stretched, creased, and smelled comfortingly of rich leather. A bag that had seen more of this country than most of its citizens.

"Do you play?"

This came from the woman in the back. She had paused in her knitting, her eyes on the guitar case in his other hand. The other item.

"Since I was a child," he told her. "Few things in life bring such comfort as music."

"When I was younger, my parents bought a piano and paid a neighborhood woman to teach me to play. Two lessons per week for nearly a year, and I could barely pound out 'Twinkle, Twinkle, Little Star.'"

"It's not for everyone." He nodded at her hands. "You've found other ways to occupy your time."

"Idle hands, right?" She held up half a sweater. "I sell them on Etsy."

Possibly the ugliest sweater he'd ever seen. "Lovely."

The train lurched and came to a stop.

He adjusted his grip on the handle of the guitar case; the weight of the item inside was nearly twice that of an actual guitar.

The doors opened and as he stepped past the infant, he smiled down at her. He could only hope the baby would never know the weight of such a bag or the feel of such a thing in her hands.

CHAPTER SIXTY-NINE

MICHAEL

I WOKE IN A bed.

A dark room.

A motel room.

Not a very nice one.

Thin light reached around heavy drapes at the window.

The scent of the musty sheets and quilt drifted to my nose.

Faded green paint on the walls. Several paintings depicting old schooners at sea amid crashing waves.

The familiar ache in my head now cold, dull.

I sat up and pulled back the sheets.

I wore nothing but my underwear.

I looked to the back of the room, already knowing what I'd find, although my heart still leaped in my chest when I saw it—my clothes, wet and dark. in a pile against the wall.

I sat there, willing this to be a dream, hoping this room would fade away and be replaced with something else, anything else, but nothing changed. My senses grew keenly aware of the layer of dust covering damn near everything, of the mold my mind pictured feasting inside the walls, and of the faint sound of water dripping. A single drop, followed by another half a minute later.

The bathroom light was on.

An exhaust fan whirred.

The door closed all but a crack.

I told my body to move, but it didn't, wouldn't, not at first. When my legs finally went over the side of the bed, they felt as if they each weighed a hundred pounds. My toes curled into the worn carpet. I forced myself to stand.

Another drop of water.

I forced myself to move.

The room seemed to stretch out in front of me, growing longer with each step I took toward the bathroom. I passed my clothes, but I didn't look down. I couldn't. I refused to take a breath, knowing it would bring with it the familiar scent of copper, the scent of blood.

When I reached the bathroom, my hand rose all on its own and touched the door; my fingertips quivered on the wood.

The door opened all too easily.

Water filled the tub to the rim. There were several puddles on the scuffed white tile.

Another drop fell from the tub's faucet and struck the water with a plop, sending ripples across it.

She was several inches below the surface.

Eyes closed.

Brown hair floating slightly, nearly still.

Her toned legs were folded awkwardly, her knees protruding from the water and resting against the wall. Her arms were at her sides, one hand gently pressed against her thigh.

A single air bubble rose from her pale lips.

Oh God, what have I done?

CHAPTER SEVENTY

WRITTEN STATEMENT, MEGAN FITZGERALD

I opened my eyes to find Michael standing over me, wearing nothing but boxers and a blank stare. He looked down at me with his mouth open and eyes I didn't recognize. A stranger in a brother mask.

Just the sight of him sent a shiver over me, brought on this instinctive need to run. The bath had been steaming when I got in, but now it felt like ice.

Fragile, Dr. Bart had said in his notes.

I don't know why the thought popped into my head at that very moment, but it did, and I couldn't help thinking of Michael that way. But the way he looked at me...

I sat up in the bathtub and pulled my knees to my chin. "Jeez, Michael, knock much? Kinda naked here."

He remained still. Didn't move.

He was fucking creeping me out, if I'm being honest.

I thought of the scissors on the counter just outside the door.

I hated myself for thinking of that.

Crazy.

This was Michael.

"Michael, say something. Are you okay?" *You're frightening me,* I nearly said.

"I thought..." he began, the words trailing off.

Then I understood.

I'm such an idiot. "Oh! No! You were still sleeping and I really just wanted a bath! I didn't mean—"

I stood, forgetting to keep myself covered, splashing water all over the small bathroom in my hurry to get out. Water pooled at my feet, disappeared in the gray and fractured tile grout.

Michael's eyes drifted over me.

I met his gaze, held it as long as I could, then looked away.

"Your hair," he finally said flatly. "You cut it."

I took a step toward him. "Can you pass me a towel?"

He took one down from the rack just outside the door and handed it to me. I quickly dried off and wrapped it around my body. I ran my hand through what was left of my hair; I had gotten a cute pixie cut. "The real question is, why haven't you? You've got half the world looking for you, and you haven't changed anything. I can't believe you were driving your own car."

"Nobody knew to look for it."

I pushed past him to the counter. "You're the worst fugitive ever." I grabbed the pharmacy bag from the corner near the sink and dumped out the box of Ms. Clairol's finest. "Your turn."

He stared at me blankly.

I snapped my fingers in front of his face. "How's your head feeling?"

Michael seemed to ponder this.

"You look like a drunk trying to play *Jeopardy!*"

His hand went to his head, rubbed his temple. "Better, I think. Still foggy, though. Like a hangover."

I moved over the box of hair dye and picked up the bottle of Excedrin Migraine I had wrestled from his hand in the SUV. "Where exactly did you get this?"

He reached for the bottle, and I pulled it back.

His eyes narrowed. "It will help with the headache."

"Oh, I don't think so." I popped the cap and dumped a couple pills on the counter. "I don't know what those are, but they're not Excedrin Migraine. If they were, they'd be white with a big *E* stamped on the side. We take them on campus when we need a pick-me-up before class. They're like drinking five cups of coffee at once."

I rolled one of the pills over with my finger. "These aren't even marked. They look like someone made them in a basement."

Michael's brain still appeared to be moving in low gear. He processed what I said, but I couldn't tell if he understood the words. I cupped my hand around the bottle and dropped the pills back in. "Wheeeere . . . did . . . youuuuu . . . get . . . them?" I dragged out each word and waved my hands in slow motion in front of his face.

"Roland Eads's house," he finally said. "They were in the medicine cabinet."

"Wonderful. What else did he have in there?"

Michael's eyes glazed over; he seemed to be losing focus.

I clapped my hands. "Michael!"

That seemed to do it. His body stiffened. A light flickered behind his eyes. "He had Ambien and mirtazapine on his nightstand. I think I remember asenapine and lurasidone in the medicine cabinet. Clozapine too."

"Jesus," I muttered. "Those are all antipsychotics. If he had them out in the open, what exactly do you think he'd hide in a bottle of over-the-counter pain pills?"

"I . . . I don't know," he stammered.

"It's been nearly a day, and you're still, like, brain-damaged." I crossed the room to my purse, rummaged around inside, and returned with a small pill bottle. "This is what you're supposed to be taking. Dr. Bart had his issues, but he had your medication right."

"I don't know, Meg. Maybe I should just flush it all out. Not take anything for a while."

"Look at you, stringing full sentences together like an actual human. I'm so proud. Here." I pulled a single pill from the bottle, held it out. "Dr. Bart prescribed one every four hours. How about we do one every eight instead?"

He stared at my hand. "What is it?"

"Dorozapine," I said. "It'll level you off. I need you thinking clearly if we're doing this."

"I haven't taken anything in years."

And you haven't been you. "Please, Michael. For me?" I pleaded. "I'll let you sneak another peek at my boobs."

"I wasn't looking at your—"

"Save it. You totally checked my ladies. Frankly, you really need to see my ass. It's fantastic." My fingers teased the bottom of my towel.

Michael's face went red.

He took the pill from my palm and swallowed it dry, then opened his mouth so I could see it was gone. "Happy, Doctor?"

I nodded and gestured toward the scissors and hair dye. "Are you ready for your makeover, sir?"

An hour later, Michael stood in front of the mirror, running his hand through his hair. "It's so...blond."

"I like it," I told him. "Your natural color is dark. We had to go with something different."

"Feels so short too."

"You've got a lot of beauty opinions for someone on the run. I don't think anyone cares about your coiffure in the clink. Put these on." I handed him a pair of black wire-rimmed glasses. "They're meant for reading. It's the lowest magnification I could find, everything else made my eyes all swimmy."

I had pulled a light blue Gitman button-down from his bag along with a pair of dark slacks. With the glasses, he looked like a new man. I nodded at the television droning behind us. Aside from commercial breaks, Michael's picture hadn't left the screen. Two of the news channels were now running my photo too. I guess you finally figured out we were together, Jessica—gold star for you!

"We look nothing like those two," I told him.

He pushed the glasses farther up the bridge of his nose. "Jeffery Longtin or Nicole Milligan?"

"I made good time while you were sleeping. We're closest to Jeffery," I said.

He reached for his watch and slipped it on.

I frowned.

"What is it?"

"I guess I've never seen you wear a watch on that arm before."

Michael shrugged and moved the Breitling to his other wrist.

CHAPTER SEVENTY-ONE

THE MAN WITH THE scar on his hand had selected a car from the extended-stay parking garage attached to Gateway Station. A white Toyota Camry, about ten years old. Nothing special, nothing that would stand out. Judging by the speckling of bird droppings on the weather-beaten paint, not a car that would be missed anytime soon. The owner was most likely on an extended trip.

Both his bags fit in the trunk with room to spare.

He tuned the radio to 90.7. Mozart's Symphony no. 20.

Nice.

From Gateway Station, he took I-55 South for about an hour, passing several small towns with unremarkable names. In Leadington, he left the interstate for a series of smaller roads. Those smaller roads gave way to blacktop afterthoughts riddled with potholes. He turned left off the third such road onto a path paved with gravel, then pulled off the edge into the grass and weeds, put the Camry in park, and killed the motor.

The Mark Twain National Forest sprawled out before him, a sea of green treetops over rolling hills. A small lake in the distance. Several hiking trails.

He hadn't seen another person in more than forty minutes.

According to his GPS, the address Patchen had given him was less than half a mile away.

He transferred the contents of his guitar case to a lightweight nylon carrying bag tailored specifically for this use, slung it over his shoulder, and set off into the woods.

Twelve minutes later, the house appeared. A small cabin nestled in a narrow valley beside a meandering creek. No neighbors. One car.

He moved through the brush soundlessly, circling the structure, to a ridge on the west side—slightly elevated, offering a clear view not only of the house but of the dirt path that served as a driveway.

Remaining low, close to the ground, he pressed his thumb down on the zipper of the nylon bag and pulled it back slowly to ensure the least amount of noise.

Polished and oiled, the DVL-10 M2 sniper rifle glistened.

He removed the weapon, extended the stock, snapped the scope into place, and spread the legs of the bipod. The suppressor screwed into the barrel without resistance. His movements were practiced, fast but not hurried. The rifle was assembled, loaded, and in place in under thirty seconds.

Lying on his belly, he viewed the cabin, the approach, and the surrounding area through the scope.

Clear line of sight to all.

CHAPTER SEVENTY-TWO

GIMBLE

THE SUV HIT ANOTHER pothole and Gimble's head cracked against the roof.

"Sorry," their driver muttered. A young kid, couldn't have been more than a year out of the FBI academy. Several raindrops smacked the windshield; the sky looked like it was about to open up.

In the back seat, Sammy somehow kept his eyes fixed on his MacBook screen—Judge Rines had approved their warrant, and patient files had been coming in one at a time. "Okay, I've got the file on Darcey Haas."

"She's the one Kepler threw down the stairs," Vela said over the open communications link. He was in the SUV behind them. U.S. Marshal Garrison and his team occupied the two vehicles at the rear. They'd flown to St. Louis in an FBI charter and driven nonstop from the moment they touched down. If Kepler and his sister were driving, and they almost certainly were, the FBI had a few hours' lead time on them.

The SUV swerved hard to the left, then jerked back over. "Sorry," their driver muttered again.

"This is more of a deer path than a road," Gimble said, rubbing the bump on her head. Large live oaks loomed above them. Thick branches swayed across the sky, painting their way with shadows.

"Half a mile out," Garrison said over the communications link. "Look sharp."

"This guy lives in the middle of nowhere."

"Darcey Haas," Sammy continued, reading aloud. "She was arrested several times for public intoxication. Court-ordered to see Fitzgerald. He filed six reports. Minimal notes. He filed just enough to satisfy the courts but didn't include any substance. Last known address was about three hours from here in Springfield, Missouri. That's where Kepler killed her."

"Fitzgerald's hiding something," Vela broke in. "There's a common thread. We're close."

When their SUV came to the top of the rise Gimble said, "I've got visual on a house. Small, single story. Red Honda Accord in the driveway. Several lights on inside. Smoke coming from the chimney. Garrison, hang back with your team. Secure the perimeter, but stay out of sight. We don't want to spook him. Sammy and Vela, you're with me."

The kid pulled to a stop behind the Honda, blocking it in, and shifted into park. Vela's driver pulled up behind them.

"Wait here," Gimble told the kid as she stepped out of the SUV, her leg muscles groaning. Sammy got out behind her, and they started toward the front porch.

As they neared the small cabin, the hair on the back of Gimble's neck stood on end and her skin prickled—something wasn't right. Her hand instinctively brushed the butt of her gun. Her fingers were on the leather release strap when she heard a shotgun cock behind them.

CHAPTER SEVENTY-THREE

WRITTEN STATEMENT, MEGAN FITZGERALD

"Who's Mitchell?"

When I said it, I took my eyes off the windshield for only a second. We were going too fast, and the rain was picking up again. The road—if you could even call it a road—was shit.

Michael was in the passenger seat, the contents of my backpack spread out over the center console and spilling over his knees onto the floorboard. He was leafing through his file for what must have been the third or fourth time. He'd listened to the tapes but hadn't said anything. He just put my tape player and headphones aside and returned to Dr. Bart's notes, his finger skimming each page as he went.

"This can't possibly be true," he finally said.

"Which part?"

"All of it. Any of it. It's crazy."

"Michael, *who* is Mitchell?"

"He's nobody, just somebody I made up when I was a kid. An imaginary friend. You heard Dr. Bart; he said Mitchell was a common toddler developmental solution. Those are his exact words. Something I created to help deal with my mom and Max."

Gooseflesh crawled over my skin. The temperature had

fallen with the arrival of the rain. I reached over and turned up the heat. "When he locked you in the dark room with the scissors and the girl, you said you wouldn't hurt her, and he told you Mitchell would. Also his exact words, 'Mitchell would.' That's what he said."

Michael's eyes dropped to his hands. When he finally spoke, his voice was soft. "He used a stun gun on me. Did I ever tell you that?"

"What?"

"Sometimes he'd force my head underwater. He had this big metal bin, the kind you'd use to bob for apples at a kid's party. We'd be in the dark room, just talking—pitch-black, couldn't see a damn thing. I'd be midsentence, and he'd grab me by the hair and force me underwater. I don't think I was more than five or six the first time. When I started to expect it, he'd change things up." His finger rubbed the corner of one of the pages from his folder. "That's what these abbreviations are in his notes—SG is stun gun, WT is water treatment, AD is air deprivation."

"Air deprivation?"

"He'd zip-tie my hands and feet, then put a plastic bag over my head."

"Jesus, Michael! Why? What was the point?"

"I'd be so scared," Michael went on, ignoring my question, "especially when I was a little kid. Then as I got older, it became like this challenge thing—could I get through another of his dark-room sessions without showing any fear? When I did, boy, did that piss him off. He wanted me scared, and if he couldn't get me there, he tried harder the next time. He'd come up with something new. Like the sessions with the girl on your tape."

"Did he really give her a hacksaw?"

Michael shrugged. "I have no idea. I don't know if she was even in there with me. He'd do that sometimes too. Tell me I wasn't alone before he'd lock me in. Or he'd tell me I *was* alone, lock me in, and after a few minutes, I'd hear someone else breathing in there or feel fingers brush over my arm. Other times he told me the dark room represented the closet in that motel room, and I'd hear these noises coming from the other side of the door, *his side*, sounds meant to be Max cutting up..."

His voice trailed off, and he turned toward the window. "He tortured me; there's no other way to describe it. I don't remember half the stuff in this file; I blocked it out. That's if it's even true. This entire folder could be just another one of his mind games. Something he meant to show me at some point but never did." Michael closed his eyes, rubbed at his temples.

"Magic pills working for you?"

He nodded. "I feel hungover, but the fog is lifting, almost gone now."

He reached over, slipped his hand into mine, and squeezed. A smile touched his lips. "Thank you."

His skin felt rougher than I remembered. Warm, though. It was nice. I squeezed back, didn't want him to let go. That's when I put my foot in my mouth. "If there's no Mitchell, then who killed your mother?"

I shouldn't have said it, and I wanted to take it back. Michael looked like I'd slapped him. He pulled his hand from mine and inched away, his eyes on the rain rolling down the passenger window.

"It was Max, had to be."

"But that's not how you remember it."

"I don't remember it at all; I was just a kid."

"On the tape, I mean. When Dr. Bart first interviewed you. You said it was Mitchell."

Michael glanced down at the map on the seat beside him, then squinted out at the sign coming up on our right. "Slow down; I think that's our exit up ahead."

CHAPTER SEVENTY-FOUR

GIMBLE

WHAT THE HELL ARE you doing on my land?"

The voice was gruff, a dry rasp. The barrel of the man's rifle was less than an inch from Sammy's ear.

"Federal agents! Drop the weapon!" Gimble shouted from up ahead. She stood in the path leading to the front door of the house with her gun out and pointing past Sammy. Vela stood beside her, his palms up.

"Badges, right now," the man said.

"Lower your weapon!" Gimble said, unflinching. "I've got people all around you."

Vela took a step forward, his right hand slowly reaching to his back pocket. "I'm taking out my identification."

"Slow."

Vela nodded. His wallet out, he held up his badge. "I'm Special Agent Omer Vela, this is Agent Gimble, and the man you're pointing your shotgun at works in our IT department. Are you Jeffery Longtin?"

"Why are you here?"

"Put down the shotgun and we'll talk about it," Vela said.

"I haven't done anything."

"I know you haven't," Vela told him. "We believe your life is in danger. That's why we're here. We want to protect you."

"Who would want to hurt me?"

"Michael Kepler," Sammy said, slowly turning toward him. "You may have seen him on the news."

"I said don't move," he said firmly.

Sammy froze.

"I don't know any Michael Kepler. Don't have no television or radio out here. I just want to be left alone. Why won't everyone just leave me alone?"

"You may know him as Michael Fitzgerald," Vela said.

The man thought about this, then said, "Fitzgerald? Like Doc Fitzgerald?"

"His adopted son," Vela replied. "Dr. Fitzgerald passed away a few days ago."

"Doc Fitzgerald's dead?"

"Aneurysm," Vela said. "Back at his home in New York."

As he lowered the shotgun to his side, Jeffery Longtin did something none of them had expected. He began to sob.

CHAPTER SEVENTY-FIVE

GIMBLE

LONGTIN'S HOUSE WASN'T VERY large, but it was comfortable. A fire burned steadily in the hearth, thick logs crackling under bright flames. A couch and two chairs surrounded a small table made of milk crates and pine boards stained dark. The furniture was threadbare, the cloth faded and worn through in parts, pulled taut and stitched by hand in others.

Sammy said he'd found something strange in the GPS data from Kepler's truck but wasn't ready to share it yet. He had cleared a spot at a small table just outside the kitchen to work on whatever it was, pushing aside dozens of leather-bound books and paperbacks, most of them horror novels and thrillers from the late eighties, nothing recent. The table also held a plate with the remains of a sandwich and several stacks of unopened mail.

Outside, Longtin had dropped the shotgun to his side but had been unwilling to give it up. Several of Garrison's marshals had worked their way through the trees, ready to come up from behind. Gimble ordered everyone to stand down and let him keep the weapon once he'd agreed to engage the safety.

He'd nodded, ushered them inside the house, and collapsed into a chair.

Gimble sat on one arm of the couch. She'd seen grown men cry but she always found it unsettling. Longtin was large, at least six two, and around two hundred and twenty pounds, all of it muscle. Fifty-nine years old, according to their records. He kept his gray hair closely cropped. Hadn't shaved in several days. Judging by the smell, he hadn't bathed in equally as long.

"You're sure he's dead?" he finally said, wiping his nose on the back of his hand.

Gimble looked around for tissues, didn't see any.

"We're sure," Vela told him. "When was the last time you spoke to him?"

"August twelfth, 1987," Longtin said, without missing a beat. "Thirty-one years, one month, five days."

A voice came over the communication link in Gimble's ear. "Gimble? It's Garrison. Copy?"

"Go, Garrison," she replied.

"We're moving all the vehicles to a small logging road about an eighth of a mile into the woods to get them out of sight. My team is positioned around the perimeter. I've got a lookout stationed back at the main road. We should have about a three-minute warning on his approach."

"Understood."

Garrison's voice dropped off for a second, like he was talking to someone next to him. When he came back on the line, he said, "There's something else, probably nothing, but you should be aware."

"What is it?"

"A truck driver just flagged down a state trooper outside Kansas City. Got up behind him and started flashing his headlights. He claims a man jumped into the cab of his truck back at the Flying T, put a gun on him, and forced him to get on the interstate. That was a few minutes after the roadblocks went down. He rode with him for about half the day, made the man take him downtown—said he had a train to catch—then tied him up in the back of the truck. The guy's not sure how long he was back there but says it was four or five hours at least. He ID'd Kepler from a photo lineup."

"What about the sister?"

"Only Kepler," Garrison replied. "Here's the thing, though—the state police said the truck driver kept bringing up the reward money, trying to claim it. The trooper who interviewed him thinks he just saw Kepler on television and was trying to line his pockets."

"So you don't believe him?"

"I didn't, but…"

"But what?"

"This guy told the truck driver he had to catch a train," Garrison said. "Amtrak has a direct route from Kansas City to St. Louis. It's called the Missouri River Runner. It pulled into St. Louis about two hours ago."

Gimble exchanged a look with Vela. "Understood. Have someone check the security footage on the train and the stations. It's probably bullshit, but I don't want to discount it. Let me know what they find."

"Copy."

Longtin watched all this, appeared confused, then saw Gimble's small earbud. "Is that a phone?"

"It's linked to my phone," Gimble told him.

"Every time I go to town, seems like things just get smaller."

Vela asked, "How long have you been out here?"

"I bought this place with the settlement money in '87." Longtin's eyes were still red and puffy. "If he's dead, do you know if the checks will stop?"

"He sends you checks?"

"Two thousand a month. That was part of the settlement."

"From your malpractice claim?" Gimble asked.

Longtin nodded. "Last time I actually saw him was at the mediation. He agreed to the fifty-thousand-dollar lump payment and the monthlies."

There were Post-it notes everywhere, on cabinet doors, on chair backs, on the walls. One on the lamp beside Gimble read *Grocery pickup—9/18, 4 p.m.* Tomorrow. Another had the name of the president scrawled on it. Some just had dates and times with a brief description, others were filled with tiny handwriting, nearly illegible.

Gimble's eyes met Vela's; he had seen them too.

"Why would Doc Fitzgerald's son come after me?"

"I was hoping you might be able to tell us," Vela said.

"I have no idea."

Gimble said, "Do any of these names mean anything to you? Alyssa Tepper, Darcey Haas, Issac Dorrough..."

She ran through all of them, all of Kepler's victims. Longtin stared at her blankly, slowly shaking his head. "I...I don't leave here much. It's quiet here; I like that."

"You prefer to be alone," Vela said.

Longtin nodded.

"Do you have trouble interacting with other people?"

"Sometimes."

"What did you do yesterday? Can you walk me through your day?"

Gimble gave Vela an impatient glance.

Longtin pursed his lips, then looked down at several Post-it notes on the table. "I read from ten in the morning until noon. Then I made a sandwich—roast beef on white with American cheese. At two, I went for a walk. Walked for about three hours—"

Vela picked up a book and set it down on top of the remaining notes.

Longtin went quiet, his eyes still fixed on the table.

"Are you able to remember without the notes?"

Longtin didn't answer.

"Mr. Longtin?"

"Sometimes, but the notes help."

"But you remember the last time you saw Dr. Fitzgerald?"

"August twelfth, 1987," Longtin said with confidence. "Thirty-one years, one month, five days."

Gimble saw it then. Before responding, Longtin had glanced quickly at a calendar hanging near the door. Each day was crossed out with a solid red *X*. The marker hung next to the calendar on a string.

Vela reached down, picked up one of the other notes, and crushed it in his fist.

"What did you read yesterday?"

Jeffery Longtin remained silent.

"From ten in the morning yesterday until noon, what did you read?"

His eyes brightened then. "*The Collector,* by John Fowles. I've read it seven times. It's fantastic. Many people believe it's the book that inspired Thomas Harris to write *Red Dragon.*"

"Do you actually recall reading that particular book yesterday, or did the contents of your note just come back to you when I offered the time you had written at the top?"

Longtin went quiet again.

"Have you ever been told you have trouble with contextual memory?"

Longtin eyed him but didn't respond.

Vela continued, "You recall certain autobiographical data, facts you've picked up throughout your life, but you have trouble with time. Your memories drift. Events from thirty years ago sometimes feel like they just happened, while recent events sometimes feel extraordinarily old."

Longtin finally nodded.

Vela took one of the notes from the table. "'Pick up laundry from Morgan,'" he read aloud. "'Six o'clock on September twentieth.'" He set the note back on the table, upside down. "I'm going to ask you another question, and I want you to be completely honest with me. Do you remember dropping off your laundry?"

Again, Longtin nodded.

"When was that?"

Longtin's eyes jumped around the room, going from note to note. The answer wasn't there. Finally, he shook his head. "I'm not sure. The memories get jumbled, like you said. Sometimes I black out too."

"Are you seeing someone to help with that?"

Longtin's body stiffened; his eyes went wide. "No way. I'm fine with the notes. I get by just fine."

Vela pulled the paperback copy of *Fractured* from his back pocket and set it on the table. Longtin glared at it.

"This book is about you, isn't it?"

Longtin looked from the book to his shotgun standing against the wall, then back to the book again. "I don't think I want you people here. I can take care of myself."

"Fitzgerald treated you for dissociative identity disorder. Multiple personalities. Did he cure you?"

At this, Longtin snorted, leaned back. "*Cure me?* Doc Fitzgerald didn't want to cure me. He wanted to understand how it happened, what made me that way...he wanted to re-create it."

CHAPTER SEVENTY-SIX

DR. ROSE

IN THE MASTER BEDROOM, Dr. Rose Fitzgerald pulled the curtain aside, only an inch or so, just enough to see out.

Four cars now.

No, wait—five. She could see the back of a van at the far end of their driveway, near the bend. At least a dozen or more people. It was hard to tell exactly how many—they kept coming and going, ducking into this vehicle and climbing out of that one. People in cheap suits with their discount haircuts, chain-store jewelry, and state-school educations paid for with debt and grants probably funded by the exorbitant taxes she and Barton paid. By the various trusts and scholarships she and Barton had created over the years.

They paced the driveway like rats caught in a maze, twitchy noses and beady eyes looking up at her, cell phones pressed to their ears.

Who could all of them possibly be talking to?

So wrapped up in their little lives.

A television droned behind her, the volume low. The local CBS affiliate. When last she'd looked, the image on the screen was of her home, some young thing with perfect blond hair standing in her street talking some nonsense.

From the driveway, a man pointed up at the window, at her.

Dr. Rose dropped the edge of the curtain.

This man had arrived a few hours ago and immediately started in on her doorbell. She didn't open the door, though; she would not. Bickley, Barkley, Begley—yes, that was it, Begley. Special Agent Waylon Begley. Poor man, to be saddled with a name like Waylon. No doubt he was down there working on a warrant just as he'd promised.

He'd get one. Dr. Rose was certain of that. The only real question was when. Judging by the growing crowd, it wouldn't be long.

She didn't have much time.

She crossed the room, picked up the phone, and dialed Lawrence Patchen again.

Four rings.

Six rings.

Ten.

Twenty.

She hung up.

Damn him.

He had always been such a weasel of a man. Barton said if he was ever backed into a corner, he would just hang his head and cry rather than face his responsibilities. How they'd ever trusted him, even in the slightest, she'd never know. She could only hope he was busy doing what was necessary, as she was.

She stepped over to the far corner of the room and tugged the corner of the Aguirrechu watercolor; the magnets disengaged and the painting flipped aside on hidden hinges. The safe was open a moment later and she began carrying the contents over to the king-size bed and dropping them into a red Bosca duffel—the files, cassettes, videotapes, thumb drives. At the back of the safe were neat stacks of hundred-dollar bills, banded and crisp, fresh from the bank. Twenty-six in total—two hundred and sixty thousand dollars. Their rainy-day money. Their emergency fund. She carried the money over to the bed and dropped the bundles into the bag along with everything else.

When finished in the master bedroom, she went to Megan's room. She'd handle the offices next. She'd call Patchen again when she got downstairs—the bastard had better pick up.

CHAPTER SEVENTY-SEVEN

GIMBLE

HE WANTED TO *RE-CREATE* it?" Vela repeated, giving Gimble a quick look.

Longtin nodded. "Not at first. At first, I think he genuinely wanted to help me. We spent over a year identifying all of my personalities, their individual traits and mannerisms, their characteristics." He looked down at the book. "The stuff in there." He twisted his fingers together, quickly pulled them apart, rested his hands at his side, then moved them to his lap, not sure what to do with them. "Without him, I might be locked up somewhere now or, more likely, dead. You gotta understand, I was completely lost when he found me. I had this sickness, but I wasn't aware of it. I blacked out constantly, lost time. I couldn't hold down a job. I'd black out on the bus on my way to work and wake up again hours or sometimes days later, either back home or in some strange place. I remember once back in 1980, I was working for a pest-control company, spraying houses, in Buffalo. I carried my gear into this little duplex, and then I was in Chicago. Just like that. Three days gone. My clothes all muddy. I woke up on a bench with no memory of how I got there. My wallet was empty. I knew I'd had sixty-three dollars in there. I didn't know if I spent the money or it got stolen. That kind of thing happened to me a lot. It happened so often, the blackouts became my normal. When I'd wake up, I'd just try to pick up where I'd left off. When Doc Fitzgerald found me, I'd been arrested for breaking and entering. I'd woken up in a house outside of Scranton, and the owner came home and found me in her bed. She nearly shot me. She didn't know who I was, and I had no memory of how I got there. I tried to get out, but she had already called the police. I blacked out again in the car on the way to the station, and when I woke up, Doc Fitzgerald was there. Two more days were missing. Apparently I kept giving the police different names when they tried to interview me. They said my accent kept changing, from Boston to New York to Irish. Said I pretended to be a woman at some point. The court-appointed attorney called Doc Fitzgerald for a consult, figured I'd had some kind of crack-up."

Longtin looked Vela dead in the eye for a moment, then turned away again. "That was lucky for me. Like I said, I'd probably be dead if it weren't for him. If someone in prison didn't kill me, I might have done it myself. I was very suicidal back then."

"You weren't aware of the other personalities," Vela said.

Longtin shook his head. "Nope. No idea. That came later, after Doc Fitzgerald identified them all. He convinced the courts I wasn't fit for trial and got me transferred to a facility in upstate New York, near the school where he taught."

"Do you recall the name of the facility?"

He studied the notes again, his eyes drifting around the living room. The answer wasn't there, though. "Something British— Essex House, Lennox House..."

Gimble said, "Was it Windham Hall?"

Longtin considered this, then shook his head. "No, I think it was Essex. I was heavily medicated back then, especially when he first brought me in. Prior to that, I had been self-medicating with pot, alcohol, LSD, painkillers, anything I could get my hands on. It seems stupid looking back on it, but at the time I felt that if I drugged myself to the point of passing out, I wasn't losing time. I was in control. I'd wake up in the same place." He waved a hand through the air. "They had to get all that crap out of my system, detox me, before Doc Fitzgerald could start a proper medication regimen."

Gimble found it odd that the man could piece together such a cohesive history yet had to refer to notes to figure out what he'd done a few hours ago. His gaze bounced all over the room. He couldn't maintain eye contact.

"Do you take anything now?" Vela asked.

"Not for nearly twenty years," Longtin told him. "Not even a drink. The notes keep me straight, and I try to live a clean life, keep to myself." He looked down at the book. "Early on, Doc Fitzgerald discovered my shifts in personality were triggered by stress or changes in my environment. Each person living inside me was unique, manufactured by my mind to handle a particular type of situation. Mary handled love, Joey was a fighter, Kevin was good at math, solving problems...thirteen different people all living in this one body. Each would come forward when I needed them, then retreat and rest when I didn't. They'd take turns."

"They'd step to the mark," Vela said.

Longtin nodded, scratching at his thinning hair. "Yeah."

Vela glanced over at Gimble, then back at the man in the chair. "Who is on the mark right now?"

For the first time, Longtin smiled. "That question isn't as easy to answer as it used to be."

CHAPTER SEVENTY-EIGHT

WRITTEN STATEMENT, MEGAN FITZGERALD

Michael picked up one of the cassettes and fidgeted with the tape, absentmindedly winding it with the tip of his little finger. "I don't remember almost any of the conversations on these tapes. I don't remember what happened in that motel room when I was a kid. Same with the notes for all my sessions with Dr. Bart—according to these files, we spoke at least three times each week, sometimes more. I remember a few of our sessions, but once he started medicating me, everything got blurry. There are hundreds of hours accounted for here, and I barely remember any of it. How can I be missing so much?"

I squeezed his hand in mine again.

Michael's voice dropped low, and for the first time, he sounded like the kid on those tapes. "Megan, my missing time, the headaches, the blackouts...does that mean it worked?"

I was shaking my head before he even got the entire question out. "No way. That's not possible. You can't just mind-fuck someone and create multiple personalities."

Michael dug Jeffery Longtin's file out of the pile at his feet and opened it next to his own. "Our histories are nearly identical—both of us lost our fathers at a very young age. Neither of us was in a stable home. My mother was a drug addict. From what it says here, Jeffery was removed from his home twice as a child when his mother was arrested for prostitution and heroin use. Both our mothers were with dirtbags. Both of us were abused. Jeffery only learned he was abused after Dr. Bart found a personality within him, this Kevin, who was able to talk about it—Jeffery himself had no memory of the things his stepfather did to him."

Michael was quiet for nearly a minute, then forced himself to go on, but he covered his face with both hands, muffling the words. "Megan, I don't remember the things Max did to me. Not one. I didn't know those things happened until Dr. Bart told me. He assured me they happened. He gave me graphic details and reminded me of it nearly every time we talked."

"Maybe you weren't abused at all. He might have just made it up," I offered. "Dr. Bart was deranged. I can see him doing that just to observe how you'd react."

Michael sighed and shook his head. "I pulled the police reports a few years ago. It wasn't easy, but they had to release them to me. The reports said there were clear indications of sexual abuse. There was evidence of scarring, repetitive abuses over an extended period. There were photographs. Just like Dr. Bart said on that tape. He might have made up some of the things he told me, but there's no way he faked a police report. Or the court orders. Occam's razor—the simplest explanation is usually the correct one. I was abused. I blocked it out. But what happened to me during those blackouts?" His palm fell on the Longtin file. "We know what happened to Jeffery Longtin."

"You're saying you're Mitchell. You're really saying that? You're willing to accept that?" I wasn't buying it. No way. I'd known Michael my entire life; I would have seen it. I would have seen *something*. "Even if I were willing to believe that, what are the odds you would be placed..." As I said the words, it clicked. "You went to Windham Hall first."

"Windham Hall placed me with Dr. Bart. Maybe that wasn't a coincidence."

"You think he had someone there watching out for a case like Jeffery's?"

"Roland Eads worked at Windham Hall." He reached into the back seat and pulled a sheaf of paper from his bag. "I found these at Roland's house. They're visitation logs. According to the time stamps, Dr. Bart went back to that place several times a month for years. His last visit was only three weeks ago."

"Why would Roland have them? He busted you out of jail, remember? If he was part of some conspiracy, working with Dr. Bart to somehow cover it up, why would he help you?"

" 'This is what you paid me to do,' " Michael muttered.

"What?"

"That's what Roland Eads said when I asked him why he was helping me. Right before..."

"Before? Before what? Before someone shot him? You said someone shot him." I slowed the car as we came to a stoplight. Rain began to pelt the windshield. I found the switch for the wipers and turned them on.

Michael had gone silent again; he was looking down at the footwell and fidgeting with his watch.

I turned and glared at him. "Michael, you said *someone* shot him," I repeated. "Someone else."

His voice was thin again. Childlike. "I see things some-times, Meg, things that aren't always real."

CHAPTER SEVENTY-NINE

GIMBLE

WE'RE ALL ON THE mark now," Longtin said. "I guess that's the simplest way to look at it. When Doc Fitzgerald started treating me, I wasn't aware of the different people living inside my body. Many of them weren't aware of each other. He described all my personalities as living in this giant room, a room so big that even if they shouted, they couldn't hear each other. A room too dark to see. In the center was a single spotlight. Whoever was on the mark stood there. If they left, someone else would take their place. Only one personality talked to everybody, and that was Kevin. A few months into treatment, Doc Fitzgerald found Kevin. He eventually convinced him to bring some of the other personalities forward. And over time, they all got to know each other. Then he began a process he called fusion. As he identified each personality, he'd fuse them with my core. Over time, Mary became part of Jeffery, then Joey...all thirteen, one at a time. He told me it was like the pieces of a puzzle slowly coming together to create one image, one core personality. Jeffery's."

"You're speaking about yourself in the third person, do you realize that?" Vela asked.

"I am?"

"Yes."

Longtin glanced at Gimble, offered an uncomfortable smile, then turned back to Vela. "I do that sometimes."

Gimble understood. The look on Vela's face said it all.

This man wasn't cured at all.

Outside, heavy raindrops began to beat on the window and the metal roof of the house.

Vela leaned in closer. "Jeffery, you said Dr. Fitzgerald never meant to cure you, that he only wanted to understand what made you this way. Did he figure that out?"

Longtin nodded.

"Did he share that with you?"

Longtin bit his lower lip. "Kevin told him."

"The dominant personality? The one who spoke to all the others?"

He nodded again. "I didn't remember it. I couldn't. Or I didn't want to. I suppose that was the real reason." He peeled a blank note from the Post-it pad on the table and began to fold it and unfold it. "My father died when I was two, car accident. And my mother remarried about two years later. My stepfather did things to me. He'd take me to this abandoned barn on the property next to our house. I like to think she didn't know, but looking back on it, I don't understand how she couldn't. I . . . I didn't remember any of it, not until Kevin. Kevin told Doc Fitzgerald all about it. He hadn't forgotten anything. Then Doc Fitzgerald told me. My mind would just shut down, and I'd black out, or at least I thought that's what happened. Kevin said I wasn't blacking out at all—he just stepped in to take the abuse because I couldn't. When it was over, he'd go away again."

Longtin wiped a tear from the corner of his eye. "My mother couldn't have known, right? Who would . . . she just couldn't . . ."

"Probably not," Vela said, although he didn't sound very convincing.

Longtin shook it off and went on. "Once Doc Fitzgerald figured out what had caused my personalities to split, his treatment shifted. I didn't see this at the time. I couldn't. Between the medications and the blackouts, I still had trouble focusing. He became fixated. He told me it was important I remembered every moment of that abuse, every horrific thing my stepfather did, and Doc Fitzgerald would push for it. The work he had done, the fusion, all began to unravel. Kevin got protective, told the others not to trust the doctor, said none of us should. He even told me—and Kevin *rarely* spoke directly to me. Mary suggested we all stop taking the medications, so we did that That only made Doc Fitzgerald angry. He instructed the nurses to inject my medications rather than administer them in pill form. I was confined to my room . . ."

As his voice trailed off, his eyes shifted to the floor.

"You're remembering something," Vela said. More of a statement than a question.

Longtin nodded. "My room at the treatment center. He put me on restriction so I couldn't leave. I couldn't watch television. The TV set was in the common room, and I wasn't allowed to go there. He took away my books. The only window was this small little slit in the door to the hallway. He covered it up from the outside so I couldn't see anything, and then he'd turn out my lights. The room would go pitch-black. He didn't allow other patients or members of the staff to see me. He began to administer my medications on his own. He delivered my meals too, but he didn't stick to the schedule. At least, I don't think he did. Sometimes it felt like I went days without food. I'd get so thirsty. I think Kevin and some of the others took turns on the mark to make it all bearable. I began to black out again, lose time. I don't know how long this went on, but at some point someone in the center must have figured out what was happening and put an end to it. I didn't see Doc Fitzgerald again for months. My attorney came to see me, said the court considered my time for the breaking and entering to be served, and told me I was free to go. When she heard what he had done to me, she filed the malpractice claim on my behalf. She got me into a halfway house, even helped me find this place when the settlement money came in. She was a very good person."

"What was her name?" Vela asked.

Longtin's eyes narrowed and his brows pulled together as he searched his memories. After about twenty seconds he gave up, shook his head, and rolled up his right sleeve. He looked down at a tattoo on his forearm. A name written in thin black script: *Margaret Tepper.*

CHAPTER EIGHTY

WRITTEN STATEMENT, MEGAN FITZGERALD

"Are you saying you shot Roland Eads?"

"I'm saying I don't know who shot him. I can't remember any details. I had one of my headaches. It started back at my apartment and just got worse as the night went on. I remember hearing the shot, looking over, seeing him dead. The gun was in his lap. I thought I saw somebody, but I don't know for sure, not anymore. Everything is just so hazy."

A car beeped behind us.

The light was green.

I peered through the strengthening storm and stomped on the accelerator. The wheels spun on the wet pavement, caught, and we started forward again. "He said you paid him to bust you out of police custody."

"I have no memory of that either. I'd never met him before. At least, I don't remember meeting him."

"So you think what? This alternate personality did it? Paid Roland, shot Roland . . . you think this was all Mitchell?"

"Erma Eads recognized me too, and I had no idea who she was," Michael pointed out. "How else do you explain that?" Michael was rubbing at his temples again. His eyes were squeezed shut.

"Are you getting one of your headaches now?"

He nodded.

"Take another dorozapine. Where are they?"

"I don't want to."

"Take one," I insisted. "Whatever this is, we need to hold it off."

A sign for Mark Twain National Forest came up on our left. We were close now.

Michael pulled the pill bottle from his pocket and took one. I fought the urge to ask him to open his mouth and show me that he'd actually swallowed.

The bottle went back into his pocket. He wouldn't look at me. "That would mean that I killed Alyssa Tepper, I just don't remember doing it."

"No way."

"Meg, she had a key to my apartment. She kept some of her things there. The police found them. They found a phone in my trash with messages between the two of us going back months. They found my clothes at her place. *My clothes*, Meg. Clothes I recognized. There were pictures of the two of us together. There was a video—a damn sex tape. It was me. Me and her. How else do you explain any of that? I'd clearly been with this girl for months, and I don't remember a second of it."

"You remember going to the movies the day you found her body, right?"

"I don't remember the movie, not really. I fell asleep."

"But you remember going?" I pressed. "You remember being at the theater. Waking up there, leaving there, going to the grocery store after...that gives you an ali—"

"I lost time, Meg," he said. "The movie was two hours and thirty-eight minutes long and I barely remember the opening credits. I had plenty of time to go home and—"

"I'm not gonna believe you got up from a movie, ran home, drowned your girlfriend in the bathtub real quick, then slid back in to catch the ending."

"If I needed to create an alibi, going to a movie and sneaking out makes perfect sense."

"Assuming you're the kind of person who kills people, why would you want to kill your girl? I mean, who are you going to bang on the off-weeks if you put the gas to your steady girlfriend? That's just poor planning."

"I'm serious, Meg!"

"So am I!"

He fell silent for a second. "You're asking the wrong question. What we really need to figure out is why *Mitchell* would want to kill her."

Now *I* was getting a headache.

The GPS dinged, and I made another left. Longtin's house wasn't on the main road. It was up some side road so small, it turned into a mud track a quarter mile into the woods. We were less than a minute away, and I couldn't see a damn thing.

"Pull over here," Michael said.

"What?"

"We can't just drive right on up. I'm gonna check it out first."

"Not a chance. We're going together."

Between the heavy rain, the muddy road, and the low overhanging branches, we were moving at a crawl. Michael opened his door and jumped out. He disappeared into the trees before I could stop him.

CHAPTER EIGHTY-ONE

GIMBLE

AT THE MENTION OF the name Margaret Tepper, Sammy glanced up from his MacBook for the first time in nearly an hour. He exchanged a quick look with Gimble and Vela. "I'm checking, hold on—"

It took him only a moment. "She was Alyssa Tepper's mother. Looks like she passed away about ten years ago, breast cancer."

Gimble turned to Longtin. "I asked you if you knew the name Alyssa Tepper, and you said you didn't."

"You asked me that? I'm sorry."

Gimble stood, started pacing.

Vela reached into his back pocket and took out the feather they had found in the book. "Have you ever seen this type of feather?"

Longtin's face went white. He reached for the feather, his hand shaking. "Where did you get that?"

Vela ignored the question. "You recognize it?"

Longtin's fingers closed around the feather. He raised it to his cheek and stroked his skin with it. His eyes filled with tears again. "Early on at the treatment center, before I was confined to my room, I'd walk the grounds. I found a baby sparrow at the base of a willow tree. It fell from a nest about nine feet up. Doc Fitzgerald let me keep it, nurse it back to health. I had to feed it with an eyedropper for nearly a month, but eventually it got better and we had this little ceremony where I released it back into the wild." He paused, wiping at his eyes with the back of his hand. "At the settlement hearing, Doc gave me a feather just like this, but it had dried blood on it. He told me, 'Broken things don't always deserve a second chance.'"

With a loud pop, the power went out.

The small cabin went dark.

The only remaining light came from the fire, which was nothing but glowing embers now.

A single shot echoed outside, and Gimble whipped around to the window.

CHAPTER EIGHTY-TWO

WRITTEN STATEMENT, MEGAN FITZGERALD

Michael was out the door.

One moment he was there and the next he was gone, disappearing into the wind, rain, and dark like he'd never existed at all. His door thudded shut behind him; the woods swallowed him whole, and I was alone. The steady thump of the windshield wipers was the only sound louder than my own breathing.

One beat.

Two.

The windshield cracked.

A small hole appeared with a pop in the top corner, just below my visor, and things began to move in slow motion. A spiderweb of cracks spread from the hole outward.

Something slammed into the leather just above the armrest in my door. Another hole there too. I felt something—a bullet, I realized—rush past my head, a thin streak of warm air.

I threw the SUV into reverse and hit the gas. The wheels spun, throwing mud, and the car lurched backward. I scraped a tree and almost went into the woods, but by some miracle— or maybe my latent badass driving abilities—I managed to stay on the path.

Another hole in the windshield.

My left arm was snapped back.

Then searing heat halfway between my elbow and shoulder.

The next shot hit the SUV in the back, the driver's-side rear tire.

The SUV slumped to the left.

When I hit the gas again, the steering was off, the car pulling hard to the left. I gave it more gas, too much. I'd dug a hole in the mud, and within seconds I knew I wasn't going anywhere. The next shot, the one that took out the other rear tire, confirmed that.

My left arm was a screaming, bloody mess, so I tugged at the door handle with my right hand. When the door opened, I tumbled out into the muddy grass and weeds and lay still. Who knows what kind of gross bugs were down there. I felt something wriggle under my palm. I pretty much have to be dying or sedated to lie around in the wilderness with shit crawling on me, so you know it was bad.

After a few seconds, I tried to get to my feet.

Another shot.

The bullet smacked into the mud less than an inch from my hand.

I couldn't see where the shots were coming from; it was too dark. Even when lightning crackled across the sky, I saw nothing, only the giant trees leaning over me.

When I tried to move again, there was another shot.

Somewhere, through the rain, I heard a single word:

"Don't."

CHAPTER EIGHTY-THREE

GIMBLE

GIMBLE TOUCHED HER EARBUD. "Garrison, do you copy?"

No response came back. "Garrison?"

Vela looked up at her. "I can hear you in mine."

Sammy's pale face glowed in the light of his MacBook screen. "I can too."

"What's happening?" Longtin said. He sat up stiffly, his head swiveling around.

Gimble's hand went to the gun on her hip. She stepped over to the side of the window, pressed tight against the wall, and looked out from the corner. "This is Special Agent Gimble. If anyone copies, please respond."

"Was that a gunshot or thunder?" Longtin asked. "The generator usually kicks in when the power goes out. Why isn't the generator coming on?"

"I can't see anything," Gimble said. "It's raining too hard."

Sammy said, "Garrison has six people out there. Even with the rain, no way all their comms are down."

"Where's your breaker box?" Vela asked Longtin.

Longtin's eyes had glazed over.

Vela snapped his fingers. "Mr. Longtin?"

Longtin shook his head. "Breaker box, right. It's on the side of the house. Out the front door, to the left, around the corner."

"Is the generator there too?"

He nodded.

"Stay off the comms." Gimble drew her gun and started for the front door. "I'm going out there. The rest of you stay here. Keep away from the windows."

"I'm still connected to the satellite," Sammy said. "Do you want me to call for backup?"

Gimble nodded, then slipped out the front door into the pouring rain as another shot cracked through the night.

CHAPTER EIGHTY-FOUR

WRITTEN STATEMENT, MEGAN FITZGERALD

I don't know who yelled it. Sounded like a man.

I leaned against the bullet-pocked SUV completely still, my eyes fixed on that last bullet hole in the ground. In the glow of the headlights, I watched it fill with rainwater and disappear into the mud like it had never been there.

My arm throbbed; I couldn't even look at it.

My left leg was behind me, my right folded under me. My right arm was holding up much of my weight, helping me keep my head and shoulders up, and it began to twitch, wobble.

A rock flew through the air and landed at my side with a muddy splash. A piece of paper was secured to it with two rubber bands. "Seriously?" I looked in the direction it had come, up and to my right, but saw nothing except a steep hill covered in brush and weeds. More trees. More woods.

With my good hand, I picked up the rock, peeled off the rubber bands with my thumb and forefinger, and unfolded the note, pulling at the edge of the paper with my teeth. An ear-bud fell out, dropped into the mud. It was tiny, no bigger than a hearing aid—I almost lost it. The words of the note smeared as the unrelenting rain smacked the paper.

Put the radio in your ear. Stand. Walk toward the cabin. Call your brother's name. Anything else = bullet to the head.

CHAPTER EIGHTY-FIVE

GIMBLE

THE RAIN PELTED HER. Tiny icy needles jabbing at her exposed skin.

When had it gotten so dark?

Gimble knelt just outside the door and tightened her grip on the Glock. She waited for her eyes to adjust to the dark. Shadows became shapes; shapes became trees, branches, a stack of logs next to a picnic table off in the distance, an ax buried in a stump with its handle pointing at the black sky.

Lightning splintered dark clouds, followed by the deep rumble of rolling thunder.

Gimble darted around the left side of the house in a crouch, gun leading. She smelled propane before she came upon the generator. Someone had cut the line, and the wet air stank of rotten eggs from the gas.

The door to the breaker panel was open. All the breakers were flipped to the off position. A thick wire jutted out from the main switch at the top of the box, ran down the wall, and disappeared into the damaged gas pipe. Someone had rigged it—if you flipped the breaker, you sent a charge down into the gas. Whoever had done it hadn't taken the time to hide his handiwork; it was left as a warning, or maybe it was a decoy—disable this little trap and a not-so-obvious second one blows the whole thing when the power clicks back on.

Gimble didn't touch any of it. Her eyes had already moved on to the body slumped on the opposite side of the generator.

The name on his black Kevlar vest was MONTGOMERY. His throat had been slashed, left to right, from behind—Gimble had spent enough time with the coroner to recognize the wound. The cut was fresh, the rain hadn't had time to wash away the blood. Probably within the past ten to fifteen minutes, at most.

Gimble raised a finger to her earbud. "Garrison, do you copy?"

Silence.

"This is Special Agent Gimble to any U.S. marshal, respond."

Nothing.

Gimble slipped her Glock back into the holster and took Montgomery's weapon, a Heckler and Koch MP5. Standard-issue; the other marshals would be carrying the same. It was a compact nine-millimeter submachine gun—not the source of the shots she had heard. Those had sounded like they came from a high-powered rifle. Had Garrison brought a sharpshooter and not told her? No, he would have said something. It had to be Kepler.

Remaining low, Gimble rounded the corner of the cabin, ran to the side yard, and ducked behind the large log pile. She found another slain marshal lying in the grass, partially hidden behind a tree. His throat was also cut; there was a second stab wound near his kidney. She took the magazine from his MP5 along with both his spares and dropped them in her pockets. She slung his weapon over her shoulder and tapped her earbud again. "Garrison? Any marshal, do you copy?" Gimble said, fighting to keep her voice from cracking. Her heart felt like it was going to burst through her chest.

"Garrison isn't available, Agent Gimble. Would you like me to take a message and have him get back to you? It may be a while."

Kepler's voice.

Gimble pressed her back tight against the logs and peered at the trees surrounding the house. No light; she saw nothing but shadows. The marshal beside her had a Maglite clipped to his belt. She snatched it up with her free hand but didn't dare switch it on.

Kepler said, "I count six, does that seem about right to you? Three around the cabin, one back on the road near the start of the driveway. Another with your vehicles, and then your friend Garrison wandering around here in the woods. Did I miss anyone?"

Here in the woods. Gimble's eyes went back to the tree line.

Lightning cracked across the sky, a bright flash, then nothing again.

"You shouldn't have come here, Agent Gimble. You put your people in danger for no reason. I don't want to hurt you or your friends. I'm nearly done with my work. You just keep getting in the way."

Gimble tapped her earbud. "Lay down your weapons and step out into the clearing with your hands on your head, Kepler."

"Or what?" Kepler laughed. "You'll repeat what you just said? We both know the score here. You're a lousy liar. Send out Longtin. He's all I want. Send him out and you can wait in the cabin with the other two for your backup to arrive. The nearest sheriff's station is thirty-seven minutes away. That means they're thirty-two minutes out if they left the second you called, which I imagine was about the time the lights went off. Of course, the rain might slow them down a little."

Another shot rang out. The rifle again.

"Shooting at ghosts, Gimble? Who is that? Did I miss someone?"

Gimble had assumed Kepler had the rifle. If it wasn't Kepler, then who? His sister?

"Send out Longtin and I'll let your shooter live too. I think enough people have bled today, don't you?"

"You know I can't do that."

"You're a stickler for rules. I get it. Let's be honest, though—Longtin isn't really contributing to society. Frankly, he's a drain. You've got Doc Fitzgerald sending him money, and he also gets food stamps, welfare...who knows what kind of handouts this guy picks up when he runs into town. Don't ask him; he won't be able to tell you. His brain is Swiss cheese. I just killed six of your people—six well-educated, useful citizens, gone. Just the thought of it made me a little sick. Felt like the scale tipped a bit in the wrong direction, but it had to be done. I gotta draw the line somewhere, though. You've got a psychologist in there, a computer wiz, yourself. I really don't want to kill the rest of you, not for him. Don't make me do that. It's not worth it. They don't pay you enough, none of you. Send out Longtin, I let the rest of you walk. There's honor in saving your own skin. There's none in dying for a scumbag like that."

Gimble peered into the trees, her eyes searching for the slightest of movements, but if Kepler was close, nothing betrayed his position.

She did the only thing she could think of. She tapped her earbud. "I'm not dying today. Let me walk back into the cabin to talk to my friends. I'll see what I can do."

CHAPTER EIGHTY-SIX

WRITTEN STATEMENT, MEGAN FITZGERALD

The note fell from my fingers into a puddle at my side, and the last of the words melted in the rainwater.

The next bullet hit the ground less than two inches from my left foot.

Another cracked into the metal of the door to the right of my head.

Warning shots.

I looked down at my black dress. An Oscar de la Renta I'd bought at the airport. Yeah, the money wasn't mine, I used Dr. Rose's plastic, but that dress was a work of art and now it was ruined because some lunatic was shooting at me in a muddy hole in the sticks. I was missing a shoe too. I didn't know if it came off in the car or when I not so gracefully exited. I didn't see it anywhere. I shook the other shoe off.

I twisted my fingers around the hem of the dress and tore off a two-foot-long strip of the soft wool fabric. I pinched one end between my torso and my damaged arm, then wrapped it around as tight as I could. The bullet had grazed me, leaving a trench in my arm. Whoever had shot me must have had a collection of Boy Scout badges for anything that involved excellent aim. He was watching me, letting me tie my dress around my arm.

I tied a knot in the material, pulled it tight with my teeth.

Stand. Walk toward the cabin. Call your brother's name. Anything else = bullet to the head.

I slowly stood. White washed over my vision. I moved toward the cabin with tiny steps, my toes sinking in the mud. Michael's name dropped from my lips.

CHAPTER EIGHTY-SEVEN

GIMBLE

I THINK I'D PREFER you stay right there," Kepler replied over Gimble's earbud.

Remaining low, Gimble pointed Montgomery's MP5 toward the tree line and slowly swept it back and forth. Rain rolled off the barrel, over the stock, and she fought the urge to wipe off her hands or readjust her grip. "Where's your sister?" Gimble said. "That was a neat little trick she pulled back at the truck stop with all the alarms. That was her idea, right? From what Dobbs tells me, you're not smart enough to come up with something like that."

Gimble saw a movement out of the corner of her left eye. She spun around, leveled the gun, and pulled the trigger three times in quick succession. *Pop! Pop! Pop!*

The reports echoed off the trees, the log pile beside her, muffled only by the rain.

"Not even close, Agent."

"Can't blame a girl for trying."

The echo of the shots faded and died, lost in the storm.

"Megan!" Gimble shouted. "If you're out there, it's not too late to turn yourself in and walk away from all this. Don't let your brother drag you down with him. It's not worth it. You're throwing your entire life away, and for what? Unless you killed those people, unless you killed someone tonight, I can protect you. I can help you. I can keep you safe! Your brother has dug himself a very deep hole, but you don't need to get caught in it. Pulling a couple fire alarms, that's misdemeanors, a slap on the wrist. Aiding and abetting, on your clean record, I can make that go away. Help us bring in Michael. Your father clearly thought he was ill. Let me get him the help he needs. You obviously care for him—do the right thing!"

As Gimble spoke, she squinted back at the trees, searching. She expected him to move while she was speaking. They usually did. If the sister was still helping him, she might be circling around right now—that's what she would do. Between the rain and gusts of wind, Gimble was damn near deaf and blind. This was no good. She needed to get back inside the cabin.

The front door was about thirty feet away.

She imagined Kepler holding one of the other MP5s, waiting for her to make that run. Thinking that's what she would do.

She tapped her earbud. "Why are you killing them, Kepler? What did Fitzgerald do to you? Why take it out on his patients?"

The moment his voice came back over the comm, she pulled the earbud out, held it away from her head, and closed her eyes, attempting to hear Kepler's actual voice from somewhere in the trees, pinpoint him. She heard only his tinny voice through the small speaker, though.

"You finally pieced that much together? Was it the book? Is that what clued you in? I've dropped so many hints for you over the years, did everything but write out a manifesto. I'm really not a manifesto kind of guy. Maybe I'm just crazy. That would be the easy way out, right? Or maybe I'm not. Maybe there are reasons.

Damn good reasons. Tell you what—give me Longtin and I'll fill you in on everything. We can chat about it while we wait for your backup to arrive."

"I can't give you Longtin."

"I could have killed you already, you and the rest of your team. Longtin dies either way. Are you going to make me do that? If you'd rather go that route, we'll need to get started. By my clock, we've got only about twenty-one minutes."

Six shots.

They pelted the log pile from the left to right, sending shards of wood through the air.

Before the echo died on the last shot, Gimble had her weapon pointing in the direction the shots had come from; her finger flipped the switch to full auto, and she unloaded the magazine with an arcing sweep over the trees as she ran toward the cabin through the mud and rain.

CHAPTER EIGHTY-EIGHT

GIMBLE

GIMBLE FLEW THROUGH THE door, slammed it behind her, and dropped to the floor near the corner window. She expected Kepler to fire, but he didn't. The logs constructing the cabin were at least ten inches thick. "We should be able to hold out in here; just stay away from the doors and windows."

Sammy glared at her, his face pasty white. Both he and Vela had heard everything on their comms. "He's bluffing, right?"

Gimble crossed the room, set one of the MP5s on the table beside him, then stacked the spare magazines beside it. "I found two dead marshals out there, both with slit throats. There's no sign of the others. I think we have to assume he killed them. So no, I don't think he's bluffing."

"We can try and get to the vehicles," Vela suggested.

"Garrison said he moved them to a logging road. We don't know exactly where, and Kepler probably has the keys." She scooped up Longtin's shotgun, handed it to Vela, then turned to Longtin. "Do you have any other weapons?"

Longtin didn't move, not at first. When she asked again, he only looked at her.

"It's the stress," Vela said. "I think it's triggering some kind of episode. He's retreating."

To Sammy, Gimble asked, "Did you reach someone for backup?"

"The local sheriff. But like Kepler said, they're more than thirty minutes out. He said it could take closer to an hour if they run into flooding. The St. Louis field office is trying to get a chopper in the air, but they need a break in the weather. Wind gusts are topping forty knots. They're grounded. They're allowed to fly if they can get above five hundred feet, but they can't take off or land in wind like that."

Gimble was looking back at the windows. "Get me some sheets. We need to cover these."

"What about the Honda outside . . ." Sammy's words trailed off as he rose and started toward the bedroom.

Gimble quickly dismissed the idea. "Too exposed. That's probably what he's waiting for us to do. We're better off staying in here."

Another rifle shot.

"If that's not Kepler, who is it?" Vela asked, turning to the window. "He's firing from a fixed position. The shots aren't getting closer. If all the marshals are dead, who is this guy even shooting at?"

"Could be a poacher shooting, maybe, or a hunter. We get a lot of those up here." The words came from Longtin, but the gravel had left his voice. He sounded like a child speaking.

Vela's brow furrowed. He knelt in front of the man. "Who is on the mark?"

Longtin didn't reply, only stared at him with watery eyes.

Sammy returned with a thick quilt. "It's got to be one of Garrison's people," he said. He helped Gimble tear the corners and secure the blanket by tying the ends to a beam above the window.

"Why else would he still be shooting? We're in here. That means he's targeting Kepler, not us."

"Kepler didn't sound too concerned."

"If it was one of Garrison's, he'd respond on the comm, compromised or not," Gimble said, lifting up the bottom of the quilt so she could see outside. "Who else would be targeting Kepler?"

None of them had an answer.

"I think I see Kepler," Gimble said. "Northwest corner. Look across the lawn about five feet to the left of the picnic table."

Sammy followed her gaze through the rain and swooping branches. "He's just standing out there."

Gimble checked the magazine on her MP5—six shots left, but she had the spares. "He might be trying to draw fire. He's about two hundred yards out. That's the edge of the effective range for these weapons."

"We don't know where the sister is. Maybe he's just a distraction."

Gimble snapped the lock on the window and raised it several inches, just enough to get the muzzle out. She lined up the shot—Kepler ducked to the left and disappeared behind the trees. "Shit."

"I think he's circling around," Sammy said.

Gimble looked down at the gun in her hands. "Have you used one of these before?"

"Not since training at Quantico."

"There's not much to it." She pressed a button and released the magazine into her palm. "To reload, you drop your expended magazine, pull back the charging handle like this, slap in a new magazine, then slide the charging handle forward again. Done. This switch on the side is your new best friend—safety is on in this position, this is auto, this is full-auto. Point and shoot. Understood?"

Sammy had never looked so uncomfortable.

"You'll be okay." She nodded toward the extra MP5 on the table.

"Take that one, and one of the spare magazines too, then find a window on the other side of the house. Cover it like this one if there's nothing on it. Don't waste ammunition. Only take a shot if it's clean. All we need to do is hold him off until our backup gets here. No heroics, Sammy. We just want him to know we have guns on him if he tries to approach."

Sammy swallowed, then awkwardly picked up the extra gun and magazine and disappeared down the narrow hallway into the bedroom.

"Fifteen minutes, by my count," Kepler said over the comm. "How's our boy doing? I imagine he's not much help under pressure."

Gimble glanced over at Longtin. His breathing seemed shallow.

Kepler said, "Can you ask him a question for me? Ask him how much propane he's got in the tank for the generator. Looks like it holds at least two hundred and fifty gallons."

Another shot rang out. Not the rifle this time. From the sound, Gimble knew it came from one of the MP5s.

"I think I can hit it from here. I missed it by only a few feet with that one. I wonder if it would go up like they do in the movies. Some kind of big fireball. That would be cool, wouldn't it? Save me the trouble of getting in that cabin. No need for Longtin to come outside in this nasty weather. Seems like a win-win for everyone."

Another shot. This one dug into the side of the cabin with a deep thump.

Longtin twitched, began to hyperventilate, his gaze blank.

Vela knelt at the man's side and snapped his fingers about an inch in front of Longtin's face. "Jeffery, can you hear me?"

"I'm fine," he answered. He didn't look fine, though; not at all. His pupils were dilated, and he wasn't blinking. His skin had taken on a damp, feverish pallor.

Vela placed a hand under the man's shoulder and helped him to his feet. "Let's splash some water on your face." He led him to the small bathroom and sat him down on the edge of the bathtub. "Take deep breaths, Jeff. Hold it for a count of three, then let it out. Think you can do that?"

Longtin nodded and drew in a breath.

"Good. That's good."

Some of the color returned to Longtin's face.

Gimble shouted to Sammy from the other room, something about spotting Kepler a hundred feet over from where she'd seen him last. Vela closed the bathroom door, sealing out their voices, and knelt on the floor in front of Longtin. "You were very helpful before, Jeff. Those things you told us. I'm sure that wasn't easy for you."

"He's going to kill me, isn't he?"

Vela forced a smile and shook his head. "That woman out there, Special Agent Gimble, she's one of the best I've ever worked with. She won't let him near you. He won't get in this house."

"I'm glad he's dead," Longtin said softly. "Doc Fitzgerald. He was a bad man."

"Those things you told us about how he studied you and your illness, how he wanted to re-create it—have you ever told anyone else that?"

Longtin's eyes had gone blank again, his gaze fixed on the floor.

Vela snapped his fingers. "Jeffery?"

"Only the girl, when she came to see me."

Vela frowned. "What girl? When was this?"

"She said Doc Fitzgerald would be very angry with me if he knew, but she said she wouldn't tell. She said it was a secret."

Longtin's voice had shifted again, gone back to a childlike tone. He looked up at Vela and smiled. "She said it was *our* secret."

"What was her name?"

Longtin's brow wrinkled as he tried to remember. "She had a silly name. It was a boy's name."

"Nick? Was it Nicki? Nicole?"

Longtin didn't reply. He looked back at the floor.

"Did you tell anyone else?"

"No."

"Even though it probably felt good to tell, you never told *anyone* else?"

Longtin shook his head.

"That's good, Jeff. That's really good." Vela reached into his jacket pocket and took out a hypodermic syringe and a small glass vial. "I'm going to give you something to help you relax. It will calm your nerves."

At the sight of the needle, Longtin shrank back against the tile wall. "I don't take meds, not anymore. I feel much better since I stopped. I don't need them."

Vela plunged the needle into the vial, drew up five milliliters, then snapped his finger against the tip to remove any air bubbles. "You look awfully stressed. This will help."

With years of skill and practice behind him, Vela moved quickly. The needle was in Longtin's neck, the plunger depressed, and the needle out again before the man could object.

Longtin pressed his hand against the tiny wound. "What is it?"

Vela placed the syringe and vial back in his pocket. "Potassium chloride. It will stop your heart, Jeffery. In a moment, you'll find peace." He smiled down at him. "Dr. Fitzgerald's work is so important, so close to conclusion. We'll always be grateful for your participation. I want you to know that."

Longtin's body spasmed. He fell off the edge of the bathtub. His right leg shot out and kicked at the wall.

Vela took a step back, removed the satellite phone from his pocket, and typed out a quick text:

Longtin dead. Call off your dog.

* * *

He pressed Send, returned the phone to his pocket, and opened the bathroom door. "I think he's having a heart attack! We need an ambulance!"

Sammy was yelling too—something about a girl covered in blood.

CHAPTER EIGHTY-NINE

GIMBLE

GIMBLE LOOKED OVER FROM her position at the window only long enough to make eye contact with Vela in the hallway behind her. "Can you help him?"

Vela shook his head. "I tried CPR, but without the proper equipment and medication, there's nothing I can do...could do...he's gone."

"Gimble!" Sammy called. "What do you want me to do about her? I think it's Megan!"

Gimble looked back out her own window. "What is she doing?"

"Just standing out there," Sammy replied. "She came out of the woods. Her left arm is covered in blood. Looks like she bandaged it with some kind of material."

"Does she have a weapon?"

"I don't see anything. She's crying. Something's wrong."

Another rifle shot.

"Oh, shit!" Sammy exclaimed.

"What is it?"

"Whoever is shooting pegged the ground a few inches from her feet. She's moving again. The shooter is driving her forward."

Gimble tapped her earbud. "Longtin's dead, Kepler. Heart attack, just now. Don't hurt Megan. There's no need to hurt anyone."

No reply.

She scrambled to her feet. "Vela, watch this window."

Before he could reply, she ran through the small cabin and found Sammy hunched down near a window in the bedroom; it was covered with a sheet. He lifted the corner and nodded at the glass.

Gimble looked out.

Definitely Megan Fitzgerald. Her dark hair was plastered to her head by the rain. She made no attempt to move it from her eyes. Her left arm hung limply at her side; streaks of blood ran from a makeshift bandage above her elbow to her outstretched fingertips. She wore a black dress, no shoes, and one of the most frightened expressions Gimble had ever seen on a person's face.

Another shot cracked through the air. The mud at the girl's feet splashed. She took several more steps.

"Who the fuck is shooting at her?"

Sammy shook his head.

Near the front of the cabin, another shot rang out. The bullet pinged off the metal propane tank.

"Jesus, we need to get out of here," Sammy muttered.

"That's what he wants," Gimble replied. "To make the tank explode, he'd need to hit it dead on, and he'd need a spark. It won't work. It's just a scare tactic."

"Well, it's working damn well. And this isn't a *he*," Sammy said. "We're dealing with a *they*. Unless Kepler is really fast and shooting both of those guns on opposite sides of the cabin, there are two people out there, maybe more. You said all the marshals are down?

He didn't do that on his own. He's not John Rambo, he's a truck driver from LA."

Outside, Megan stopped moving. She was saying something, but Gimble couldn't make it out.

Gimble hit her earbud again. "Kepler, who is shooting at your sister?" The words came out louder and faster than she'd meant them to; her emotions were getting the better of her.

When Kepler replied, his voice was the opposite of hers—slow, calm, nearly reserved. "Tell her to get in the car."

Gimble's eyes darted over to the red Honda sitting in the driveway about half a dozen steps from where Megan Fitzgerald stood.

Two more shots. The first came from the opposite side of the house; it ricocheted off the propane tank again. The second smacked into the earth less than a foot behind the girl.

Two shots.

Two different weapons.

Two shooters.

Megan yelped and took another step forward.

A third shot came a moment later and shattered the window. Both Gimble and Sammy fell back and went down, crouching low behind the wall. Shards of glass spilled around them. The wind yanked at the exposed sheet, snapping it outward and blowing it back in again, and the rain followed, nearly loud enough to drown out Megan's sobs.

"Tell her to get in the car," Kepler repeated.

Gimble's grip tightened on the MP5 still in her hands.

Sammy craned his neck toward the window. "Megan! He wants you to get in the car!"

Gimble shot him a look.

"Make him stop!"

"Get her in the car," Kepler said, his voice low.

"He said he'll shoot me!" Megan screamed. "Michael!"

Not "Michael said he'll shoot me," but "He said he'll shoot me."

"He won't!" Sammy shouted over the storm. "He wants you in the car. He won't hurt you, not if you get in the car!"

"Somebody is using Megan as bait, trying to draw Michael out," Gimble said under her breath.

"What? Why?" Sammy said, his eyes fixed on Megan.

"Gimble! I smell gas!"

This came from Vela in the other room. One of the shots must have punctured the tank.

This can't be happening, Gimble thought. "Kepler's got the MP5. Whoever has the rifle is trying to use Megan to get to Kepler," Gimble said. "Kepler's trying to get her out of the line of fire."

"Then what do we do?"

"I'm not letting her get away," Gimble replied. "I have no problem using her as bait."

Sammy shook his head. "No way." He peered back out into the storm. "Megan, do as he says! Get in the car!"

Megan sucked air in through slightly parted lips, then nodded quickly and wiped the snot from her nose with the back of her good hand. She took a step toward the Honda, froze, and looked at the woods.

"Keep going, Megan!" Sammy shouted.

Megan did. She took another step and another after that.

With each, Gimble waited for the crack of a rifle, but it didn't come.

Megan reached the car, put her trembling hand on the door handle.

"Tell her to get in and leave," Kepler said over the comm. "She shouldn't be here. She's not supposed to be here."

"Damn it, Gimble! We've got gas in the house!" Vela shouted from the other room.

Gimble ignored him, her fingers beginning to twitch on the side of her gun.

Sammy called, "Get in the car, Megan! Get the hell out of here! Now!"

Her eyes were wide, red, and puffy with tears. With one last look back at the woods, Megan yanked the car door open, scrambled inside, and pulled the door shut behind her. She became a dark silhouette behind the wheel, her shoulders shaking with sobs. Longtin must have left the keys in the ignition, because the motor sputtered and came to life with a puff of smoke from the exhaust.

Gimble exchanged a look with Sammy, then she stood, raised her weapon, and fired two quick shots at the Honda. The first missed; the second struck the right rear tire, and the car slumped to the side.

Gimble dropped back to her position under the window. "I'm not letting her go."

"Christ, Gimble!" Sammy was glaring at her.

"You shouldn't have done that," Kepler said over the comm.

Another shot pinged off the propane tank with the rattle of a rusty bell.

"Step out of the woods and turn yourself in, or my next bullet goes right through her," Gimble replied without any hesitation.

Another ping off the propane tank.

"You're a federal agent."

"People die in friendly fire all the time." Gimble pointed at her eyes, then at Sammy, then at the window. "With a mess like this, whatever I put in my report will end up being the final word. My people will cover for me."

Vela had been right. Gimble could smell gas now too.

A third shot rang out from an MP5 in the woods to the right. The bullet slammed into the passenger door of Longtin's car.

"Maybe I'll do it," Kepler said.

The Honda dropped into gear, lurched forward, started limping down Longtin's driveway, Megan clearly struggling with the wheel.

"You won't kill her," Kepler stated.

"I see him," Sammy said.

"Where?"

"Five o'clock. He's down low at the base of an oak just past the edge of the driveway, sighting on the propane."

They both rose up at the window, weapons high.

Neither fired a shot; the explosion came too fast.

CHAPTER NINETY

WRITTEN STATEMENT, MEGAN FITZGERALD

When I pulled the car door handle, I didn't actually expect it to be unlocked, but it was.

When I fell into the seat, I didn't expect the keys to be in the ignition, but there they were.

I definitely didn't expect the rust bucket of a Honda to start, but it did.

And all of these things happened while I waited for a bullet to rip through my chest and splatter my blood all over this cracked plastic faux-leather interior while an old eighties tune from Joan Jett blared from tired, rattling speakers.

The bullet didn't come when I started the car—although someone shot at the right rear tire—it didn't even come when I managed to get the Honda in gear and head down the driveway. That didn't mean it wouldn't.

When I tried to wiggle my left fingers, they barely twitched. My arm felt cold, like something just removed from the refrigerator, something detached and not my own.

My vision kept clouding, going white, then black, filling with floating specks that did not belong. My equilibrium was off. I felt like I was tipping to the left, then back again. I couldn't decide if I wanted to vomit or faint or both.

I had no business operating heavy machinery.

The Honda was an automatic, which was good. It didn't have power steering, which was bad. Between the slippery mud, the flat tire, and ruts in the path, the wheel kept yanking under my good hand and pulling in one direction or the other. I wanted to floor the gas and couldn't. Conditions forced me to move at a crawl.

I kept waiting for the next bullet.

I was maybe a third of the way back to the main road when I spotted someone in the rearview mirror—Michael, about a hundred feet back, darting across the path behind me, his light blue shirt a blur. He glanced at me and at the car and was gone a second later, back into the woods.

My foot hovered over the brake; I let the car coast.

Just that slight movement of my head as I looked in the rearview brought another flurry of white and then black over my vision.

Loss of blood. My rational mind weighed in from high up in the cheap seats. *You're gonna pass out.*

I turned the wipers on, and for some reason, this made me think of Mrs. Lutwig, my tenth-grade driver's ed teacher. I could see her sitting next to me with her lips pursed, slapping a solid check mark across the paper on her clipboard. She wasn't done with me, though. She nodded at the windshield. *What else, Ms. Fitzgerald?*

Oh, Christ, the headlights!

I saw the switch. My right hand reached up and over the steering column to the left side while my muddy knee held the wheel straight. I fumbled with the control, which felt thick and unwieldy under my fingers.

The headlights blazed on, cutting through the rain.

Michael was standing about twenty feet in front of the

Honda, his narrow eyes peering at me, a rifle dangling from his right hand and a bag slung over his back.

The worn rubber of the wiper blades smeared the rain on the glass. Left to right, and back again.

Michael started running toward the car.

Then the world exploded in a blinding flash of white light.

CHAPTER NINETY-ONE

WRITTEN STATEMENT, MEGAN FITZGERALD

Michael had been sprinting toward me, the rifle swinging.

Then the explosion.

My right foot came down hard on the pedal. At first, I wasn't sure which pedal my foot had selected because my mind was stuck somewhere between autopilot and holy-hell-do-something.

The wheels locked up.

The Honda slid several feet in the mud and came to a stop.

Michael bounced off the hood of the car.

I screamed his name.

Thought I screamed his name.

It might have just been in my mind.

I didn't see him get up, but he must have, because he was at my door; he had it open, and his arms were sliding under me, lifting me up and out of the Honda and into the rain.

Where did you get the gun? I tried to say, but what came out was more like "Word da du git de hun?"

He seemed to notice the blood for the first time. His mouth fell open. He reached for my Girl Scout Superfly in the Field Bandage and touched it tentatively with the tip of his finger. "He shot you?"

I nodded and immediately regretted the movement. *He most certainly did*, my mind agreed. *Wait, who shot me?*

I blinked, and when I did, Michael was in the driver's seat of another car—no cracks in these seats. Somehow, we had changed cars. I was in the passenger seat, buckled in, and we were moving down a dark road. He was talking.

"I don't know what I saw back there," he said as the wiper blades swished back and forth.

Half-conscious, I watched him. I tried not to look away, couldn't let myself look away, because I knew *exactly* what I'd seen back there. Right before that explosion, I'd seen two Michaels. And I wasn't sure which one was sitting next to me.

That was the last thought to flutter through my head before the car and everything else went dark.

PART 5

ASHTABULA, OHIO

There is no hiding from the past. It's the driving
force behind all we do.
                              —Barton Fitzgerald, MD

CHAPTER NINETY-TWO

DOBBS

EIGHT HUNDRED AND EIGHTY-TWO miles away from the events in Missouri, Dobbs stared up at the Fitzgeralds' large home. He'd practically worn a path in the cobblestone driveway with his pacing back and forth. Begley was on the phone. He had wandered halfway down the drive and was working his way back now, weaving through the various federal agents standing around, waiting.

The house was eerily quiet, although lights were on in nearly every room. Along with everyone else, Dobbs had watched them flick on one at a time. First upstairs, then downstairs. It started shortly after the housekeeper left. The older woman had rushed out from a side door around dusk, made her way to her car, and drove off with her head down the entire time, unwilling to make eye contact with any of them. Maybe she was an illegal... people always assumed the worst. He was fairly certain they would talk to her, but not yet.

Another light came on, this one from a room on the far west end of the house. A shadow moved past the window. The blinds moved again. Dr. Rose Fitzgerald peered out for several seconds before disappearing. She'd done the same in nearly every room, at every one of those windows. A wraith haunting the halls of a castle.

Begley finally disconnected the call and made his way back to Dobbs. "We got our search warrant."

He turned to the crowd behind them, placed two fingers in his mouth, and blew. A shrill whistle cut through the various conversations. He raised his other hand above his head and made two quick circles in the air, then pointed back at the house. "Let's go!"

CHAPTER NINETY-THREE

WRITTEN STATEMENT, MEGAN FITZGERALD

When I was eight, I broke my left arm. We had a tree house in the backyard with a climbing rope that ran up to a trapdoor that opened into the center of the little structure about ten feet off the ground. There were knots in the rope about every foot or so, these big thick knots Michael had tied for me when I couldn't shimmy up the rope on my own. Michael had no such trouble; he'd gone up and down that rope a hundred times prior to tying the knots in an attempt to show me how easy it was.

"Come on, Meg. It's cake. Like this—"

It wasn't easy. It certainly wasn't cake.

Hence the knots.

He convinced me this wasn't cheating. He said it was no different than the training wheels that had come off my bike earlier that summer. I was late to that party too. Michael had been riding without training wheels since he was five.

He was always the voice of reason.

"You'll never learn if you leave the training wheels on," he'd told me two months earlier.

It took an hour of convincing after that. Three minutes with a wrench. And another twenty minutes of practice, and then Michael was a hundred feet behind me, standing in the driveway, his hand no longer holding on to my seat, a giant grin on his face. I was riding on my own.

Dr. Rose watched from the foyer, and I could have sworn I saw her smile, although Michael told me it was probably just gas or maybe the sun had caught her at a weird angle. Couldn't have been a smile, because miserable old bags don't smile.

Michael had been right about the training wheels. When he tied the knots in the rope, I figured he had to be right about that too. I wasn't completely convinced, though.

"Why can't I just climb stairs?" I asked him. I always took the stairs to get up to the tree house. That's why they were there, after all. Civilized people used the stairs. They didn't climb trees, ladders, or ropes to get into their house. They took the stairs and went in through the front door.

"Pirates climb ropes," Michael replied, tying the last knot.

I'd forgotten we were pirates today.

"I'll stand under you. You'll be okay."

He showed me how easy it was after he tied that last knot. He shot up the rope and back down again as if it were nothing. Cake.

My turn.

I stood there for at least a minute, my head craned up, looking at the open trapdoor. Then I kicked off my shoes and reached for the rope.

"Put one hand here above this knot, then step on the one at the bottom, get both feet on it. Use your feet to hold on. When you've got a good grip, reach for the next one with your other hand and pull up. Like a caterpillar or an inchworm, only vertical."

Vertical and *horizontal* were Michael's words of the week on the calendar in his room, and he appeared committed to wearing them out.

I gripped the rope above my head as tight as I could, then I stepped on the bottom knot with one foot, then the other. Cake. Yellow with chocolate frosting.

I started up the rope, going hand over hand, my feet searching for the next knot and the next one after that. The muscles in my thighs burned, but I kept going because Michael had done it, and Michael said I could do it too. When I was about four feet off the ground, he crouched down below me and held the rope steady. When I got higher, he stood and looked up at me. "You're almost there, Meg!"

My arms shook, my legs vibrated, but I kept going. One knot at a time.

I would have made it if I hadn't reached for the mouth of the door early. I was so close, and that wooden edge felt like the finish line, so I made a grab for it. Had I been a few inches higher, my fingers would have hooked it, and I would have pulled myself right up. I wasn't quite there, though, and instead of wrapping around the lip of the opening, my fingers brushed it and went past, and my balance went with them.

I tipped forward, and my other hand stretched for the door too, but it was even farther away, so it found nothing but air. I dropped toward the unforgiving ground, looking nothing like the graceful pirate I had promised to be.

Michael was still beneath me, but I came down hard and fast and at this weird angle. I hit him first, then the ground hit me. I tasted dirt and grass, and then somehow I stood right up, thinking everything was just fine.

I'd knocked Michael over, and he stood too, and I knew immediately from the look in his eyes things were not fine. When I followed his gaze to my left arm, I understood why he was so pale and why his mouth was hanging open. My left arm did not look the way it was supposed to. While a normal arm had a single joint at the elbow, I now had two—my arm bent at the elbow and again right under it. Something white and sharp poked out of my skin behind my elbow, and I think if someone had told me it was my bone, I would have puked on my bare feet.

My legs wobbled under me, and I toppled over.

Michael caught me.

I know he shouted, screamed for help, but what I remember most is how he held me so close, put his lips right at my ear, and said, "Pick a number between one and five, Meg."

"It hurts, Michael," I said between the sobs that came whether I wanted them to or not.

"It only hurts because you're thinking about it," he told me. "Pick a number between one and five. Concentrate on that, and the pain will go away."

He was a liar, but I appreciated the effort.

My left arm felt no better right now, and that was the least of my problems.

CHAPTER NINETY-FOUR

WRITTEN STATEMENT, MEGAN FITZGERALD

I didn't remember passing out, but that's how that kind of thing works, right? You don't flip a switch or pull the covers up around your neck and slowly drift off. Someone else's hand is manning the power button, and that individual is not big on giving you warnings.

My eyes opened.

I heard breathing.

First my own, then from the seat next to me.

The digital clock above the car's radio read 5:35 a.m. The sun was creeping out.

I was facing forward, and this was a problem because I wouldn't be able to see the person in the driver's seat without turning my head, and I couldn't turn my head without tipping off that person to the fact that I was now awake.

"You've been out for a while."

Shit.

Michael's voice. Calm. Sounding half asleep too.

We weren't moving. The motor wasn't running. The car was parked on the side of the road—a narrow residential street with small houses in neat little rows, each one nearly identical to all the others, as if they'd been planted by some kind of large machine with only paint color and landscaping to set them apart.

"Where are we?"

"Nicole Milligan's house."

"I didn't give you her address."

"I found it in her file. Dr. Bart kept tabs on her."

"Oh."

I still hadn't turned my head. I wasn't sure I wanted to. My mind played the footage back like a DVR—Michael running across the path; Michael in front of the car. An impossible distance to cover in only seconds.

"What color was his hair?"

Michael asked the question as if he'd just been poking around in my mind. I'd never been able to keep secrets from him. He read me like yesterday's paper. It had been like that since we were kids.

" 'I saw two Michaels. I saw two of you,' " he went on. "You kept repeating that while you were sleeping. I didn't want to wake you. I figured restless sleep was better than no sleep."

I did turn then. I looked right at him.

He wasn't looking at me, though. He was staring at a house across the street. Dark windows. A yellow Volkswagen Bug in the driveway. A house not much different from all the others on the block. In the space between the houses, I could see a giant expanse of water. Nicole Milligan lived someplace called Ashtabula, Ohio. This would be Lake Erie.

"How long was I out?"

"Hours."

He'd rebandaged my arm, wiped away all the blood. I wiggled the fingers of my left hand. They worked again. Still a little numb, but they moved. My filthy dress had been replaced by a white tank top and jeans. A pair of tennis shoes were on the floor next to my feet. All things from my bag. From the corner of my eye, I saw my bag perched on the back seat, Michael's beside it. Dr. Bart's files too. All our stuff from the SUV. There was also a black nylon bag, one I didn't recognize. A rifle was on the floor, the barrel resting on the transmission hump. "Whose car is this?"

"I found it. Not far from Jeffery Longtin's house."

I noticed the steering column then—the plastic around the ignition was missing. Several wires dangled under the dash near Michael's legs, their ends twisted together. "When did you learn to hot-wire a car?"

He didn't turn to me. His gaze remained fixed on the house. "I didn't. It was already like that."

"When you *found* it?"

"Yeah."

"Where did you get the rifle?"

"I took it from the man who was shooting at you."

"Is this his car?"

"I think so. I bashed his head in with a rock."

He said this nonchalantly, as if it were nothing. As if he'd just mentioned he'd made the guy a sandwich.

"What color was his hair?" Michael asked again.

I thought about this for a second, tried to focus the images in my head, but the truth was, I couldn't tell. His hair looked dark, but it had been matted down by the rain. Everyone's hair looked darker when it was wet. Besides, it wasn't exactly a moment for attention to detail. I looked at the back of Michael's head as he looked out the window. Blond hair. The color I dyed it. Dry now. "Where are the glasses I gave you?"

"I lost them in the woods."

My eyes fell on his right wrist.

No watch.

His left arm was resting on the open window. I craned my head slightly to get a look at that wrist.

No watch there either.

"I'm going to ask you a question," I said. "It may seem weird, but I need you to answer. It's important to me. Important for us. Understand?"

He nodded slowly in the pale light. "What is it?"

"When I broke my arm, when we were kids, whose fault was it?"

"That's your question?"

"It is."

Michael considered this, still watching the house. "Johnny Depp. If it wasn't for that stupid movie, we wouldn't have been playing pirates. Although you've always been clumsy. Not much of a climber either."

We'd always blamed Depp—our little secret. Only Michael would have known that. Some of the tension slipped from my body.

Michael added, "Meg, I saw him too. In the woods."

CHAPTER NINETY-FIVE

DOBBS

DOBBS WATCHED BEGLEY POUND on the front door of the Fitzgerald home with the back of his fist for the third time, five quick hits in succession. "Dr. Rose Fitzgerald, this is Special Agent Waylon Begley with the FBI! I have a search order for the premises and an arrest warrant for your daughter, Megan Fitzgerald! Open the door immediately or we will have no choice but to break it down!"

Back in Los Angeles, a warrant serve-and-search would have played out a little differently, Dobbs thought. The battering ram would have cleared the door, concussion grenades would have flown through the opening following the team leader's half-assed shout of a warning, and a dozen SWAT officers dressed in full battle gear would have plowed inside, destroying everything in their path while disabling anyone they encountered. The good doctor would have been on the floor chewing on carpet with her arms pinned behind her back before the first tear from the gas fell from her eye.

Not in the burbs.

Not in this ritzy neighborhood.

Here, they get a subtle knock and the chance to extend an invitation. No need to damage a hand-carved, ten-thousand-dollar door.

"We know she's in there," Dobbs told Begley. "You've given her plenty of time to respond. She's not answering. We need to use the ram."

Begley nodded.

Half a dozen agents stood behind them at the ready. Begley beckoned to an agent holding a two-and-a-half-foot-long black cylinder. Dobbs recognized it as a Blackhawk Monoshock Ram, not unlike the ones his department used. Newer, though, and missing the telltale scratches of near daily use. This one spent most of its life in the trunk of someone's car.

The agent stepped up, held the ram by both handles, and swung it with an arc at the door about an inch to the inside of the dead bolt. The wood splintered and cracked; the heavy oak door swung inward.

Begley stepped inside first. "Dr. Fitzgerald, this is the FBI— we're coming in!"

Dobbs followed after him, the palm of his hand resting on the butt of his gun. He didn't draw the weapon, but he had unsnapped the leather clasp. There was a round in the chamber, and the safety was disabled. He hoped to God he wouldn't have to shoot some old woman today.

With hand gestures, Begley signaled for two of the agents to go upstairs, another toward the kitchen, two more down a hallway on the right. He motioned for Dobbs to follow him.

They found Dr. Rose Fitzgerald in what appeared to be a library sitting at the end of a plush leather sectional sofa. A bottle of Scotch rested on the table beside her next to a half-empty glass and several nine-volt batteries. There was a cordless phone in her hand. She appeared to have just finished up a call, had a disgusted look on her face.

She dropped the phone onto the cushion beside her, reached for the glass, and raised it to them. "To the finer things and the trials that pave the road to them."

The doctor drank down the Scotch, dabbed at her mouth with the back of her hand, and set the glass on the table. With a heavy sigh, she stood, smoothing the pleats of her pressed slacks. "You said you have an arrest warrant. Does it extend to me?"

Begley took a card from his pocket and handed it to her. "You can access the warrant with this URL. It includes a full search of the premises here and your offices at the university, and there's also an arrest warrant for your daughter, Megan Fitzgerald, for aiding and abetting your son, Michael Kepler Fitzgerald, in connection with more than a dozen homicides."

This news didn't seem to faze her. The stony expression on her face didn't falter. She took the card and set it on the table beside the bottle. "Those two were never my children. They don't have my blood, my DNA. I share nothing with them other than my home. They were leeches, feeding off me. Parasites in a petri dish. Something you scrape off the bottom of your shoe on the stoop before stepping inside. I hope you put bullets in both of them."

Dobbs glanced over at Begley. Neither of them was quite sure what to make of this.

Dr. Fitzgerald went on. "My attorney has advised me that if the warrant includes no arrest for me, I'm to leave the premises."

"We may have questions," Begley said.

She raised an eyebrow. "I should hope so. And you're welcome to ask them of my counsel. You wouldn't question me without an attorney present, would you?"

Begley didn't respond to that.

"Nor would you attempt to detain me without the proper

authority to do so. Imagine the public relations mess that would create. I am a public figure, after all."

She offered them both a cold, snakelike smile, bitter, full of bile. She stepped past them and started down the hallway in the direction of the garage. At the corner, she paused, the smile gone. "While you're welcome to stay, I strongly suggest you gentlemen exit my home immediately."

That's when Dobbs smelled it.

Smoke.

CHAPTER NINETY-SIX

WRITTEN STATEMENT, MEGAN FITZGERALD

"I want you to see something," Michael said, reaching into the storage compartment of his door. He took out a cell phone and handed it to me. It was a cheap disposable, like the ones both Michael and I had now, the kind you could buy anywhere—prepay and toss when you're done.

"Is it yours?"

"It belonged to the man who was shooting at you."

I bashed his head in with a rock.

I pressed the power button. The screen flashed some Chinese logo, then asked for a pass code.

"It's one, two, three, four."

"How'd you figure that out?"

Michael shrugged. "People are lazy. If they don't use four zeros, it's one, two, three, four. If that's not it, it's usually the last four digits of their Social or their street address. Same thing with bank PINs."

I made a mental note to change my PIN code when this was all over.

I keyed the numbers in, and a menu came up.

"Go to his text messages."

Texts were the second option on the menu. I pressed the

button, and a single conversation appeared. "He was in contact with only one person?"

Michael nodded. "Read it."

The conversation wasn't very long—

You didn't tell me there would be federal agents involved.

You didn't ask.

You didn't tell me about him either.

?

You should have told me what he was capable of.

?

At least six dead marshals here, maybe more.

It's under control.

You need to pull back.

Are you there?

Are you there?!?

"You think they're talking about whoever we saw?"

"I know it wasn't me," Michael replied.

"Would you remember if it was?"

Michael didn't answer.

I bashed his head in with a rock.

"I didn't see his face, Michael. Not really. I saw a blue shirt like yours. I wanted it to be you, but then I saw you in front of the car." I looked back down at the phone. "It was pouring rain. Pitch-black out. I'd lost blood, I was crashing from adrenaline. It really could have been anyone."

"You're making excuses now."

I didn't want to say it, but I did anyway. "You read the files, Michael. You heard the tapes." I turned to him. "Tell me the truth. Did you lose time back there?"

Michael looked like I'd punched him in the gut. He didn't answer my question, though. I'm not sure he knew the answer.

I went back to the phone. "Maybe we should call whoever this is."

"And say what? 'Sorry we killed your friend'?"

"Okay, text, then. Pretend to be him."

Michael didn't reply, just kept glaring out the window.

I keyed in a quick message. Michael heard the tones and turned to me but not before I hit Send.

"What did you say?"

"I said, 'Sorry, here now.'"

He seemed ready to object, but a reply came in before he had the chance.

What happened? Where did you go?

"Write 'I pulled back, like you said,'" Michael told me.

"Yeah, that's good." I keyed it in.

Where are you now?

I thought about this for a second. "Awaiting instructions," I said aloud as I typed.

A moment passed. Then:

They'll go to the girl next. Like I told you.

Both our faces were glued to the small screen. I think we both knew what was coming.

I typed in, *Address?*

I gave it to you.

"Tell him you lost it," Michael said.

I typed that.

Nothing.

No response.

Then an address filled the screen: *148 Summerset, Ashtabula, Ohio.*

Both Michael and I turned to the small house across the street. On the mailbox, in large reflective numbers, was *148*.

"Shit," I muttered.

Michael took the phone from me and typed in, *What do you want me to do?*

No answer. Then the phone began to ring in his hand.

"Don't answer it," I spat out.

"He knows we're not him."

"How can you be sure it's a him?"

Michael said, "We should answer."

"Don't."

Michael's finger hovered over the answer button, but he didn't accept the call. The phone rang half a dozen times, then went to voice mail. The caller didn't leave a message.

Another phone rang somewhere. Loud, obnoxious. One of those old-school landlines with actual bells inside. It was coming from inside the house.

A light turned on. A window on the far left side.

A shadow moved past the window.

Michael dropped the phone and grabbed the rifle from the floor in the back seat. He snagged the bundle of wires sticking out from under the dash and pulled them apart, and the engine died. "Come on—"

He was out the door and walking swiftly toward the little house before I could respond.

CHAPTER NINETY-SEVEN

DOBBS

FROM THE FITZGERALDS' GARAGE, Dobbs heard the throaty growl of a car starting. The tires chirped as they quickly reversed. Through the window, he saw Dr. Rose Fitzgerald behind the wheel of a black BMW, 7 Series, maybe 8. She performed a quick three-point turn and weaved through the various law enforcement vehicles toward the road.

Inside the house, the air became hazy, thick with smoke. It trailed in from each of the hallways, dark and black, crawling across the ceiling. The silence of the place was broken by a low hum, a slight crackle, as several fires took root throughout the home.

Dobbs's eyes landed on the nine-volt batteries on the table. She'd removed them from the smoke detectors.

Upstairs, someone shouted.

Footsteps, running, thumped on the second floor.

Begley tossed Dobbs his keys and yanked out his cell phone. "I'll get Fire and Rescue! Follow her!"

Dobbs was out the door, his eyes stinging from the smoke.

Outside, agents scrambled. Fingers pointed up.

Dobbs jumped into Begley's rented Nissan Rogue, and as he shot down the driveway after Fitzgerald, he hazarded a glance in the rearview mirror.

Three windows blew out of the second floor, followed by a belch of black smoke and flames.

By the time he reached the end of the driveway, he knew the fire department wouldn't make it in time.

He hadn't seen Begley come out—only about half of those who'd gone in were back out front.

CHAPTER NINETY-EIGHT

WRITTEN STATEMENT, MEGAN FITZGERALD

I wasn't a fan of what happened the last time Michael had left me alone in a car, so I scrambled out after him, raced up the cracked concrete path behind him.

We were halfway to the door when the shrill clatter of the phone inside stopped.

When Michael reached the house, he turned the rifle around and beat on the front door with the butt end. "Hey, Nicki! Knock-knock!"

He slammed his shoulder into the door, hard, all his weight behind it.

The frame rattled, but the door didn't give.

"What are you doing? We can't break in!"

He slammed the door again.

"Michael, stop!"

Ignoring me, he took several steps back, got a running start, and barreled into the door with a heavy push off his legs. This time, the frame splintered and the door snapped open. Michael stumbled inside, nearly lost his balance, but found his footing in a small living room.

"Was that our buddy Larry on the line? Did you say hello for me?"

A door slammed somewhere deep in the house, toward the

back; that was followed by a crash. "Don't worry about me, Nicki! I'll make myself comfortable!"

Michael grabbed the end of a dining-room table, yanked it up, sent it crashing against the wall. A bowl of fruit, some kind of glass centerpiece, and a few smaller items shot through the air and clattered all around.

"What are you doing?" I shouted.

Three more slamming doors.

He ignored me. He crossed the room and started down a hallway toward the sound.

All the doors in the hallway were closed.

When Michael reached the first, he rested the barrel of the rifle on his shoulder and leaned in close. "Are you in there, sweetie? I can smell your drugstore perfume. It's that same cheap shit I remember from years back, but it's *your* cheap shit. Brings to mind so many fond memories. I used to love the way you dabbed it behind your ears and right between your breasts. Hmm—those other places too. Why didn't you keep in touch? I've missed you."

He kicked the door. The drywall shuddered. It was a cheap, hollow-core plank. His foot nearly went through as the door flew open and cracked against the wall.

A home office. Cluttered with boxes and filing cabinets. There was the old phone, a red plastic box sitting on the corner of a scratched-up wooden desk.

Michael swung the barrel of the rifle off his shoulder as he stepped into the room and slowly swept the gun back and forth. "I haven't played hide-and-seek since I was a kid. This is exciting! Come out, come out, wherever you are! Come out, come out, you little whore!"

I took a step back.

Michael looked at me, tilted his head to the side, pouted. "What's wrong, Meg? You don't want to play?"

I shook my head, but when I opened my mouth, nothing came out.

Michael smiled.

"You should run now," he said softly. "I would."

CHAPTER NINETY-NINE

DOBBS

THE GATE TO THE Fitzgerald estate was wide open and had been since they'd arrived yesterday.

Dr. Fitzgerald didn't slow as she reached the end of the drive. In fact, she picked up speed. The BMW's rear wheels bit into the blacktop as she made a hard left onto Danby Road.

Dobbs's borrowed Nissan was top-heavy and took the turn with less grace, the back end sliding. He yanked at the wheel, tried not to overcompensate, and straightened back out. By the time he'd gotten behind her again, she had added several car lengths to the distance between them. At half the size and a fraction of the horse-power, the Nissan was no match for the BMW. The irony was, she didn't appear to be trying to outrun him. She was speeding along at a good clip—at least twenty miles an hour over the posted limit—but she was just driving fast. If she wanted to lose him, she could.

The doctor took another right onto Whitetail and vanished momentarily behind a hill. He almost didn't see her turn right again on East King. If a slow-moving pickup truck hadn't pulled out in front of her, he surely would have lost her. She weaved back and forth in an attempt to pass the lumbering vehicle, but he was towing a wide trailer carrying several golf carts, the road was narrow, and at this hour, he didn't expect a need to share it.

Dobbs got up behind her and flashed his headlights on and off, high and low. Hit the horn several times. She looked up at him in her rearview mirror, then her eyes went back to the road.

When the truck lazily swung to the right, she jerked into the left lane and floored the accelerator. The BMW shot past before the truck had a chance to come back in the other direction.

Dobbs crossed into the left lane and jammed the gas pedal of the Nissan down to the floor, but rather than producing the smooth purr of the BMW, the Rogue sounded like a lawn mower bogged down in thick, wet grass. He thought it might stall, but it lurched forward. When he was halfway past the truck and trailer, the driver started to roll into his lane.

Dobbs slammed his palm down on the horn.

The driver looked up from the phone in his hand, offered an apologetic wave, and got back into his own lane.

He didn't see her turn on Fall Creek Drive. He blew right by. If he hadn't caught her out of the corner of his eye climbing out of the car, he would have lost her.

Dobbs threw the Rogue into reverse, churning up loose gravel, backed up to the missed turn, and saw the BMW parked up ahead in the wash of his headlights. Fitzgerald gave him an irritated glance, then scrambled down a small footpath without bothering to close her car door.

Dobbs parked behind her, blocking her in, and chased after her. At the mouth of the path, he caught a glimpse of a sign that read CORNELL, with an arrow.

WRITTEN STATEMENT, MEGAN FITZGERALD

Michael started for the only closet in the room. He yanked open the bifold door and began poking around inside with the barrel of the gun.

I ran to the kitchen and started tugging open drawers, one after the other. "Come on, everybody's got—" Then I found a junk drawer with a large pair of scissors on top. I snatched them up and ran back down the hall.

Michael broke open another door.

A small bathroom.

He gave me a sideways look. "I thought I told you to run."

"I'm not gonna let you hurt her!"

"No?" He glanced at the scissors in my hand, amused. "That's so sweet."

He stepped into the bathroom, pulled back the shower curtain.

Nobody.

He reached down and jerked hard enough on one of the vanity doors to break off the hinge. The door fell to the side at an awkward angle. He knelt and looked inside.

Nothing.

"I bet you're hiding someplace dark, Nicki. You always did like the dark. That's where you were at your best."

"You're him, aren't you?"

Michael smiled at this. "I'm just me. Nobody special."

He pushed past me into the hallway, ignoring the scissors in my hand.

"You're Mitchell," I said behind him.

He eyed the next door, this one on the right. "I'm whoever Dr. Bart wants me to be." His foot came up, smashed into the door. It flew open and cracked against the wall inside the room.

Bedroom. Double bed, unmade. Clothes piled on the floor. A magazine. A pizza box sitting on the dresser. The scent of day-old pepperoni wafted across the room. "Why do all the women in my life have filthy bedrooms? You're the psych major, Meg. What does that say about me? Am I attracted to untidy women?"

He hooked his free hand under the mattress, pulled it up and over, stood it on end against the wall. The box spring went next. He shook his head and glared down. "What a mess."

Probably a hundred books. Hardcovers, softcovers. Magazines too. A couple socks, a few pairs of panties, a single black leather glove. Lots of dust bunnies. Nicole wasn't there, though. He dropped the box spring and turned his attention to the closet. Another bifold door.

"Stop and talk to me for a minute!"

"About what?" He said this casually, as if we were playing Scrabble.

"Why do you want to hurt her?"

He was facing the closet door. He tilted his head to the left, then to the right, stretching his neck muscles. "Who says I want to hurt her? I'm just excited. I haven't seen her in such a long time. I just want to give her a hug and a big sloppy kiss."

He tore open the closet doors with enough force to rip them from their track. One fell to the side with a clatter; the other hit against the wall. The floor was filled with boxes and shoes. Clothes were packed so tight on the wooden rod, it bowed at the center. He shuffled the blouses and dresses around, but it was clear she wasn't in there.

"Wow, Nicki, have you ever considered donating some of this stuff? This is how you end up on that show *Hoarders*."

He gripped the rod in the middle and pulled. The sagging rod let go. Clothes spilled around our feet.

He went back into the hall.

Next door.

He opened it with another kick and stomped inside.

Another bedroom.

The phone started to ring, the bell nearly deafening.

He cocked an ear. "Nicki, you gonna get that? I bet it's Larry again."

I ran back into the home office, grabbed the receiver, and pressed it to my ear. "You need to send help! He's going to kill her!"

There was silence.

"Are you there?"

On the other end of the line, I heard Dr. Bart's gravelly voice.

WRITTEN STATEMENT, MEGAN FITZGERALD

"We're so close," Dr. Bart said. "Do you feel it? Like electricity in the air. It's damn near palpable. Thick and tingly. The hair on my arms is standing up."

"Hello?" The word slipped from my mouth into the old receiver, nearly a whisper.

In the other room, a mattress hit the wall and rattled the house.

Dr. Bart went on. "If you have to kill her, you can. I promise you, there will be no repercussions. I'll dispose of her body. You need not worry about that. She won't be missed. Isn't that right, sweetie? Nobody loves you. Poor little trashy thing."

Another tape. Had to be. "Who is this?"

"Do you feel it?" Dr. Bart asked again, his voice anxious, a fever to it. "Who is on the mark?" he asked softly.

Silence then.

The longest silence.

"Mitchell. Mitchell is on the mark."

"How can I be sure?"

"Who the hell is this?" I screamed into the receiver.

"I have no reason to lie," the voice told Dr. Bart.

I heard him cluck his tongue the way he used to do. Twice. Then another. "If you kill her, I'll believe you."

"Okay."

The line went dead then.

And four shots rang out from the other room.

Pop! Pop! Pop! Pop!

CHAPTER ONE HUNDRED TWO

WRITTEN STATEMENT, MEGAN FITZGERALD

I dropped the receiver and ran down the hall toward the gunfire.

Michael was in the second bedroom, his back pressed against the wall. There were four splintered holes in the closet door next to him, all grouped close together about two feet off the floor. The rifle was hanging from his back; he hadn't fired. His eyes were wide, and a thin layer of sweat covered his forehead.

If he'd been hit, I didn't see a wound. No blood anywhere.

We both heard the next sound.

Click.

Followed closely by two more: *Click. Click.*

Michael reached over, grabbed the handle of the bifold, and yanked it away. Nicole Milligan was on the floor, her knees pulled up tight against her chest, some kind of revolver in her hand pointing forward. Her face was streaked with wet mascara, her entire body quivering. Stringy long brown hair hung down her back and shoulders, partially covering her left eye.

"There you are!" Michael beamed.

He reached down for her, pulled her up with a fistful of her tank top in his right hand while snatching the revolver from her with his left. He tossed the gun off to the side, then lifted her off the ground and slammed her against the wall.

Nicole's frightened eyes glared at him, her head shaking from side to side.

Michael leaned forward and kissed her even as she squirmed. Nicole bit his lip, and he pushed her away, slammed the back of her head into the wall again. He wiped his mouth with his free hand and looked at the holes in the broken closet door. "A little higher and to the left, and you might have pegged me!"

Nicole's feet dangled about a foot off the ground. Michael had her around the throat now, and when she tried to speak, nothing came out. Her eyes found me, pleaded. She kicked, bucked at him, thrashed, but he was too strong.

"Where is it?" Michael asked calmly.

Nicole glared at Michael as she gasped for air.

Michael loosened his grip and lowered her just enough so her toes could touch the ground. "It's mine, Nicole. You stole it, but I'm a forgiving guy. Tell me where it is, and I'll look past all of this. I'll walk right out of here. No harm, no foul."

She still said nothing.

Michael's grip tightened again. "Or I can snap your dainty neck and find it myself."

Nicole's eyes darted to me, then back to him again. She finally looked toward the dresser on her left. "Music box."

Michael's eyes followed hers to a small wooden box with a mirror embedded in the top. He went over to it, dragging Nicole along as if she weighed nothing. When he opened the lid, a tiny ballerina popped up, and some song I knew I'd heard before but couldn't name began to play.

"Under the tray," she said, her voice raspy, raw.

Michael tugged the felt-covered tray from the box and tossed it to the floor, spilling several rings, earrings, and a necklace around his feet. He reached inside and took out a folded piece of paper, opened it with his thumb and forefinger.

The paper was cream-colored with an intricate pattern along the edges in gold. The text was large, in black ink. I couldn't make out the words.

"Nobody is real without one of these," he said. "You don't exist. Not in today's world."

"What is it?"

He folded the paper again and shoved it deep into his pocket. "My birth certificate."

Michael's gaze dropped back to Nicole. The lines of his face tightened and burned red. "This whore stole it. Figured she could use it against me. Thought she had some kind of leverage over me."

Nicole was shaking her head again. "Dr. Bart gave it to me. Told me to protect it. I would never take it. I'd never do anything to hurt you."

His fingers tightened around her neck again, slowly, like the patient grip of a python. He was choking her.

I held up the scissors, point out. "She gave you what you wanted. Let her go."

"You gonna stab me, Meg? How 'bout you give her a good poke instead? I'll hold her still for you, just like this. You remember how to do it, right? I'm sure Dr. Bart showed you."

I did remember.

I shot forward and, putting my weight behind it, buried the scissors up to the bright purple handle in Michael's back.

None of us moved. Michael stood perfectly still, his stiff arm pressing Nicole up against that wall. My fingers were still wrapped around the handle of the scissors and didn't seem to want to let go. They'd gone in so easily. I guess I'd expected some kind of resistance, but the sharp blades slipped right into him. Through the shirt, the skin of his back, fat, muscle, and whatever was on the other side of all that.

The moment passed, and Michael's face turned white.

His fingers loosened, and Nicole sagged to the side.

I let go of the scissors.

I grabbed her hand and pulled her out into the hallway as Michael's left hand fumbled around the air behind him, his fingers searching for the scissors, as he spun in a slow circle. "You've done some stupid things in your life, Meg. But that was epic. I'll give you a solid ten count, and you'd better hope you can find a more creative spot to hide in than little Nicki did on her first shot out."

Hallway.

Living room.

I pulled Nicki behind me—she was partially unconscious from the choking. Her feet were dragging, kept catching on the carpet. "Do you have a car?"

She tried to talk, but nothing came out except for a choked gasp. She shook her head.

"Another gun?"

She shook her head again and pointed toward a door off the kitchen. "Basement," she managed.

Back down the hall, I heard a loud grunt from Michael.

I left Nicki balanced against the sofa, ran into the kitchen, and opened the basement door several inches, hoping he'd think we'd run down there. I opened one of the cabinet doors too.

In the living room, Nicki was shuffling toward the ruined front door, her strength slowly coming back.

The blast of a rifle.

The plaster to the left of the door exploded.

Michael was in the hallway behind us. The scissors fell from his hand. A deranged grin filled his face. "Five, one thousand. Six, one thousand. Seven…"

His bloody hand reached for the charger on the rifle and pulled it back. The spent shell ejected, bounced off the wall, and fell to the floor. A new round replaced it. He started toward us, slowly at first but picking up speed with each step.

I shoved Nicki through the broken door and pulled it closed behind me.

Michael slammed into the other side.

The doors to the Toyota Michael and I had arrived in were still open. Nicki scrambled around to the passenger side, got in, and yanked the door shut behind her. I was in the driver's seat and pulling the door closed when Michael finally came out the front, that grin growing on his face. He took his time, moving with slow, lumbering steps. Blood dripped from his back, although not as much as I'd hoped, leaving a trail in the concrete.

My eyes dropped to the bundle of wires hanging at the base of the steering column. I had no idea how to hot-wire a car. Four of the wires were stripped at the end. I grabbed them at random, touching metal to metal. The second pair sparked.

Michael tapped at the window of the driver's-side door. He puckered his lips, blew me a kiss, then smashed the glass with the butt of the rifle.

Tiny bits rained down on me, slammed into my cheek, got caught in my hair.

Nicole screamed.

Michael said, "The Johnny Depp thing, Meg? It's in your file."

He raised the butt of the rifle again. I remember it coming toward my head, but nothing after that.

CHAPTER ONE HUNDRED THREE

DOBBS

DR. ROSE FITZGERALD PROVED to be much faster than Dobbs had expected. He caught a glimpse of her through the swaying branches and trees, a red bag at her hip, but she vanished a moment later as she lumbered over a hill and down the other side. The path was relatively worn, clearly frequented, but in the dark he was leery of moving too fast and turning an ankle on a root or some unseen divot in the earth.

He heard rushing water long before he saw it, but he hadn't been prepared for what he found when the path dipped down and turned a hard right.

A gorge—four, maybe five hundred feet deep. Several waterfalls, a rushing river running beneath, and the lights of a power plant nestled in the rock near the bottom on the far left. The trees opened up, the sky reached down, and Dobbs felt his legs go weak at the sight.

A suspension bridge connected that end of the gorge to the far side, at least three hundred feet long and six feet wide. Thick cables, wood, and wire held in place by who knew what dangling across a slice of Mother Nature where it had no business being.

Dobbs hated heights.

Hated wasn't a strong enough word.

The cold, still air. The dark. The loud, rushing water far below. All of it somehow made this place seem both large and small at the same time. Another sign, like the one at the start of the path, read CORNELL, with an arrow pointing toward the bridge, but he couldn't see the university from here. There was nothing but the gaping mouth of another path at the far end. Nothing but isolation.

Fitzgerald was about a third of the way across, the cables and wooden boards gently rocking back and forth with each step she took.

"Doctor, stop!" Dobbs shouted.

To his surprise, she did. Nearly at the halfway point, she froze and turned toward him, one hand gripping the railing, the other on the strap of her bag.

"We need to go back, Doctor—to the house!"

She smiled then. Even from this distance, Dobbs could see it, and that smile frightened him. Unlike the smile back at the house, this one was genuine. She wiped the smile from her face a moment after it appeared, as if she thought showing her true emotions was some kind of weakness. "I can't go back. None of us can. You don't see that yet, but you will."

Dobbs took several steps out onto the suspension bridge.

"Don't." Fitzgerald raised her free hand. "Right there is fine. Not another step."

Dobbs stopped moving, but the bridge didn't; it continued to sway. Not much, just enough to remind him solid ground was ten feet at his back. The center where Fitzgerald stood swayed far worse, but she seemed oblivious to it. Her eyes remained fixed on him. "You need to let it all burn," she said. "Fire is one of the few things in life that can truly cleanse. Anything else is no better than slapping a coat of paint on a rusty car. You can hide the cancer for a little while, but eventually it eats right through, worse than ever. Fire, though; fire is final. There is no coming back, no resurrection. Maybe that's what Barton should have done years ago. Set fire to the whole damn thing. I told him to. God knows I told him to more times than I can count, but he was always so damn stubborn. He couldn't see past the moment. He couldn't see where it would all go. I could. And rather than smother that child with a pillow when I had the chance, I let Barton continue his work. I allowed it to fester. That kind of blood doesn't wash off. It's under my nails, where the water can't reach it."

A wire safety mesh rose from the railing to the cable high above the bridge. Dobbs watched as Fitzgerald grabbed it, pulled it apart, exposing an opening. "I cut this two days ago. I told myself if someone fixed it before I came back, I wouldn't do it. I suppose I gave myself an out."

Dobbs started toward her.

"Don't!" she shouted, leaning into the opening. "You're not fast enough. Don't even try. Don't give me a reason. Stay right there."

Dobbs froze. She was right. He was more than a hundred feet away. "Jumping isn't the answer."

"There is no answer," Fitzgerald said, shaking her head. "He's coming home, and I have no intention of giving him my last breath. I don't owe that to him. I owe no one."

"Megan needs you," Dobbs said, edging closer. "We can protect you. Let me help you."

"Give Larry my regards." Fitzgerald smiled again. "I always liked this bridge."

Dobbs ran. He forced every ounce of energy down into his legs and shot toward her. The bridge jerked beneath him with each step. He ignored the height, the rushing water below. His only focus was her. He grabbed for her, reached across the impossible distance, fumbled for her arm, her clothing, anything, but she was right—he wasn't fast enough.

CHAPTER ONE HUNDRED FOUR

DOBBS

IN HIS MIND'S EYE, Dobbs saw her fall. Her determined eyes never left him as she fell through the air, down toward the water, then bounced off the rocks below with an almost silent thud. The current didn't so much take her as wash over her, white water folding over her like a liquid blanket, enveloping her, tucking her in for the night. In his mind's eye, he saw all this, but he hadn't actually seen it. She was simply gone by the time he reached the place she had jumped, nothing left to indicate she had been there, nothing to see but the white frothy water rushing angrily below.

Dobbs stood on the bridge as minutes passed, leaning over the edge with one hand wrapped in the broken mesh, just staring down at those rocks. When he finally pulled himself back through the opening and collapsed on the wooden planks, he remembered to breathe.

His phone started to ring.

He fished the cell from his pocket and pressed the answer button without looking at the caller ID. "Yeah?"

"Bring her ass back here. We've got her on arson. Probably obstruction. I don't care how many attorneys she throws at us."

Begley.

Dobbs forced himself to stand. He started back down the bridge, the path, toward the cars. "She's dead."

"What?"

Dobbs told him.

Begley was silent a moment, processing this. He finally said, "The house is gone. Well, not completely, not yet. The fire department is here, but at this point, they're just trying to contain it. She spread some kind of accelerant inside. One of our guys said the upstairs carpet went up with a blue flame that rolled down the hall and up the sides of the walls. Probably gasoline or alcohol. I'm sure the fire marshal will figure it out. The roof collapsed a few minutes ago. If any worthwhile evidence survives, it will be days before we can dig it out. Hold on a second..."

Dobbs stepped off the bridge, went past the sign that said CORNELL, and walked toward the cars.

He could hear a dinging chime coming from the open door of Fitzgerald's BMW.

Begley came back. "I told one of the patrolmen she jumped. He's going to scramble the locals and take care of things there. I need you to get back here. We've got to figure out our next step."

Dobbs leaned into the BMW. It smelled vaguely like Fitzgerald's perfume. "What was the name of the guy Vela said ran that orphanage? Do you remember?"

Begley thought about this for a second. "Patchen, Lawrence Patchen. Why?"

Give Larry my regards.

On the passenger seat of the BMW was a visitor's pass for Windham Hall.

CHAPTER ONE HUNDRED FIVE

GIMBLE

THE EXPLOSION HADN'T BEEN the propane tank but a rented SUV about halfway up Longtin's dirt driveway.

The local sheriff showed up ten minutes later, followed by three deputies; the helicopter was twenty minutes behind them. U.S. marshals and federal agents out of the various St. Louis field offices filtered in too. They were combing the woods in pairs. Several large floodlights had been erected around Longtin's cabin. The chopper flew over for what must have been the dozenth time, tethered to the ground by a beam of light sweeping the trees. Gimble pressed her hand over her ear and shouted into her phone. "What do you mean, she jumped?"

Begley told her. The fire at the house. The bridge.

"Christ," she muttered.

Two EMTs wheeled Longtin's body out of the cabin to a waiting ambulance. Vela was right behind them, talking to the older of the two. She couldn't make out the words. The coroner had two vans en route. In addition to the murdered marshals she had found on the side of the house and near the woodpile, they had found four others. Two were still missing. Garrison's body had been lying beside his SUV not far from the cabin, a deep stab wound in his left leg at the femoral artery, another across his neck. He'd bled out before he could get a shot off.

The sheriff walked over. He'd come out of the woods. A tall, skinny man in his late fifties with a thin, graying mustache and dark eyes magnified behind small, round glasses. Rather than a typical wide-brim hat, he wore a baseball cap with SHERIFF across the front. She'd forgotten his name. Didn't really care.

"There's something you need to see," he said. His accent was more Texan than Midwest. He didn't wait for a response, just turned and started back toward the woods.

"Begley, I'll call you back." Gimble hung up and followed after him. The ground was a spongy, muddy mess. She tried to step on weeds and fallen leaves, but it did little good. Her tennis shoes sank into the earth, each step making a sucking sound in the mud. The sheriff wore tall rubber boots that came halfway up to his knees. He didn't seem to care where he stepped. Although the entire area was considered a crime scene, the rain had made the collection of shoe prints all but useless.

He led her up a hill, through a small clearing, and onto a ridge overlooking a portion of Longtin's wooded driveway and cabin. A crime scene photographer and two local CSI investigators were huddled over another body. Yellow tape had been strung around four trees, creating a large box around them. Two battery-powered floodlights illuminated the area.

Gimble felt her chest tighten. "Is that another marshal?"

"No, ma'am. We're not sure what we've got here," he replied.

He ducked under the yellow tape and stood several feet from the body. He took off his baseball cap, scratched at the top of his bald head.

Gimble came up beside him.

The body—a man—was lying on his stomach, his legs stretched out straight behind him, his arms reaching forward. The back of his head had been crushed. Rainwater pooled in the cavity, a mix of loose hair and flakes of brain matter.

Gimble asked, "Did you find a rifle?"

"A rifle? No. Why?"

She ignored the question and pointed at a large rock lying about a foot from the body in the mud. "Is that the murder weapon?"

The older of the two CSIs nodded. "Most likely. The rain gave it a good wash, but I found a few hairs caught in the surface." He pointed toward the rock with the tip of a pen. "The body didn't collapse like this; the limbs would be more random, bent. This person was already lying on the ground in a straight, prone position, and someone came up from above and behind with the rock. Took him completely by surprise with a single blow."

The sheriff understood then. "This is one of your shooters," he said. A statement, not a question. "That's why he's lying like that." He pointed back down the hill. "Clear line of sight to the driveway and the front of the cabin. So if he was the one taking potshots at you and the girl, who killed him? Your boy Kepler?"

My boy Kepler.

"Why was he shooting at any of you?"

"Turn him over," Gimble said. "I need to see his face."

The CSI looked to the sheriff, who nodded. With the help of the other investigator, they grabbed the body at the shoulder and down near the waist and rolled him over. The rain sloshed in the crater of his skull. Gimble fought the urge to throw up.

Dark eyes. Blond hair. Forties. Not someone she recognized. She snapped a photo with her phone. "Any identification?"

He shook his head. "Nothing on him. Nothing in his pockets at all. We'll run prints back at the coroner's office. He's got an old scar on his left hand, nasty-looking thing. No visible tattoos."

Gimble glanced back at the cabin. The propane tank was around the other side. No line of sight from here. At least two hundred feet to where she thought she saw Kepler in the woods when she was at the log pile. No way he covered that kind of ground that fast, not through the trees in the rain. No way.

He's a truck driver from LA. Some kid who grew up in the burbs.

What the hell were they dealing with?

The radio attached to the man's shoulder squawked. "Sheriff?"

He reached up and pressed the button on the side. "Go."

"We found the red Honda. About a half mile from your current location. Tire's gone, drove it on the rim. She ran it off into the weeds under a canopy of live oaks. Damn near missed it. There's blood on both seats, on the steering wheel. No sign of the girl." The voice paused, then came back. "I've got another set of tire tracks near it. Looks like a second vehicle had been parked here. Something small, judging by the wheelbase. I don't see tracks driving in, only driving out, so whatever it is, I think it was parked before the rain started."

"Blood in both seats?" the sheriff said into the mic.

"Yeah. Could be a second person. Hard to tell. The rain did a number on the ground. We're pulling prints from the interior."

The sheriff's eyes were fixed on Gimble. "Copy that."

Gimble was still looking at the cabin.

The sheriff's eyes narrowed. He nodded at the body. "You know what this is."

"Shooter number one," Gimble replied flatly, turning back to him. She told him about the rifle shots, Megan Fitzgerald.

"We've got a missing weapon, Sheriff. A rifle. I suggest you find it." Gimble's fingers were twitching. This didn't make sense.

Before he could ask her another question, she turned and went back down the hill.

Sammy caught up with her as she approached the back of one

of the FBI vans parked next to the cabin, his ever-present MacBook under his arm. "According to the fire marshal, the bullets didn't pierce the tank. Looks like he rerouted one of the gas lines through the dryer vent. That's why we smelled gas inside."

"Wonderful."

"I need to go to the St. Louis field office," he told her. "I need access to several databases I can't reach remotely."

She waved him off, only half listening to him. "Go."

None of this mattered to her. Not right now. The only thing that mattered was the person who had walked out of the woods with his hands held above his head shortly after that explosion

Gimble tugged at the door handle on the back of the FBI van, opened it, climbed inside, and tugged it shut behind her. She sat on a small bench above the rear wheel well and stared at Michael Kepler. "You need to tell me what the hell is going on."

CHAPTER ONE HUNDRED SIX

GIMBLE

HE'S GOT MY SISTER," Kepler said, attempting to lean toward her. He managed to move about two inches—his hands were cuffed to his feet, his feet were shackled to the floor of the van. The links of metal clanked as they rolled through the heavy eyebolt.

"Who's got your sister?"

Michael Kepler didn't say anything at first. He opened his mouth, ready to speak, thought better of it, then just shook his head. "You'll think I'm crazy."

"I *know* you're crazy. It's well documented. My people told me all about your medical history. You've killed, what, two dozen people? Three? I'm not even sure anymore." Her face flushed red. She turned away from him for a moment, then looked him square in the eye. "Do you know how many of the bodies lying in the dirt out there were my friends?"

"I haven't killed anyone."

"There will be a line of people drawing numbers to stick the needle in your arm." She lowered her voice. "If this place weren't crawling with cops, I'd drag your ass out of this van and put a bullet in your head myself just to be sure some lowlife attention-seeking lawyer didn't get the chance to get you off on some insanity plea, you crazy fuck."

"I saw him," Kepler said. "In the car with her."

"Your sister drove out of here under her own power."

Kepler quickly shook his head. "No. I saw him get in the car with her. That's why I turned myself in. You need to help her."

"Saw who?"

"Mitchell," Michael said softly.

Gimble's eyes narrowed. "Who the hell is Mitchell?"

"I think he might be my brother," Michael said, but even as the words came out of his mouth, he seemed unconvinced.

"You don't have a brother."

"I remember him. I thought he was some kind of imaginary friend when I was little, something I made up. Now I'm not so sure."

Gimble reached into her pocket, pulled out a bottle of pills, and slammed it down on the floor between them. "Recognize those?"

Michael hesitated, then nodded.

"Dorozapine. An antipsychotic. *Your* antipsychotic. My people tell me it's meant to treat schizophrenia, dissociative disorder. It's meant for people like *you*. It's one of many prescribed to you."

Michael tried to lean forward again. "If Mitchell did all this, if he killed all those people, including your friends, he'll kill Megan. You need to stop him."

Gimble snickered. "*You* did all this. I saw you walk out of the woods holding an MP5. The same gun you used to shoot at me and at the propane tank—and at this sister you seem so worried about."

Kepler shook his head again. "I found the gun. Right after I saw him in the car with Megan. I picked it up, but I never fired it." He yanked at the chains on his wrists. "Test me. You can do that, right?"

Gimble didn't reply.

"I know where he's going next."

Gimble stared at him for nearly a minute without a word, anger burning under her skin.

Kepler's eyes fixed on her. "Nicole Milligan."

She couldn't take this anymore. She got out of the van, slamming the door behind her.

She found Vela on the outside, listening.

"I didn't want to interrupt you," he told her. "But I needed to hear what he said."

"Tell me this is all bullshit," Gimble said, her fingers twitching.

"You heard what Longtin told us. Fitzgerald studied Longtin in order to understand his illness. He said the doctor wanted to re-create it. If that's true, and that's a big *if*, somebody like Kepler would provide the proper template. His childhood trauma, the death of his mother, what her boyfriend did to her body while he was hiding in the closet...all of that makes him susceptible to a psychotic break. If there is a Mitchell, he exists only in Kepler's mind. He'd see him as a real person. There's a good chance they might even interact. Or the other personality could take over completely. It's very possible a Mitchell personality took over, committed the crimes in Kepler's history, and he's totally unaware of it."

"He said he saw this other person in the car with his sister," Gimble pointed out.

Vela shrugged. "It's very possible he did. That doesn't mean he's real. Hallucinations are common among those suffering from his condition."

The coroner's vehicles must have arrived while she was talking to Kepler. Two men in white were loading up body bags.

"There's not a drop of blood on him," Gimble said. "These people were all killed with a knife. We didn't find that either. How do you explain that?"

Vela shrugged again. "The knife is probably out there in the woods somewhere. All this rain, maybe that washed the blood away. I don't know. Forensics isn't my specialty."

Gimble flagged down one of the FBI investigators, a young agent, early twenties. She wore white coveralls, and her jet-black hair was pulled back. "There's a man in this van. I need you to collect his clothing and test everything for GSR. Can you do that?"

The agent nodded.

Gimble added, "Take someone else with you. I want a weapon on him at all times. The cuffs stay on—cut the clothing off him if that's what you need to do."

"Yes, ma'am."

Special Agent Gimble, Agent Gimble, or just Gimble, but never "ma'am," she thought. But she had much bigger problems. She knew the name Nicole Milligan. "Milligan was on that list of patient files you pulled, wasn't she?"

Vela nodded. "Fitzgerald treated her after she was raped."

"I need an address," she told him. "Whatever contact information we have." Gimble started to walk back toward the cabin, then stopped and turned to Vela again. "If there was a brother, there'd be a record, right?"

"There is no brother," Vela replied.

"That wasn't my question."

"Kepler's birth certificate was issued by that orphanage, Windham Hall. He wasn't in the system when they brought him in. He was most likely born outside of a hospital. If his mother gave birth to a second child, there probably wouldn't be a record of him either."

"Where are you on getting into that place and pulling records?"

"They're not returning my calls."

Gimble frowned, turned away. "I told you to get the local field office out there. Did you do that?"

"I haven't had a chance. Things have moved too fast," Vela replied.

Gimble felt her face flush red. She hated repeating orders. "Get it done, right now. I want a warrant within an hour."

"We've got Kepler in custody. What's the point?"

Gimble turned to him, and apparently just seeing her face was enough.

Vela raised both hands. "Okay, okay."

His phone was out and pressed to his ear when she stepped back into the cabin.

WRITTEN STATEMENT, MEGAN FITZGERALD

It was the sun in my eyes that woke me. A bright red on the other side of my eyelids. I didn't open them. I didn't want him to know I was awake.

We were driving again.

Beside me, Michael was drumming on the steering wheel, humming along to "Angela" by the Lumineers, and for one fleeting moment, everything was all right again. Michael and I were just on another road trip, one of his deliveries for work, windows down, morning air blowing through our hair.

The side of my head throbbed, and I remembered the butt of the rifle coming down on me, crashing into my skull, Michael at the other end of it.

"Christ, Meg, why did you make me do that?" he said from beside me. "You're the last person I want to hurt."

I felt his hand on my leg. He squeezed my knee. "You're all I've got."

His fingers were cold.

I opened my eyes.

Shards of glass from the shattered window sparkled in the carpet, on the dashboard, the center console. This was the second time I'd woken up in this car.

Michael gave my knee another squeeze and smiled at me. "There's my girl."

My hands were bound with duct tape; my ankles too.

I was wearing a different pair of blue jeans.

"I'm afraid you wet yourself earlier, when you fell asleep," Michael said. "I had to change your clothes, clean you up. Couldn't have you sitting in that filth." He smiled again. "Don't feel bad about it or embarrassed. It happens, I understand. It would have been better if it didn't happen, but it did, so I took care of it."

I tried not to react to this, but the muscles in my legs clenched anyway. Michael must have felt it. His hand left my knee and returned to the steering wheel as the Lumineers made way for Mumford and Sons. He started humming again.

"Michael, what are you doing? Where are we going?"

Speaking aloud, the movement of it, caused my head to ache. I squeezed my eyes shut against the pain for a moment.

Michael glanced at me, a sympathetic look in his eyes. "I'd offer you a painkiller, but I'm afraid I don't have anything."

"Where are you taking me?"

He smiled again, his gaze back on the road. "We're going home, Meg. We still need to have a chat with Dr. Rose and Mr. Patchen. Of course, there's Dr. Bart's funeral today. Neither of us should miss that. Dr. Rose would be horribly upset, don't you think?" He glanced down at the dash. "We're making great time, though. I think we'll be able to knock out everything with time to spare as long as we don't run into any traffic or weather. And look at that sky . . . it's shaping up to be a spectacular day."

"Michael, I think we should go to the police," I said. "Turn ourselves in."

He only stared forward.

I craned my head to look in the back seat. Our bags were still there. "We've got Dr. Bart's files. If we turn in everything, they'll understand. They'll have to listen to us. None of this is your fault. He did this to you."

"You make it sound like a bad thing."

"You've hurt people, Michael. A lot of people."

"I've freed us. *You* and *me*. Don't you see that? All of this is for us. With Dr. Bart out there, his patients out there, Dr. Rose—we'd never be free. Someone would always know about us. With them gone, we're free. Finally free. All I've done is fix things, restore to us what is rightfully ours. I've taken our lives back." He turned to me briefly, then looked back at the road. "They locked you up at night like some kind of animal. That will never happen again. I won't let it."

"If we turn in the files," I said, "they will listen to us. They'll help you. Michael, please—I don't want to see anyone else get hurt!"

He clucked his tongue. "You really need to stop calling me Michael."

He pulled the wheel hard to the right and just barely made the off-ramp for a rest stop. The tires wrestled with the pavement as he slammed on the brakes and skidded. Somehow, he managed to maintain control. He steered the car off to the edge of the parking lot, next to a metal trash barrel, and threw it in park.

"What are you doing?"

He just shook his head. "Stay there."

As if I had a choice. As if I had a say in my current location.

Michael reached into the back seat, grabbed my bag with Dr. Bart's files, and got out. He dumped the contents of my bag into the trash barrel.

"Michael, what—"

"I'm not going to tell you again—stop calling me that."

He pulled a lighter from his pocket, ignited it, and lit one of the pages. The flames ate the paper, curling the page, glowing red, black, to gray dust. And when he couldn't hold it any longer, he dropped it into the barrel with the rest. Within moments, flames were leaping up into the air. He watched it all, expressionless.

I tugged at the tape on my wrists, but I couldn't get it loose.

From behind me, from inside the trunk of the car, someone started to beat against the back seat.

WRITTEN STATEMENT, MEGAN FITZGERALD

"Michael, what's that?"

Michael gave me a sideways glance and waved a finger through the air. "Nope, nope, little sister. What did I tell you?"

"Is that Nicole Milligan?" I craned my head toward the back seat, but I couldn't see anything.

" 'Is that Nicole Milligan . . . Mitchell.' "

"You seriously want me to call you Mitchell?"

"That would be the polite thing to do. It's my name."

I looked around the seat, at our bags in the back. "Take one of your pills, Michael. The dorozapine. That will help. It's not too late to fix this."

"Are you trying to make me go away already? We've got so much catching up to do. I've missed you." He closed his eyes and took a deep breath. "I've missed fresh air. I've missed the sound of traffic. You have no idea what it's like to be hidden away from the world, not even forgotten, but unknown, a footnote nobody wants to write. I've been trapped in a jar. A caged rat locked away in the lab. It's my time now. I've earned that." Opening his eyes, he walked back to my side of the car, the fire burning behind him. His hand came in through the window, and he stroked my cheek. "It's our time, Meg. Finally. When this is over, we can go wherever you want. I've got money stashed away. Passports and credit cards for both of us. We can disappear, just the two of us, and put everything else in the rearview mirror."

"There's no escaping this," I told him. "Your picture is all over the news. You're on the cover of every newspaper. Websites. The last time I checked, the reward was around five hundred thousand dollars. Where do you think you can hide?"

He was shaking his head. "Not my picture—*his*. They're looking for Michael, not me."

"But you're—"

He pressed a finger to my lips. "Don't say it. Don't taint this for me. They wanted to hang a Kepler by the neck, so I gave them one. I'd be willing to bet they're not even looking for me anymore."

I shook my head away from his finger. "What are you talking about?"

"You read the files, Meg. It's all right there."

"Michael, I don't—"

The back of his hand crashed across my jaw, slamming my head into the headrest. I raised my bound hands to my face and felt the warm trickle of blood from the corner of my cracked lip.

"Michael is dead." He said the words slowly, deliberately. Restrained. "Don't call me that. Never again. Do you understand? They have their Michael, their one hundred and eighty-five pounds of flesh. He's dead. There's just us now, and as long as we stay together, as long as we have each other, everything will be okay."

"Mitchell..." The name felt wrong on my lips, but I said it

anyway. "What about me, Mitchell? They're looking for me too. I can't hide from this. I'm all over the news too."

Nicole Milligan was beating against the back of the seat again, kicking the lid of the trunk. I could hear her muffled cries. I think I figured it out a moment before Mitchell said it aloud.

"Nicki always reminded me of you, Meg. I'm not gonna lie—there were times when I pretended she was you. When I wanted her to be you. Seems fitting, don't you think?"

He looked back at me, determination in his gaze. "Aside from her, there are only two other people left who know the truth. I'll make quick work of them—you can help me if you want to. Then we'll be free. Finally free."

His hand ran through my hair, brushed it back. When his touch went to my bare shoulder, when I felt his fingers against my skin, my body tensed. "The two of us together, Meg. Can you imagine? I hope you can. I've thought about nothing else for as long as I can remember. That's what kept me going, got me through it all. All those sessions with Dr. Bart. His little games. I'd have gone mad without you there. Knowing you were so close. I used to have a sweater of yours. I'd bury my face in it when Dr. Bart finally left me. I'd lose myself in your scent. I'd think of your smile, your delicate hands."

He reached to my lip, wiped the blood away. "I love your laugh, Meg. I always have. I promise, when this is all over, you will laugh again. I'll make you so happy. You're all that matters to me."

He looked down at his right wrist, then his left. His watch was gone. "We need to get moving. Patchen will be expecting us by now. After that, we've got a funeral to attend. We'll say our final goodbyes to Dr. Rose and be on our way. Two adopted lab rats, finally free."

He leaned through the window.

Mitchell leaned through the window.

And he kissed me. As Nicole Milligan screamed from the trunk, he kissed me, and I thought good and hard about biting him. In the interest of self-preservation, I held still.

CHAPTER ONE HUNDRED NINE

GIMBLE

TEST HIM AGAIN," GIMBLE said with frustration, staring at the tech.

The investigator just stood there. "I've tested him three times. There is zero gunshot residue on him or his clothing. He hasn't fired a weapon recently. I tested for blood spatter too, and that came up negative."

"The rain washed it all away—had to be all the rain," Gimble said, thinking out loud.

The investigator shook her head again. "It doesn't work that way. Visible signs, maybe, but barium and antimony can't be washed away. You can't even *scrub* them away. A casual douse in the rain wouldn't do it, no way. I'm confident in the results."

Gimble said, "Maybe he wore gloves and tossed them in the woods?"

"I tested his neck and his face in addition to everything else. People assume GSR only appears on the hands, but that's not true—it gets everywhere. There's blowback. Minute traces, mind you, but it would be there."

"This man hasn't fired a gun?"

"No, ma'am. I don't believe so."

She hadn't heard Vela come up behind her. He was holding his phone out. "I'm on with the local PD at Milligan's place. You'll want to hear this." He raised the phone to his mouth. "Officer, I've got you on speaker with Special Agent Jessica Gimble. Can you repeat what you just told me?"

Gimble pressed a hand over one ear and leaned in close to try and hear him over all the noise.

Vela's thumb pressed the volume button several times, raising it to the maximum.

" . . . arrived here about thirty minutes ago in response to a neighbor's noise complaint. Looks like someone busted out a car window in the street out front. The vehicle is gone but plenty of glass left behind. I found obvious signs of a break-in at the house—the front door was kicked in. The interior has been substantially vandalized. I've got a bullet buried in the wall near the front door. Looks like a rifle slug. Interior damage indicates a possible struggle. Four more bullet holes in the wall of a back bedroom from a small-caliber weapon. I've got blood on the floor in that room too, more on the floor in a hallway. Not enough to be fatal. We recovered all four slugs from the wall, no blood on them, so whatever caused the injury didn't originate with those shots."

"What about the woman? Nicole Milligan."

"We cleared the house when my backup arrived. There's no sign of her."

Gimble frowned. "What kind of timeline are we looking at? Can you tell?"

"The complaint call came in at about ten to six this morning. That's around twenty minutes before I arrived. The blood hasn't dried, CSI isn't here yet, but I'd be willing to bet it's under an hour old."

Gimble glanced at Vela. "Where is Milligan's house?"

"Ashtabula, Ohio. Just off Lake Erie."

"How far is that? What kind of distance?"

"Almost six hundred miles," Vela replied. "There's no way—"

Gimble wasn't listening. "That's less than nine hours' drive time. With limited stops, exceed the speed limit by just a little, it can be done."

"You can't possibly believe this guy," Vela said, nodding at the FBI van behind them. "He's just buying time. Maybe trying to set up some convoluted defense."

Gimble leaned back over Vela's phone. "Officer, the neighbor who phoned in the complaint—did she see anyone?"

"No, ma'am. She was in bed. Her bedroom backs up to Milligan's house but she was afraid to look out the window. She didn't want anyone to see her. She said she heard a loud bang—I'm guessing that was the front door. That was followed by shouting, a man and woman, the gunshot, glass shattering, then nothing. Those things, in that order. By the time she got up the nerve to look outside, nobody was there. She didn't see their vehicle."

Gimble eyed Vela. "A man and a woman? Two voices. She's sure of that?"

"Yes, ma'am."

Gimble's eyes had drifted back to the FBI van containing Kepler.

The officer continued. "Oh, and the mirror—I need to tell you about the mirror."

"The mirror?" Vela repeated.

"In the bathroom. Someone wrote, 'Some things stick. It's time to go home, Meg,' with a piece of soap on the glass."

Gimble and Vela exchanged a glance, then she leaned back toward the phone. "We'll need fingerprints, blood samples, copies of whatever you pull out of that place, understand? Agent Vela here will put you in touch with our crime lab to coordinate. If we can get a team out there fast enough, we will, but we're in a time crunch here. Your people may need to handle the collection. Are you comfortable with that?"

The officer was quiet.

"Officer?"

"Our lead detective just arrived on scene. I'll have him call you back in a minute."

The line went dead.

Vela put the phone in his pocket. "There has to be another explanation."

"And what if there's not? What if Kepler is telling the truth?" Gimble asked. "If there is a twin, and I agree, that's a big *if*, how could we tell them apart?"

Vela looked down at his shoes. "If they're dizygotic, fraternal, they would have developed from two different eggs. There would be obvious physical differences. They are no different than any other siblings, really, except they are born at the same time. Monozygotic, however—identical twins—share the same DNA. The same physical characteristics. We'd have to rely on external differences such as behavior, personality, scars." He paused for a second, then looked back at her. "Fingerprints aren't a genetic characteristic. The patterns and swirls are influenced by the developmental environment of the womb. Fingerprints would be different in identical twins."

Gimble thought about this for a second. "We've got Kepler's DNA at every crime scene, but not a single matching print. This is possible."

"A man can't hide for twenty-six years," Vela replied. "No way."

"Okay, the sister, then," Gimble countered. "She left here, drove straight to Milligan's house, and abducted her."

"You said she was hysterical, had a gunshot wound, so she was in no condition—"

"Give me another theory, then, anything," Gimble interrupted. "Give me something that makes sense. Either way, this isn't over. We've got another missing woman, possibly another victim at this point. Maybe two if Kepler is telling the truth."

Vela smoothed his hair back. He had nothing. He looked as tired as the rest of them.

Gimble climbed back into the van and pulled the door shut behind her.

Kepler was wearing an orange jumpsuit now, one specifically designed to be put on without removing restraints. Rows of snaps ran up the arms and legs. "Do you believe me now?" he said, rubbing at the cuffs on his wrists.

Gimble ignored the question. "How did you know about Nicole Milligan?"

"You weren't fast enough, were you?" Michael said, lowering his head. "He's already been there."

"How did you know about her?"

"Is she dead? Did you find Megan? Please tell me Megan is okay."

Gimble told him what they'd found. She knew she shouldn't. She had no reason to humor this man, but she told him anyway. Whether he was delusional or not, she needed to know what he knew.

When she finished, Kepler said, "You know about the feathers, right?"

"Longtin said Fitzgerald gave them to his patients."

"Not all his patients, only certain ones. When Alyssa Tepper was found in my apartment, I asked Megan to go through Dr. Bart's records. The patients who received feathers after sessions all had blue dots on their files. We found Alyssa Tepper's file and several others marked with the same dot. From what we pieced together, Mitchell has been systematically killing off those specific patients. Jeffery Longtin and Nicole Milligan were the only two still alive — that's why we came here."

"You want me to believe you came here to help Longtin, not kill him? You want me to ignore all the evidence against you and believe that?"

Kepler said, "You know I didn't shoot at you. I didn't stab anyone. If it wasn't me, who was it? You don't have to believe me, I won't ask you to do that. Just look at the facts, at the evidence. I turned myself in. You've had me locked up for hours and nothing has changed. It's still going on. Mitchell plans to finish this and at this point, I don't think he cares if you think it's me anymore." He looked up. "Did you find Nicole Milligan?"

Gimble saw no reason to lie to him. "Ashtabula, Ohio. Near Lake Erie."

"He's heading back to New York. He's going home."

It's time to go home, Meg.

Gimble said, "Who's left?"

Kepler looked down at his hands. "Maybe Dr. Rose? I don't know how far he's willing to take this."

Gimble looked at him then and realized he didn't know. There was no way he could, really. She had probably killed herself within minutes of Kepler turning himself in. Nobody would have told him, so she did. She waited for a reaction, any reaction, but there was none. Kepler clearly displayed two of the telltale signs of a sociopath—lack of emotion and lack of empathy. He took her death as a fact, another piece to an incomplete puzzle. He finally said, "If the house is gone, so is the room."

"What room?"

"The dark room. Where he'd lock me for . . . for treatment. Some of his other patients too." His face fell. He was shaking his head. "We had all the doctor's records, proof of what he was doing, but they were in the SUV that exploded. All that's gone now too."

The chopper flew over again, the loud *whoop* of the blades drowning out all else for nearly a minute before drifting off.

Kepler looked up toward the sound. "You're wasting time. They're obviously gone. Somebody else is going to die."

Gimble studied him; the two of them stayed quiet for some time. She wasn't sure if she believed any of this, but it was clear Kepler believed it. He wasn't exhibiting any outward signs of deception. Of course, that could be faked, but he seemed so tired and run down, she wasn't sure he was capable of such a thing right now.

She reached into her pocket and took out his bottle of pills. "Do you need one of these?"

His blank gaze fell on the bottle, then he looked back at her. "I will if you want me to, but I don't feel like I need them. I'd rather keep my head clear so we can find Megan."

"You're not finding anyone," Gimble told him. "You're going to prison."

Kepler looked her dead in the eye. "He doesn't know I turned myself in. You can't let the press know—he thinks I'm still on the run. If he finds out, he might change whatever he has planned. He might just kill Megan and Nicole and run. Disappear."

"You're wanted for multiple murders."

Kepler raised his hands and rattled the chains. "You've got me. I'm in federal custody. I'm not going anywhere. You've chased him for what? Two years? I'll help you. You can't risk him escaping again."

"You don't know his endgame, not really."

"If he's my brother, I understand him better than anyone else. I told you he'd go after Nicole Milligan and I was right."

"But you don't know where he's going next."

Kepler tilted his head slightly to the side. "What day is it, Agent?"

Gimble had to think about it for a second; she hadn't stopped moving in nearly a week. "Tuesday."

"Tuesday," Kepler repeated. "Dr. Barton's funeral is today. If anyone else connected to this is still alive, they'll be there. We need to get to New York. Get me eyes on that crowd and I can help you identify the people there. That's how you get ahead of him. If you lock me up instead, the press gets wind I'm in custody, tomorrow you'll be cleaning up more bodies and he'll be gone."

Gimble kept her glare trained on his face.

"You know I'm right," Kepler said. "You'll never catch him without me."

When Gimble got out of the van, she found Vela standing in the same spot as earlier. He glanced down at her twitching fingers as she closed the door.

He held up both palms deferentially. "This is obviously your call, but for what it's worth, I think he's working you."

"Call the airfield. I want the jet fueled and ready to go in twenty minutes," Gimble replied.

"Are we going to Los Angeles or New York?"

"New York," she said. "I don't know how Kepler is involved and I need to. Until then, we keep the fact that he's in custody under wraps. He stays in play. We see this through."

She took out her own phone and dialed first the assistant director, then the local Bureau branch in Erie. Gimble gave them Milligan's address and instructed them to take over the local investigation, treat it as a kidnapping, and send copies of all findings directly to her. Then she whistled for Vela, climbed into an FBI SUV, and said, "Come on."

PART 6

HOME

Sometimes, the only thing separating false from true is perception.

—Barton Fitzgerald, MD

DOBBS

I DON'T LIKE THIS; we should run it by Gimble first," Begley said.

They were parked on Browning Street, the tall peaks of Windham Hall visible through the branches of the old oaks a block down the road.

Dobbs had waited for a patrol officer to arrive at the bridge and secure the scene before heading back. He found Begley pacing the drive at the Fitzgerald gate, and he was in the passenger seat before the Nissan even stopped moving. He smelled of smoke. Now it appeared the agent was having second thoughts about coming here.

"You told her about the pass I found in the car, right?"

Begley shook his head. "She cut me off before I got the chance."

"Call her back, then," Dobbs replied. The visitor's pass was in his right hand; he found himself absently turning the plastic card in his fingers.

"She's not answering. They're still in the air." He glared at the pass. "That should be in evidence."

"I'll log it when we get back," Dobbs replied. "Want me to

return you to the house? If you'd rather stand around that place and watch everyone pick through the ashes, you're welcome to do that." Dobbs nodded toward the large brick structure. "I told you what Dr. Fitzgerald said before she jumped."

"That's hardly conclusive."

"There's the uniforms too." He held up the pass. "Her husband was here recently."

"You don't know that—maybe he left the pass on his seat months ago."

Dobbs shook his head. "The interior of that car was immaculate. There was nothing inside. Not even a pen or coins lying around. People like that don't leave things on the seat unless they recently used them or planned to use them soon."

"She was so cryptic on the phone," Begley said. "Guarded. Like she didn't want to talk on an open line."

"Gimble?"

"Yeah."

"But she did tell you she thought Kepler and his sister were heading back to New York, right?"

"Yeah."

"And you updated the BOLO? Locals, feds, everyone has eyes on this area?"

Begley nodded.

"Then I think you've done everything by the book. She'd want you to be right here, following a lead. She wouldn't want you sitting around waiting for the press to find him."

Begley looked out the window at Windham Hall and considered this.

"If she has a problem with it, you can always blame me. I work for LAPD; I don't answer to her. You can tell her you tried to talk me out of it and I'm some crazy rogue cop unwilling to listen to reason. Say you came along to keep me in check."

"That sounds about right."

Dobbs looked at him. "In or out? Last chance."

Begley gestured toward the building. "Just go."

Dobbs pulled out onto the quiet street and turned into the Windham Hall driveway. The large wrought-iron gate was closed. He stopped beside the call box, lowered his window, and pressed the button.

No response came.

"Looks abandoned," Begley said, peering through the gate.

He was right. The grass hadn't been mowed in some time. Several wooden benches lined the driveway on the other side; one of them had collapsed and was overgrown with weeds.

Dobbs pressed the button again. When he still didn't receive an answer, he took the visitor's pass and pressed it against the electronic card reader. A beep came from the speaker, a small blinking LED changed from red to green, and the large gate swung open. He waited for Begley to object again, but he didn't.

Dobbs eased the car forward.

Windham Hall was larger than he'd expected. Only the façade was visible from the street, but as they neared the building, it was clear it extended deep into the property from the back. Three stories tall with windows at the basement level, the building had once been a mansion and had been substantially added to over the years. Ivy covered the deep-red brick and climbed the outer walls, even some of the windows. It hadn't been cut back in a while. Thick vines hung from the trees like heavy green teardrops.

Dobbs followed the cracked driveway around, carefully avoiding several potholes, and parked near the front door. A small lot stood off to the side, thirty feet away. A silver Volvo was parked in the space nearest the building; there were no other vehicles.

"Somebody's here," Begley said.

"Patchen?"

"Maybe."

They got out of the car.

The front door was locked. When Dobbs knocked, nobody answered.

Next to the door, mounted in the brick and worn after years of exposure to the elements, was another card reader. A little red LED blinked patiently up at them.

WRITTEN STATEMENT, MEGAN FITZGERALD

"Talk to me, Meg."

I glanced over at Michael, Mitchell, whoever, in the driver's seat and raised my bound hands. "Cut away the duct tape, and we can chat."

"It's not on your mouth."

My hands dropped back into my lap. "What do you want me to say?"

"Tell me how much you missed me. How happy you are to see me. How you've longed for this moment your entire life, and you finally feel free," he said.

"Fuck you."

Mitchell beamed. "There'll be plenty of time for that later."

"Ew."

He reached over and squeezed my knee. "I'm just trying to lighten the mood."

We were driving fast. Blowing the limit by twenty, easy. I expected a police car to come screaming out from behind some trees or fly up behind us, but none did.

Nicole had stopped beating on the trunk lid about twenty minutes ago. She'd gone quiet again.

We'd flown past the first sign for Ithaca about five minutes earlier.

"You can't kill her," I said.

His hand left my knee and went back to the wheel. He signaled and passed a slow-moving minivan.

It must have been the adrenaline or the hysteria or just the general loss of my marbles, because I laughed at that. He's speeding with one girl tied up in the passenger seat, another in the trunk, half the country's law enforcement officers looking for him, and he signals before passing a soccer mom. To me, this seemed the equivalent of a bank robber holding the door for the SWAT team.

He smiled again. "It's good to see you happy. I've missed you, Meg."

"Promise me you won't kill her."

The smile grew.

"*Mitchell,*" I forced myself to say. "Promise me."

"I don't plan to do it alone. We'll kill her together. That's what Dr. Bart would have wanted. He'd be so proud if he could see us right now, you and me working together. Don't you think?" His smile grew wider. "Oh God, it just feels so good to be out. To be with you."

His hand went to my knee again, then slipped a little up my thigh.

I pulled away, got closer to my door.

The smile left his face. "What's wrong, Meg?"

"Why did you kiss me back there?"

"I don't understand. Why wouldn't I kiss you?"

"You're going to make me say it?" I frowned. "You're my brother!"

The car slowed. He stared straight ahead.

"Not my *real* brother," I went on. "But still. It's weird."

He looked over at me, the corner of his lip rising. "You still think I'm him, don't you?"

"You're sick, Michael. You're not taking your meds, and you're not thinking straight. You're allowing your illness to—"

"Ask me," he broke in. "Go ahead and ask me. I know you want to."

I looked at him. "Who's on the mark?"

"Mitchell," he stated flatly.

This was hopeless. "That's what I mean. You think you're Mitchell. You need your meds."

His hand left my leg again. "Michael is my brother. We left him at Longtin's little wooden shit shack back in St. Louis. I'm Dr. Bart's dirty little secret. The one he kept in a cage for twenty-six years."

DOBBS

THE FIRST TIME DOBBS pressed the ID card to the reader, nothing happened. Nothing happened the second time either.

"Hold on," Begley told him. Using the tail of his shirt, he wiped the screen of the reader. "Okay, try again."

This time when Dobbs pressed the card against the reader, the LED switched from red to green, and there was an audible click. He rested his free hand on the butt of the Glock on his hip and eased the door open. The bottom scraped against the marble floor, the wood swollen. Morning light spilled in from outside, illuminating a dark-paneled foyer with wood benches built into either side and empty coatracks filling the space above. The floor was covered in a dusting of dirt; several fall leaves fluttered against the baseboards, caught in spiderwebs.

"Federal agents!" Begley called out. "Is there anyone here?" His words echoed off the wall. The air smelled stale. "Is this place abandoned?" Begley asked, stepping inside.

Dobbs found a switch on the wall and flipped it. Fluorescent bulbs ticked to life from above, illuminating the foyer, a central hallway, and at least half a dozen other corridors leading away from the main room. "I don't think the power would be on."

A sign on the wall read DORMITORIES TO THE LEFT, ADMINISTRATION TO THE RIGHT. There were two staircases, one set leading up, the other down.

"Come on," Dobbs said, heading down the hallway to the right, toward administration. Begley followed, his hand resting on his gun too. Their footsteps were much louder than either man would have liked.

WRITTEN STATEMENT, MEGAN FITZGERALD

"That's not possible," I shot back.

Mitchell had slowed to the speed limit. "I don't understand. You know this. You know me."

I just shook my head.

"Did Dr. Bart mess with you too? Make you forget somehow?"

Before I could answer, he continued. "You read all his files, right? You read them?"

"The ones you burned back there? Our evidence? Those files?"

He said the next words slowly, driving them home. "There was one for Michael Kepler, and one for—"

I knew where he was going with this. "M. Kepler."

He nodded. "I've seen them too. Dr. Bart would let me read them—yours, mine, Michael's, Nicole's, all of them. All the others. Years' worth of data. I've seen it all. It started with Longtin. Patient zero, I guess you could call him. You read his file, right?"

I thought about what Michael and I had considered earlier in the car, but it seemed so crazy. "He studied Longtin's condition and wanted to produce dissociative identity disorder. He wanted to create multiple personalities."

Mitchell nodded again. "He just needed fertile ground. He got that with Michael and me. The way our mother died. The trauma of that. It left us wide open. You heard the tapes..."

The car was still slowing down. I don't think he had his foot on the gas pedal anymore.

"Michael doesn't have a brother," I said. "You are Michael."

He shook his head. "They found Michael in the closet at that motel, and child services called Windham Hall. Patchen came out to pick him up. I saw him load Michael into his car, and when he started to drive off, I ran out. I'd been hiding behind the Dumpsters, watching the police. But I saw him taking away my brother, and I ran. I couldn't let him take away my brother. When he stopped, I got in the car too. I didn't think twice about it. I yanked open the door and scrambled in beside him. At first, I thought he was going to tell me to get out, the way he looked at me. But he didn't; instead, he just drove off. He took us both back to Windham Hall. We were only four years old. I never considered the fact that nobody else saw me. I just couldn't bear to be separated from Michael. We only had each other. I was probably in shock too. After seeing what Max did."

He reached into his back pocket and took out the paper he'd retrieved from Nicole Milligan's jewelry box. He tossed it into my lap.

"Michael and I were born in a crack house on a filthy mattress in Brooklyn. That piece of paper is the only proof I even exist."

I unfolded the document. It was a birth certificate, issued by Windham Hall four years after the stated date of birth. The name read *Mitchell Aaron Kepler*.

DOBBS

THERE WERE BOXES EVERYWHERE.

Stacked against the walls, on top of the furniture.

Every room they passed was in some form of disarray. Chairs were stacked on tables. Sheets covered cabinets. Large rugs had been rolled up and were standing against the walls or balanced precariously in corners. Paintings stood in piles, the walls above them darker in the spots where they'd once hung. At the windows, heavy draperies were pulled tight, sealing out the light.

They found the door to the administration office open. Several wooden chairs sat outside of it, their surfaces marred with the scribbling and scratches of the children who'd occupied them over the years.

Dobbs caught movement inside the room. Begley saw it too. A shadow against the back wall, there for only a moment, then gone.

Dobbs motioned for Begley to move to the left of the door. He neared the wall on the right and eased closer to the opening, releasing the leather strap on his Glock with the thumb of his right hand. In position, he nodded at Begley.

"Federal agents," Begley called out. "Step out where we can see you!"

There was a loud thump, followed by a crash. Someone swore in a gruff voice.

A thin, wiry man in his mid-sixties came out of an office in the far back corner, a confused look on his face. "Can I help you, gentlemen?"

He held a revolver in his hand.

Λ big one.

CHAPTER ONE HUNDRED FIFTEEN

WRITTEN STATEMENT, MEGAN FITZGERALD

"Is this real?"

I held the birth certificate awkwardly in my bound hands, my fingers running over the intricate trim pattern in gold foil along the outer edges, my eyes glued to the name.

Mitchell Aaron Kepler.

Nicole Milligan began thumping on the trunk again. One fist, over and over. *Thump, thump, thump . . .*

His foot found the gas pedal, and we began to pick up speed. We passed another sign for Ithaca—next exit, two miles.

"When we got to Windham Hall, Patchen rushed us inside to his office. He told Michael and me to sit in chairs outside his door. He closed it, but I could still make out the words, some of them, anyway—'How fast can you get here? We don't have much time. Double, it will cost double.'"

He fell silent for a moment. "That's the part I remember most, 'it will cost double.' I think it stuck out because Max's dealer had told Max the same thing the night before when he'd tried to buy some smack or weed or meth or whatever he needed to satisfy his latest jones. Michael was completely silent beside me, probably in shock. I remember somebody had carved a name into the arm of the chair. He kept running his fingers over the letters, following them like a little track.

Over and over; he wouldn't stop. I'd pull his hand away, and he'd just do it again. Fitzgerald showed up about an hour later—Dr. Bart, we were told to call him. When he came in, he knelt down in front of us, took our hands in his, and told us everything would be okay."

He clucked his tongue and glanced out the side window. "For a second there, I think I even believed him. I know I wanted to believe him. I'm sure Michael did too. At that age, you want to trust adults, but every adult in our lives had let us down, had lied to us, and I guess we built up a wall because of it. I should have known they were both lying when they separated us, but even then, we wanted to believe."

He eased the car to the right, following the Ithaca exit.

After several more turns, I knew where he was going.

We spotted the smoke a minute or two after that. My house, a smoldering ruin off in the distance.

CHAPTER ONE HUNDRED SIXTEEN

DOBBS

PUT THE GUN DOWN!" Begley shouted, his own weapon out and pointing at the man in an instant.

"How did you get in here?" the man replied, the barrel of his revolver leveled at Begley. "This is private property. You're trespassing."

Dobbs raised both his hands, palms out. "We're with the FBI. We have reason to believe Michael Kepler might be coming here. Are you familiar with Michael Kepler?"

"Of course. I watch the news."

"Lower your weapon," Dobbs said in the most soothing voice he could. "Are you Lawrence Patchen?"

He nodded. "Show me your identification. Slowly."

Dobbs reached into his back pocket, withdrew his badge, and held it up.

The man squinted at the badge and ID card. "You're LAPD. You don't have any jurisdiction here. I want you both to leave immediately."

"I'm afraid we can't do that," Begley said, circling slowly to his right.

"Don't!" the man shouted. "Neither of you move!"

The gun, a Colt Python, was too big for him. His hand was shaking from its weight or from nerves or both. His finger grazed the trigger.

Begley continued to move around him. The man followed him with the barrel, his narrow eyes darting from Begley to Dobbs and back again.

"I'm a federal agent," Begley said. "This man is a homicide detective. Like he said, we're both in pursuit of Michael Kepler, and we have reason to believe he's coming here."

If this meant anything to the man, his face didn't give it away.

"Put your gun down," he said to Begley.

"I'm afraid I can't do that."

The Python went off with the blast of a cannon; the bullet struck Begley in his upper chest. He fell back, knocking over several boxes behind him as he crashed to the floor. When the gun came around toward Dobbs, he dived to the side, landed hard on the marble. A second shot exploded; the bullet buried itself in the wall above him. He rolled and had his own gun out and pointing up before he stopped moving.

Patchen was gone.

Dobbs scrambled to his feet and went to Begley. A large red stain was spreading over his sky-blue shirt. A puddle grew underneath him. He opened his mouth to say something, but nothing came out. His lips were flecked with blood. He was choking, choking on his own blood. Dobbs pulled out his cell phone and dialed 911 with one hand while pressing on the wound with his other.

When the operator picked up, he didn't give them a chance to speak. "This is LAPD Detective Garrett Dobbs. I've got a federal agent down at the Windham Hall orphanage in Lansing. Gunshot wound to the chest, possible punctured lung. Send help immediately. Suspect armed and on the premises."

There was no response.

He looked down at the display—

CALL ENDED.

He had only one bar.

He dialed again, but this time he just got dead air.

The first call had dropped while he was talking. He had no idea if the operator had heard any of what he said.

Begley's arm came up slowly. He pointed at the door, toward the hallway. "Go." The word was thin, barely a whisper. Blood pooled in his mouth, staining his teeth, and dripped down his cheek.

Dobbs shook his head. "No way."

Begley's hand went to his chest; he pushed away Dobbs's hand and covered the wound himself. Blood oozed out between his fingers. "They'll find me. Go."

"I'm not leaving an officer down."

Begley stared up at him. His lips parted again, but the life left his eyes, and he didn't utter another word.

CHAPTER ONE HUNDRED SEVENTEEN

WRITTEN STATEMENT, MEGAN FITZGERALD

Mitchell pulled to the side of the road when my house came into view. He hadn't turned down our street but instead had taken Hickory and followed it up to the top of the hill. The property was visible in the valley beneath us; the driveway was still filled with ambulances, fire trucks, and other vehicles most likely belonging to law enforcement.

The car jerked as he shifted into park before we had come to a complete stop. I heard Nicole Milligan roll in the trunk, thud against the back seat. She let out a muffled sound of complaint.

Mitchell was out the door and standing next to the car, his face turning red.

He stared down below.

My stomach sank at the sight of it. It didn't seem real; it was like watching a scene from a movie. The roof was a skeleton of sticks. Half the walls were missing. All the windows were destroyed. Black smoke poured out from every opening, staining the sky and what little still stood of the outer shell.

When he got back in the car, I asked, "Do you think she was in there? Dr. Rose?"

He ignored me and pulled back onto Hickory, followed the quiet street down to Danby Road, and made his way back to NY-13 toward Lansing.

"Do you think she was in the house?" I repeated, craning my head back toward the smoke. "She must have gotten out, right?"

He kept ignoring me. I watched as he reached over and flicked on the radio. He pressed the scan button, and kept punching it with his fingertip until he came to a news station.

"...Cornell University security has been asked to prevent the student body from approaching the bridge while local and federal authorities attempt to piece together the events unfolding this morning. Why the Cornell instructor would jump from the beloved suspension bridge to her death in Fall Creek Gorge is still unknown. Dr. Rose Fitzgerald, a practicing psychologist, recently lost her husband, Dr. Barton Fitzgerald, a renowned psychiatrist and author. Perhaps his death was too much for her. We have learned a substantial police presence has gathered at her home in South Hill. A fire has been reported at the residence as well. We will continue to keep you apprised as events unfold. Dr. Rose Fitzgerald is survived by two adopted children, her daughter, Megan, and son—"

Mitchell shut off the radio, beat his fist on the steering wheel, and screamed so loud your buddies at Quantico probably heard him.

CHAPTER ONE HUNDRED EIGHTEEN

GIMBLE

THE WHEELS OF THE Gulfstream G550 hit the tarmac at Ithaca Tompkins Regional Airport with a chirp. Gimble felt the jet engines reverse, heard the brake flaps deploy, sensed the pressure of deceleration. Rather than look out the window, she continued to stare at the back of Michael Kepler's head.

He was chained to a seat two rows in front of her in the small jet, his fingers gripping the armrest. He'd barely moved during the flight. He may have even slept. She couldn't bring herself to talk to him, not once. All the facts of this case rattling around in her head and running into each other had given her a terrible headache.

Vela sat across from her, his eyes closed.

As the plane slowed and maneuvered toward a small terminal, her mobile phone beeped with an incoming text message, then immediately rang with a call. She glanced down at the display, saw that it was Sammy, and answered. "Gimble."

"Okay, this is weird so I'm not exactly sure what I've got, but you need to know about it. What do you know about tractor trailers?"

Gimble said, "They drive ridiculously slow and love to cut me off in traffic, and at least half of them seem to be owned by Walmart."

"Have you ever driven one?"

"Sammy, I'm really not in the mood for twenty questions. What are you getting at?"

"When we were at Longtin's cabin, I noticed something very strange in the GPS data we pulled from Kepler's truck. The data recorder captures a lot of different things—full GPS, speeds, engine data, starts, stops; I've been focusing on RPMs. Tractor trailers like the one Kepler drove max out at around nineteen hundred, much lower than cars. You'll never see one break two thousand. It's not possible without redlining, burning out the engine. When I isolate the data for each of the murder victims we traced back to his routes, there is a stop somewhere near the highway. When the vehicle starts moving again, the RPMs are anywhere from one thousand to four thousand. They stay in that range to and from each of our murder scenes, then drop down to below two thousand back at the highway. Every time."

Gimble squeezed her eyes shut. "I don't follow. Are you saying he changed vehicles to commit the murders?"

"Not only did he change vehicles, but he took the time to remove the Trux Data recorder from his tractor trailer and plug it into the secondary vehicle—some kind of car, can't tell what. When he returned after the murder, he pulled the device again and placed it back in the truck," Sammy explained.

"Why would he do that? It just makes him look guilty. Draws a clear line right to each murder."

"Yeah," Sammy said. "Exactly. Doesn't make sense for *him* to do it at all."

Gimble was staring at the back of Kepler's head again. "But if somebody wanted to frame him..." Her voice trailed off.

"Yeah."

Gimble blew out a breath.

I don't think he cares if you think it's me anymore.

"Did you find any proof he has a brother?" she asked.

"Nothing," Sammy replied. "It's like Vela told you. There's no record of his birth. His birth certificate was issued by Windham Hall when they brought him in at four years old. It's very possible his mother gave birth to another child too and it was never recorded. It happens a lot, particularly with the homeless or low-income women. I couldn't find anything to indicate where he was born. No shots—no medical records, period. Nothing for those first four years. He didn't exist until they brought him into that orphanage."

"That orphanage," Gimble repeated. "Do you know if Vela's warrant got approved?"

"He hasn't applied for one yet. I checked the system right before I called you. Do you want me to do it?"

Gimble looked over at Vela. His eyes were still closed. She'd told him to do it for the umpteenth time back at Longtin's cabin. "Yeah, rush it through. Call me as soon as it gets approved."

"You got it," Sammy said. "Oh, and boss? One other thing."

"What?"

"Kepler's birth certificate. The physician's signature is Dr. Barton Fitzgerald."

She frowned. "Are psychiatrists allowed to do that?"

"Dunno, but he did."

The plane lurched to a stop.

Vela's eyes snapped open.

Outside, a black SUV rolled onto the tarmac about twenty feet away. The driver got out and opened the doors.

Gimble looked over at Kepler. "Call me back when you get that, Sammy."

"You got it."

The call disconnected, and Gimble checked her text messages. The last one to come in was from Begley thirty-five minutes ago—

At Windham Hall with Dobbs.

She dialed him but got voice mail.

"What's going on?" Vela asked, rolling his head, stretching.

"How far is Windham Hall from here?"

"I have no idea."

She unbuckled her seat belt, nodded at Kepler, and stood. "Get our prisoner in the car. We're heading there first."

CHAPTER ONE HUNDRED NINETEEN

WRITTEN STATEMENT, MEGAN FITZGERALD

Driving again.

Fast.

Too fast.

"Michael, slow down," I said, barely able to hear my own voice over the straining engine.

"Don't call me Michael," he growled.

"Mitchell, stop!"

He slammed his foot down on the brakes, and the rear of the car fishtailed. I flew forward, but my seat belt yanked me back. Nicole Milligan thumped against the back seat. He didn't stop, but he slowed just enough to avoid hitting a little boy on a bicycle probably on his way to school. The kid rolled off into the bushes to avoid us and held up his middle finger as we sped past.

Michael was already accelerating again.

"Where are we going?"

Houses flew past us on both sides. He was doing at least twice the speed limit through a residential neighborhood.

"Dr. Rose needed to die. I was supposed to kill her. I *deserved* to kill her. It was my right." The words came from him rapid-fire. He just spat them out, not necessarily for me, just to get them out there. His hands were shaking, his face

435

bright red. "All of them." He fumed. "Every damn last one of them."

"You said he kept you in a cage," I said, attempting to change the subject, calm him somehow.

"What?"

"Dr. Bart. You said he kept you in a cage."

His fingers drummed on the steering wheel. He didn't look at me when he spoke, just stared ahead. "They gave you everything. You and Michael. That big house. Good schools. The perfect life. They gave you and him everything, and he locked me away in a hole."

"I don't understand."

"She knew all about it. She knew everything that man did."

"Dr. Rose?"

He nodded. "Separating us, that was her idea. That's what he told me."

"Separating you and Michael?"

"His plan had always been to use what he learned from Longtin to try and re-create dissociative identity disorder in someone else, but when he told Dr. Rose there were two of us but a record of only one, she told Dr. Bart and Patchen to separate us immediately, like two groups in an experiment. It was her idea to take Michael back to the house and leave me at Windham Hall. Michael and I had both suffered the same traumatic experience. He'd have two chances. That bitch not only mapped out a detailed plan to fracture what was left of our minds but also convinced Dr. Bart of what should be used as a model for each of our secondary identities. They sealed the decision the moment my twin brother and I started to lead separate lives. They'd convince me I was Michael and twist him into believing he was me. Between the three of them, they meticulously documented both our lives," he said. "Dr. Bart would make me read Michael's journals, listen to his interviews, relive his every experience, and repeat them back to him over and over again until he felt I was convinced it happened to me. He called me Michael, and heaven forbid I referred to myself by my real name. You heard the tapes, the horrible things he'd do. He'd put me in that room, find some way to convince me, break me, make Michael's experiences my own..." His voice trailed off. "When he'd leave, I'd spend hours just repeating my own name, running through my day, my own experiences, as limited as they were, to try and hold on, but it became so hard. I felt myself slipping away. It was all Michael, Michael, Michael. I was kept in the dark. I ate, I slept. I was allowed to read what Michael read. I could only know what Michael knew. Live what Michael lived. They created these detailed narratives accounting for every moment of our fake lives, drilling them into our heads." As if to punctuate this, he twisted his fist against the side of his skull, then rapped against his temple, three hard taps. "With Michael, they tried to twist him into me—forced him to believe he was Mitchell for countless sessions until neither of us knew who we were anymore."

I found myself looking at his hair as he spoke, as he did this—his blond hair.

I had dyed Michael's hair blond back at the motel.

He caught me looking at his hair.

CHAPTER ONE HUNDRED TWENTY

DOBBS

DOBBS TRIED CPR, BUT he knew it was useless. Begley was gone. The bullet had gone straight through, and when he tried to roll him to get a look at the exit wound, he found a two-inch hole in the man's back.

He set him down gently.

Dobbs's hands were covered in blood. He wiped them on his jeans.

He heard a metal door clunk open and then close somewhere down the hall, back the way he'd come.

He scrambled to his feet, shoved his phone into his pocket, pulled his own gun, and ran toward the front door.

A light blinked off at the bottom of the stairs.

Dobbs took the steps two at a time. The light came back on about a third of the way down, tripped by a motion sensor in the far corner of the stairwell. The metal door was at the bottom. Solid steel with a push bar in the center, no window. He knelt low, squeezed into the corner beside it, reached up, and depressed the bar. He gave the door a hard push, then came around fast, sweeping right to left and then back again with his Glock. Although the long hallway was lit by bare fluorescent bulbs strung from the ceiling, each began to darken. First the closest to him, then the next, and the next after that, switching off in sequence.

More motion sensors.

Each set with a short timer, maybe thirty seconds.

No sign of Patchen.

The hallway seemed to stretch the length of the building with more than a dozen doors at intervals throughout, all metal, none labeled. At least, not that he could see from where he crouched.

Each door vanished with the light, swallowed by the growing grasp of total black.

The last light to remain on was two-thirds of the way down. The next light, the one hanging at the end of the hall, had never come on. Patchen had disappeared behind one of these doors. He'd gone no further. Dobbs bolted down the hall, the lights coming back on with him. A door to his left, another to his right. One on each side of the hallway.

Dobbs reached out and touched the doorknobs. Neither was warm or damp or felt different from the other. He twisted each one slightly. Both turned. His eyes quickly scanned the wall; he located the manual switch for the light above him and turned it off. Then he dropped to the ground and looked under each door.

He caught a hint of light under the door on his left a moment before it switched off, and all went dark.

His hands went to the doorknob again.

He counted to three in his head, then twisted and pulled the door open.

The motion triggered the light on that side, and it switched on again.

Stairs.

Black rubber treads dropping down into more darkness with an old black metal handrail on the wall at the right.

From somewhere in that darkness below, Patchen shouted, "I didn't mean to shoot him! The gun just went off!"

"Then drop the gun and come up slowly with your hands on your head!" Dobbs shouted back.

Silence.

Dobbs could hear dripping water down there. It was some kind of subbasement. "Now, Patchen!" he shouted down the stairwell, tightening his grip on the Glock, pointing it into the absolute nothingness below.

When Patchen spoke, he sounded closer. "Okay. I'm coming up."

Remaining low, Dobbs pressed into the doorjamb, tight against the wall.

The water dripped again.

Patchen fired.

The muzzle blast was a blinding white light, the sound deafening.

WRITTEN STATEMENT, MEGAN FITZGERALD

He ran his hand through his hair. "You left the box from the dye in your trash at the motel. I bought the same one. How does it look? I think I like being a blond."

I wasn't sure I believed anything he was telling me.

"I'm not him," he said when I didn't speak. "I can still tell the difference, even if you can't."

He snatched the birth certificate from my hand and shoved it into his pocket.

My eyes narrowed. "If you're not Michael, why continue to pretend to be him? Why kill all those people and frame your own brother?"

"I didn't exist. I still don't. The birth certificate is the only proof I have. Michael, Michael, Michael, all those years as Michael. I had no television, no news, nothing. My life was a void. They didn't allow me to exist. They kept me in my hole while Michael lived. While the two of you *lived*. They stole everything from me. Twenty-six years gone, while Michael lived. Don't you get it? He's had his life. It's my turn now." He rattled off names: "Alyssa Tepper, Darcey Haas, Issac Dorrough, Selena Hennis, Cassandra Shatley, Katrina Nickols, and the lovely Nicki Milligan bouncing around in the trunk—every single one of them helped the Fitzgeralds and Patchen cover this up. He bought them all off—a couple extra dollars in their pocket. They stole my life just as much as the Fitzgeralds did, so I stole theirs. I took it back. I made it right. If I could kill them all again, I would. What I did to them was merciful compared to what they all did to me."

He turned to me and said something I didn't expect. "I was there for your ninth birthday, Meg. We met four times when you were ten. Dozens more after that. We've eaten dinner together. As part of his therapy, Dr. Bart would sometimes bring me back to the house and I'd be Michael for the day. Those were the moments I'd live for. You were always so kind to me. Of course, you had no idea I wasn't him. I can't imagine what the Fitzgeralds would have done if I'd told you. If I violated the rules of their tests. I slept in Michael's bed once. I got up in the middle of the night and crawled in beside you—do you remember that? You wrapped your arms around me, held me. You were so peaceful. To this day, I still remember the sounds you made while you were sleeping that night, each gentle breath. The warmth of your body next to mine. You have no idea how I've clung to that moment, how many times I forced my mind to go back to that moment to escape Dr. Bart's torture, his sessions. You were the only bright light for me."

He reached over and squeezed my hand. "Everything I've done has been for you, Meg. You're the only thing that has ever really mattered in my life. The little life I've been allowed to live. And pretty soon, after Patchen is dead, when they're all finally dead, I'll have peace. When they find what's left of Nicole's body, they'll think she's you, and you'll be free too. Both of us, finally. We can be happy. I promise you, I'll make you happy."

What did he expect me to say to that? My mind was swimming. I turned back to the window. I'd been to Windham Hall only a few times with the Fitzgeralds, but I recognized the road and I knew we were close.

CHAPTER ONE HUNDRED TWENTY-TWO

DOBBS

THE BULLET STRUCK THE metal door on the opposite side of the hallway above and behind Dobbs with a loud *ping,* then ricocheted off to the side.

His eyes had grown used to the dark, so the white flash of the muzzle blast was blinding—a strobe that left all else dark with bright flecks floating through his vision.

Before the echo of the blast died down, Dobbs fired the Glock, four shots, then three more, all down toward the base of the stairs. Each time he pulled the trigger, his own muzzle blast added to the confusion. When he fired that seventh shot, he forced himself quickly to his feet and started down the steps two at a time, firing four more times as he went.

Motion-activated lights came on with each step, chasing him, and when he got to the bottom, he threw himself forward, leaping across the room. He crashed into some old wooden chairs stacked against the wall and fell to the ground in a heap. He shot wildly, his arm swinging from left to right in a wide arc until the gun did nothing but click.

He ejected the empty magazine from his Glock, pulled another from his back pocket, slammed it into the butt of the gun, and racked the slide, all while his eyes fought the confusion of light and dark and tried to take in the room.

Damp concrete floor. A large boiler and HVAC equipment against the wall to his left next to the stairs. There were folding tables piled high next to the chairs he was tangled up in. A large drain was at the center of the room. The entire space smelled musty.

He crouched behind the tables.

No sign of Patchen.

If he'd hit him, the man hadn't made a sound. Dobbs didn't see any blood on the floor.

"You have no idea what you're stepping into, Detective. You should get out of here while you can. Just go. I'm a walking dead man. Stick around long enough, and you'll join me." Patchen's voice echoed off the concrete block walls. It came from everywhere and nowhere.

The basement lights began to tick off, one at a time, thirty seconds after the last detected motion. Dobbs forced himself not to move. "You killed a federal agent, Patchen. You're going to prison. You'll get the needle."

Patchen laughed. "That child is coming for me. I can feel it. A needle would be a blessing. I'm more likely to eat my own gun before the day's out."

"I can protect you from Kepler."

"Think so? You have no idea what Fitzgerald created."

"Put the gun down and step out where I can see you."

Another light went dark. Two left.

"I've got work to do, Detective," Patchen replied. "And you're slowing me down. If you don't let me go, I'll have no choice but to kill you. You know I will. I've got nothing to lose. What do you have to lose, Detective? Who's waiting for you back in Los Angeles?

Is someone going to cry when I put a hole in your chest to match your partner's?"

The last two lights flicked off in quick succession.

The basement went totally black.

Both men went quiet.

Water dripped.

WRITTEN STATEMENT, MEGAN FITZGERALD

Mitchell passed Windham Hall, his foot never leaving the gas as we flew by. He made a right turn on Graham, then another on Winton. He followed the narrow lane nearly to the end, then turned right onto an unmarked blacktop road. The surface was cracked, riddled with potholes. Weeds and long blades of grass poked up from the various openings as Mother Nature worked to reclaim the ground.

"Where are we going?" I asked.

"Dr. Bart never took you this way?"

I shook my head.

"I couldn't go through the front door. Particularly at odd hours. Somebody might have seen me. There were too many children running around, too many little eyes. The adults too. The employees. They hid me from everyone. Only Michael could pass through the front door, only Michael, and I wasn't always Michael. All my time here, and I don't think anyone other than Patchen and the Fitzgeralds ever knew. Well, Roland too."

"Roland Eads?"

"When I needed to get out, when I needed time alone, Roland got me out of my cage. He'd sneak me out this door and help me get back inside. He knew what they were doing was wrong. I don't think he understood why I came back. Every time he snuck me out, I always came back."

"Why would you?"

"Where else would I go?"

He slowed to a crawl. Thick branches reached down from above, scratched at the roof of the car. A field came into view, overgrown and wild.

"I'd sometimes see the other boys playing out there, but then Fitzgerald would make me duck down before they could see me. I'd hear them laughing, shouting, off in the distance while I was pressed against the carpet in front of the seat. One time, he made me wait down there for over an hour."

The car came to a stop at a tall stone wall with a metal gate at the center. He shifted into park, pulled apart the wires under the steering column. The engine sputtered and died. "End of the road, little sister."

From a compartment in his door, he took out the scissors with the purple handle. The blades were stained with dried blood. He rolled his shoulders against the seat back and winced. "You got me good, Meg. I'm not gonna lie. Hurts like a son of a bitch, but I can't fault you for doing it. I probably would have done the same. I'd have gone for the kidneys, though. Much lower, on the right or left. When stabbing the back, always go for the kidneys."

He said this like he expected me to break out my note-pad and take notes, draw a little diagram, prepare for a pop quiz later. I'd probably choose a different option, though. If I had those scissors, I'd put them nice and deep into his neck, or maybe his eye. Kidneys seemed a little too slow, too compassionate.

He leaned forward and snipped away the duct tape from

my ankles. My bound hands were on the door handle when he said, "You run, and I'll kill little Nicki. I'll gut her like a pig in a slaughterhouse."

"You're going to kill her anyway," I replied, my hand still on the handle. "And I don't know her. Maybe she has it coming to her. What makes you think I care?"

"Because I know you better than you know yourself. I read all your files too, remember? Dr. Fitzgerald shared everything with me. I know all your deep dark secrets, your desires, your mistakes, your regrets. I know about that cute little birthmark on your inner thigh, the one shaped like a heart. I know you hated it enough to try and cut it out when you were ten, and I know whenever someone puts his head down there for the first time, you wait for the inevitable comment about it, some snarky remark." He leaned forward, close enough I could smell mint on his breath. "I know you so well, I'm certain that even if I walked around and opened that door for you, you'd keep your butt planted firmly in that seat. Not because you want to protect that bitch in the trunk, but because you're curious to see what happens to her. You want a front-row seat for the show."

He reached over and stroked my cheek with his long fingers; his palm felt warm. My skin tingled. I tried to deny this, tell myself it was fear, the adrenaline. I was an excellent liar. Not good enough, though. I learned long ago, you can lie to others, but it's impossible not to see right through your own bullshit no matter how many times you repeat it. I closed my eyes and let him touch me, and deep down, a part of me didn't want him to stop.

He whispered, "In a few more hours, this will be over, Meg. They'll all be gone. I'll take you someplace safe and I'll show you what it really means to be loved. You and I were always meant to be together. Fate saw to that, brought us together all those years ago and kept us together ever since. Doesn't matter who or what tried to get between us. It's always been you and me. It always will be."

My eyes still closed, I pressed my face against his palm and raised my bound hands. "If you really trust me, cut this tape away too. Let me help you."

His fingers slipped down from my cheek to the curve of my neck, dipped under the thin material of my top. "Not yet, but soon enough. We still have work to do. I need you to get me something out of the glove box."

When I opened my eyes, he was back in the driver's seat, a mischievous grin on his face like he had a secret bubbling inside, and it was all he could do to keep from telling me.

I pressed the button on the glove box, but it didn't move.

"It sticks a little. Tug at the top."

So I did, and it came open. A thin metal chain kept it from tilting too far and spilling the contents on the floor. A ziplock bag sat on top of tattered manuals for the car. Several aged receipts were crammed in there too. Oil changes, new tires, Taco Bell.

I took out the bag.

Four feathers were inside.

"Bring them with us. I hope we have enough. I'm expecting several guests. Then there's Nicki, of course."

"Of course," I heard myself say, because what do you say to that?

He kissed my cheek, pressed the trunk release, and got out of the car. I climbed out too. Eyed the overgrown field. I could so easily run. Instead, I watched as he swiftly rounded the back of the car to where Nicole Milligan had already managed to scramble out to the ground. She twisted on the blacktop like a dying worm. Mitchell had not only taped her ankles but continued to wrap the duct tape all the way up to her thighs. Her arms were taped up to her elbows. Another piece of tape covered her mouth and circled her head numerous times; half her hair would probably come out when it came off. She wasn't going anywhere without help.

Mitchell tucked the scissors in his back pocket, picked up her squirming body like a bag of dirty laundry, and threw her over his shoulder, wincing under her weight. He hadn't changed shirts, and a large, dark bloodstain covered a good portion of his back. Through the hole I'd made earlier when I stabbed him, I could see more duct tape. He'd used it to close the wound. Versatile stuff, duct tape.

"This way, Meg," he said, starting toward a metal door painted brown. "Bring your backpack."

I snatched up my backpack and followed a few paces behind him.

Nicole Milligan's wide, bloodshot eyes drilled into me, pleaded with me, but I couldn't do anything but listen to her muffled screams. I looked back at her, a little part of me curious at what point anger would give way to fear, at what point fear would give way to regret, at what point she'd finally surrender. I wondered if I'd recognize those shifts in her eyes.

CHAPTER ONE HUNDRED TWENTY-FOUR

DOBBS

A LIGHT ON THE far end of the room blinked to life.

Dobbs raised his gun to fire but not before Patchen shot three rounds from somewhere on the opposite side of the room, all at the ceiling. His motion triggered two of the basement lights to come back on; his bullets struck the fluorescent bulbs in sequence, quickly plunging the room back into darkness.

Dobbs rose, pointing his barrel in the direction of the other man's muzzle flash. He fired three shots of his own, then dropped back down. Like the rounds fired by Patchen, the shots were horribly loud, echoing off all the concrete and then slowly fading, leaving Dobbs with a ringing in his ears, a high-pitched whine. Then he heard the drip of water.

And silence.

Dobbs closed his eyes, tilted his head, listened.

Ringing in his ear.

Drip.

Shuffling of feet.

Drip.

Patchen pulled the trigger again, but only a click came, followed by four more. Empty.

Dobbs opened his eyes.

He rose slowly, crouching, remaining low. He held his gun out ahead of him, led with it, as he slowly rounded the stack of tables and made his way out to the open floor, careful not to make a sound.

Soft footsteps on the far end of the room.

Dobbs raised his gun, prepared to fire. His eyes desperately attempted to find a target in the darkness, but with the complete absence of light, he saw nothing, only murky black.

A door squeaked open. There was the clatter of something crashing against a wall.

Another light came on, this one from a room just off the large central chamber. A door closing, twenty feet ahead and to his left, a shadow shrinking on the other side.

For one brief instant, Dobbs glimpsed the basement again before the door closed completely, sealing the light away behind it.

He shuffled across the concrete to the door, pressed his ear against it.

Patchen came at him from the opposite direction at a run. The gun was no longer in his hand. Instead, he held a hatchet. The blade came down through the air in a sweeping arc toward Dobbs's gun, his right arm. He pushed back and crashed into the door behind him; the sharp blade cut into his skin just below his shoulder as he fell into the room.

Dobbs landed on his back; his gun clattered across the concrete floor, and he scrambled toward the far end of the room on his hands and feet in a quick, awkward crab walk, warm blood soaking his sleeve, dripping to the floor, trailing behind.

Patchen came at him again, huffing hard now, and swung the hatchet down and to the left. When it whistled past Dobbs, Patchen immediately swung back again in the opposite direction, driving Dobbs deeper into the room. His eyes were wild, wide. He swung a third time, and pain shot down Dobbs's arm as he smacked against the far wall. With more instinct than thought, he rolled to his left. The blade came down and cracked into the concrete inches from where he'd been.

When Dobbs rolled back in the other direction, he expected Patchen to strike again, was prepared to kick at his shin, take his leg out from under him, but Patchen was darting across the room to the door. He was out a moment later, slamming the door behind him.

A bolt slid into place.

A lock clicked tight.

Half in shock, Dobbs pushed back against the wall and sat up, staring at the door. He pulled his knees tight against his chest. His heart thudded against his rib cage. His left hand reached for his damaged arm, squeezed, held the wound. Blood flowed through his fingers. He sucked in a ragged gasp; pain radiated out from his torn shoulder, down his arm, to his fingertips.

The world tilted, his vision clouded, his body attempted to shut down. He forced himself to focus, he grasped at the present.

His eyes drifted over the walls of the small room.

Pictures.

Hundreds of pictures.

And he instantly knew that if he were to shout, nobody would hear him, not here.

That's when the lights went out.

CHAPTER ONE HUNDRED TWENTY-FIVE

GIMBLE

WHAT DO YOU MEAN, they won't approve it?" Gimble said into her phone. She was in the front passenger seat of the SUV. Kepler and Vela were behind her. They were racing through a residential neighborhood. According to their driver, they were only a few minutes from the orphanage.

"I've tried two different judges," Sammy replied. "Both came back and said we had insufficient cause for a search and seizure. A judge in Tompkins County, name of Rhodes, said he was familiar with Windham Hall. He told me the place had been shuttered due to budget cuts. An old building, just got too expensive to maintain. The kids were relocated a few months ago and the structure is set for demo. We've got a double whammy—they housed children and medical records. Everyone seems particularly protective of both. He's got a clerk trying to determine where their records were shipped, said he'd get back to me."

Gimble felt her face flush. "I don't give a shit about their records. I just want access."

"I told him that. He just said he'd have someone get back to me."

Gimble sighed; her fingers twitched. "Keep trying. Any luck reaching Dobbs or Begley?"

"Both go straight to voice mail."

"Keep—"

"—trying," Sammy interrupted. "Yeah, I get it."

Gimble hung up.

"That's it on the right," their driver said, pointing out the window.

Gimble looked up at the building, at least a story taller than the surrounding homes. A large wrought-iron gate blocked the driveway. The driver pulled up to a call box and lowered his window. He reached out and pressed a button. After a moment, he pressed it again. Then he turned to Gimble. "No answer."

She got out of the SUV and went to the gate, peered up the drive. "I see two cars. Do we know what Begley and Dobbs are driving?"

Nobody answered.

In the back seat, Vela was saying something to Kepler.

Gimble grabbed hold of the gate and shook it. It was sealed magnetically at the top and bottom. She took out her phone and dialed first Begley, then Dobbs. Both calls went straight to voice mail. She didn't know Dobbs well, but it was unlike Begley to go silent for so long. If they were in there and not responding, they could be in trouble.

She looked back at the driver. "Can you push it open? With the SUV?"

He shook his head. "I'm not authorized to do that."

"I could order you."

"You could, and I'd call my supervisor for approval. Without a warrant, we need probable cause."

"I've got two unresponsive agents possibly in that building," she shot back.

He was young. Obviously uncomfortable. He hesitated, looked

back at the gate. "If I were to get out of the SUV to place a call to SAIC Grimsley, and you took control of the vehicle while I was otherwise engaged, there'd be little I could do to stop you."

He had his door open before she responded, his phone out.

From the back seat, Kepler said, "I know the gate code."

Gimble turned and faced him.

He reeled off the numbers.

Her eyes remained on him for a moment, then she looked back at the driver. "Try it."

He leaned into the call box and keyed in the number.

Nothing happened.

"It's not working," he said.

Kepler leaned forward. "Press the pound sign."

He did.

The large gate clicked and began to swing inward, slow and lumbering.

Gimble and the driver got back in the SUV. They started forward. She turned back to Kepler, but he spoke before she could say anything.

"It spells out *Mitchell* on the keypad."

"Your brother's name," she stated flatly.

Kepler nodded.

"When were you here last?"

He turned and looked out the window.

They parked behind a white Nissan Rogue. The other car was a Volvo. Gimble texted both plates to Sammy. His response came back a minute later:

The Volvo is registered to Lawrence Patchen. Rogue is a Hertz rental—Begley.

She replied:

Get me everything you can find on Patchen.

Gimble took her Glock from her shoulder holster, checked the magazine to ensure it was fully loaded, then pulled back the slide, chambered a round, and put it back under her arm. "Vela, you're with me." She turned to the driver. "I need you to stay out here with the prisoner. If we're not out in ten minutes, call for backup. Understand?"

"Yes, ma'am."

Gimble groaned and got out of the SUV.

Had she looked into the back seat, she would have seen Vela slip a handcuff key to Kepler. She didn't, though. She was too busy stomping off toward the front door.

WRITTEN STATEMENT, MEGAN FITZGERALD

"Tighten her feet," Mitchell said, circling the bed.

He had opened the brown metal door with a security code. I tried to memorize the numbers, but his fingers moved too fast. The door opened on a small antechamber, like a mudroom, with another door leading toward the main level of the building, and two staircases, one going up, one down. He carried Nicole Milligan's squirming body past the second-floor landing all the way up to the third. Between the wound on his shoulder, the woman's weight, and the steps, he was breathing heavily by the time we reached the top, and I considered trying to overpower him, but I wasn't sure how. If I tried to push him, Nicole could get hurt, *bad*. The scissors were in his back pocket, crimson-stained blades glistening with each motion-activated light. I could grab the scissors and stab him again.

Kidneys this time.

Both kidneys, you fuck.

But again, he'd probably drop Nicole.

The steps were narrow. Steep. Concrete. Any fall could prove to be fatal.

So I did nothing. I followed behind him with my hands taped together, clutching my bag of four feathers like an offering, to the top floor. From there, he pushed through another metal fire door into a hallway with doors lining both sides.

"This is where *they* got to sleep," he'd said as we passed bedroom after bedroom. Each contained bunk beds—some two, some four; one large room even housed six—but the mattresses were gone, and only the frames remained. Drawers were missing from the dressers. Empty closets hung open, naked hangers left behind.

"Do you smell that?" I asked.

I didn't see him nod, but I imagined he did. "Gas. Patchen is probably following Dr. Rose's lead. Fire cleanses everything. The building is set for demo, so he'd be doing them a favor."

Another light blinked on as we made our way down the hall. One behind us turned off. They stayed on for only twenty or thirty seconds.

"What if he starts a fire while we're still up here?"

He ignored me. "Last door on the left, Meg. That's where we're heading."

The last door on the left was another bedroom. A single bed was pushed back against the far wall. An antique desk sat opposite, a drawerless bureau beside it. This was the only room I'd seen with a mattress. Mitchell had rolled Nicole off his shoulder and dropped her in the center of the bed. He produced zip ties from his other pocket, cut the tape from her hands, and secured each wrist to one of the bedposts. Then he cut the tape on her legs, forced them apart, and secured those too.

"Tighten her feet," he said again.

I was busy staring at the floor. The wood was soaked with gasoline; the walls too. Puddles in the corners. The wallpaper. Gasoline had been splashed everywhere.

I reached for the zip tie on her left foot, pretended to tighten it.

Mitchell frowned, rounded the bed, and tugged at the plastic tie hard enough to get a wince out of Nicole. "Like that," he said, pulling at the one on her other foot next.

The scissors were in his other hand, the blades opening and closing as he absentmindedly worked the handle. He raised them toward Nicole's face. She shook her head violently back and forth.

"I suppose you remember these. Dr. Bart loved to play with them in that little room of his, in the dark. Remember what he'd make you say? He'd make you whisper it in the dark before you'd lash out with these and try to cut me. How did it go again?"

Nicole didn't answer him. Of course, she couldn't because of the duct tape. But it was clear she knew what he meant.

Mitchell leaned in close, whispered in her ear, "'I'm the night. I'm death. I'm rot. I'm you.'"

She glared at him, her body trembling.

"You'd whisper that over and over again. And in that damn little room, sound carried, so I could never quite tell where you were, not in the pitch-black. There were only the whispers. Then you'd cut me—"

He moved so fast. The scissors sliced her cheek in one quick, fluid motion and were back at his side again before the first sign of blood appeared. He didn't cut her deep, but it was enough. She jerked at her bindings, twisted, arched her back. She couldn't get away, though. She wasn't going anywhere.

I remained still.

I watched.

What else could I do?

Mitchell laughed. "You got me good. More times than I

can count. I still have the scars to prove it. Hours of that. You wouldn't stop, he wouldn't let you stop, not until my personality retreated and the other one came out. His little game as he scribbled down notes, as he checked his various recorders. 'Mitchell, Mitchell, come out and play!' And if it wasn't Mitchell, it was Michael, and then back again. So many times, so often, I didn't know who I was. How could I?"

He leaned into her; his lips brushed her forehead. "How much did he pay you to make me scream? Was it worth it? All those times? How 'bout we play a game? Let's see how much you can handle before you become someone else. Before you want to *be* someone else. Today you get to be Mitchell, and I'll play you. No need to pay me. I'll take on the role pro bono. It's all for science, right? For knowledge. Let's see if we can take Dr. Bart's research to the next level."

CHAPTER ONE HUNDRED TWENTY-SEVEN

DOBBS

DOBBS RAISED HIS LEFT arm, his *good* arm, above his head and waved it around. The movement hurt like hell but it worked—the light above him flicked back on, illuminating the room.

He didn't want to look at his other arm but knew he had to. When he glanced down, he winced. The hatchet blade had left a cut at least an inch deep and four inches long in the upper part of his arm, just below his shoulder. He could still move the arm, his hand, but he barely felt his fingers—they were numb and prickly, as if asleep. Blood flowed freely down his arm with each pump of his heart. His head was spinning. If he didn't stop the loss of blood quickly, he'd black out, or worse.

The light blinked back out.

Dobbs cursed, waved his hand again, and turned it back on.

He took the material from his torn shirt and tied it around the wound. Pain raced down his arm, up his back; he pressed against the wall, closed his eyes, waited for the nausea to pass and the cloud of white to leave his vision.

The room went dark again.

Dobbs waved.

He looked at his arm.

The flow of blood hadn't stopped, but it slowed substantially. This was good. He was worried the blade had cut an artery. Although, if that was the case, he'd probably be dead by now.

Using the wall at his back to maintain his balance, he stood carefully.

The world spun.

Dobbs spotted his gun in the far corner and picked it up. His right hand was useless, and he was a shit shot with his left, but a gun in any hand was better than no gun. He tucked it back into his holster.

The lights went out again.

"Shit," he muttered. He reached into his back pocket and took out his cell phone—he wasn't surprised to see he had no signal. He switched on the flashlight app. The walls appeared to be stone with a layer of concrete. They were covered in photographs. Photographs of Michael Kepler and Megan Fitzgerald, hundreds of them, from when they were children through the present. There was no particular order to them. It looked like they had just been taped up over time, wherever space could be found. Some were yellowed and frayed with age; others appeared to be no more than a few weeks old. In some places, they were several layers thick.

A cot sat against the far wall, filthy soiled sheets balled up on top. Several milk crates were lined up against another wall, and when Dobbs peered inside them, he found clothing. One contained nothing but Windham Hall uniforms, faded with age. Another contained men's clothing. The third held women's undergarments, bras and panties of various colors and sizes. Like the photographs, some were old; the older ones looked like they'd belonged to a teen. There was a pair of red lace thong panties too. They looked brand-new. Dobbs knew at once they all belonged to Megan Fitzgerald—trophies of some sort, pilfered over time.

He went to the metal door and beat on it. "Open the door, Patchen!"

At first, there was no reply. When Patchen did speak, he sounded like he was on the opposite side of the basement. "That's where he kept that godforsaken child. That room."

"Michael?" Dobbs shouted back.

"No, the other one. The one he called Mitchell."

Dobbs frowned. "Who's Mitchell?"

Patchen didn't reply. Instead, there was a loud *twang*. Metal striking metal.

Dobbs shook the door handle but it did no good. "Let me out of here—cooperate and I can still help you!"

Another *twang*. Harder, more forceful.

"I felt it was important for you to see that room, Detective. For *someone* to see it, before all of this is gone. Fitzgerald's greatest success, our success, is one that will never be talked about. Perhaps behind closed doors, in professional circles, but never publicly. Who would believe such a thing?"

Twang!

"What are you doing out there?" Dobbs called out.

Patchen's reply sounded strained. He was slightly out of breath. "Fitzgerald truly was a master of the mind. He was taken from us far too soon. I can't imagine what else he might have accomplished had he been given another decade or two. I'm honored to have helped in what little ways I could. Rose helped too—she was instrumental, of course. But Bart opened doors in the field most researchers either didn't know existed or didn't have the balls to consider. A true pioneer who deserves to be up there with Jung and Freud."

Twang!

"Ah, there it is!" Patchen cried out. "These old gas lines are cast iron, tough as nails!"

"Open the door, Patchen!" Dobbs shook the door, kicked the base. It barely rattled in the solid frame. His legs felt like rubber; he was weak from the loss of blood.

"Not much longer now, Detective. Get comfortable. I suggest you make peace with your God, if you believe in that sort of thing."

CHAPTER ONE HUNDRED TWENTY-EIGHT

GIMBLE

KEPLER'S CODE WORKED ON the front door of Windham Hall like it did at the gate—the numbers on the keypad that corresponded with *M-i-t-c-h-e-l-l*. Gimble was standing in the foyer when she heard a metallic clanking noise from somewhere deep within the building.

Vela came up behind her and cocked his head. "What the hell is that?"

Gimble drew her weapon. "Federal agents! Identify yourself!"

Her words echoed off empty halls. No reply came.

Vela took out his own gun and pointed toward several signs on the wall next to some staircases. "Administrative office is that way," he said.

Gimble nodded and started toward the hallway, her gun at the ready. Something in the air felt off, too still. The hair on the back of her neck stood up, and she shivered.

They found the administrative office.

They found Begley.

Gimble gasped at the sight of him, lying still in a large pool of his own blood. Blackened hole in his shirt, his chest. She motioned for Vela to check on him, silently pointing toward Begley with two fingers. As he knelt beside the body, she swept the small room—behind boxes, under the desk, anyplace someone could hide.

They were alone.

She turned back to Vela.

His fingers were pressed to Begley's neck. He shook his head.

The loud, metallic *ping* again. The sound echoed through the building. She couldn't pinpoint the source.

The nameplate on the door read DIRECTOR LAWRENCE C. PATCHEN. Another on the desk said the same. There was a framed photograph, too, next to a half-filled cardboard box, a gilt frame displaying three young men wearing smug smiles and matching Cornell sweatshirts. The first man was clearly the younger self of the man in several other photographs on the office walls—thin with a large forehead and ears that were a little too big for his head.

Lawrence Patchen—had to be.

She recognized the second man from the author photograph on the paperback of *Fractured*. Like Patchen, Dr. Barton Fitzgerald was much younger here, an early version of the man she'd become familiar with over the past several days. He had one arm around Patchen's shoulder, the other around the third man. At first, she didn't recognize the third man. There were several reasons for that—he was just a kid in the photograph, and at least forty pounds lighter. He wasn't wearing glasses. His hair was thick and in a completely different style. Even the color was different. She didn't recognize him for all those reasons along with one other, the one her brain screamed out at her—she didn't recognize him at first because he shouldn't have been there. He had no business being in that photograph. Special Agent Omer Vela had told her he'd gone to Berkeley.

When she turned back to him, he was no longer crouching

beside Begley's body. He was standing beside an empty bookcase, his gun leveled at her chest.

"Patchen always was a nostalgic idiot," he said. "Packs up this entire place and leaves something like that out for the world to see."

Gimble moved slowly, her grip tightening on her gun, her finger slipping around the guard to the trigger. "What is this?"

He waved his own gun at her. "Set your weapon down on the floor and kick it over to me."

"No."

"I don't want to kill you, but I will."

Eighteen inches. That's how high she'd have to raise her Glock in order to get a chest or head shot in. A quick swing of her arm. A flick of her wrist. No chance to aim, not really. Pure Wild West.

"You'll never get the shot off. Not before me."

Gimble knew he was right, but that didn't make what she did next any easier.

She lowered her gun, dropped it by her side, and kicked it away. The Glock skirted across the floor into the blood pooled around Begley, came to a stop near his waist.

His eyes remained on her. "Step around the desk. Take a seat in his chair."

Gimble stepped back instead, toward the door.

Vela pursed his lips. "You're going to make me kill you, aren't you?"

Gimble took another step back. "You're a special agent with the Federal Bureau of Investigation."

"I was a scientist first, a psychologist foremost. Some things aren't so black-and-white. Not in a way someone like you might prefer. Some things are bigger."

Vela stepped toward her.

Gimble took another step back. "You've been part of this from the beginning?"

His face was smug. "I've had an interest for a very long time."

"You could have stopped him. None of those people had to die."

"Every experiment has its share of dead lab rats." Vela pulled the trigger. The bullet buried itself in the wall about an inch from her left arm. He nodded toward the wooden chairs just outside Patchen's door. "Take a seat, Gimble. I'm not going to ask again. We don't have time."

Gimble looked down at the chair on the left. As she did, her eyes fell on a word carved into the armrest. She read it several times before looking back over at Vela.

He was smiling. "That's where it all started, right there."

The word wasn't really a word at all, but a name—*Mitchell*.

The metallic *ping* echoed again, louder than the last, followed by a *thunk*. Something broke with that last one.

From somewhere in the building, a woman screamed.

Vela looked up toward the ceiling and smiled. "Mitchell's here. He's early."

Gimble took another step back.

"Don't."

Gimble's finger twitched. She dived through the opening onto the floor to the right of the doorway.

Vela fired two quick shots—*bang-bang!*

Both sailed over her and embedded themselves in the wall on the opposite side of the hallway.

She rolled, came up in a crouch.

Vela ran toward her.

Gimble reached to her right, grabbed the base of a tall wooden coatrack, and swung it around like a long baseball bat. It cracked against Vela's shin, throwing him off balance, and he flew forward, his arms flailing. His head crashed into the marble with a sickening crunch. His gun skittered across the floor.

Vela didn't move.

There was blood. Not at first, but it came—a puddle spreading out from under his temple. His leg jerked.

Gimble stood, breathing hard. Her right hand was shaking. She reached for it with her left, massaged her wrist.

She took out her phone.

No signal.

When she started back down the hallway toward the door, she felt someone watching her. She froze.

Michael Kepler was standing about halfway down the hall, utterly silent, a Glock in his hand. His eyes met hers. Neither moved.

CHAPTER ONE HUNDRED TWENTY-NINE

WRITTEN STATEMENT, MEGAN FITZGERALD

Mitchell drew the blade of the scissors down Nicole Milligan's forearm, from the inner part of her elbow to her wrist, pressing just enough to draw blood but careful to avoid the veins beneath. She tried to jerk away from him. She pulled as far to the side of the mattress as she could, but her bindings wouldn't allow her to move much. Her head thrashed back and forth; she glared at both of us.

I screamed again.

I didn't want to—it just came out.

Mitchell was getting off on this. He smiled at me. "You want to try?"

I shook my head.

"She's done it to you; I've seen your scars," he said. "When Dr. Bart locked you in the dark room, who do you think was in there with you?"

I looked down at my own arms, at the thin white lines—a dozen or so on the left, eight more on the right. Had I been wearing sleeves, I would have pulled them down, covered them up, but in my tank top I was exposed. I rubbed at them instead. I folded my arms over my chest. "That was a long time ago."

"That doesn't make it right. What he did to you. What she

did. You were just a little girl. He had no right. You trusted him—same as I did, same as Michael—and he treated all of us like objects, like things he could use up and toss out with the trash."

I looked down at Nicole, at her pleading eyes. "He used her too."

"Not like us."

"She wanted to be a psychologist. He told her he'd help her—put in a good word with her instructors at Cornell, write her a letter of recommendation. He even said he'd cite her help in his research when he published."

Mitchell laughed. "He never intended to publish. Not about all this."

"Not in traditional circles," I replied. "But there's a place for it."

"How do you even know that?"

I rounded the bed and ran a finger over Nicole's palm. "We talked, didn't we, Nicki? All that time alone in the dark room. It wasn't always about what Dr. Bart wanted. Sometimes we talked."

Nicole nodded her head.

"She's not your friend," Mitchell shot back. "We were tortured—by him, by her, by all of them." He lashed out with the scissors and slashed Nicole's other arm. She flinched, tried to pull away again. Her fingers tightened around mine.

I squeezed my eyes shut. Turned my head away.

"I want you to watch," Mitchell said.

"Why?"

"Because it's for you."

"It's not what I want."

"It's what you *need*."

Mitchell rounded the bed. His eyes fixed on the blade of

the scissors, a little bead of red dripping down the metal. He twisted them ever so slightly in the air, watched the blood roll back down the other side. When he reached Nicole's feet, he pulled off her shoes and socks, threw them to the corner of the room. He ran the tip of the scissors over her heel, across the sole of her right foot. Left a faint line but didn't break the skin. "Ticklish, Nicki?"

Her toes curled back, her feet jerked, but the zip ties held them in place.

Mitchell slashed in fluid, quick movements. First the right foot, then the left. Cuts across her heels, deep this time. Nicole yelled beneath the duct tape on her mouth. Her eyes filled with tears.

We all heard a loud bang, then—a gunshot from somewhere downstairs.

Mitchell's head jerked up.

Two more quick shots.

"They're here," he said. "We need to hurry."

"Don't kill her. Please."

Mitchell ignored this; he licked his lips and looked around the room. "Where's your backpack?"

I glanced down at my feet. My backpack was leaning against the side of the bed.

"Take everything out, scatter it all around the room. Put some stuff on the bed too. When they pick through all this, after the fire, we'll want them to believe she's you."

Gunshots meant police.

Gunshots meant help.

"We're up here!" I screamed out.

GIMBLE

KEPLER STARED AT HER.

Gimble's hand instinctively went to her shoulder holster.

Empty.

Her Glock was back behind her, next to Begley's body.

Her eyes jumped to Vela's gun, lying on the ground at least eight feet out of reach.

Kepler didn't move.

"I trusted you," Gimble told him. "I brought you here."

She tried not to look at the gun in his hand; she focused on his face. "Where did you get that?"

She already knew, though. She thought about the young agent she had left alone with him in the SUV.

Kepler glanced down at Vela's body on the floor behind Gimble, at the growing pool of blood around the man's head. His eyes found Vela's gun off to the side. He caught Gimble looking toward it too. He raised the gun in his own hand and pointed the weapon at her. "You killed him?"

Gimble slowly raised her palms. "Put the gun down, Michael."

"We're up here!" someone cried out. A female voice, echoing from somewhere up above.

Kepler looked over his shoulder. "Megan!"

Gimble dived for Vela's gun. She hit the marble hard and slid across the floor. Her fingers found his Glock, gripped the butt, wrapped around the trigger. She rolled onto her back, sat up, and thrust the barrel toward Kepler.

He was gone.

"Shit!" She scrambled to her feet and ran down the hallway after him.

She'd started up the staircase near the entrance when she heard gunfire from below.

Distant.

Buried.

Dobbs.

Had to be Dobbs.

DOBBS

DOBBS HAD HEARD GUNFIRE upstairs, he was sure of it. He waved his hand, turning on the motion-sensing light.

His own gun was still in the corner of the room where he'd dropped it. He picked it up in his left hand and pointed it at the ceiling. He squeezed the trigger and fired off three quick shots. Bits of plaster fell to the floor.

He knew shouting was useless, but someone would hear the shots.

"Do you really want to draw them down here, Detective?"

Patchen sounded like he was right on the other side of the door.

Heavy metal. No way a round would make it through. His weapon was loaded with hollow points, which were meant to shatter upon impact. They weren't designed for penetration. If he shot at the door, he was more likely to injure himself with a ricochet or fragment than hit Patchen.

"Shoot the door, and it might spark. Trust me, Detective, none of us want that right now."

The motion light blinked off.

Dobbs waved again, turning the light back on. "What are you doing out there?"

"Have you ever come to a crossroads? Reached a decisive moment in your life that called into question all you had ever done and presented you with two separate paths forward? Not necessarily a right path and a wrong path but each going in a different direction?"

Dobbs didn't respond. He had no idea what to say to that.

Patchen went on. "I found myself standing at just such a crossroads of late—after I learned of Fitzgerald's passing. Rose and I might have been privy to his research, his progress, but neither of us was ever under the illusion we could control his creation. Mitchell responded only to him. Feared only *him*. With Fitzgerald gone, the lion escaped from his cage. So I had this choice—should I attempt to cage the beast again and continue the research through some other means, or should I bring an end to the experiment? With Rose's assistance, continuation might have been possible—there's certainly more to learn. But without her...well, I'm willing to admit I'm not strong enough. When I turned on the news and saw her house burning, I knew she had made the decision for us."

"She didn't die in the house. She jumped off the bridge at Cornell," Dobbs told him, not because he had any interest in having a conversation with the man but because he knew that as long as Patchen was talking, he wasn't doing something else. Dobbs needed to buy time.

"She jumped?"

"Yeah."

"Well, she's dead nonetheless," Patchen said. "Both Fitzgeralds gone. Our funding...gone. With that, one particular path at that crossroads shone a little brighter than the other. I knew what I had to do. I'm meat for the lion, Detective. I knew he'd come for me, and it's my duty to end him. I hired someone...I hoped he could...but...well, he failed. Now it's on me. If Mitchell's not here yet, he will be soon. Fire kills even the worst virus, Rose knew that much."

Dobbs could smell the gas coming from under the door. He was getting so weak. He didn't realize he had fallen until his head cracked against the cold floor.

He heard a loud click.

All went dark again.

"Lights out, Detective."

Dobbs forced his arm up, waved—nothing happened. Patchen must have flipped the breaker.

CHAPTER ONE HUNDRED THIRTY-TWO

WRITTEN STATEMENT, MEGAN FITZGERALD

I heard Michael yell my name from somewhere in the building, yet I was staring right at him.

Mitchell cocked his head, smiled. "I told you, Meg." He grinned at me, a twisted grin. "Call out again. Draw him up here. Bring him to us."

Nicole squirmed and writhed on the bed.

Mitchell placed his hand on her chest and pressed down, held her still. The stained scissors glistened in his grip.

"No..." I shuffled back until my legs pressed against the bed frame.

"It's okay, Meg. I won't hurt him. I promise."

Oh, but I knew he would.

The lights went out. All of them.

The world went black.

I lunged at Mitchell. Leading with my shoulders, I caught him right in the belly. He was a lot bigger than me, but I took him by surprise and I heard the air leave his lungs and slip from his lips with a wet gasp. The scissors clattered to the floor, and I dropped down to my knees, searched the grimy wood. When my fingers found them, I grabbed the handle and thrust them forward. He wasn't there, though.

I heard him to my right, swung that way.

Nothing.

With my other hand, I reached out blindly. My fingers raked the air. I didn't find him. Instead, my hand hit the wall, slipped across the peeling wallpaper soaked with gasoline.

"Maybe you should light a match, Meg. Better to see by."

A light bloomed. A ferociously bright light in the otherwise dark room. Mitchell stood about five feet from me, a match flickering between his thumb and forefinger. He grinned and pinched it out.

I pushed off the floor, moving toward the light, his voice, leading with the scissors.

I missed again.

A shadow skirted across the edge of my vision, a swift phantom.

"You remember those scissors, don't you, Meg? Bet it feels good. Like the touch of an old friend. Makes you feel strong, like you're in control."

Something shuffled to my left, then sliced across the palm of my hand. I screamed and scuttled back, cradled my arm close. Warm blood flooded between my fingers.

"I brought a knife of my own," Mitchell said in a low whisper. "The dark room was always more interesting when everyone had skin in the game, don't you think? I never played with three people, though. Dr. Bart always preferred two."

He moved again, and Nicole Milligan jumped with enough force to bang the bed frame against the wall. She cried out from behind the duct tape.

He cut her again.

"I wish we had more time," he said, now somehow on the opposite side of the room.

I dropped to the floor and crawled toward the bed. Gasoline soaked through my jeans and burned where he cut me. I choked back a scream. My heart beat so hard, I felt it in my throat.

I thumped against the metal frame again and went still.

I listened.

Mitchell wasn't moving.

Nicole Milligan twisted.

The frame squeaked.

The room was stiflingly dark, pitch-black.

I reached up, found Nicole's foot, and cut away the zip tie.

The blade of Mitchell's knife swooped down through the air with a whistle, missed my hand by less than an inch, and clinked against my scissors. I kicked out, caught him in the leg, and quickly shuffled to the head of the bed. I cut the zip tie on her hand and rolled under the bed before he had a chance to take another swipe at me. I came up on the other side, cut her left hand free too.

I heard him run. Heavy steps on the hardwood.

I slipped back under the bed and quickly pulled myself along the frame to the bottom. Above me, I heard Nicole sit up.

Mitchell's blade came down hard, right where she'd been. He must have buried the knife to the hilt in the mattress, because when he yanked it back out, the entire mattress jumped with it.

I pushed out from beneath.

Got to my feet.

I sliced away the last zip tie, this one from her left foot, and pulled her toward me and off the bed. The two of us crashed down to the floor, her on top of me, as Mitchell sliced again, three quick strikes into the fabric.

"Run," I whispered into Nicole's ear. I rolled, forced her off me, and sat back up with the scissors ready, listening for him in the dark room.

Mitchell didn't move.

The only sound came from Nicole scrambling across the floor toward the door. Although I couldn't see her, she must have tried to stand because she let out a muffled scream, and I thought of the cuts on her feet, the gasoline on the floor—the burn. She fell back to her knees and crawled toward the door, the hallway.

"Let her go, Mitchell," I said.

My eyes adjusted to the gloom just enough to make him out—he was pressed into the far corner, leaning against the wall. I caught the slightest shimmer of the blade in his hand, the whites of his eyes. He was looking directly at me.

At first, he only smiled. Then he leaned forward. "I'm thinking of a number between one and five, Meg."

Another match hissed to life in his hand.

I jumped to my feet and shot for the door. I grabbed Nicole's arm and threw it around my shoulder, forcing her to stand. She flailed, punched me, tried to pull away. I yanked her hair, tugged her forward, looked back for a moment.

Behind us, Mitchell said softly, "Three. It was three."

He tossed the match into the air and started after us.

GIMBLE

EVERYTHING WENT DARK.

Gimble froze on the stairs.

She heard Michael's footsteps somewhere up above. They grew distant, quickly faded away.

Below, the echo of the gunshots died too.

She stood there in utter blackness. Silence.

Her phone was in her back pocket. Gimble took it out and switched on the flashlight. The narrow beam rolled over the walls, the steps, first up, then down. The thin scent of gasoline wafted down from the second floor.

Kepler up.

Dobbs down.

She glanced at the display on her phone—no signal.

Her fingers twitched.

Without another thought, Gimble turned and raced down the stairs to the lower level, the flashlight beam bobbing. At the bottom, she came upon a metal fire door. Leading with her gun, she pushed through and found herself in a long hallway with doors lining both sides. All closed. All metal.

She considered shouting for him but didn't. He had shot at

something or someone, and at this point, all she had on her side was surprise.

The first three doors were locked.

The fourth was a storage closet filled with cleaning supplies—chemicals, mops, brooms, paper towels. She closed the door, tried the next one.

Locked.

She walked a couple feet down the hallway to two more doors. Like most of the others, the door on the right was locked. The one on her left opened up to another staircase, this one going deeper into the building. The scent of rotten eggs rushed at her, thick and stale, the unmistakable odor of the mercaptan added to natural gas.

The flashlight beam played over the staircase. The walls were painted a muted gray. Black rubber treads covered each step; there was a metal handrail on the wall. Nothing down below but darkness.

Water dripped.

She heard a muffled thud, like someone banging on a thick wall. This was followed by a shout—barely audible, distant.

Dobbs.

Gimble switched off the flashlight.

Total darkness.

She had a decision to make.

She could descend with the light on, which would give away her position, or she could go down without it, but either way, whoever waited down there had the advantage and she knew it. She couldn't turn back, not knowing he needed help.

Gimble began walking down the stairs, slowly, methodically, allowing her eyes to attempt to adjust. She kept her gun ahead of her in her right hand. Her left was below the gun clutching the phone, one finger on the flashlight button.

With each step she took, the scent of gas grew stronger. This was mixed with the musty mildew smell of a damp basement. She reached the bottom and left the mouth of the stairwell at a low crouch. She could make out rudimentary shapes, nothing more—something stacked against the opposite wall, large equipment, maybe a boiler or air conditioner.

She heard something shuffling to her left, near the corner behind some large boxes, and she spun toward it.

"If you shoot and strike something metal, the spark will ignite the gas." The voice was low, barely audible. "Please do. I dare you."

Gimble thumbed the flashlight.

The beam cut through the dark. She'd hoped the light would blind whoever was there, but if it did, she couldn't tell. She found herself staring at a man in his sixties with thinning hair and a rumpled suit, a crooked tie, and dusty loafers. He ran toward her, face contorted. That's when she saw the hatchet in his hand, swinging toward her, cutting the air with a whistle.

CHAPTER ONE HUNDRED THIRTY-FOUR

WRITTEN STATEMENT, MEGAN FITZGERALD

The match flew from Mitchell's fingers and sailed through the air as if in slow motion, a spark of light. It bounced off the door frame and landed in the gasoline pooled in the hallway. For a second, I thought it went out. I thought maybe it had been extinguished by the force of air generated by his throw. Or maybe the liquid itself put it out. For that one moment, the flame dimmed, but then it roared to life with a swoosh, first the puddle, then the trail down the hallway. Then up the walls, the wallpaper, everywhere gasoline had been splashed.

I yanked Nicole into a room at our right just as a blue flame rushed past the open doorway where we had just stood. The two of us fell to the floor in a tangle of limbs.

"Megan!"

The shout of my name didn't come from the room we had been in or even from that direction; it came from the opposite end of the hallway.

"Michael!" I screamed back. "It's Mitchell! He's real! He's got a knife! He's trying to kill us!"

Nicole twisted beneath me, tried to get up. She was hysterical. I'd dropped the scissors near the door, and she grabbed for them, but they were out of reach. I grappled with her, got hold of both her arms, pinned her down on her back.

"Where are you?" Michael shouted back.

"In here!" Which was exactly zero help. There were too many rooms; he couldn't see us.

Nicole brought her knee up, caught me in the belly, and knocked the wind out of me. I rolled off, coughing. She scrambled across the floor. I grabbed her hair and yanked her back. She flipped over. Her hand shot forward, her long nails scratching the air, reaching for my eyes. I balled my fist and hit her as hard as I could in the side of her head. This stunned her but didn't slow her down. Somehow she got the scissors; she swung them at me, grazing my shoulder, then twisted toward the door. I punched her in the back of her head. I didn't want to, but there was no reasoning with her. I couldn't let her run out there—her feet, her knees, her legs, her whole body was soaked in gasoline.

She dropped. Her face smashed hard against the floor.

She went still.

I shook her, but she didn't move. "Shit! Shit! Shit!"

Black smoke gathered at the ceiling in a cloud. We had to get out of here. I couldn't carry her. I snatched the scissors from her hand and went to the doorway. "Michael!" I shouted again.

With my next gasp, my lungs filled with smoke. I dropped low and coughed it out. My eyes burned. I'd read that in a fire, it's the smoke that kills you, not the flames. That seems pretty unlikely until you start choking on the stuff.

I saw him then, about ten feet down the hall. He had a gun in one hand and held the collar of his shirt up over his mouth with the other. He squinted, saw me, and started toward me, carefully avoiding the flames.

From the opposite end of the hallway, Mitchell screamed, a horrible, guttural shriek. Michael appeared stunned at the sight of him. He froze. By the time he recovered and attempted to raise the gun, it was too late. Mitchell had shot past me, dived through the air, and caught Michael around his waist. The gun fell away. I lost track of the knife. They both dropped to the floor, the fire lapping at the air around them.

CHAPTER ONE HUNDRED THIRTY-FIVE

GIMBLE

GIMBLE DIVED TO HER left and crashed into a stack of metal folding chairs piled against the wall. Her phone skittered across the floor, came to a stop near the HVAC unit. The hatchet swung past her face; there was a swoosh of air as he brought it back around to strike again.

Gimble rolled to her left, the legs of the chairs digging into her back. The hatchet blade came down and cracked against one of the chairs with a loud *clank*, and she prayed to God it wouldn't spark as she threw herself to the side, away from the furniture. She landed hard on the concrete and winced as her left arm folded awkwardly beneath her, but then she scrambled to her feet, rubbed her arm, and brought her Glock back up. "I'm a federal agent!"

The man turned toward her, raised the hatchet again. A twisted smile rolled across his lips. "You're trespassing, and you're pointing a gun at me. I'm just defending myself. How could you threaten a frightened, defenseless old man?" He ran toward her, the hatchet above his head.

Gimble jumped aside and punched at his back as he flew past.

She landed only a glancing blow; it rolled right off. He crashed into the side of the HVAC unit, recovered, and turned back to her. He nodded at a door in the corner of the room. "Your friend is dying in there. Let me go, and you might have time to save him."

The flashlight from Gimble's phone pointed up at him from the ground. His shadow covered the wall and part of the ceiling, towering over her. He coughed, choked on the smoke. The smell of gas was growing thick.

Gimble pointed her weapon at him. "Drop the ax."

His head tilted to the side. "We talked about that. The muzzle flash alone will ignite the gas. You know it will."

"Maybe I'm willing to take that chance."

He coughed again. "How good a shot are you?" He raised his foot and brought it back down on her phone.

Darkness engulfed them.

Gimble ran at him.

WRITTEN STATEMENT, MEGAN FITZGERALD

Fire scurried up the walls, inched across the ceiling.

I dropped to my hands and knees and peered through the smoke.

Michael brought his knee up into Mitchell's chest. Mitchell gasped, fell back, then scrambled to his feet, the knife held out before him in an underhanded grip. The blade was red.

When Michael stood, I saw a growing stain in his side. He was wearing some kind of prison jumpsuit.

Mitchell wiped the back of his hand over his mouth. His lower lip was split. "Christ, Michael, you're so fucking sloppy. I've had to clean up after you every step of the way— Erma and that girl at the motel. You can't do anything right. I've been killing for years, and the police have been clueless, but in two days, you lead them right back here in some crazy, public shitshow. When I left Alyssa Tepper in your bathtub, I really hoped you'd find a way to dispose of her body, cover it up. You could have helped me. But no—instead, you call the cops." He shook his head. "Crossroads, Michael, crossroads. You chose the wrong path. Now I've got to give them another body. You left me with no choice. We've got Nicki Milligan in there. She's a good match for Megan, but I gotta give them you too. There's no other way out of this. We let them find you, find Nicki, Meg and I walk away, nobody's the wiser."

Michael pressed a hand over the cut in his side and just stared at him, his mouth hanging open, his eyes wide. Confused.

"You've got to take one for the team," Mitchell continued, moving the knife from his right hand to his left, then back again. "My life ended in this place. It's only fitting that yours does too. There's poetry there. Justification. Fitzgerald's notes are gone. Everyone's dead or will be soon enough. When this building goes, what they all did will die with it. I'll finally be free. I need you to do this one thing for me, this one last little thing. I've seen so many people die and they all look so relieved at the end, like a burden has been lifted. I can do that for you. God knows what you did to Mom must weigh heavily on you."

"I d-didn't..." Michael stuttered, unable to complete the sentence.

"I suppose after twenty-two years, you've found all kinds of ways to spin it, help yourself sleep, but you can't lie to me. I was there. I saw you. I saw you wait for her to fall asleep in the bathtub, then go in there and ease her under the water. You were so careful that she didn't even wake up. You were so gentle, like a vet putting a family's treasured dog down."

Michael pressed at the wound in his side and only stared. He seemed oblivious to the fire around him.

Mitchell took a step closer. "I get it—that's what you did. You put her out of her misery. And she was *miserable*. We were days away from being homeless, destitute. You did her a favor. Kudos, brother. I didn't have it in me. Not then, anyway." Mitchell smiled. "Telling him I did it, spinning it like I was some imaginary friend. That was inspired. We know the truth, though. We both know it was all you."

The heat of the fire pressed in at me, but I couldn't move. My eyes kept flying from Mitchell to Michael and back again. At my feet, Nicole groaned. I switched the scissors from my right hand to my left, wiped my sweaty palm on my jeans, then returned the scissors to my right, gripping them tight.

Mitchell's gaze never left Michael. "When you told Max he had to get rid of her body, that the police would assume he did it, you were so convincing. He was high as a kite, like Mom, but still, at four years old? To think with that kind of clarity? You inspired me, Michael, you really did. I wanted to be just like you. Fitzgerald and I talked about all that a lot. Pieced together what little you told him with what I knew, filled in the blanks. I gotta be honest, I think it all scared him a bit. Not enough to make him stop, though. I think he relished the fact that you had it in you."

"None of this is true," Michael said. "Mom . . . Mom drowned on her own. Max blamed himself. *He* thought the police would blame him. The drugs made him paranoid. That's why he . . . he did what he did. The things you're saying . . . they're not true. That's what Dr. Bart believed, and he tried to convince me that's what happened, but it's not. It's what he told me when he wanted me to become Mitchell—he tried to force me to believe it—but it wasn't true."

Mitchell shook his head, his face red, a vessel bulging at his temple. "*Become Mitchell?* You're still acting like I'm not real. Like I'm just one of your hallucinations. Your little imaginary friend come to life."

Michael blinked. His face was riddled with confusion. He glared at Mitchell, then at Nicole lying on the ground at my feet, then at the scissors in my hand. "I don't know what you are, M—"

Mitchell lunged at him.

GIMBLE

GIMBLE CLOSED THE DISTANCE between them with three fast steps. She charged at him through the dark, didn't give him a chance to move out of the way. When the barrel of her Glock pressed into the soft flesh of his belly, she leaned in, put all her weight behind it. He twisted beneath her, managed to get the hatchet up.

Gimble pulled the trigger. She couldn't see a damn thing, but she squeezed her eyes shut anyway, waiting for the entire room to go up in a giant fireball. The gun jumped with the first shot, and she fired again. She fired a third time. Each time, she forced the muzzle deeper into his abdomen.

The heavy blade came down, struck her just above the waist, and Gimble jerked to the side, knocked it away with her free hand. The hatchet clattered onto the concrete.

He collapsed against her. A grunt escaped his lips, and she pushed him away. His limp body fell to the ground.

She dropped the gun. Gimble staggered, caught herself, and leaned forward, her hands on her knees. She drew in a deep breath and coughed. The smell of the gas burned her throat, her lungs. "Dobbs! Where are you?" she finally managed to say.

She heard nothing but the steady drip of water.

Her hand went to her side, where the blade had hit. Her shirt was torn, but it hadn't broken the skin. There wasn't enough force behind the blow.

She raised her head. "Dobbs!"

Thump.

The sound came from her right; it was barely audible, like someone hitting a mattress. She turned toward it. "Again!"

Thump.

Her hands out before her, Gimble moved as quickly as she dared, shuffling her feet. When the toe of her shoe struck something, she carefully maneuvered around it. She crouched low, the air a little easier to breathe near the floor. "Keep going!"

Thump. Thump.

Her hand found a wall; she pressed her palm against it. She heard Dobbs again, still to her right, and she moved toward the sound, following the wall until she reached a hallway. A moment later, Gimble's hand traced a door frame.

The door jumped with the next *thump*.

"I'm here! Hold on—" She found the doorknob and twisted, but it didn't open. She ran her hand back up the side of the door frame and found a bolt, a heavy metal thing at least half an inch thick. She yanked it aside and pushed open the door.

Dobbs was on the floor, his arm and the leg of his jeans soaked in blood. Off to the side, the flashlight from his phone lit the room, a bubble of light.

Photographs of Michael Kepler and Megan Fitzgerald covered the walls. There was a cot. A few milk crates had been repurposed as furniture. Books. A toilet and sink in the corner of the room. The lock was on the outside of the room—someone had been kept here.

She went to him, knelt down. "Can you stand?"

Dobbs nodded, but it was clear he'd lost a lot of blood. His face was deathly white. His hair was greasy, soaked with sweat. He raised a trembling hand, touched Gimble's cheek. "I think I love you."

Delusional too.

Gimble grabbed his phone and tucked it into the front pocket of her jeans with the flashlight pointing out. She lifted his good arm over her shoulder and put her arm around his waist. "On three—" She counted down and got him to his feet. His legs nearly buckled, but she held him, waited for him to grow steady.

"He cut the gas—"

Gimble was already pulling him toward the door. "I know. We need to hurry."

She got him through the door, down the hallway, and back into the subbasement. His eyes fell on the lifeless body.

"Patchen. He killed Begley," Dobbs said between panting breaths.

"Kepler's here. He's loose in the building."

He didn't respond to that. Somehow, though, Dobbs managed to quicken his pace.

CHAPTER ONE HUNDRED THIRTY-EIGHT

WRITTEN STATEMENT, MEGAN FITZGERALD

The heat of the growing flames pressed at me from all sides. "Don't hurt him! Stop!" I shouted, hurling myself at both of them.

Nicole grabbed my leg, tripped me, and I fell to the floor. She tried to wrestle the scissors from my hand, but I kicked at her; my foot landed square in her face, knocking her back. Heat seared my skin. I rolled to the side, got back on my feet.

Out of the corner of my eye, I saw Mitchell throw himself at Michael, pushing off from his right foot and flying across the hall. Michael tried to sidestep him. The movement tugged at the wound in his side, and he winced, slowed, but it was enough—Mitchell hit him at an odd angle, and he fell against the burning wall. He pulled away but not before the shoulder of his shirt caught fire. He jumped forward and slapped at the flames until they were out.

Michael spotted his gun against the baseboard about five feet down the hall and dived for it. The moment his fingers wrapped around the steel, he pulled his hand away—it was too hot. He twisted back around just as Mitchell landed on top of him, his knee on Michael's right arm, pinning it down. He held Michael's other arm back with his left. Mitchell raised his knife and aimed it at the center of Michael's chest.

I raised the scissors.

Michael's eyes were on mine, pleading. I heard my name in his defeated gasp.

Mitchell's arm swung through the air, arcing down toward Michael.

I jumped on him.

I threw myself onto Mitchell and buried the scissors in his back. The first blow landed inches from where I had stabbed him earlier. I brought the scissors up and stabbed him again. The blade hit bone, maybe his spine. I yanked them out, stabbed him again. And again after that. He tried to buck me off, but my legs were wrapped around him. I wouldn't let go. I kept stabbing and stabbing until the back of his shirt was soaked in blood. I stabbed him until I was exhausted, and then I rolled off to the side and fell to the floor beside them.

Michael's head, only inches away, twisted toward me. He coughed and blood flecked his chin. "Fire . . . get out . . . Meg . . ."

I forced myself back up, shaking my head. "No, no, no, no."

I pushed Mitchell off him; the scissors were still buried in his back. His body rolled to the side and thumped against the wall. The flames caught his hair, and his vacant eyes stared back at me.

When I looked down at Michael, I saw the blade of Mitchell's knife in his chest, buried nearly to the hilt. His hand went to it, tried to pull it out, but he was too weak. His fingers fell away.

My eyes filled with tears. I touched his cheek. "I'll get you out, Michael. Stand with me. I'll carry you if I have to. Don't die on me!"

He looked up at me as if my words didn't make sense.

"We have to leave the blade in, though," I told him. "Taking

499

it out here might be more dangerous than leaving it in. I'll get you outside, find help..."

He blinked slowly. His lips moved. I leaned in closer, put my ear near his mouth.

"Get Nicole out," he whispered. "Save...Nicole."

I shook my head. "We'll both get her out, you and I together. Or she can help me with you...the three of us, we're all getting out."

He didn't answer.

I choked on the black smoke between sobs, coughed, wiped my eyes, and kissed his forehead, his cheek. "I love you, Michael. You know that, right? I've always loved you. Nobody else. Only you."

When I lifted my head and looked down at his face, I knew he was gone. His eyes had glazed over, his mouth hung slightly open, and he was no longer breathing.

I don't know how long I sat there—a minute, maybe two. When I forced myself to turn away, I saw Nicole. She had crawled halfway down the hall before collapsing. I pulled my shirt up over my mouth and went to her, keeping low, avoiding the smoke as much as I could. The flames had worked their way up the walls and were eating at the ceiling now. Chunks of plaster started to fall, little bits at first, then bigger pieces.

"Can you hear me?" I shouted at her.

She turned to me slowly. She was choking behind the duct tape. She had tried to pull it off, but Mitchell had wrapped it around her head so many times, there was no way to get it off by hand, we'd need—

I looked over at Mitchell behind me—the scissors were still buried in his back. He was covered in flames, his skin black and charred.

There was no time.

Michael lay so still beside him.

I turned away, couldn't look anymore.

I grabbed Nicole around the waist and forced her up. The cuts on her feet were black with a mix of soot and blood. She fought me at first, but when she realized we were heading toward the stairs, she pushed forward. The two of us hobbled, inched toward the only way down, the only way out.

CHAPTER ONE HUNDRED THIRTY-NINE

GIMBLE

DOBBS STUMBLED FOR THE third time, and Gimble tugged him back up, pulled him closer. "We're almost there," she said reassuringly.

"No, we're not," Dobbs replied. His leg buckled again, and he nearly fell. Somehow, she kept him standing.

She'd managed to get him out of the subbasement and up the first flight of stairs into the main basement level, the long hallway. She closed the heavy metal door behind them, and while that seemed to hold most of the natural gas at bay, she could still smell it. She imagined it was coming up through the HVAC vents.

"I smell smoke," Dobbs said. "You need to leave me and get out of here. If there's a fire and that gas reaches it, the—"

"Just keep moving," Gimble interrupted, dragging him along. Patchen had killed the building's power, and by doing so, he'd done them a favor. If the HVAC had still been running, pumping the gas through the building, it would have surely ignited by now.

They reached the metal fire door leading back upstairs, and

Dobbs collapsed. Gimble caught sight of his face as he dropped beside her—she saw his eyes roll back in his head.

Gimble dropped to her knees. "Dobbs! Not now, we're almost there!" She slapped him, hard, right across the face.

He groaned but didn't move.

The fabric he had wrapped around the hatchet wound in his arm had come loose, and his arm was covered with dark red blood. She pulled off her belt, wrapped it around his arm, and yanked it tight using a foot against his torso for leverage.

Dobbs's eyes shot open, and he howled.

"There he is," Gimble said, removing the belt.

His head swiveled, unsure of where he was. Then he remembered. His eyes pleaded with her. "I don't want to be responsible for your death."

"I didn't haul your ass this far to watch you die." Gimble helped him back to his feet. "One more flight of stairs. If the building blows, it'll happen fast and I'll never know what happened. I leave you, I'll have to live with that. Contrary to what my team might tell you, I have a conscience." She reached over and jabbed the wound in his arm.

Dobbs jerked away, now fully awake.

She glared at him. "Every time you slow down, I'm doing that again."

He nodded, leaned back against her.

Gimble shoved open the door, and the smoke rushed in at them, gray and black. The air was hot and smelled of burning timber. "Move!"

She pushed him out into the thick of it and pulled the door shut behind her. Gimble couldn't see a fire, but she could hear it, a low rumble somewhere nearby. She tried not to think of all the gas building up below them.

They reached the top of the steps and as they started toward the front door, Gimble heard someone coughing. Dobbs heard it too. He began to turn toward the sound, but she stopped him. "Get out of here. I'll go."

He looked as if he planned to argue with her, but then he nodded and shuffled toward the front door.

Gimble coughed, covered her mouth, and swiveled back toward the sound. That's when she noticed Vela was gone.

GIMBLE

BLOOD STAINED THE FLOOR where Vela had fallen, but there was no other sign of him.

The sound of coughing came again, harsh and relentless, followed by desperate gasps.

Kepler?

Vela?

It came from above and behind.

Gimble's hand went to her empty holster as she spun back toward the sound.

Dark black smoke roiled at the ceiling, churning and twisting like angry storm clouds. It was worse at the staircase leading to the second floor. At the top of the steps, there was a giant mass of deep gray fighting to get down, get out from above, held back only by the laws of nature but spilling into the first floor nonetheless. Tendrils of smoke reached down and out from the opening, exploring the ornate architecture in search of a meal, trying to satisfy the appetite of some beast up above, something growing larger with each passing second.

Through the haze, Gimble spotted them.

Megan Fitzgerald came through the smoke first. She stumbled awkwardly down the steps, nearly slipped, and braced herself on the wall. She had an arm wrapped around another young woman, and Gimble recognized her immediately as Nicole Milligan. Milligan's feet were bare, filthy, bloody. She had duct tape wrapped around her head, a giant mess of it over her mouth, caught in her hair, and she seemed barely conscious. Both were covered in soot, their clothing in tatters.

When Milligan saw Gimble, her eyes went wide and she tried to pull away from Megan, nearly taking them both down the stairs in a tumble, but somehow Megan managed to maintain her grip.

Gimble raced up the steps, took Milligan's free arm, and put it over her own shoulder. Heat belched down the stairs. Fire raged up above, eager to come down. She had to shout to be heard over it. "Where's your brother?"

Megan shook her head. Her soot-covered face was streaked with dried tears and snot. "Mitchell killed him. He's dead. They're both dead." As she said the words, the tears came again, rolling from her puffy red eyes, and her body shook with sobs.

From above came a loud crash, followed by a deep rumble.

Gimble thought about the gas building up below.

"We need to get out now!"

She dragged them down the steps. Even as the smoke grew worse and filled their lungs, she pulled them forward. They reached the door, fell. Then there were arms, hands, grabbing at them, pulling them down the sidewalk, across the lawn.

Gimble didn't see Windham Hall explode, but she felt it. The pressure hit her with the force of a Mack truck.

PART 7

ITHACA, NEW YORK

The most fertile soil is mixed with the ash of ruin.

—Barton Fitzgerald, MD

CHAPTER ONE HUNDRED FORTY-ONE

MEGAN

I WAS NUMB.

And I had been numb for two days.

If I spent the rest of my days numb, I thought I would be fine with that. I couldn't sleep; I didn't want to be awake. Every time my eyes shut, I saw Michael's face looking at me as he lay on the floor at Windham Hall, twisted and weak, pleading for me and Nicole to get out. Even then, in his final moments, his thoughts were on saving me. He always was the selfless one. The good one.

The cemetery before me was empty.

There was only me, a reverend I didn't know, and some worker. He skulked behind the pile of dirt covered with a sheet of cheap Astroturf and glowered at me. When I caught him looking, he didn't bother to turn away, didn't even shift his eyes. He scratched his stubbled chin, shoved his hand in his pocket, and stared.

The rain had started about twenty minutes earlier, and even though I'd brought an umbrella, I didn't open it. Each icy drop on my head, on my skin, reminded me I was still standing while

Michael, Dr. Rose, and Dr. Bart were ten feet in front of me and six feet under; they would never feel another raindrop.

The reverend droned on, but I didn't hear a word.

Dr. Bart had been buried two days ago. While I was in the hospital, heavily medicated, they'd put him in the ground. I was told the funeral was well attended. Colleagues, fans of his writing, lookie-loos. I'm not sure if anyone who came could be called a friend of his. I think they were all there for the spectacle of the thing. The papers covered it; they went on and on, all this bullshit about the loss of such a prominent force in the field of psychiatry.

Dr. Rose's suicide was mentioned on page 23 of the local paper. They'd asked me for a photograph, but I didn't supply one. They'd printed a photo no doubt procured from Cornell, an ancient headshot where she appeared twenty years younger, a little less wrinkled, and ten pounds lighter. The smug grin was there, though. That grin followed her everywhere. Today, we put her next to Dr. Bart.

The reverend must have finished speaking about Dr. Rose, because he shuffled the five feet over to the final grave in our little family plot and gestured toward the eight-by-ten of Michael in a gold frame perched precariously on an easel. The picture was far too small for its purpose, but I didn't have time to get something larger made.

How they found Michael's body, I'll never know.

When the gas in the basement of Windham Hall hit the fire on the second floor, the explosion could be heard from miles away—windows shattered for three blocks.

I don't remember the explosion. The doctors told me I was thrown nearly twenty feet and suffered a grade 2 concussion. Nicole Milligan was in bad shape. Alive, though. The police said I saved her. The last I'd checked, she still hadn't regained consciousness.

She was in the hospital room next to mine. I stopped by before I left this morning.

Jessica Gimble, the FBI agent who'd helped Nicole and me take those last few steps and get out just before the explosion stayed with me most of the night, sitting in a chair by the window. When my eyes fluttered open and I saw her, I tried to speak but she shushed me and told me to rest. She had several bandages on her face and a nasty cut on her cheek, the kind that leaves a scar. I could give her the name of a good plastic surgeon—Dr. Rose knew a few. Her left hand was wrapped in gauze. Her chestnut hair was pulled back in a ponytail, and she wore no makeup.

She'd left me a note on a pad of paper:

Write down what you remember; we'll talk when you're better. And call me Jessica. :)

So I did, with as much detail as I could muster. When she came by later to pick it up, she told me she'd be sharing it with an LA police detective named Garrett Dobbs. I Googled him—cute guy—so I added his name to the salutation of the letter; seemed like the polite thing to do. I told them everything from Michael's first phone call through the explosion. I didn't leave anything out.

As much as it hurt to relive it, I did.

Somebody pulled Michael's body from that mess. They still hadn't found Mitchell. They would, though. Who knows what else they'd find as they dug through the rubble of that place.

The reverend went on.

The filthy gravedigger continued to stare.

I looked out over the empty cemetery through the rain.

I did my best to ignore all the people shouting behind me.

I'd turned around only once, but when I did, dozens of cameras went off—clicks and flashes and cell phones held high in hopes of getting some shot of me over the heads of the others. Television crews, reporters from every imaginable newspaper and website—they were all there. They screamed questions at me, thrust their arms forward with microphones, hoping to catch something, anything for the record. The police held them back behind wooden barricades. They all wanted to watch me bury the Birdman Killer. That's what they were calling Michael in the media: the Birdman Killer. How fucking stupid was that? They'd painted him as a monster, this crazy murderer who crisscrossed the country on a mad killing spree. I'd read a couple of the articles, and that had been enough. The same rehashed bullshit. None of it was true. Not a single mention of Mitchell. It made me sick. Michael was a good man. He didn't deserve this. None of it. I'd promised the police I wouldn't talk to the press, not until they concluded their investigation, not until they'd pieced together everything I'd told them in my written statement, but I could hold my tongue for only so long. Another day or two, and I'd set the record straight, consequences be damned. I owed Michael that much.

The reverend bowed his head and recited some prayer. I wanted to leave.

A hand fell on my shoulder. "How are you doing, Megan?"

It was her, Agent Gimble...Jessica. She had a slight Southern accent—I hadn't noticed it before.

"How do you think I'm doing?"

She turned her back to the press, and her eyes fell on the three graves. "I can't imagine what it's like to bury your entire family like this. I am so sorry."

"Why did you bring him there? If you had just taken him to jail, he'd still be alive." I'd just learned about this last night on the news. There was talk of an internal investigation. I really didn't care what they did to her; it wouldn't bring Michael back.

She looked at the ground. "He was cuffed in the back of a federal vehicle. He shouldn't have been able to get out."

"He did, though, didn't he?"

"Yes, he did."

My eyes started to well up again. "Because he wanted to help me. That's all he ever wanted to do. He never hurt anyone."

She didn't respond to that.

I turned to her, my voice rising. "If he was a killer, why didn't he kill the agent you left out there to guard him? He could have easily killed him. He got the cuffs off, had surprise on his side. Instead, he just got his gun and handcuffed him to the steering wheel." I said the next words loud enough for the reporters to hear: "Michael didn't hurt him because he didn't have it in him. Michael never hurt anybody. He couldn't."

The reverend was staring at me. I really didn't care.

I sneered at her. "What's to stop me from turning around right now and telling all these people what really happened? Telling them all about Mitchell? All the Fitzgeralds' dirty little secrets?"

She squeezed my shoulder. "That's why I'm here, Megan. We know Michael didn't do it. We have proof."

My heart thumped. "Did you find Mitchell?"

She shook her head. "It's better than that. Let me get you out of here, away from all these people and back to the station. I'll show you." She leaned close to my ear. "When we're done, if you want to, I'll do a press conference with you. My office will organize it. We'll get the truth out there. We'll clear Michael's name together."

MEGAN

I RODE IN ONE of the FBI vehicles—a black sedan with dark tinted windows—and I was thankful for that. The driver pushed through the crowd at the cemetery with a vigor that suggested he had no qualms about running over one or more reporters should they happen to remain in the path of the federal vehicle. Several of the reporters smacked at the car as we rolled past. Another pressed a wide camera lens against my window and held the shutter button down in hopes of catching an image of me. I had no idea if the camera would work through the dark tint. I shielded my face behind my hand anyway and stared down at the floor, wondering what thoughts had gone through Michael's head when he'd sat in a vehicle just like this one.

Nestled between a community college and a law practice, the FBI offices were on State Street in downtown Ithaca. A squat one-story building painted a hideous beige with narrow brown windows, it looked more like a bunker than an office building and screamed *federal* from the street.

My driver pulled up to the main entrance and opened the door for me—he was quite the gentleman. Does one tip in a situation like this? Jessica got out of the car behind me and ushered me inside. At a security desk, my purse went through an X-ray machine like the ones at the airport, and I stepped through a large metal detector. Once they'd determined I wasn't a terrorist, my picture was taken and I was handed a visitor's pass.

"This way," Jessica said and led me to an elevator.

"Isn't this a one-story building?"

"There are three basement levels." She hit the button.

As we waited for the elevator, I noticed several people watching me. I glanced down at my black dress, wondering if maybe it was too short.

When the doors opened on level B2, we were greeted by a man in his early thirties wearing a Mumford and Sons T-shirt and carrying a MacBook. He smiled at me. "You must be Megan Fitzgerald. It's a pleasure to meet you."

"Megan, this is Special Agent Sammy Goggans. He works with me back at our Los Angeles office."

I shook his hand. "Mumford. Nice. The FBI lets you wear T-shirts?"

He leaned in close and lowered his voice. "They tried to reprimand me for it once, but I cited religious reasons. They never know how to react to that."

They hurried me down a series of hallways to a conference room in the back west corner. We were far underground, so the only window in the room looked out into the hall. Six chairs surrounded the round table. One of them was occupied by the police detective I'd Googled.

"This is Detective Garrett Dobbs of the LAPD. He's been working with me on this case for the past few days. I believe I mentioned his name back at the hospital."

The detective's right arm was in a sling. He had several cuts on his neck and face. As cute as his picture, though. Broad shoulders and close-cropped dark hair. Incredibly intense eyes. I wouldn't kick him out of bed.

A white file box was on the floor beside him.

He stood and smiled. "Hello, Megan. I knew your brother. I'm so sorry for your loss."

Jessica gestured toward an empty chair. "Would you like something to drink? Soda, water, coffee?"

I shook my head. "I have a lot to do today. I'm supposed to meet our family's lawyer in an hour to go over information on the estate, so I don't have a lot of time."

"I totally understand. We'll make this fast. Do you want your lawyer here with you? We can wait if you want to call him."

"Why would I want my lawyer here?"

Jessica shrugged. "Some people aren't comfortable talking to the FBI without a lawyer present, so I'm just putting it out there. If you want to call him, we don't mind; we'll wait. It's up to you."

"I'm fine," I said, settling into the chair.

Jessica closed the door, and the three of them sat opposite me. The one in the T-shirt opened his MacBook, and I heard a tiny fan whir to life.

She produced a notebook and pen and set them on the table. She had a copy of my statement too. She set that beside her notebook. A camera lens stared down at us from the far corner of the room with a blinking red light.

"Is that on?"

She kept her eyes on me. "Yeah. They record twenty-four/seven. It's not like on TV. They don't give us a way to turn them on and off. They've got cameras all over the office. I've been doing this for so long, I forget they're even there. It doesn't bother you, does it? I imagine there are cameras at Cornell too, right? Ever since 9/11, seems like there are cameras everywhere, recording everything we do."

I nodded.

"Just ignore it," she said, turning toward the detective. "Dobbs, can you hand me that..."

Her voice trailed off, but he seemed to know what she meant. He reached into the file box, retrieved a manila folder, and gave it to her. She studied the contents, then placed the open folder in the center of the table. It held three photographs. She spread them out and pointed to the first. "That's obviously your adoptive father, Dr. Barton Fitzgerald. We'll talk about him in a minute. Do you recognize these other two?"

I leaned forward. "The one on the left is Mr. Patchen," I told her. "He runs, I mean *ran*, Windham Hall."

"And how do you know him?"

I shrugged. "He'd come to the house sometimes. He was friends with my parents."

"You had no interaction with him aside from that?"

I shook my head.

Jessica gestured at the other photograph. "What about him?"

"I don't know him."

"You've never seen him?"

"No."

"Not even with your parents?"

Again, I shook my head.

She turned the photograph around and studied the man's face. "That's Dr. Omer Vela. He worked with the Bureau as a consultant. Apparently, he went to school with both Lawrence Patchen and your adoptive father. He may have been part of the attempt to frame your brother, Michael. We're still trying to piece together what his involvement was."

"Oh, I've got one more photograph I'd like you to look at."

This came from Dobbs. He took another folder from the box and handed it to me. It held a photo of a man in his mid-fifties. Heavy-set. Salt-and-pepper hair. I didn't know this man either.

I handed the folder back. "I've never seen him."

Dobbs frowned. "His name was Roland Eads. He used fake credentials to pose as an attorney and help your brother escape police custody back in LA."

"Oh." I took a closer look.

"You do know him?" Jessica asked.

"Michael told me about him. Mitchell did too. Mitchell said he used to help him sneak out of Windham Hall. I know Michael went to his house. I guess Mitchell did too when he...I never met him though."

Sammy gave Jessica a sideways glance, then said, "We've gone through his phone records. From what we've gathered, Mitchell paid him to sneak files out of Windham Hall, anything he could find to back up what Fitzgerald was doing. There was a twenty-five-thousand-dollar payment on the sixteenth. That's the most recent. We think that was to fund his break from the LAPD."

This is what you paid me to do.

Sammy went on. "Roland's sister, Erma, kept a diary. She was careful about what she wrote, though. She didn't want to incriminate her brother. There was only one entry on Mitchell a few years back. Roland told her Mitchell and Michael were nearly identical, like two people competing for the same life. He wondered what would happen if both of them were in the same room. He wanted to reach out to Michael, but we haven't found any evidence to suggest he ever did—not until the LAPD thing, anyway."

Dobbs handed me another picture. "We found Roland in his car."

When I glanced down at the photo, I immediately turned away, but not before the image became etched in my mind. A body burned, completely unrecognizable.

Jessica frowned at him. "She doesn't need to see that. Nobody does." She reached across the table and patted my hand. "Sorry about that."

I pulled my hand out from under hers and placed it on my lap.

Dobbs said, "He didn't die in the fire. Somebody shot him first." He made a gun out of his thumb and pointer finger and pointed it at his own forehead. "The fire was just an attempt to destroy evidence. To further frame your brother."

Jessica leaned forward and said, "We think it was Mitchell, like the others. We placed him in LA."

CHAPTER ONE HUNDRED FORTY-THREE

MEGAN

YOU NEED TO TELL the press! They're blaming everything on Michael."

Jessica nodded at the man in the T-shirt. "Show her, Sammy."

He clicked several buttons on his MacBook, then turned it around so we could see the screen. "This is Barton Fitzgerald's American Express account. See right here? We've got a charge on the fourteenth of September for Crossover Airlines."

I pulled the computer a little closer. "He was using Dr. Bart's credit card?"

Sammy nodded. "We think he had access to your e-mail account and possibly the text messages from your iPhone too."

I sat back in my chair. "How?"

Detective Dobbs reached back into his box and pulled out an iPad in a plastic evidence bag. "They found this in the basement room at Windham Hall where Dr. Fitzgerald kept him. It's fried, but when our techs moved the SIM card to a working iPad, we realized it was set up to mirror all your accounts."

My stomach sank. "I have an account with one of Dr. Bart's credit cards."

"And with this iPad, Mitchell had access too."

Sammy pulled up a spreadsheet on the Mac. "From what we've gathered, Mitchell monitored your communication with Michael, particularly when the two of you talked about his work, and when one of Michael's routes intersected with the location of one of Mitchell's potential victims, he'd fly out and rent a car and tail Michael. At some point, he'd remove the GPS system from Michael's truck, move it to his rental, then return it after committing the murder. He made it look like Michael drove to each crime scene."

I must have seemed puzzled, because he asked if I had any questions.

"How can you tell he moved the GPS? How do you know it was him?"

Jessica smiled. "The device also recorded RPM data. RPMs for a truck are very different from a regular vehicle's. Sammy caught that."

There was a small refrigerator in the room. She reached inside, grabbed a Coke, popped the top, and took a drink. "Are you sure you don't want something?"

I shook my head. "I'm fine."

Sammy gave Jessica a wry smile. "Can I ask her?"

She rolled her eyes. "Go ahead."

He turned to me. "How did you trick the cameras back at the truck stop?"

I might have shrunk back a little in my chair. "I didn't..."

Jessica waved a hand. "It's okay, you can tell him. Nobody is prosecuting you for that."

"I can't get in trouble?"

"Nope."

I looked at all three of them. It didn't really matter; they couldn't prove it. "I tapped into the truck stop's DVRs and used facial-recognition software to find video of Michael. It wasn't hard; he visited that truck stop on nearly every trip. Then I clipped the footage, changed the time stamp, and uploaded it back. Piece of cake."

Sammy asked, "How did you access their system? It's a closed network secured with two-fifty-six-bit encryption."

I stifled a laugh. "If you try to go in from a terminal or the internet to gain access to the network, sure, it's nearly impossible. The people who install these things aren't idiots."

Sammy didn't say anything, and the cute detective seemed confused, so I broke it down. "It's like a house—they put an impossible-to-break dead bolt on the front door but they don't worry about keeping out the person who's standing in the kitchen. I just unplugged the CAT-5 cable from one of the cameras and plugged it into my laptop. The cameras are already on the network, beyond the security. I just mimicked the camera's MAC address and I was in. Child's play. Full access to everything on their system."

Sammy considered this. "Where did you learn how to do that?"

I shrugged. "A guy named Roy turned me on to a YouTube video. Everything is on the internet these days."

It was Jessica's turn to smile. "Does that answer your question, Sammy?"

He nodded and fell back in his chair. "Yep."

Jessica took another sip of her Coke and set the can down on the table. "Did you ever ride with Michael on any of his deliveries, Megan?"

"Sure. A couple of times, I flew out and met him," I told her. "Everybody likes a road trip. It gave us a chance to spend some time together."

To the detective, Jessica said, "That explains the holes in her attendance records. Quality time with her brother."

"Brother by adoption," he corrected.

"You looked at my attendance records?"

She didn't answer me. Instead, she said, "Did you ever see Mitchell on one of these road trips when you were with Michael?"

"No, of course not. I didn't know there was a Mitchell until he showed up at Jeffery Longtin's cabin." I looked back at the detective. "What else did you find in that room in the basement?"

He glanced down at his box, then back to me. "Photographs, mostly. Hundreds of them—both you and Michael." He lowered his voice. "You were naked in some of the shots. They were hidden-camera pics, kinda creepy. He had some of your underwear too. There was a box filled with your clothes."

"Ew."

"Most of it was destroyed in the fire." He glanced down at the box again. "The rest will be locked away in evidence. You don't need to worry about the wrong people seeing any of that stuff."

I looked down at my hands. "I can't believe Dr. Bart kept him down there."

"I'm sure it was horrible," Jessica said. "Somehow he managed to get out when he needed to. Apparently with Roland Eads's help."

"Mitchell said it was like being in a cage."

Jessica and the detective exchanged a glance.

The IT guy was fiddling with his MacBook again. He turned it back to me, and a video began to play. "Have you ever seen this?"

The image was grainy. The only light in the room came from a candle on a nightstand. The camera was focused on a bed. A woman on top of a man. "Is that—"

"It's Alyssa Tepper," the detective replied. "And that is—"

I covered my face. "Michael! Oh my God, turn it off. I can't watch that!"

He didn't, though. He let it continue to play. "When we first saw this, we thought it was filmed in Alyssa Tepper's apartment. Why wouldn't we think that, right? We found the camera in her bedroom pointing at the bed. Same bedspread as in the video. The image is so dark, it's hard to make out the furniture, but if you look carefully, it doesn't match Tepper's—it's close, but not the same. See?"

He paused the video and handed me another photograph, a picture of a dresser, and said, "That's hers. Different, right?"

I looked at the photograph, then slid it back to him. "It's hard to tell. It's dark in the video."

The detective handed me another picture. "We found this one in an album in Michael's storage unit back in Los Angeles. It's old— he's just a teenager—but look at the dresser. I think it's a match. What do you think?"

I recognized Michael's room. He was sitting on his bed. The dresser was clearly visible.

Jessica's finger settled on the photograph. "That's the same bedspread too. From the video."

Detective Dobbs put the photograph back in his box. "When we caught that, we took a closer look at the tape and at the time code embedded in the tape, and we realized the video was nearly seven years old. It was shot about six months before Michael moved out of the Fitzgerald home. Alyssa Tepper was a patient of Dr. Bart's at one point. Michael told us he didn't know her, but he lied about that, didn't he?"

"Or this is Mitchell," I countered. "They look exactly the same."

"*Looked.*"

I really didn't need this. Not now. "Fine. *Looked.* Whatever."

"Again, I'm sorry for your loss," Detective Dobbs said.

I frowned. "So Mitchell somehow staged Alyssa's apartment to make this video look recent. That makes sense, right? If he was trying to frame Michael?"

Jessica nodded. "He even altered several recent photographs to make it appear the two of them were dating. Planted a mobile phone at your brother's place filled with bogus text messages. He placed some of Michael's clothes in her apartment."

Sammy added, "Flight records and credit card charges put him in Los Angeles at the time of her murder."

"Couldn't it have been Mitchell in the pictures? Posing as Michael?"

Sammy shook his head. "Nope. They were photoshopped. Edits like that leave a trace. Easy enough to tell with the right equipment."

That seemed weird to me. Why would Mitchell bother? He looked just like Michael.

I caught movement out of the corner of my eye and glanced up at the window. Our housekeeper, Ms. Neace, was standing in the hallway looking in, looking at me. When our eyes met, she quickly shuffled away. Several agents were huddled around her. "What is she doing here?"

Jessica reached into her pocket and took out a pill bottle. She set it in the center of the table. "Can we talk about these?"

CHAPTER ONE HUNDRED FORTY-FOUR

MEGAN

I SNATCHED THE BOTTLE from the table. "These are Michael's. How did you get them?"

Jessica took another drink of her Coke. "At Longtin's cabin, after Michael said he saw you get in the car with Mitchell, after he turned himself in so he could help rescue you from ... Mitchell, we found those in his pocket." Her mouth was a thin line. "Do you know what they are?"

"Of course I do. They're dorozapine. Dr. Bart prescribed them."

"That particular medication isn't common here in the States. I had to look it up. It's primarily used in Eastern Europe, the former Soviet Bloc, places like that. Less ... regulated places."

I really wasn't in the mood for a pharmaceutical geography lesson.

Jessica nodded at the bottle. "Michael did have a prescription for dorozapine; he started taking it years ago. But that bottle there, those aren't his. Are they, Megan?"

I twisted the bottle in my hand, and the pills made a sound like slow rain. I pointed back at the window. "Tell me why Ms. Neace is here."

Jessica smiled again. "We'll get to her in a minute. I want to talk about those pills, the dorozapine. It's an antipsychotic. A dangerous one. It's primarily used to treat schizophrenia and dissociative identity disorder. It can be very helpful to someone with one of those conditions. But if it's given to someone not suffering from those conditions, someone like me or Detective Dobbs here, there can be substantial adverse effects—hallucinations, memory loss, paranoia, anxiety. Are you aware of that?"

I said nothing.

She continued. "Dr. Fitzgerald was. Apparently, medications like dorozapine were key to his research, his attempts to induce psychosis, like dissociative identity disorder. That's why he prescribed it to Michael, right? To try and induce multiple personality disorder?" She leaned forward and tilted her head. "That's not why he prescribed it for you, though, is it?"

I squeezed the bottle tight. I wasn't going to look at the name on the label. I wouldn't give her the satisfaction.

Jessica eased back in her chair and turned to the guy with the MacBook. "Sammy, play our interview with the Fitzgeralds' housekeeper, please."

He nodded, clicked several buttons, and turned the laptop monitor to face me.

Ms. Neace's face filled the screen. She was twitchy, nervous. "He pushed that boy so hard from the moment he brought him home. He was only four or five at the time, but Dr. Fitzgerald would keep him in his office for hours—session after session after session. Drilling him about the atrocities he witnessed, forcing him to relive those memories. Sometimes they'd take breaks; other times he'd insist they eat their meals in there." She leaned forward and shook her head. In a lower voice, she said, "He'd lock him in that horrible little room—no lights, nothing—and pump him full of medications. The others too—he did it to all of them. Him and his damn research. Rose was no saint either. She was right there with him, encouraging him. What he did to those children, it was nothing short of torture."

Jessica's voice came from somewhere off camera. "Why didn't you report him? Say something?"

Ms. Neace huffed. "Who would believe me? Do you have any idea who was funding him? You don't report that kind of thing. Not if you want to live. I did all I could. I stayed in that horrible house and helped the boy when he was in my care. I withheld the meds when I could. Made him throw them up sometimes. Taught him to pretend he was on the meds when they were watching." She shook her head. "Little good that did. Fitzgerald was relentless. He was determined to split that boy into a dozen different parts, shatter his fragile mind. He created this entire Mitchell persona down to the smallest detail and tried to force it on him, make it part of him. He wanted to create a killer without remorse, a personality that could kill with the flip of a mental switch, then go back without any memory of what he'd done, without guilt. The perfect killing machine. Michael was so tough, so strong. He built walls. Where a weaker mind would have caved, he pushed back. It didn't work with Michael. Fitzgerald tried for years, but it didn't work. He eventually moved on—"

Sammy stopped the video.

The time stamp at the bottom was an hour earlier.

The heat flared in my cheeks.

Jessica took the pill bottle from me, then wiped away a thin line of moisture on her Coke can. "Michael knew. Didn't he? That's why he covered for you. That's why he told us he saw Mitchell take you."

I looked at the three of them. Two people I didn't know were standing at the window watching us. "What are you saying?"

"Megan, who's on the mark? Right now."

"You can't be serious."

"A few days ago, I wouldn't have believed it either."

"Mitchell kidnapped me! He killed Michael. He tried to kill me! Nicki!" I slammed my hand down on the table. The slap echoed through the room. "Mitchell killed all those people and tried to frame Michael!"

Gimble nodded at Sammy.

"On it," he said. And he loaded another video. Apparently, Nicole Milligan was awake.

CHAPTER ONE HUNDRED FORTY-FIVE

MEGAN

NICKI WAS IN ROUGH shape.

She was in a hospital bed, raised into a semi-sitting position and propped up with pillows. Her hair looked greasy, plastered to her head. She had a black eye, several cuts and bruises on her face. When she spoke, her voice was quiet, mouse-like. "Patchen tried to warn me, but by the time he called, I heard someone shouting outside my front door. A man's voice, familiar, but I couldn't place it. I hadn't heard that voice in years. Someone kicked my door in. I ran to the back bedroom, grabbed my gun, and hid in the closet. He was shouting at me. I heard a woman's voice too, and both of them were getting closer. When I saw shadows through the closet door and knew they were in the room with me, I fired. I panicked and just started shooting, kept shooting until the gun was empty. Then she yanked the door open and pulled me out."

"Where was the man?" Detective Dobbs's voice.

Nicole blinked at the camera.

"Nicole?"

She shook her head. "I didn't see him. I figured he ran off

530

somewhere in the house." Nicole licked her cracked lips. "She pulled me from the closet. Started shouting at me, 'Where is it! Where is it!' And I recognized her then—the doctor's daughter. She—"

"She's lying!" I shouted.

Sammy glanced at Jessica and paused the video.

My face burned. "Mitchell broke the door in! I chased him through the house! I wasn't even in the room when she fired the shots at him—I was—"

"You were what?"

My voice dropped lower. "I was on the phone."

"You were on the phone? Who did you call?"

"I . . . I didn't call anyone. It was Dr. Bart. He called—"

Jessica smirked. "The *dead* Dr. Bart called Nicole's house?"

I tried to remember. Everything had happened so fast, it was hazy. "Not him. Obviously not him. I think it was a recording. Had to be." I was mumbling. *Pull it together, Meg.* I looked Jessica square in the eye. "Somebody was fucking with me." I drew in a deep breath and went on as calmly as I could. "I hung up and found a pair of scissors in Nicole's drawer—I stabbed Mitchell. I got him off Nicki long enough to get her to the car. He barely slowed down. He got to us before we could drive away and knocked me out."

All three of them stared at me like I was some kind of crazy person.

Jessica told Sammy to play the video again.

Nicole said, "She slammed me against the wall. She was *so* strong, incredibly strong. I managed to get hold of a pair of scissors and I stabbed her in the shoulder. Then I ran. I got outside and made it into her car, but I couldn't get it started. It looked like it had been hot-wired or something. I tried, but she knocked me out. She had a rifle and she hit me with it."

Sammy paused the video again. The three of them looked at me.

"This is bullshit," I said, fuming. "That's not what happened."

Jessica leaned toward me. "Show us your shoulder, Megan. Your left shoulder."

"What?"

Jessica pulled the corner of her own tank top off her shoulder. "Just a quick peek among friends."

"No way."

"We'll get a warrant."

I crossed my arms.

"If she didn't stab you, what do you have to worry about?" Detective Dobbs said.

"I hurt my shoulder at Windham Hall when I was trying to get away from Mitchell."

"Show us."

I glared at all of them, then stood. "You know what? I've got nothing to hide." I reached behind my back, tugged down the zipper of my dress, turned around, and pulled the top down. "When I crawled under the bed, *trying to help Nicole,* I got caught on a nail or something sticking out of the floor. Or maybe it was on the bed frame, I'm not really sure. But she didn't stab me— *nobody* stabbed me."

A camera flashed behind me. I covered myself and spun around. Jessica set her phone down on the table. "You can get dressed now."

I turned around and pulled the top of my dress back up. "I told you."

"A doctor should look at that. It may be infected," Jessica said.

I fell back into my seat. "It's just a bad scratch. She's lying. I don't know why, but she's lying, and all of you are buying it."

Sammy was fiddling with his computer again. "Do you know what a Ring doorbell is, Megan?"

MEGAN

I'VE SEEN THE COMMERCIALS."

"It's a smart doorbell," Sammy said, "with a motion sensor and a camera. Any time the doorbell detects motion, it records it and uploads the video to the cloud. Nicole Milligan had one installed when she realized someone was killing off people associated with Dr. Fitzgerald."

Jessica tried to take my hand. I pulled away. "This will be disturbing for you, but you need to see it," she said.

Sammy turned the MacBook toward me.

The footage was grainy, shot in the dark with infrared. Black-and-white.

Me, running from the car in front of Nicole's house to the front door, a rifle in my hand.

Mitchell's voice: "Hey, Nicki! Knock-knock!"

I kicked the door in, ran inside.

Mitchell again: "Was that our buddy Larry on the line? Did you say hello for me?"

"This is bullshit!" I shouted. "It's fake! Somebody doctored it, like those photoshopped pictures of Michael and Alyssa!"

Jessica wasn't watching the video; her eyes were on me. "Show her the other one."

He clicked on a thumbnail image on the screen.

Nicole ran from the front door and scrambled into the driver's seat of the car. A moment later, I came out, the rifle in my hands. I brought the butt of the gun down into the car window, shattering the glass. Nicole screamed. I brought it down again, smashed it against her head.

"Stop!" I shouted.

Sammy did.

The screen froze with me leaning through the destroyed car window on the driver's side, my hand on Nicole's throat.

"Give me an iPhone and ten minutes, and I could put you in that video," I said. "I don't know who's doing this or why, but it's not real. None of this. Somebody is trying to frame me just like they did Michael." Then I got it. I understood. They were all in on it. "Did Mitchell work for you? Is that why you're protecting him?"

"Let's talk about Molly," Jessica said.

"Who?"

"The manager at the motel in Needles. Did you kill her because she saw your face?"

"What? No. I . . ."

"Erma Eads too, right? She could identify you. You couldn't have that. You've never left a witness. Her brother, Roland . . . it was you who shot him in the parking garage, wasn't it?"

I could feel my heart beating hard; my cheeks burned. I was trembling. I wanted to jump across the table.

Jessica produced the pill bottle again and pushed it toward me. "Are you sure you don't want one of these?"

I snatched up the medication and threw the bottle against the far wall. "I don't need the goddamn pills! Why are you protecting Mitchell?"

Jessica placed her palms on the table. "Megan, there is no Mitchell. There never was."

"You're insane," I shot back. "All of you."

Jessica ignored me and went on. "Your housekeeper, Ms. Neace, she told us Dr. Fitzgerald created a Mitchell persona, down to the finest details. He tried to instill it in Michael, tried for years, but it didn't work, so he moved on. He moved on to *you*. And it *did* work with you. Fitzgerald subjected you to the same treatment, the same torture, as Michael. You just don't remember."

"No way."

"She said you sometimes spent days as Mitchell, even weeks, and while you were him, Dr. Fitzgerald would lock you in that room in the basement at Windham Hall to observe you, to document everything. He and Patchen would sneak you in and out through the back door so none of the residents saw you. Neace said you were only six years old the first time. This has been going on your entire life. If the Mitchell persona presented while you were home, if Mitchell was *on the mark* and they didn't have time to get you to Windham Hall, they'd lock you in your room." Gimble paused for a second, considering this. "At some point, you figured out how to get out, or Mitchell figured out how to get out, and that's when the killings began. You, Mitchell—you used Michael as cover and went after everyone who knew the truth."

"I'd never hurt anyone." Then I remembered something. "Mitchell's birth certificate! Nicole had it hidden in her house, in a music box!"

Detective Dobbs gave Jessica an awkward glance. "You mentioned that in your statement, the birth certificate, so we asked Nicole about it. She said she had a cassette tape hidden in the music box and you took it, not a birth certificate. She made copies and gave us one."

He reached back down into his box and took out a microcassette recorder. He set it in the center of the table and thumbed the Play button. My heart thudded as I heard Dr. Bart's voice.

"We're so close," Dr. Bart said. "Do you feel it? Like electricity in the air. It's damn near palpable. Thick and tingly. The hair on my arms is standing up."

I'd heard it before. The conversation I heard over the phone at Nicole's house.

Dr. Bart went on. "If you have to kill her, you can. I promise you, there will be no repercussions. I'll dispose of her body. You need not worry about that. She won't be missed. Isn't that right, sweetie? Nobody loves you. Poor little trashy thing."

My heart beat against my rib cage like an angry kettledrum.

"Do you feel it?" Dr. Bart asked again, his voice anxious, a fever to it. "Who is on the mark?" he asked softly.

Silence then.

The longest silence.

"Mitchell. Mitchell is on the mark."

"How can I be sure?"

"I have no reason to lie," the voice told Dr. Bart.

My voice.

I heard him cluck his tongue the way he used to do. Twice. Then another. "If you kill her, I'll believe you."

"Okay."

The voice was deep, thick, far lower than usual, nearly identical to Michael's, *to Mitchell's*, but unmistakably mine.

I had been shaking my head without even realizing it. The word *no* slipped from my lips over and over again, and I had to bite my tongue to get it to stop.

Dobbs switched off the tape.

I twisted my hands together, pulled my index finger back, and welcomed the pain it brought, anything to distract me from this. "I killed Mitchell," I finally said in a low voice. "He was trying to hurt Michael. That's what *I* did."

Jessica's hand found mine again. This time I didn't pull away.

She said, "Megan, I don't know how to tell you this. There's no easy way, so I'm going to just come right out and say it. You killed Michael. If you somehow saw Mitchell, thought he was Mitchell, it was a hallucination. Nicole saw you go after Michael with the scissors. She tried to stop you, but you were too strong. You overpowered her."

My eyes welled up with tears. I tried to speak; couldn't. My entire body trembled, this unbelievable cold enveloping me, eating me.

"I'm so sorry," she said.

Someone knocked on the door. The three of them looked up, not me. I glanced at my wrist, at a watch that wasn't there.

Mitchell came into the room in a blur, the scissors with the purple handle in his grip. He went for Jessica first, diving through the air. He crashed into her, and the scissors sank into her neck. He pulled them out and stabbed again; her blood spurted across the wall.

Dobbs tried to stand, tugging at his gun, while Mitchell pounced on—

The knock again.

The door opened.

"Agent Gimble?"

No Mitchell.

Not now.

Not ever.

The man standing there was in his mid-fifties, bald except for a ring of gray hair. He wore a dark suit and a maroon tie, had thin glasses perched on his nose. "The assistant director would like to have a word with you." He nodded at Dobbs. "You too." He told the IT guy he was wanted on level two.

As he said these things, he glanced at me. I could only imagine I looked a fright.

Jessica was looking at me too. "Wait here, Megan. We'll be right back."

Seemed like a silly thing for her to say, since they locked the door behind them.

Michael was standing in the hallway, watching me through the window. I wiped away the tears and smiled at him.

He told me what to do.

Everything would be all right.

GIMBLE

GIMBLE AND DOBBS FOLLOWED the agent down a series of hallways; Gimble had been told his name but couldn't remember it. Her brain was a muddled mess. As they walked, he rattled off additional information—the case was moving fast.

"We've got another body."

"What?"

"A kid named Roy Beagle. He worked the Sharper Image counter at Laughlin/Bullhead International Airport near Needles, California. They found him locked inside a Mamava pod, strangled, with his pants around his ankles. He had a feather sticking out of his mouth. Been there at least four days. Cleaning crew found him."

"Jesus," Gimble muttered.

Dobbs asked, "What's a Mamava pod?"

"Nursing station for mothers. They're in all the major airports now," the agent replied. "We also found her prints on the MP5 recovered on the edge of the woods back at Longtin's cabin. The investigating officer believes she was the one firing on the propane tank and that she dropped the weapon a moment or two before she came into view. Voice analysis proves you were speaking to her, not Kepler, over the comm system. Same thing at the truck stop when you were in the helicopter."

"She sounded just like him."

"She believed she was him," the agent said. "We think she set the SUV on fire after she left your line of sight and used the explosion as a distraction to kill the sniper."

"Or Michael killed him—we may never know." Gimble's fingers were twitching.

"The ballistics are a mess. According to forensics, the round we recovered from the Honda's door was a nine-millimeter and originated from the cabin, not the sniper's rifle. The angle's all wrong."

"Vela," Dobbs said softly.

"Had to be," Gimble replied.

"That's not what I mean," Dobbs said.

And when she looked up through the open door of SAIC Paul Grimsley's office, she understood. Assistant Director Warren Beckner had flown in from New York that morning and taken over the space. He stood behind Grimsley's desk. Special Agent Omer Vela was sitting in a chair opposite him, a cup of coffee in his hand.

"What the hell is he doing here?" Gimble spat, charging into the room.

Beckner raised a hand. "Control yourself, Agent."

Her face burned. "He sabotaged this investigation! He tried to kill me! I have reason to believe he released Michael Kepler, an action that led to the man's death. We also have evidence that he took unauthorized shots at Megan Fitzgerald—this man should be in custody!"

"Lower your voice and take a seat, Agent," Beckner told her. "Detective, come in and close that door behind you."

Dobbs looked at Gimble, then closed the door.

Beckner placed both hands on the desk and appeared lost in thought. When he looked back up at Gimble, he sighed. "We seem to have extenuating circumstances."

"No shit," Gimble said.

"I left my patience back in the city, Gimble. Don't push me. Not today," Beckner said. He picked up a sheet of paper from the desk, traced the edge with his index finger, then put it back down. "Apparently, Dr. Vela is not who he originally presented himself to be when he joined your team."

Gimble glared. "No—"

Beckner silenced her with a glance. "He doesn't fall under my purview. He's not with the Department of Justice, not with the Bureau."

Her eyes narrowed. "So who is he with?"

"I'm not at liberty to say."

Dobbs took a step forward. "Defense? DoD?"

Beckner's face betrayed nothing.

Vela took a sip of his coffee.

Gimble's eyes didn't leave Vela. "That's it, isn't it? Department of Defense?"

"Things have gotten out of hand, and I'm here to put the train back on the rails," Vela said.

She turned to Beckner. "I don't care who signs his checks. Are you aware he has a history with Fitzgerald? There's a good chance he knew Megan Fitzgerald was our unsub prior to joining the investigation—he withheld information that could have prevented the deaths of more than a dozen people."

Vela took another sip of coffee. "I'm here to tell you, Megan Fitzgerald is not your unsub."

"Excuse me?"

"Newspapers, television, the internet...they all have Michael Kepler as your killer. That's the narrative we're going with. Any contradicting information you may have learned is to be treated as classified," Vela told her.

Gimble's face somehow grew redder. "Narrative? This isn't some kind of story you can shape and edit! Kepler may not be one hundred percent innocent in all this, but he certainly isn't a killer. It was Megan all along! We found propofol in her locker at Cornell—the same drug used to kill Alyssa Tepper. She planted Michael's DNA at the crime scenes. We can place her at each murder. We've got numerous phone calls between her and Roland Eads up until the hours before he was killed—looks like Eads was trying to build a case against Fitzgerald and that guy Patchen. He stole substantial amounts of information from Windham Hall. We found it hidden in a crawl space under his house. Megan most likely shot him in cold blood while her brother sat right beside him! We just found another body—some kid at the airport who—"

Vela interrupted. "The boy at the airport will be ruled an unrelated isolated incident. As far as the rest, the recently deceased Michael Kepler is your killer. Megan Fitzgerald had absolutely nothing to do with any of it. In fact, when she attempted to convince her adoptive brother to turn himself in, he kidnapped her. She was lucky to escape with her life. Somehow, she even managed to rescue his final victim. Anything she might have told you that's contradictory to this is due to her current fragile mental state—her confusion and shock. She's been horribly traumatized and is in need of care. I'm here to see that she gets that care at a properly equipped facility."

"Oh no." Gimble shook her head. "You're not taking her."

"'Do you have any idea who was funding him?'" Dobbs muttered to himself.

"What?"

"That's what the Fitzgerald housekeeper told us," he said. "'You don't report that kind of thing. Not if you want to live.' Fitzgerald wasn't some rogue doctor; he was working for someone. Whom-ever Vela here answers to."

Gimble turned back to the doctor. "Who? NSA? CIA?"

Vela said, "Kepler fits the profile. Frankly, he fits better than Megan ever could. All those bodies—the press wants someone like Kepler, *expects* someone like Kepler."

Beckner sat on the corner of the desk. "Megan Fitzgerald is mentally ill. If we attempted to prosecute, she'd never see the interior of a courtroom, you know that. She wouldn't answer for these crimes. She'd end up in the care of competent doctors, which is where she belongs. This is best for her. As far as the press goes, the people need closure. Kepler provides that. This is the proper solution to protect all interests."

Gimble huffed. "I don't believe this! Whose orders are you following?"

He held up the sheet of paper. "If I could show you whose signature is on this document, you wouldn't be arguing with anyone right now."

"Then show me."

"You know I can't do that."

"I can't go along with this," Gimble said.

"You've caught one of the most prolific serial killers of the twenty-first century. Your methods will be taught at Quantico. This puts you on the path to take my job one day," Beckner told her. "Don't blow this, Agent. This is a make-or-break moment for your career."

Gimble took out her badge and gun. "Agent Begley died working this case. So did many U.S. marshals. Their families deserve to know the truth."

"Discussing any of this with anyone outside this room will be considered an act of treason," Vela said. "Don't commit career suicide over the reputation of a dead man. Kepler is your killer."

Beckner stood. "Your reports have been vetted. Do the right thing here. Believe me, this *is* the right thing. It's bigger than personal feelings of right or wrong."

"I'll take care of her," Vela assured Gimble.

An alarm blared through the office, a high-pitched alternating tone accompanied by flashing strobes in the ceiling.

"Megan!" Gimble shouted, bolting from the room.

CHAPTER ONE HUNDRED FORTY-EIGHT

GIMBLE

ONE DAY LATER, GIMBLE stood in the rain. Thick icy drops whipped to a mild frenzy by the fall wind beat on her from above. Her hair was plastered to her head. Water had found its way under her coat, soaking her clothing. She'd catch a nasty cold, but she really didn't care.

She glanced at the expansive cemetery grounds, then back to the three fresh graves before her. Somebody had spray-painted a large red *X* across the front of Michael Kepler's black granite tombstone. She tried to wipe it away, but the paint had already dried.

Deep in her pocket, her fingers snapped.

When an umbrella appeared above her, she didn't turn. "For a cop, you're not very stealthy," she said.

"I figured you'd be here," Dobbs said.

"I really don't want to talk to you."

"You need to talk to someone."

"Vela's a shrink—maybe I'll talk to him."

"Good luck finding him."

Gimble said, "You just stood there through all of that. You didn't back me up once."

Dobbs stepped closer, squeezed under the umbrella with her. "Working for LAPD, I've learned to pick and choose my battles. I've also learned there is a right time to fight. In that room, we were outnumbered, and we didn't have all the facts. Personally, in this case I think it's best to lie low, gather additional intel, and come back to fight another day. This isn't going anywhere."

"It's already gone," Gimble told him. "They moved her this morning."

"Moved her where?"

"Exactly."

"Is she—"

Gimble shook her head. "She's still in a coma. The machines are keeping her alive. Zero brain activity."

"It's not your fault."

"It's *all* my fault. I didn't spot Vela—two years, and I had no clue. And I left those pills in the room with her."

"We all did," Dobbs said.

Gimble's stomach was in knots. "I tried to get in to see Nicole Milligan this morning, and they wouldn't let me. I read her statement instead, but it's already been altered. Goes on and on about Michael Kepler kidnapping her, dragging her to Windham Hall, Nicole killing him to save her...completely whitewashed."

Dobbs said, "Neace's statement is the same way. She called Michael a bad seed. Said the Fitzgeralds did their best to rehabilitate him, but he was too damaged by what happened to his mother. She even said he admitted to killing her. Who knows if that's even true. I'm sure both their bank accounts are recently flush."

"I had the same thought. Sammy could check, but every time I call him, I get voice mail."

"I saw him this morning. He gave me this—told me to give it to you." Dobbs pulled a piece of paper from his pocket and handed it to her.

Gimble unfolded the scrap of paper, doing her best to shield it from the rain.

Intercepted a text conversation between the sniper and Patchen:
Unknown: You didn't tell me there would be federal agents involved.
Patchen: You didn't ask.
Unknown: You didn't tell me about her either.
Patchen: ?
Unknown: You should have told me what she was capable of.
Patchen: ?
Unknown: At least six dead marshals here, maybe more.
No calls. Talk back in LA.
—Sammy

"She flipped the pronouns in her written statement," Gimble said. "She must have killed the marshals before the sniper shot her, then she killed him, the only witness. Christ, a girl covered in blood—she probably walked right up to them." She paused for a second. "I bet she killed that trooper at the truck stop too. Winkler."

"We'll regroup back home," Dobbs said, reading over her shoulder. "Fight another day. All of this will come out eventually. We need to work smart, under the radar."

Gimble didn't respond. She shoved the note in her pocket.

"You kept your gun and badge for a reason," he pointed out.

Gimble felt the weight of her Glock under her shoulder. Maybe he was right. "What could they possibly have planned for her?"

Dobbs said, "I've got a long flight back to California. On my way to the airport, I'll stop at a bookstore and pick up copies of all Fitzgerald's books. Figured I'd start there."

"Gonna build a profile?"

"Something like that."

For the first time, she looked up at him. "Call and share it with me? When you get something together?"

Dobbs smiled. "I'll do that, and you need to do something for me."

"What?"

"Dinner. Back home."

"Dinner?"

"Yeah, that thing people do a few hours after lunch."

"Like a date?"

"Yeah, like a date."

Her voice dropped lower. "You don't want to date me, Dobbs. I'm a mess."

"I'm no prize either, but I'm pretty sure we both need to eat."

Gimble shrugged. "Okay."

"Really?"

"Too easy?"

"Yeah, a little."

"I'm still a federal employee. I'm not gonna turn down a free meal."

"Then we'll find her."

"After dinner?"

"Eventually," he said.

"Fight another day."

"Yeah."

Dobbs moved closer. He felt the warmth of her body. The rain rolled over the top of the umbrella and cascaded down around them, their small cocoon. He leaned forward and smelled her hair.

Gimble said quietly, "Working on a second date?"

"Maybe we should get out of the rain," he told her.

"Not yet," she said. "Let's just stand here awhile."

When his hand found hers, she didn't pull away. For the first time in weeks, her fingers relaxed, and Gimble thought of nothing else but that moment.

EPILOGUE

MEGAN

YOU DID SO WELL, Meg."

I didn't see Michael at first; my vision was filled with clouds, white, hidden behind a thin curtain of gauze. The material melted away, broke apart, a dissolving veil, as my eyes adjusted and my mind awoke from deep slumber. I spotted him then. He sat slumped in a chair to the left of my bed, his legs stretched out and crossed at the ankles. There was a magazine in his lap—*Psychology Today,* I think.

I tried to sit up, and my head started swimming. "Whoa."

"You shouldn't do that. Give yourself a minute."

I nodded, but that was a mistake. The blood swooshed around in my skull.

A rack of machines whirred on my left, a mess of beeps and hisses and little dancing lights and lines across displays. Just looking at it made things worse. When I turned away, I found myself staring at an IV bag fixed to a pole, a thin plastic tube running from the bag to my arm carrying transparent liquid.

"Where am I?"

"The university hospital." This came from Dr. Bart, and when I forced myself to sit up, I found him standing at the foot of my bed, looking at a clipboard. "You gave us a considerable scare, but I think you're through the worst. We had to pump your stomach, but we got most of it out fast. I'll hold off on the lecture, but I guarantee you one is coming, along with punishments—grounding, no electronics except what's needed for your schoolwork, and others. I'm sure Rose is working on a list. She'll be here in about an hour. She got caught in traffic."

Michael stood up from the chair, came over to me, and took my hand. "I can't leave you alone for a minute."

Dr. Bart glared at him. "She shouldn't have been there in the first place."

"It was just a party."

"With college kids, alcohol, and obviously a wide assortment of drugs," he shot back.

"She didn't take anything. I think someone put something in her drink."

"Is that supposed to make me feel better?"

I coughed. My throat felt like I'd swallowed glass. "It hurts…"

"Try not to talk," Michael said. "You need to rest."

He looked young, far younger than he should have. Eighteen, nineteen, no more than twenty, for sure.

Dr. Bart stepped around to the opposite side of my bed. "Your throat hurts because a gastric lavage consists of forcing a large-gauge tube down your throat, filling your stomach with saline, sucking it all back out, then pushing activated charcoal down in its place to absorb whatever is left. I had half a mind to try and wake you up at the start to ensure you'd remember it and think twice about drugs next time."

Michael's face went red. "I told you, she didn't take anything."

"And I told you, she shouldn't have been there," Dr. Bart shot back. "All actions have consequences, good and bad. We're each the architect of our own fate."

Michael knew better than to argue with him. We both did. He said, "Do they know what it was?"

Dr. Bart replaced the clipboard on the end of my bed. "The lab is analyzing it for me, but I haven't received the report yet."

Michael turned back to me. "Do you remember what you were dreaming? You were tossing and turning so much, the nurse thought she might have to put restraints on you. You screamed too, a couple hours ago. I couldn't quite make it out, but it sounded like you said *Trimble* or *Nimble*."

"I don't remember."

"Aw, hell," Dr. Bart muttered. He was standing next to a vase filled with roses, sucking on his thumb. "Damn things still have thorns on them."

He reached over to a table near the door, picked up a pair of scissors with a purple handle, and began stripping the thorns from the stems. "The more beautiful, the more vicious the bite."

I didn't remember the dream, but something else popped into my mind. I looked at Michael. "You didn't leave Nicki there, did you?"

He shook his head. "Mitchell gave her a ride home."

"They're talking again?"

He grinned. "More than talking. You don't remember?"

"Last night is kind of a blur."

Michael glanced over at Dr. Bart, who was still occupied with the roses. He lowered his voice. "After they killed that kid at the airport, Roy something, they—"

My eyes snapped open.

All was dark.

Pitch-black.

Stagnant air, so still that it weighed on me, moist and thick. Warm, too warm.

There was no sound. I heard absolutely nothing but the rush of blood pumping in my ears, the steady thump of my heart.

Where will you be when your life ends?

The thought came into my mind as a whisper across a vast field, barely there and gone before I could fully grasp the words or determine who said them. This was followed by a deep pain, the sickening squeeze of migraine taking root at my temples, waking with me.

When I tried to sit up, I realized I couldn't—my hands, my arms, were restrained. My legs too.

Why was it so dark?

"Hello?" I spoke the word, but hardly a sound escaped my lips. My vocal cords didn't want to work; it was as if they had gone unused for days, weeks, months.

I might have been in a room or a box or a grand hall. There was no way to be sure. I waited for my eyes to adjust to the gloom, but they didn't. The darkness was utterly complete.

I knew a place like this. I was intimately familiar with it, but I couldn't be there. Dr. Bart's dark room burned down with the house. I'd seen it myself—it was nothing but a smoldering ruin. Dr. Bart was gone; they were all gone.

"Megan?"

The voice was thin, metallic. Whoever spoke my name hadn't done so in the room with me but over some kind of intercom. The single word was followed by an audible click. Then: "Remain still, please."

As if I had a choice.

Lights blazed on above me, incredibly bright. I squeezed my eyes shut, saw nothing but pink and dancing blotches of white.

Behind me, a heavy-sounding door opened with a whoosh of air.

I heard the click of heels on tile from my left, around the back of my head, then to my right. I tried to turn my head toward the sound, but I couldn't. A band of some sort across my forehead held me still. "Who's there? Say something . . . please."

When nobody spoke, I told my eyes to open. *Made them open.* The blinding light with the migraine was worse than a steak knife to the cornea, but I did it anyway, and through a haze of building tears, I took in what little I could see.

A stark room.

No windows.

A single chair barely visible to my left. A bag atop that chair, one I recognized. A red Bosca duffel.

The footsteps came nearer. Right behind me now. Someone leaning over, close—a shadow crawling over me as whoever it was spoke.

"Who is on the mark?"

I didn't answer her, not at first, because it couldn't be. When I did, her name fell from my lips with the stark crash of shattered glass. "Dr. . . . Rose?"

"You've been asleep for some time."

"You're dead."

"Am I?"

I needed water. My throat was so dry. "Where are we?"

Someplace safe.

Only that wasn't what she'd said. When I told my mind to focus, when I grasped each word, I realized I had heard her wrong.

"Someplace we can safely continue," she said. "Now. Who is on the mark?"

ABOUT THE AUTHORS

JAMES PATTERSON is one of the best-known and biggest-selling writers of all time. His books have sold in excess of 385 million copies worldwide. He is the author of some of the most popular series of the past two decades – the Alex Cross, Women's Murder Club, Detective Michael Bennett and Private novels – and he has written many other number one bestsellers including romance novels and stand-alone thrillers.

James is passionate about encouraging children to read. Inspired by his own son who was a reluctant reader, he also writes a range of books for young readers including the Middle School, Dog Diaries, Treasure Hunters and Max Einstein series. James has donated millions in grants to independent bookshops and has been the most borrowed author in UK libraries for the past thirteen years in a row. He lives in Florida with his family.

J. D. BARKER is the international bestselling author of numerous books, including *Dracul* and *The Fourth Monkey*. His novels have been translated into two dozen languages and optioned for both film and television. Barker resides in coastal New Hampshire with his wife, Dayna, and their daughter, Ember.

Read on for a sneak peek at the next gripping stand-alone novel
from the world's bestselling thriller writer

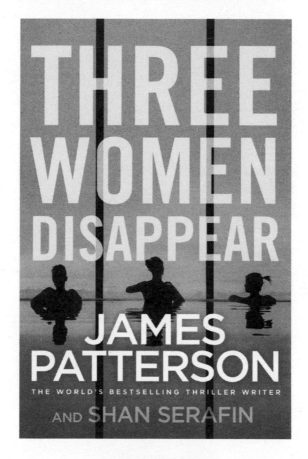

Out October 2020

DETECTIVE SEAN WALSH

"LET'S KILL him again in slow motion," I said.

I took a coffee cup from the sink, started the faucet running.

"Assume for a second that it *was* a female killer," I began. "I'm Anthony Costello, accountant to the mob, nephew of top dog Vincent Costello. It's early in the morning, and either the help's asleep or they haven't arrived yet. I'm probably ticked off at having to do my own dishes."

"As ticked off as I am right now?" Detective Heidi Haagen asked.

I ignored her. This was my wife we were talking about. I wasn't going to let the department pin a murder on her—especially not when it was me who sent her to work for Costello in the first place.

"The lady assassin approaches me from behind," I continued, "as I'm rinsing my mug. I've got the water running full throttle because I'm Anthony Costello and I never do anything halfway. The sound makes for nice cover. Lady Assassin tiptoes up behind me and plunges a big old kitchen knife deep into my left shoulder. Probably she's aiming for my neck or spine, but she's no pro—that's obvious from the mess she left behind. Her hands are sweating, and she closes her eyes at the last second."

"We've been over this," Heidi said.

Heidi, my onetime partner, now boss. She was the one who shut me out of this case. Now I was trying to claw my way back in.

"I know," I said. "I know we have, but bear with me. Costello's a big guy. About my height, but a hundred pounds heavier. That first blow brought him down, but it didn't kill him."

I spun away from the sink, dropped to my hands and knees. Heidi rolled her eyes.

"Lady Assassin sidesteps, gets me in the center of my back, but not as deep this time. I drop to my belly and start crawling, trying to get away, maybe headed for the living room, where I keep that Glock stashed in the coffee table drawer."

I pulled myself forward on the tile mosaic floor, grunting and grimacing, playing the part.

"This isn't necessary," Heidi said.

But it was. I had to make her understand—Sarah wasn't capable of killing Anthony Costello.

"She keeps coming at me, again and again, but she's out of breath, losing force. These are just puncture wounds she's inflicting now. I'm Anthony Costello. I'm not going to be done in by my own chef in my own kitchen. So I reach for a chair and pull myself up. Maybe I manage a threat: 'It's my turn now' or 'You're a dead woman'—some stock phrase to make her tremble. I start toward her, then stumble, brace myself against the sink. And now it's me who's scared, because I'm looking at her eyes, and it's clear a switch has flipped. She charges, stabbing wildly. I shield my face with my forearms. The blade finds my gut, my ribs, my thighs. And then she lines up for the kill shot, the tip of the knife pointed at my sternum. In a final burst of energy, I hurl myself out of the way, then stagger and drop. Her final thrust hits the countertop. Here."

I pointed dramatically to a deep gouge in the polished oak. Heidi yawned.

"Sean," she said, "Sunday mornings are sacred. I told you when you called that you'd better have something—"

"Solid and irrefutable, I know."

I went over to the knife block and found one with the same make and model as the murder weapon. Heidi took a step back, which almost made me smile. I held the knife out to her, handle first.

"Sean, I—"

"Just take it."

She did.

"I know you've seen the photos," I said. "I know there were measurements taken, and I know those measurements suggest that the killer was 'above average in strength.' Here's the thing: I asked you to meet me at the scene today because I want you to try it."

"Try what?"

I gestured to the stray hole in the counter.

"You're about five foot ten, right? You hit the gym daily. Bench your own weight. Hell, you could probably bench *my* weight. I challenge you to take the same knife and, with just one thrust, make a hole that deep."

She was less than enthusiastic.

"Even if the department would allow a—"

"Half as deep," I said. "The same gouge, half as deep. Forget what's allowed: I'm fighting for my wife's freedom here."

She glared at me.

"This isn't going to prove anything," she said.

"Just make sure you grip the handle tight. I don't want the blade sliding up your palm."

She gave in. She repositioned the handle in her fist, switched her weight to her back foot, and lunged with everything she had.

THE RESULT?

Not even one-quarter the depth of the original. The hole was barely noticeable when she pulled the knife back out. We stood staring at the counter. No words were exchanged, no meaningful glances. Then she dropped the knife in the sink and started for the door.

"We're leaving," she said.

"That's it?"

"I told you: it doesn't prove anything."

I followed her outside, onto the wraparound porch of what had begun as a plantation house, rebuilt and renovated over time into a multimillion-dollar mansion. Drive time to either Tampa or Orlando was roughly an hour, but the immediate area looked like the land that civilization forgot. Nothing but kudzu, palm trees, and now police tape in every direction. Heidi lit a cigarette, probably just so she could blow smoke in my face.

"Sarah Roberts-Walsh is a small-boned diabetic who couldn't lift a twenty-pound barbell off the floor," I said. "She *couldn't* have made that gouge in the counter."

Heidi turned to face me.

"Open your eyes, Sean. Stop ignoring the obvious."

"Nothing's obvious."

"Your wife disappeared the same day Anthony Costello was murdered. Maybe the same hour."

"She isn't the only one who went missing that day."

"Yeah, and maybe when we find her she'll have a real good story."

She walked down the porch steps and started toward her car, then turned and came striding back.

"Just what exactly was the wife of a homicide detective doing working for a mob accountant?"

"She was his chef."

"I'm not talking about her job title. How did she meet him in the first place?"

I didn't say anything. I was surprised it had taken Heidi this long to ask the question. I'd had run-ins with the Costello family before. A little over a year ago, I'd arrested Nicholas Costello, Anthony's nephew, for holding up a liquor store on the outskirts of Tampa. After the arrest, evidence went missing, witnesses recanted. It looked bad. It made me look bad. And then Sarah started working for Anthony. Rumors were flying around the squad room: Detective Sean Walsh on the Costellos' payroll. Me, who'd given fifteen years to this job.

"That's your story?" Heidi asked. "Silence?"

"She isn't involved," I said.

"Maybe. Either way, I don't want you anywhere near this."

I watched her drive off, then took out my cell phone and speed-dialed Sarah.

"Hey, it's me again," I told her voice mail. "I'm praying you can hear this. It's been two weeks now. I miss you. I need to know you're okay. I need you to come home. Whatever happened, you need to come home."

I hung up, headed for my car. My phone rang just as I stuck

the key in the ignition. I grabbed it off the dashboard without checking the caller ID.

"Sarah?" I said.

"Next best thing. You got something to write with? 'Cause I got an address."

It was Lenny Stone, ex-cop turned PI. I'd hired him to track down Sarah.

"Where?" I said. "Where is she?"

"About a hundred miles south of the middle of nowhere. Nearest town is Kerens, Texas. Time to dust off that Stetson, partner."

SARAH ROBERTS-WALSH

October 12
9:30 a.m.
Interview Room C

"FORENSICS FOUND traces of Costello's blood on your clothes, so why don't you tell us what happened?"

We were sitting in a plain white room with a drop ceiling and a mirror I assumed was two-way. Me and Detective Heidi Haagen. She leaned across the metal table.

"This is serious, Sarah," she said. "Your own husband brought you in."

"Where is Sean?"

They were the first words I'd spoken since we sat down. My voice cracked like a teenage boy's.

"Doesn't matter," Haagen said. "He can't help you."

"But I didn't do anything."

"Then just tell the truth."

"Where do you want me to start?" I asked.

"That day. Everything you remember. Begin at the beginning and don't hold back. No detail is too small."

All right, I told myself. *You can do this.*

I gripped the sides of my chair, took a breath, started talking. I kept my eyes pointed straight ahead, away from the mirror. I knew damn well who was standing on the other side.

*   *   *

The morning of Anthony Costello's murder, I woke up to find myself lying on a moss-covered boulder, surrounded by kudzu. I had no idea where I was or how I'd gotten there. I made to stand but my legs were wobbly and my feet kept slipping on the moss. I felt my pockets: no phone, no wallet. For a long while I just sat there, trying to think things through. Maybe I'd gone camping with friends, wandered off by myself, and gotten lost. Maybe I'd forgotten to bring my insulin with me, which would explain why I'd blacked out.

"You're diabetic?" Haagen interrupted.

"That's right," I said. "If I miss an injection, life can get real fuzzy."

She jotted something in her notebook.

"Go on," she said. "What did you do next?"

I yelled for help. I figured if I'd come here with friends, they couldn't be too far away. I shouted and kept shouting, but no one shouted back. I took a deep breath, ordered myself not to panic.

"Anybody hear me?" I tried again. "Please, I need help."

Silence. Nothing but birds fighting off in the woods.

All right, Sarah, I told myself. *It's up to you.*

I lay on my belly, slid down the boulder, and landed ankle-deep in a thick patch of marsh grass. The front of my blouse was stained green. I started to brush myself off, looked down, noticed for the first time that there was blood on my sleeves, blood on my jeans, blood all over my white sneakers. Not wet, but not dry, either. Had I fallen? Been attacked? I scanned my body for any hint of a wound, felt the back of my head for lumps or abrasions. Nothing. The blood wasn't mine.

So whose was it? I struggled to push my mind back but came up empty.

I wasn't wearing a watch, had no idea how long I'd been

unconscious. I looked up at the sky. The light seemed to be growing stronger. I figured it was somewhere between 8:00 and 9:00 a.m. Where would I normally be between 8:00 and 9:00 a.m.? I couldn't remember. I could remember my name, my age, my weight, the fact that I was a diabetic—but where I lived and what I did all day were gone.

I felt dizzy and a little nauseous. Assuming I was right about the time, my last insulin injection would have been late last night, maybe eight hours ago. Eight hours wasn't the end of the world. If I'd passed out atop that boulder all on my own, it might have had more to do with dehydration than blood sugar.

I needed water. I needed insulin. I looked around for a path or a landmark. Nothing. The boulder was lodged at the summit of a small incline. If I was looking for civilization, then downhill seemed like the best bet. I started to walk, then run. The running set off a sharp pain in my right calf. I stopped, knelt down in the grass, and rolled up my pant leg. There was a gash, maybe an inch wide. Something had pierced the thick denim of my jeans. I was wounded after all, though this cut didn't begin to explain all the blood.

"Keep moving," I told myself.

The morning was cool by Florida standards, but my forehead and the small of my back were soaked. I'd been walking for what felt like hours when I passed through a wooded area and emerged in a wholly different world: a painstakingly landscaped and manicured world. Palm trees instead of kudzu, a freshly mowed lawn instead of swamp grass and weeds. And at the other end of that lawn, a house. More than a house: a mansion. An old-fashioned plantation manor refurbished to look as though it were built yesterday.

I'm on someone's estate, I thought. *I have been all along.*

"Hello?" I yelled.

Once again, no answer.

There was a fence along the back of the house separating the lawn from a colorful maze of perennials and fruit trees. I hurried over to the back gate, feeling I'd made it to safety, only to find something that brought me up short and made me wonder if I'd ever be safe again: there was blood on the handle, blood spotting the gate's white wooden planks.

Little by little, then all at once, my memory came alive. I'd been to this house before. I'd been here every day for the last year. I was personal chef to a man named Anthony Costello and his wife, Anna. This was their house. This was where I made three meals a day for them, where I'd made breakfast for Anthony as recently as this morning.

My legs wanted to buckle, but I kept moving forward, through the gate and up the steps to the wraparound porch. The sliding back door was open. I stepped inside.

"Anna?" I called out. "Anthony?"

Nothing. The silence scared me more than waking up on that rock. This time of day, the place was normally bustling. Serena, the maid, would be singing to herself as she polished the dining room table; Anna would be watching *Good Morning Florida* with the volume turned full blast; Anthony would be pacing the marble hallway, cursing into his phone.

"Serena?" I tried.

Still no answer. Something was seismically wrong. I crept like a cat burglar through the dining room, the laundry room, the family room, the living room, the parlor, Anthony's office. Ten thousand square feet of real estate and not a whiff of life.

"It's Sarah," I called upstairs. "Anyone home?"

I'd climbed a handful of steps when the dizziness hit me hard. *Water*, I reminded myself. *You need water*.

I made my way to the kitchen. And that was where I found him. Anthony, facedown on the floor, outlined by a pool of his own blood, a kitchen knife lying not three feet away.

'CLINTON'S INSIDER SECRETS AND PATTERSON'S STORYTELLING GENIUS MAKE THIS THE POLITICAL THRILLER OF THE DECADE'

LEE CHILD

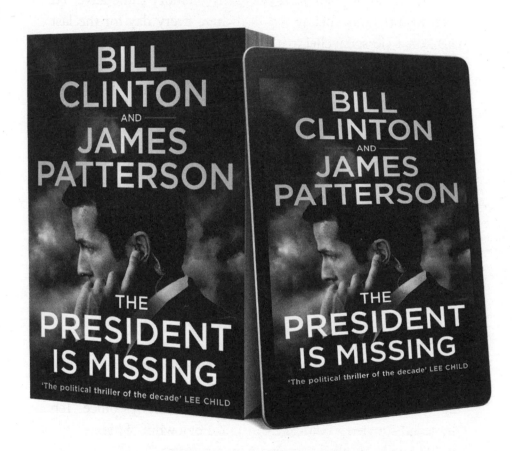

'Difficult to put down'
Daily Express

'Satisfying and surprising'
Guardian

'A quick, slick, gripping read'
The Times

'A high-octane collaboration . . . addictive'
Daily Telegraph

Also by James Patterson

ALEX CROSS NOVELS

Along Came a Spider • Kiss the Girls • Jack and Jill • Cat and Mouse • Pop Goes the Weasel • Roses are Red • Violets are Blue • Four Blind Mice • The Big Bad Wolf • London Bridges • Mary, Mary • Cross • Double Cross • Cross Country • Alex Cross's Trial (*with Richard DiLallo*) • I, Alex Cross • Cross Fire • Kill Alex Cross • Merry Christmas, Alex Cross • Alex Cross, Run • Cross My Heart • Hope to Die • Cross Justice • Cross the Line • The People vs. Alex Cross • Target: Alex Cross • Criss Cross

THE WOMEN'S MURDER CLUB SERIES

1st to Die • 2nd Chance (*with Andrew Gross*) • 3rd Degree (*with Andrew Gross*) • 4th of July (*with Maxine Paetro*) • The 5th Horseman (*with Maxine Paetro*) • The 6th Target (*with Maxine Paetro*) • 7th Heaven (*with Maxine Paetro*) • 8th Confession (*with Maxine Paetro*) • 9th Judgement (*with Maxine Paetro*) • 10th Anniversary (*with Maxine Paetro*) • 11th Hour (*with Maxine Paetro*) • 12th of Never (*with Maxine Paetro*) • Unlucky 13 (*with Maxine Paetro*) • 14th Deadly Sin (*with Maxine Paetro*) • 15th Affair (*with Maxine Paetro*) • 16th Seduction (*with Maxine Paetro*) • 17th Suspect (*with Maxine Paetro*) • 18th Abduction (*with Maxine Paetro*) • 19th Christmas (*with Maxine Paetro*) • 20th Victim (*with Maxine Paetro*)

DETECTIVE MICHAEL BENNETT SERIES

Step on a Crack (*with Michael Ledwidge*) • Run for Your Life (*with Michael Ledwidge*) • Worst Case (*with Michael Ledwidge*) • Tick Tock (*with Michael Ledwidge*) • I, Michael Bennett (*with Michael Ledwidge*) • Gone (*with Michael Ledwidge*) • Burn (*with Michael Ledwidge*) • Alert (*with Michael Ledwidge*) • Bullseye (*with Michael Ledwidge*) • Haunted (*with James O. Born*) • Ambush (*with James O. Born*) • Blindside (*with James O. Born*)

PRIVATE NOVELS

Private (*with Maxine Paetro*) • Private London (*with Mark Pearson*) • Private Games (*with Mark Sullivan*) • Private: No. 1 Suspect (*with Maxine Paetro*) • Private Berlin (*with Mark Sullivan*) • Private Down Under (*with Michael White*) • Private L.A. (*with Mark Sullivan*) • Private India (*with Ashwin Sanghi*) • Private Vegas (*with Maxine Paetro*) • Private Sydney (*with Kathryn Fox*) • Private Paris (*with Mark Sullivan*) • The Games (*with Mark Sullivan*) • Private Delhi (*with Ashwin Sanghi*) • Private Princess (*with Rees Jones*) • Private Moscow (*with Adam Hamdy*)

NYPD RED SERIES

NYPD Red (*with Marshall Karp*) • NYPD Red 2 (*with Marshall Karp*) • NYPD Red 3 (*with Marshall Karp*) • NYPD Red 4 (*with Marshall Karp*) • NYPD Red 5 (*with Marshall Karp*)

DETECTIVE HARRIET BLUE SERIES

Never Never (*with Candice Fox*) • Fifty Fifty (*with Candice Fox*) • Liar Liar (*with Candice Fox*) • Hush Hush (*with Candice Fox*)

INSTINCT SERIES

Instinct (*with Howard Roughan, previously published as* Murder Games) • Killer Instinct (*with Howard Roughan*)

STAND-ALONE THRILLERS

The Thomas Berryman Number • Hide and Seek • Black Market • The Midnight Club • Sail (*with Howard Roughan*) • Swimsuit (*with Maxine Paetro*) • Don't Blink (*with Howard Roughan*) • Postcard Killers (*with Liza Marklund*) • Toys (*with Neil McMahon*) • Now You See Her (*with Michael Ledwidge*) • Kill Me If You Can (*with Marshall Karp*) • Guilty Wives (*with David Ellis*) • Zoo (*with Michael Ledwidge*) • Second Honeymoon (*with Howard Roughan*) • Mistress (*with David Ellis*) • Invisible (*with*

David Ellis) • Truth or Die (*with Howard Roughan*) • Murder House (*with David Ellis*) • The Black Book (*with David Ellis*) • The Store (*with Richard DiLallo*) • Texas Ranger (*with Andrew Bourelle*) • The President is Missing (*with Bill Clinton*) • Revenge (*with Andrew Holmes*) • Juror No. 3 (*with Nancy Allen*) • The First Lady (*with Brendan DuBois*) • The Chef (*with Max DiLallo*) • Out of Sight (*with Brendan DuBois*) • Unsolved (*with David Ellis*) • The Inn (*with Candice Fox*) • Lost (*with James O. Born*) • Texas Outlaw (*with Andrew Bourelle*) • The Summer House (*with Brendan DuBois*) • 1st Case (*with Chris Tebbetts*) • Cajun Justice (*with Tucker Axum*) • The Midwife Murders (*with Richard DiLallo*)

NON-FICTION

Torn Apart (*with Hal and Cory Friedman*) • The Murder of King Tut (*with Martin Dugard*) • All-American Murder (*with Alex Abramovich and Mike Harvkey*) • The Kennedy Curse (*with Cynthia Fagen*)

MURDER IS FOREVER TRUE CRIME

Murder, Interrupted (*with Alex Abramovich and Christopher Charles*) • Home Sweet Murder (*with Andrew Bourelle and Scott Slaven*) • Murder Beyond the Grave (*with Andrew Bourelle and Christopher Charles*) • Murder Thy Neighbour (*with Andrew Bourelle and Max DiLallo*)

COLLECTIONS

Triple Threat (*with Max DiLallo and Andrew Bourelle*) • Kill or Be Killed (*with Maxine Paetro, Rees Jones, Shan Serafin and Emily Raymond*) • The Moores are Missing (*with Loren D. Estleman, Sam Hawken and Ed Chatterton*) • The Family Lawyer (*with Robert Rotstein, Christopher Charles and Rachel Howzell Hall*) • Murder in Paradise (*with Doug Allyn, Connor Hyde and Duane Swierczynski*) • The House Next Door (*with Susan DiLallo, Max DiLallo and Brendan DuBois*) • 13-Minute Murder (*with Shan Serafin, Christopher Farnsworth and Scott Slaven*) • The River Murders (*with James O. Born*)

For more information about James Patterson's novels, visit www.penguin.co.uk